D1147329

MISTRESS OF
THE COURT

Also by Laura Purcell:

Queen of Bedlam

MISTRESS OF THE COURT

Laura Purcell

MYRMIDON

MYRMIDON

Rotterdam House
116 Quayside
Newcastle upon Tyne
NE1 3DY
www.myrmidonbooks.com
Published by Myrmidon 2015

Copyright © Laura Purcell 2015

Laura Purcell has asserted her right under the Copyright, Designs
and Patents Act 1988 to be identified as the author of this work.

A catalogue record for this book is available from the British Library.

ISBN 978-1-910183-07-6

Set in 11/14pt Adobe Garamond Pro by Reality Premedia Services, Pvt. Ltd

Printed in the UK by CPI Group (UK) Ltd, Croydon, CRO 4YY

All rights reserved. No part of this publication may be reproduced,
stored in a retrieval system, or transmitted in any form or by any
means, electronic, mechanical, photocopying, recording or otherwise,
without the prior written consent of the publishers.

This book is sold subject to the condition that it shall not, by way of
trade or otherwise, be lent, resold, hired out or otherwise circulated
without the publisher's prior consent in any form of binding or cover
other than that in which it is published and without a similar condition
including this condition being imposed on the subsequent purchaser.

1 3 5 7 9 10 8 6 4 2

CCBC
AMAZON
03 /2019

For my parents

FAMILY OF GEORGE I & GEORGE II (simplified)

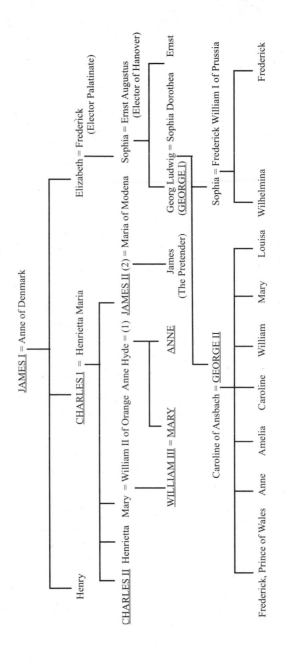

1712

CHAPTER ONE

～ Beak Street, London ～

Pain cracked across the back of Henrietta's skull, filling her vision with white light. As her body smacked against the floor, her skirts ripped. She spluttered and tried to roll over, but Charles planted his boot in the small of her back. 'Give it to me, bitch!'

Noise fragmented into shards. A cry soared, cutting through her husband's voice. It was Henry – poor boy. He would be so afraid. 'What?' she gasped. 'What do you want now?'

'You know what!'

Money. Money for the bottle, money for the faro table, money for his whores. Money he never earned. A pitiful amount of interest on her dowry, intended for her sole use.

Her hand flailed across the floor, trying to find purchase. Only mouse-droppings met her fingertips. 'I have none.'

'You do!' His breath hit her ear, stinking of tobacco and alcohol. 'You feed the child, don't you?'

Resentment boiled up inside her but she could not let it show. Submission was the only safe path. She had tried the other way more than once – and barely escaped with her life.

1

'Henry!' she called out to her son. 'Tell Papa when we last had something to eat. It wasn't today, was it?' she prompted. 'Nor yesterday . . . '

Charles's boot pressed down, choking the breath from her. Her ribs mashed into the floor. With no fat to cushion them, they threatened to burst through her wasted skin. 'What? Starving my son?'

The pressure on her back lifted for an instant before Charles stamped upon her shoulder blades. Vision flickered. Henrietta tasted vomit in her mouth and suddenly it was all around her, sticking to her cheeks. Her consciousness retreated, fleeing the squalor and pain. *Hanover*. She had to think of Hanover: the sparkling court, the fine dresses. Fountains that danced in the sunlight. It was her only hope of escape.

'For God's sake, woman! Look at the state of you.' Charles spat on her prone form. 'I won't have this mess in my house. Get it cleaned up by the time I return.'

'Yes, Charles.'

He slammed the door, shaking the thin walls and rattling the windows in their frames. Henrietta waited a few moments, testing the silence against his return. Nothing. The void was like the sound of angel wings.

She struggled up and leant one arm against the wall. Another chip, another piece of torn wallpaper. At least it wasn't a bloodstain this time. She grabbed a rag from the chair and wiped her face. Her woollen gown was past repair; soiled, torn and shiny at the seams. The frayed linen around her elbows caught up dust and dead flies. She would have to go on wearing it: the humiliating rag that marked every step she had fallen from her place as Miss Hobart of Blickling Hall. It was the only piece of clothing she owned.

A whimper broke the bruised silence. Henrietta looked up from her gown to see Henry, watching her. His eyes brimmed with tears.

'Henry. Henry, it's all right. Look, Mama isn't hurt!' She spread

2

her arms and moved to embrace him, but he dodged out of the way. She couldn't blame him. She was a frightening figure, covered in scratches and vomit. She wished she could light a fire, give him something sweet to take the edge off the shock. But she had nothing – nothing except her love. And it wasn't enough.

'Mama has a plan,' she told him. 'A plan to get you food and an education. You'd like to go to school, wouldn't you?'

He didn't answer.

She knelt softly and put her head level with his mop of dirty hair. 'I'm going to tell you a story,' she crooned. 'A story of a sad old queen called Anne who was very, very ill. Winter drew near and her days fell away like autumn leaves. She wished and wished for a child to take her throne, but it didn't come.' Henrietta had a vivid memory of her own mother, putting her to bed with a fairy-tale. She swallowed. 'But then, guess what happened? The queen found a magical place, across the narrow sea. A place where there were generations of princes and princesses, just waiting to keep her country safe.'

Still on her knees, she shuffled over to the bed. As she pushed the frame, straw burst from the mattress and fluttered down on her head. 'Now, your Papa's name is a key to that magical place. You only have to say *Howard* and the doors will open. We need to go there and serve the princes and princesses. Then, when they come to England to take their throne, Mama and Papa will be right there beside them.' Henrietta rapped the floorboards with her knuckles. One returned a deep, hollow sound.

'But how do you get to the magic place?' Henry's voice was a tiny thread. 'How do you cross the sea?'

Henrietta laid a finger on her lips. 'It's a secret. You mustn't tell Papa.' Her nails closed around a loose piece of wood and wriggled it free. 'But at night, the fairies come and . . . '

Breath left her in a rush of anguish. *No. It cannot be.* Her careful hoard, the stash she had starved for, was gone. A yawning gap met her frantic gaze, her groping fingers.

Somewhere out there, she knew, Charles would be sitting on a battered stool, drinking her dreams into oblivion.

∼ ∽

Something had to change. With her secret reserves plundered, Henrietta had no choice. She ripped open the mattress, dug through the straw and removed a handful of dull gold. The last relics of her mother: two bracelets and an ornamental hair comb.

She took Henry with her to the pawnbroker. Without the constant reminder of his gaunt face, she feared she would lose her nerve. She didn't look at the man who exchanged her memories for dirty coins. As soon as she had a fist full of metal, she bit each piece and hurried from the shop.

She ducked her head under cold drops of rain and tugged Henry back toward Beak Street. A sweet, nutty scent wound its way through the stench of wet bodies and dung. *Gingerbread*. Henry's stomach fizzed and whirred beneath his torn shirt. Her own belly quivered, yearning for something to churn. It had been so long . . . With an iron self-denial, borne from years of practice, she ignored the demands of her body and pushed on. Rumbling carts jolted past, the oxen straining at their traces. A wounded soldier scrabbled on the pavement, dragging his legless body across puddles to beg. Yet through it all, the deep, seductive pull of that gingerbread remained.

Henry tugged on her skirts. 'Mama! Mama!' He stared at the vending stall with his poor sunken eyes.

Temptation crept up from her stomach and knocked her thoughts askew. No matter how powerful its wrench, no matter how she wanted to feed her son, she couldn't give in – not now. 'You know I don't have enough money.'

'But you just sold your jewels,' he whined. 'I saw them give you coins. I'm *so* hungry.'

The pawnbroker's ticket burnt in her hand, branding her with guilt. She intended to buy the bracelets back, one day. She couldn't bear to think of her mother's gold, dangling around the wrist of some merchant's wife. 'I have a little money, but I need to save it. Remember the land across the sea?'

Henry groaned.

Carefully, they picked their way across the street. The crowd was thick and angry, jostling for shelter. On the other side of the road the aroma of baking was stronger than ever. Her head floated, high above the mud and dripping eaves. Giddiness took her in a wave. She stumbled and put out a hand to brace herself against the glass of a shop window.

'Mama, Mama! Oh please, please can I have some? I'll be good forever.' Henry jammed his fingers into his mouth and gnawed on them. 'Please Mama, my tummy hurts!'

His plaintive words coursed through her. Her little one. In pain. Being punished for something that was not his fault. Could she really let him suffer? Her head pounded as she tried to think straight, to command the body that screamed out for food. If she didn't get to Hanover, Henry would have no future. All the biscuits in the world would not signify then. But how to explain that to a boy?

Henrietta raised her head and looked into the shop. Faceless, wooden heads stood in a line – a doll's imitation of the traitors on Tower Bridge. Copious locks spilled from their crowns and flowed down to the chin; blacks, browns, fiery ginger, gold like spun sugar. Wigs finer than anyone she knew could afford.

She blinked and her focus changed. The wigs fell into the background; she saw herself reflected in the glass: a long face that would be handsome but for the pinched cheekbones; stormy, brooding eyes; hair the colour of chestnuts in autumn. Her fingers strayed

5

to her neck, twirling the loose strands. It was the exact shade of her father's. Could she sell it? A part of herself, her past?

Henry stamped his feet. 'Please, Mama? Please?'

She turned to her son and pressed a coin into his palm. 'You go fetch some gingerbread, my love. There's something Mama needs to do.'

~ ~

Blades of sunlight fell across the empty room. Henrietta sat cross-legged on the floor as motes danced around her. Henry knelt in the corner, drawing in the dust and chattering to himself. She could not even smile at him. Her knees shook so violently that they clacked against the boards. If there was anything left inside her, she would have thrown it up.

What had she done? Charles would be home any minute. When he stormed in the door and saw the furniture was all gone . . . She closed her eyes and swallowed. She had signed her own death warrant.

Even selling her hair had not been enough. She'd only been able to barter two passages to Hanover and three sets of good second-hand clothes – one for each member of the family. Everything she owned, reduced to scraps of paper and material. Substances Charles's hands could so easily rip. What had possessed her to do it?

The door burst open. Charles blew into the room with a gust of wind, obliterating Henry's dust picture. He had been drinking again. The sharp scent of alcohol leeched from his coat into Henrietta's nostrils. To her, it was the rank scent of her own fear. This was it. She either won, or lost all hope of escape. For good.

Charles staggered forward two steps and recoiled. 'God's blood! What the hell happened to you?'

Her pulse leapt like a leveret. 'I've sold everything,' she rasped out.

'Even your hair?'

'Yes – even that.'

To her surprise, Charles laughed. 'I always knew you were addled in your wits.' Henrietta tensed herself, ready for the words she knew would come next. 'Where is it, then, you mad slut? Give me the money.'

Terror turned her vision white. 'I don't – I don't have it. There's none left.' She clenched her hands into fists, burrowing her fingernails into her palms. 'I bought two tickets to Hanover.'

'Hanover!' Quick as a dart, he spun and hit her in the face. She fell backwards; her spine whacked against the floor, knocking the breath from her. She couldn't afford to lay stunned. Groaning, she rolled onto her side and curled up into a ball, protecting her face and the precious tickets. 'Bloody Hanover! I wish you'd never got that maggot into your head! What the hell do you think you're going to find over there?'

Freedom. Life. 'We could serve the court,' she said. Her voice spiked as he kicked her back. 'Get a regular income.'

He paused. She heard him heave for breath. 'And what exactly do you propose to do with my boy, while you're gadding about the court?'

'Edward has agreed to care for him.'

His fingers burrowed into the rags of her hair and jerked her head up. Pain screamed over her scalp. 'Edward? Pompous, preaching Edward?' Spittle landed on her cheek. 'No. Even you couldn't be that stupid. You know I'd pull your head off if you wrote to him.' He yanked tighter. Her neck gave an ominous crack.

'Think what's due to our son! He's the grandson of an Earl, the nephew of an Earl. Edward's house is a proper place for him – not here.'

Through her wavering vision she saw Henry, still in the corner, with his hands over his eyes.

Charles growled and dropped her to the floor. 'You had no

right to sell my property. Much less to go snivelling to my damned brother. I ought to take you out in the street and whip you.'

A shiver ran through her. 'Charles – '

'But you're in luck,' he continued, pacing to the window. 'It just so happens I have need of that ticket.' He glanced outside darkly. They were below street level; all that passed were hooves and feet. 'The duns have caught up with me. If you don't have money for them, we need to move on.'

She was breathless. Shakily, she propped herself up on her elbows. 'Does . . . does that mean . . .?'

Charles narrowed his eyes. 'It means I'll go, since you have my arm twisted behind my back. But don't think you'll escape unpunished. If this doesn't make our fortune . . . by God, woman you will pay.'

CHAPTER TWO

∽ Hanover ∾

Every jolt of the wheels rattled Henrietta's bones. The passengers' rancid breath and body odour made her queasy. A suspicious man wearing a muffler was squashed beside her and dug his elbows into her ribs at each turn. From across the coach, an old lady with a chicken on her lap regarded her with a steady gaze.

Henrietta shrank within herself. Now she was finally treading the path she had planned for so long – and she was afraid. It did not feel like her dreams of escape – there was no elation, no soaring sense of freedom. She was in a trance, watching from afar as some other Henrietta crossed the waves and travelled over the Continent.

She stared at the straw-littered floor of the coach. She missed Henry's presence like a limb. He had been the spur to her side, forcing her to press on. Without him she lost focus. At least Charles's brother would care for him well. It would be a treat for the boy to see how the upper class lived – how he should have lived.

In the corner, two men were arguing. Henrietta focused on their lips, trying to make out their harsh, grating words. Her German was good, but amongst these native speakers she felt like a novice. There was a speed, a lilt to their language that no classroom could teach.

At least with correspondence she would be safe. With her education, she could easily compose a letter to the Dowager Electress Sophia at the palace of Herrenhausen and ask for an audience. And yet . . . Cramping anxiety seized her every time she considered setting pen to paper. Addressing the next Queen of England – the woman who held all of her hopes in the palm of her hand. How on earth would she begin? There were no letters, no lines and dots of ink sufficient to convey her desperation. What if she failed?

It occurred to her for the first time that she had gambled everything on one toss of the dice. Until now, she had only experienced the wild rapture that such a risk brings. But as she looked on her fellow passengers and their scowling faces, she realised she could lose. Without royal favour, she wouldn't have enough money for the journey home. She could be stuck here, among strangers, while Henry . . .

A snort drew her eyes to the corner of the coach. Charles slumped against the battered upholstery, a thread of drool hanging from his lip. Whatever foreign liquors he had imbibed, they kept him comatose. That was something to be thankful for, at least.

The woman holding a chicken exchanged a flurry of words with a child next to her. Her plump hand pointed to the window. 'Herrenhausen.'

Henrietta could not help it; she pushed past the muffled man and strained to see out of the window. Frantically, she spat on her handkerchief and scrubbed the smeared glass. Images rose up from the grimy mist. Ornate hedges, stretches of water, gates with golden fretwork. Marble statues peered down from plinths, assessing the flowers below. Green. So much greenery. Her hand, clutching the stained handkerchief, fell limp at her side. The gardens expanded, filling the window. Planted in careful patterns, the bushes twisted and turned until their foliage transformed into a living damask. Here and there, a jet of water shot up from the fountains and sparkled in the sunlight. Henrietta's gaze travelled down an avenue of limes to where the palace sprawled in proud white stone. She was transfixed. It was unlike anything she had seen before – more elegant than the crumbling St James's Palace in London. Two storeys of frescoes and glittering windows. She drew a breath, blinked – and it was gone.

She fell back into her seat. It was as if she had blown out a lamp. The coach rumbled on, looking darker and dirtier than ever. The chicken lifted its tail and messed on the old woman's lap. She didn't even flinch.

Henrietta glanced at her own travelling dress. Her train carried a cargo of straw. Her fingernails were black-tipped and chewed to the quick. What had she been thinking? They would never accept her in a place like Herrenhausen. She felt her unworthiness creeping like a stain over her flesh.

'What's wrong with you?' Charles's voice startled her. He was worse for wear after his nap, with bloodshot, bleary eyes.

'I – I saw the palace.'

'And?'

'It was beautiful.' The skin on her forehead tightened with unbearable pressure. 'Just – beautiful.'

'Good. The Elector must be thick in the pocket.' His nose wrinkled as he looked her up and down. 'Better clean yourself up before you go there. Can't have you disgracing me.'

She was almost sick with shame. She wanted to weep and tell him she could not go; that she had been wrong with her wild dreams.

'Hetty?'

Henrietta raised her eyes to his face. Just around the mouth, she saw a whisper of Henry creeping through. 'Yes?'

'I only agreed to this hare-brained scheme because the duns were closing in. *You* sold everything without my leave. Remember?' Charles placed a heavy hand on her shoulder.

'Yes, Charles. I – '

'You promised me this would be the making of us. A palace, an apartment, wine. You *promised*.' He leant close enough for her to see the flecks of stubble on his cheeks. The mere scent of him made her shudder, bound up as it was with the memory of pain. 'And you know what happens to women who break their promises. Don't you?'

～ ～

Henrietta plunged her fingers into the cheap pomade and squinted. The mirror was filthy, speckling her face. She tried her best to paste her poor, cropped hair into some semblance of a style and thanked God for the mobcap and hat that hid the worst of it.

'Eighteen guineas,' Charles scoffed from the sofa. 'It wasn't worth that much. What else did you do to make that wigmaker pay up?'

Henrietta nipped her bottom lip. 'There was a time when you thought my hair lovely enough.'

He had been handsome back then. But to look at him now, sprawled on the cushions like a marionette with its strings cut, she would never have believed it. His lips were loose and wet from too much drink, his skin mottled. The dashing young soldier she married had disappeared; Charles dropped the act as soon as the church bells clanged to a halt. 'Why do you not dress for court?'

Charles snorted. 'I'm not going. I have business to attend to.'

Blood pulsed in her head. She heard it like a drum, pounding out her wrongs. The Dowager Electress Sophia had graciously invited them both to wait upon her. Failure to attend would be an insult. 'Please, Charles. Please.' Desperation made her voice jagged. 'Why stay here? You can't visit the tavern or the whore house. If you become a topic of gossip in Hanover, all our chances are ruined.'

She ducked as he flung a cushion at her. It bounced off the wall and skidded across the floor. 'Damn your impudence!'

'But – without you, how can I possibly – '

'You want me to work for the next Queen of England?' he roared. 'Well go and get me a place!'

'I need you with me! Please, Charles. If you ever cared for me, even a little bit, please do this one thing. It is all I will ever ask of you.' He pouted. 'Charles!' She fell on her knees before him and searched his red face. Surely there was some sense, some shred of decency inside? 'I beg of you! What do you think will happen if we don't get into court? We sold everything. We will be ruined. Out on the street. Starving.'

He pushed away her imploring fingers. 'Pull yourself together, woman. I'm sure Edward – '

'We have exhausted your brother's hospitality!' Henrietta wailed. 'It's a miracle he agreed to look after Henry. He threw us out once before when you didn't pay the rent! Or have you forgotten that, in your drunken stupor?' His blow was instant, pushing her back across the room and driving her teeth into her cheek. Black shapes, like smuts from a fire, danced before her eyes. Henrietta raised a hand to her ringing ear. Her fingers came back spotted with blood.

'I would have your entire dowry at my disposal, if it wasn't for your meddling uncle and brother,' Charles snarled. 'It's your fault we are poor. You find the remedy.'

Wobbling, Henrietta grasped the bureau and dragged herself to her feet. Without another word, she picked up her hat and left the room.

～ ～

She had forgotten the feel of a carpet; how it made her shoes sink, the gentle pad and whisper as she glided over it. She found she could not walk properly.

13

Her unimpressive dress drew strange looks from the Usher of the Presence who guided her, and the guards who raised their halberds to let her through. She stared at her feet and focused on moving them forward. She couldn't risk quailing beneath the hostile glances, or gasping at the flock wallpaper and intricate gilding. She had to look like she belonged here. Portraits of long-dead dukes sneered down at her, their oily eyes disdainful. She was not good enough. Her stomacher was too plain, her shift too coarse and devoid of frills. The steel improvers that held out her skirts were small and drooping. Of all the jewellery a lady could possess, she had only her wedding ring left – and God knew that was more of a shackle than an ornament.

The usher led her through a burnished door into a closet. Sofas of duck-egg blue stood beside the wall, while courtiers lounged against their golden frames. Ornate mirrors reflected shelves of books. The veined marble fireplace, empty in the mild weather, bore the largest carriage-clock Henrietta had ever seen upon its mantelpiece. Each tick echoed in the hollow grate.

'Wait here.' Her guide vanished, leaving only the faintest trace of sandalwood cologne behind him.

She stood, shipwrecked in the centre of the rug. Two stout female courtiers gawped at her. They had gold and silver thread in their clothing, fine pocket-watches and exquisite lace. Their disdainful gaze slithered over her, taking in the splashes of mud on her shoes and the dull paste buckles. Little pins of mortification pricked under her skin and behind her eyes. Bowing her face beneath the brim of her hat, she stumbled over to a sofa and sat down. The upholstery sighed.

'New to court?'

She jumped. A man with small features and arching, intelligent eyebrows sat beside her. His dress was smart but unadorned. There were no black patches on his face, no diamond pins in his jacket.

'I am sorry.' He put out a hand, looking abashed. He spoke the

14

court language of French with an English accent. 'I didn't mean to frighten you.'

'No, no, it was my fault. I was . . . somewhere else.'

He smiled. 'I cannot blame you. Dreadfully dull, all this waiting. Still, it builds character.'

'Have you been here long?'

He laughed. 'Do you mean today, or in general? The answer to both questions is pretty much the same. I have been here for ages. If you cannot buy yourself a place at court, you have to pay for it another way. With your time.'

'But you have met the Electress Sophia, at least?'

'Dowager Electress,' the man corrected. 'Sophia still thinks she rules the roost, but in fact it's her son, Georg Ludwig.'

Henrietta winced. She had known that. But Sophia was more important in Britain, since she was the next heir to the throne. Her son was still in the shadows. 'The Elector, Georg Ludwig – he has a wife?'

The man sucked in his breath through clenched teeth. He glanced around before stealing closer. 'You must not mention her,' he whispered. 'Caught in adultery – banished to a castle in Celle.'

The scandal sizzled in Henrietta's ear. 'I thank you for the hint,' she said. 'I would have made a blunder there.'

'Not at all.' The man offered a hand. 'John Gay. If I can be of any further assistance, do let me know.'

She shook his hand quickly. 'Henrietta Howard.'

'Ah, Howard! That's an ancient English name. Sophia will love you. She is very proud of her English heritage. Wants people to call her the Princess of Wales! But if you cannot gain a place with Sophia, you should try for the Princess Caroline. She is an excellent woman.'

'Princess Caroline? Is she Georg Ludwig's daughter?'

'Daughter-in-law,' he amended. 'Married to Georg Ludwig's son, Prince George.'

Her head reeled. It was too much to take in at once. She had only considered courting Sophia, not a son, grandson and grand-daughter-in-law. But she would have to commit the relationships to memory fast . . .

'The Honourable Mr and Mrs Howard.'

Henrietta spun around. A powdered gentleman with a bored expression on his face held the door open. She fumbled to shake out her skirts and stand. 'Just – just Mrs Howard, actually.' Once again, she felt critical eyes upon her. What a sight she must look, poorly dressed and unaccompanied.

'Very well, *just Mrs Howard*. The Dowager Electress has asked for you.'

Henrietta held her breath. Her feet wobbled on her heels as she stepped forward. She had taken no leave of Mr Gay, but she couldn't look back over her shoulder now. Her vision had become a tunnel. The threshold was the only thing that existed. Shaking, she followed the page and passed through the doorway, into the warm embrace of a sunlit room. A hush fell at the sound of her footsteps. The gentle hum of an orchestra, which had been playing when she entered, faded away. She focused straight ahead, trying to stop her legs from shaking. A great chair stood by the window with a thin figure hunched against the upholstery. Sophia – it had to be. Henrietta's insides turned to liquid.

'Come.'

As she moved forward, rays of sunlight bounced off the glass, dazzling her. She could not squint or turn her face to the side; she could only stumble blindly on into the light, toward the woman who would decide her fate. She curtsied low, the scent of herbs rising to greet her from the floor.

'Mrs Howard.' The voice was warm and caressing, like a summer breeze. 'We have been waiting to meet you.'

16

CHAPTER THREE

Herrenhausen

'I wish she would hurry up and die. What's she waiting for?'

Caroline's laugh rang around the gardens of Herrenhausen, bouncing off the clipped hornbeam to join the tinkling fountain. 'Oh Grandmamma, you do not mean it. Poor Queen Anne. Give her a few more days.'

Sophia scowled, deepening the wrinkles in her face. 'In a few days she can change her mind. Cut the House of Hanover from the British succession completely.'

'If she does that, she will not have to wait long for death,' Caroline pointed out. 'For I'm sure you would kill her.'

Sophia chuckled, but the trouble didn't leave her watery brown eyes.

It wasn't fair. Britain's throne was so close to Hanover now, you could practically taste it. But even as Queen Anne's life trickled away, death was snapping at the heels of her successor. Caroline's stomach pitched as she considered her husband's frail grandmother beside the vibrant gardens. Spring bloomed; flowers opened, shedding their scent on the balmy air, yet Sophia curled and decayed.

Every day scored her, marking a living tally of years on her skin. Achieving her dream should be simple: all she had to do was live. But even Sophia's indomitable spirit would struggle to keep this scraggly, bony body alive.

Caroline sighed and looked over to her children playing beside the topiary figures. Frederick, her eldest, tickled his sisters and made them squeal. The familiar ambition surged through her as she watched him. Here was her contribution to the glory of their house – a vessel to keep her blood forever in the veins of the British monarchy. If he could. Maternal affection did not blind her; Fred was not the son she had hoped for. She wanted a ruddy-faced, harum-scarum boy with a powerful presence. But as Fred grew older, he looked less and less like a future king, with a narrow chest that heaved as he ran and legs slender as twigs beneath his stockings. Even out in the sun, his skin was so pale. She chewed her lip. She needed another boy. There was no guarantee this sapling would grow to take his place.

As they walked on, a palette of foliage spread before them: white and pink blossom, purple leaves, the dark emerald of the Cyprus, all shot through with sticky buds. It was a peaceful, beautiful scene, but Caroline couldn't appreciate it. Sophia kept fidgeting at her side.

'If death took me tomorrow, I would go content so long as it said *Queen of England* on my tombstone.' Sophia twisted the curls of her wig around a finger. 'I'll settle for outliving Anne a day – an hour.'

Caroline saw her own prickling desires reflected in Sophia's aged face. 'It *will* happen,' she said. 'I will always have hope for our house. You and your grandson are destined for great things.'

A childish shriek rang out. Caroline's eldest daughter, Anne, dodged Frederick's advances and shoved him into a hedge. She looked so triumphant, dusting off her little gloves, that Caroline did not have the heart to scold her. Better her daughter learnt to push men about than be pushed by them.

Sophia sniggered as Frederick wormed his way back onto his feet, green sprigs stuck to his hair. 'And your little Fretz? Is he destined for great things?'

'Fred,' Caroline corrected. 'The English will think Fretz sounds too German – we will start calling him Fred.' One of the many changes she planned. In England, show was everything. Military force would not be enough to impose a new dynasty on the country – the House of Hanover needed to win the people heart and soul.

'Excellent!' Sophia clapped her gnarly hands. 'Let us make him English! We cannot be too English for my taste. Speaking of which . . .' She flicked her eyes over the train of ladies and dogs dawdling in their wake. 'I have a new English lady. Did you see her?'

'Really, how would I know? You have a new English lady each week. I wonder if poor Queen Anne has any courtiers left.'

Sophia grinned; even this was a small victory over her rival. A breeze fluttered past them, making the flowers bob. 'This one is not from the court, I think. Look toward the back, you will spot her instantly.'

Caroline turned her head and pretended to admire a statue. Her eyes darted forward and back like the wasps sipping nectar from the flowers. Yes, she saw the lady at once; you could not miss her. That dress, so remarkably plain in this court of gold and silk. The bodice sagged a little over her chest; her waist seemed slim, but the gown failed to shape it. Perhaps it was second-hand. Were they really starting to admit waifs and strays like this into their court?

Caroline had to concede that the woman's figure was good; slender and just above average height. There was little else to recommend her. Hunks of short, chestnut hair stuck out beneath the saucer of her hat. As if aware of her failings, she kept a little apart from the other ladies, her eyes trained on the gravel.

Abandoning the statue, Caroline walked forward. She splayed her fan and whispered to Sophia. 'Good Heavens! What *is* that?'

'That is The Honourable Mrs Howard, my dear.'

Caroline baulked. She recognised the name, but surely she was mistaken . . . 'Howard? Was that one in our book of English peers? I seem to remember . . .'

Sophia raised her eyebrows, ploughing furrows into her forehead. 'You are right to look surprised. The Howards are Earls of Suffolk. They own a grand house in Essex.'

The ancient name of Howard, yet dressed like a pauper? It didn't make any sense. 'And she always wears a dress like that?'

'*That* dress. She has been here a week and I have seen no other.'

Caroline chuckled, but in truth she was uneasy. The poor creature must have fallen on hard times indeed. It would take a lot of courage – or desperation – to turn up day after day in that outfit and be sneered at. 'Perhaps she is one of those English eccentrics?'

Sophia plucked a fallen petal from the hedge and ran it through her fingers. 'Actually, she is rather sweet. Very eager to please. Learned, certainly. I rather think I might keep her.'

'Yes, you would.' She smiled. 'You do love a good puzzle. What of her husband?'

Sophia moistened her lips. Before she could speak, a cry rent the air. A page ran cringing from the palace with his arms clasped in a protective arch over his head.

'Ruined! The whole blasted thing is ruined!' It was a voice that could flay skin. A wig sailed from the window and bounced off the page into a hedge. 'What did you do, use it to dust the shelves? I've seen more powder on a baby's arse!'

Caroline and Sophia exchanged a look.

'Perhaps it is time you returned to George,' said Sophia.

One hour – she left him a single hour and he fell apart. No doubt his father had been stirring the cauldron in her absence, prodding him with fresh slights and malicious words. She groaned. 'It is Georg Ludwig, your *dearest* son.' Sophia smirked – she did not love him any more than Caroline. 'He is the cause of this.'

'Ah. I suppose he won't let George go to England and receive his honorary titles?'

'No. I haven't had a moment's peace since he found out. It's been like appeasing a baited bear.'

Objects tumbled from the window in quick succession; a hat, a book, a pair of gloves. The ladies tittered. Mrs Howard stood at the back, her eyes wide.

Sophia's face twitched as she struggled to contain her amusement. 'Well, you had better go to him now. I would like *some* servants left alive.'

Caroline sucked in a breath and girded herself. She had weathered many such storms before. Taking the wig from a tangle of branches, she brushed off the leaves and started toward the palace.

～ ⁓

Henrietta pulled another stitch through the embroidery silk and secured it with a knot. At least her blistered, calloused hands were good for something; she worked with more speed and accuracy than the other ladies. Not that it made them like her any better. She was careful to keep her eye fixed on the needle so that she did not see their scathing looks, the hard grins that told her she was beneath their contempt. Humiliation was a constant companion. She had never felt so much like a dog begging for scraps at the table. Were it not for Sophia's kindness, she believed she would flee the court entirely.

Sophia sighed as she leant back in her chair, already bored from inactivity. 'Look at him there, my grandfather, staring down at me.' As one, the ladies gazed at the portrait brooding above the mantelpiece. James I of England stared back at them in oil paint with his pointed beard and knowing eyes. 'I wonder what he would make of all this. Would he want me on his throne?' She turned. 'Mrs Howard,

I've seen you with a history book on your lap. What do you think?'

Silk rustled as everyone swivelled to stare at Henrietta. Her tongue suddenly felt too large for her mouth. 'I . . . I am sure he would feel for you, madam. He had to introduce a new ruling dynasty to Britain too, did he not?'

Sophia's face became a map of wrinkles. 'Yes. But the people tried to blow him up, and then they beheaded his son.'

The ladies laughed. Each jangling note was a pinprick in Henrietta's skin. As if these Hanoverians knew the least thing about English history. She cleared her throat. 'How right you are. Perhaps you should ask the Princess Caroline. I am sure her knowledge is superior to mine.'

'Yes!' Sophia clapped her hands. 'Come. Let us go to her.' She was up and out of her chair before Henrietta had a chance to lay down her sewing. Astonishing, that an eighty-two-year-old woman could move with such speed.

Used to their volatile mistress, the other ladies rose and followed, blocking Henrietta's passage with their hoops. She hung behind and walked alone, at the very back. She was always at the back.

As they made their way down the corridor, a window opened upon the gardens. Through the glass the Elector Georg Ludwig and his mistress, Madame Melusine Schulenburg, could be seen taking the air. They made a strange couple; serious and unattractive. Georg Ludwig walked as if he were late for an appointment. Heeding neither the flowers nor the butterflies, he kept his head high and straight. The lady minced after him. She was so thin she looked almost ill.

Sophia glowered at them as she swept past. 'Pah! Look at that maukin! I never thought my son would conceive a passion for such a scarecrow!'

There was certainly no love lost in this family. Henrietta could not keep track of the petty jealousies that wreathed the palace. The only person on good terms with all was the Princess Caroline. That was understandable; she was not a woman Henrietta would want to cross.

Since first glimpsing the princess, Henrietta had held her in a state of church-like awe. Oh, she was cordial enough, offering a ready smile and tinkling laughter to every gathering. But there was something behind that cheerful expression that pierced like a blade.

As they sailed into Caroline's private chambers, they saw the princess sitting beside her husband on a damask sofa. Pale blue silk stretched over her buxom figure and frothed into lace around her bosom. The curves of her ample breasts showed creamy white. She had a prominent, sloping nose and tilted feline eyes. They flashed over the ladies for a second but gave nothing away.

The prince's face was slim and earnest looking, dominated by round blue eyes. He would be handsome but for the mottled colour of his skin and the veins that stood out like cords in his neck.

Caroline rose and smiled with even white teeth. 'Ah, Grand-mamma. What a pleasant surprise.' Long blonde hair tumbled down her back in waves, powdered to the hue of winter sun.

Sophia hobbled over, infusing the space with her scent of dried lavender and faded roses. 'My dear.' She looked at Prince George, sitting on the sofa. 'Have I interrupted you?'

'No.' It was clear from the speed of his answer that she had. 'I am leaving now. I must take my exercise before it gets too hot.'

'Your father is in the gardens,' Sophia warned.

'Then I shall ride.' Springing to his feet, he made a brief nod to the ladies and sped through the door.

Caroline fell back on the sofa with a sigh. 'You may guess what that was about. The same argument, again and again.'

'I can understand his frustration.' Sophia sat down beside her. 'It would do us so much good to have a presence in England at this time. If he could only go and receive his titles, it would be one foot in the door.'

Henrietta nodded. Much as the British wanted to keep Queen

Anne's Catholic brother away from the throne, they were unnerved by the idea of bestowing their crown upon a foreign power. These Hanoverians were strangers who did not understand the customs, the history – even what it meant to be British. The longer they stayed away, the more alien they seemed.

'You agree, madam? You nod very decidedly?'

Henrietta jumped to see Caroline looking at her with those piercing blue eyes. She suddenly felt naked. 'I . . . '

Sophia smiled. 'Ah, yes. I have not presented Mrs Howard, have I? Come forward, dear, meet the Princess Caroline.'

She took a few wobbling steps, aware of every eye upon her. As she curtsied, the dull material of her cheap gown pooled on the floor beside Caroline's cornflower silk. She could not bring herself to raise her eyes. Sophia might be charitable enough to see past oddities of dress and appearance, but she had a feeling this glamorous princess was not.

'Why, you look fit to faint, child. Come, give me your hand. I do not bite.' A few ladies tittered. Gingerly, Henrietta took the princess's fingers and kissed them. They had the honeyed scent of attar of roses. 'The Dowager Electress tells me you are recently arrived from England. You will be best suited to tell me about the political situation there. I saw you nod so earnestly as we spoke of sending my husband over. Do you think it would be a good plan?'

Her mouth was suddenly full of ashes. It had been so long since she had been pressed for her opinion that she had forgotten how to give it. The clock ticked, accentuating every second of her silence. 'I . . . I do not know how much Your Highness already understands about the state of my country.' She darted a glance up. Caroline watched her with unblinking concentration. 'Perhaps you have heard of the two political groups, the Whigs and the Tories?'

'Oh, yes. But I do not thoroughly understand them at present. Do go on.'

That was the last thing she wanted to do. It was as if someone had wiped the slate of her mind perfectly clean. Had Caroline asked Henrietta her name, she would have struggled to answer. 'Well . . . The Tories are in power. They have been loyal to Queen Anne. But – but they stand by the Stuarts. They are not . . . It is the Whig party that favours your family's claim to the throne.' She ploughed through her thoughts, turning up nothing but thick soil. She could not decide if it would be less foolish to speak or stay silent, but her mouth kept moving and made the choice for her. 'In general the Tories represent the interests of the landed squires. The Church of England. But you see there are so many schisms and factions, it is hard to explain . . . The Whigs favour freedom. That is, they believe the constitution is more important than the rights of kings . . .' She blushed, wishing the carpet would let her sink into its plush folds. 'Forgive me, I am not making much sense. I am trying to remember what my father told me. He was a Whig, but he died when I was nine. I do not perfectly recall his words.'

Actually, her only memory of her father's political forays was the noise of raised voices travelling through the house up to the nursery storey; her mother's high-pitched scold about the huge sums of money spent in the previous election.

Caroline wore the false, closed-lipped smile of indulgence that she conferred upon her children. 'Never mind, Mrs Howard. I am sure you will be able to tell me more when you are not taken by surprise. I have rather put you on the spot.'

Her nervous laugh gurgled in her throat. 'All I meant to say was that the Tories can suggest many things about your family while you are not there to contradict them. Seeing a prince in the flesh would put many rumours to rest.'

'I agree. But the Elector does not mean to let my husband go.'

'Nor does my cousin Queen Anne,' Sophia pointed out. 'I am sure she would have found an excuse to stop the visit. She does not want us over there, reminding her she must die.' She snickered. 'Ah, if only she and my son had made a match of it. They are both pig-headed and stubborn. What a couple they would have been!'

Caroline adjusted her position on the sofa. 'But the Countess d'Eke looks as if she has an opinion. Pray, tell me what it is?'

Henrietta slipped back to allow the countess her place in the sun. The others shouldered her behind them without a second glance. Failure left her hollow. If only she had spoken to her brother John and found out more about the state of parliament before she came. But that had been next to impossible; Charles forbade any visits to John until he relinquished her dowry. Their correspondence could only continue in secret; long letters were too much of a risk.

She took her place on the edge of the group, hidden from view. The sun shifted outside and cast a shadow across her. Disappointment drained her until all that remained was a bitter tang of self-loathing. She had been given her chance to impress – and fallen at the first fence.

∾ ∾

Company packed the salon. Rivulets of sweat trickled down Henrietta's legs as she took another warm and unpleasantly sweet sip of ratafia. She had always imagined the inner sanctum of court to be like a paradise, but it was as hot and stinking as a circle of hell. Dice clattered against the tables, followed by cheers and groans. Red, laughing faces swirled past her eyes. She wondered what Charles was doing, back in their tiny rooms. If he knew how freely the wine flowed here, perhaps he would come to court after all.

Most of the ladies played at cards with the princess. Caroline sat with a hand fanned before her face, masking all but her dancing eyes. Her gown glowed emerald in the candlelight.

Henrietta rubbed at her ear, pressing through the folds of lace and hair that covered it. If she could overhear a conversation, she might join in. But on one side of her head there was nothing but a high-pitched whine. It had been that way for a few weeks now. She recalled Charles's heavy hands and the blood brought away on her fingertips. She shuddered. Perhaps this time he had damaged her beyond repair.

'Mrs Howard, isn't it?'

She jumped round, almost spilling her drink. To her astonishment George, the Electoral Prince, stood before her. He cut a handsome figure in his long coat frosted with silver. His features were pointed and almost feminine as they opened up in greeting.

Henrietta bobbed a hurried curtsey. 'Yes – yes, Your Royal Highness. I am Henrietta Howard.' Panic spiralled through her. She had only ever seen this man shouting or throwing servants out of the room. His temper was infamous. If she brushed him up the wrong way, she was done for.

'How do you do? How do you do?' He took her hand and pumped it in his own. 'My grandmother speaks of you very often.'

His touch caused a tingle inside. These men of the court dazzled her with their glamour. Such a vivid contrast to the dirty, tatty Charles. Henrietta curtsied again, feeling as if she had two left feet. 'That is very kind of her.'

'She was right – you do have a soft, remarkably clear voice.' Henrietta felt her cheeks grow warmer. 'She believes – and so does my wife – that you would be the perfect person to help me with my English. What do you think, eh? Can you do anything about my accent?'

A spasm of horror cramped her stomach. How could she spend hours alone with this man without sending him into one of his rages? She would never dare to contradict him for a mistake. 'How you honour me,' she said in a small voice. 'I am, of course, always happy to help where I can.'

She looked down his sharp nose to his full, pouting lips. They broke into a smile. 'Excellent! I will summon you tomorrow. Only let us not make it too hum-drum. I cannot endure long lessons. They put me in a devil of a mood.'

Henrietta swallowed. She had thought Herrenhausen a haven from Charles, but it seemed she was only swapping one man with a short fuse for another.

As if reading her thoughts, George spoke again. 'And your husband, madam? Where is he? I should like to meet The Honourable Mr Howard.'

The ringing in her ear picked up a notch. 'Indisposed, Your Highness. But I'm confident he will be at court very soon.'

'My wife tells me he's a soldier?'

'He was. A Captain of the Light Dragoons.'

The prince's face lit up. 'Capital! What uniform did he have?'

'Uniform?'

'Yes.' He nodded vigorously. 'How many buttons? Gold braiding?'

A painful memory played behind her eyes: Charles, clean-shaven, with his helmet under his arm. The man she had fallen for and never seen since. 'Dark blue, edged with gold.'

'Is that all you remember? You women never pay attention to these things!'

She held herself taut, afraid she might have angered him. Thinking quickly, she diverted him down another path. 'Have you seen military action, sir?'

'Yes! I had a horse shot out from under me at Oudenarde, poor beast,' he said with relish. 'Somersaulted right over him and landed on my feet. I kept on fighting. Wouldn't let the brutes have the satisfaction of seeing me wounded.'

'That sounds extremely brave.'

'It was the War of the Spanish Succession, back in the year eight.

We fought to put Archduke Charles of Austria on the throne.' His voice quickened, warming to his theme. 'I never thought I would see the day I fought for Archduke Charles! You know, I expect, that he wanted to marry Caroline before I did? If he wasn't Catholic, he would have been a good match for her.'

His words turned to a gabble in Henrietta's ear. She nodded politely, but he rambled on about the Archduke's lineage – obscure royal relations who meant nothing to her. Evidently he was a man who enjoyed the sound of his own voice. She could just envisage these English lessons he proposed: hours of tedium. She would present a few new words, then he would launch into one of his stories and she would not venture to interrupt him.

But was that really so bad? It was a chance, after all. She had failed to impress Caroline, but George was not half as quick. By showing patience, she could worm herself into his good graces. She would be a fool not to latch onto this opportunity like a limpet.

George paused. His bulging blue eyes blinked expectantly.

'Fascinating,' Henrietta supplied quickly. 'Just – fascinating. However do you remember all that?'

He beamed. 'Wait until I tell you the connection through my mother's side of the family.'

Henrietta watched the prince's lips move. She schooled her features into an expression of rapt attention and made encouraging noises. She saw instantly that he was pleased with her.

She was struck by the way he looked into her face, carefully watching the effect of his words. She had not experienced such close attention from a man since . . . she could not remember.

Something flickered inside her, a tinderbox trying to strike a flame. It was a feeling she had almost forgotten. Blushing, she lowered her eyes.

CHAPTER FOUR

Herrenhausen

Soft coos drifted on the summer air. Henrietta stood at the centre of the maze, watching doves poke their heads through heart-shaped holes in their cote. They reminded her of her son: all wide-eyed innocence.

Shouts drifted over the hedges; ladies squealing, still lost in the labyrinth, and beyond that the gentle lap of gondolas on the moat. She sighed. If she shut her eyes and inhaled the scent of foliage, her mind transported her. She soared over the lime trees, looking down on the pike ponds where golden scales glimmered beneath the water. She flew across the roaring Channel, all the way back to Henry. How often she had dreamed of being in Herrenhausen – away from Charles, safely enclosed behind golden gates. But now she was here she could only mourn what she had left.

Behind her, a footstep crunched on the gravel. She wheeled round so fast that the birds fluttered inside, leaving her standing in a swirl of feathers.

'Ah, Mrs Howard. We meet again.' Caroline ambled into the heart of the maze. Henrietta froze. The princess, with her honeyed smell and sharp beauty, still filled her with a sense of unease. Her gown swept up leaves and pebbles as she walked. She stopped by the dovecote, peeled off her gloves and teased a bird onto her finger.

Giggles drifted toward them. Caroline tilted her head in unison with the dove on her hand. 'Do you know, my ladies have been in this maze thousands of times? I mean it literally. Thousands. They do not remember the twists and turns.' She shook her head. 'I cannot understand the dullness of their wits.'

'The ladies of the court lack Your Royal Highness's skill.'

Caroline looked at her. 'You do not. You reached the centre before me.'

Henrietta's insides clenched, as if Caroline was viewing something deeply private. Blushing, she inclined her head.

Caroline ran her fingers through the dove's feathers. 'You were very nervous when I spoke to you the other day, but I believe you understand more than you reveal. That is wise. A lady must conceal any learning she has, the same way she would hide a limp or a deformity. It is only then, when men think she is a pretty little fool, that she can make them do what she wants.'

Henrietta smiled – there was some wisdom in that. 'I do not know. I cannot make the prince pronounce *Hampton Court Palace*. I certainly cannot make my husband do what I want.'

A breeze whistled through the hedges and snatched a curl from her cheek. Caroline's gaze intensified. Realisation came to Henrietta with a stab of horror: the bruise. Her hand flew to her face, but it was too late.

'Oh.' Caroline replaced the bird amongst its friends. 'What a contusion you have there, Mrs Howard. I suppose . . . ' Seeming to change her mind, she took a step toward Henrietta. Her voice dropped to a whisper. 'My dear, how long has your husband been treating you thus?'

The hedges swirled. Even in his absence, Charles had found a way to ruin her. She had an absurd impulse to fall at Caroline's feet and sob. The burden of her secret was an intolerable weight she had carried alone for too long. But she did not have the luxury of confession. If she admitted what Charles truly was, the royal family would never employ him. With a supreme effort, she rearranged her tight face into an expression of surprise. 'I beg your pardon? I do not have the pleasure of understanding – '

Caroline held up a hand, making her rings glint. 'Hush. Be truthful, child.' She paused, as if choosing her words carefully. 'You are not much acquainted with me, Mrs Howard, but I can tell you that my mother was married twice. Her second husband was a brutal man. He left his mark . . .' Her plump lips quivered.

Panic rattled in Henrietta's ribcage. Every one of Caroline's compassionate words was a door slamming in her face. 'I can assure you, Your Royal Highness is quite mistaken. My candle went out on the way to bed; I was foolish and thought I could manage without it, but –'

'My mother was not the only one he beat.'

The breath mangled in her throat. She sagged into a hedge. Only its dense, scratching branches held her up; her legs were useless. Years of work undone by one stray bruise. With Charles unemployable, she would never save enough to make her way back to Henry. Nothing beckoned ahead but the cold pavements, splashed with mud and filth. Fighting with dogs over offal in the street. Her thoughts turned to the River Leine; its swirling eddies, its dark depths.

'Is this why we never see Mr Howard? Did you run from him?'

Her throat was in a knot. She could only shake her head.

Caroline extended a knuckle and fluffed the white croup of the bird nearest to her. 'So what was your plan? To get a place in the next queen's household, I suppose? That would make sense. You would be safe, under our protection.' She rested her chin on her bare palm, tapping her fingertips against her cheek. 'But the husband . . . What did you propose doing with him?'

'I thought he might find a post too,' she wheezed. 'But he would not come to court. He would not even try.' She hung her head. 'Not that it matters, now.'

'Of course it matters!' Caroline's voice was sharp. 'For shame, child, do you give up so easily?'

'I . . . ' She shook her head, utterly lost. All the fight and sense seemed to be dribbling out of her, feeding the sturdy hedge. 'Surely I must give in, now.'

Those piercing eyes pinioned her. 'Do you think I would tell your secret?'

'No, madam. I trust you are too good for that.' She closed her eyes. 'I cannot say what you plan. All I know is that you will never employ my husband.'

'Not I. Nor Sophia. But the Elector might.'

'The Elector?' Henrietta pictured the grim-faced, dour-looking Georg Ludwig. She could not imagine a man less likely to favour Charles. 'I do not understand. What are you saying?'

'I will speak to him.' Caroline pulled her gloves back on. 'He listens to me, though he pretends he does not. I will get Mr Howard a place with him.'

'But – Your Highness . . . '

'Do not fret. I will ask it as a favour, for myself. All you have to do is get the scoundrel here. If he works for the Elector and you work for Sophia, you will be kept apart often. Safe.'

Henrietta couldn't trust her senses. Her mouth hung open, trying to form words. A moment ago her dreams had capsized, but now the world had flipped again – too fast. The princess, help a wretch like her? 'You would do that for me?'

'Of course.'

The sun moved behind the hedges, gilding Caroline's profile. Henrietta wanted to kiss the hem of her skirt. 'Your Highness. . .'

There were no words.

The princess pressed a finger to Henrietta's lips. Her glove tasted of rosewater. 'Hush, now. I will keep you safe, Mrs Howard. Trust in me.'

⤳ ⤴

Caroline sailed down the corridor, gripping her children's hands. Little Frederick fell behind with his skinny legs. He trailed his spare fingers across the panelling, not walking like a prince at all. She sighed. What could she do for him? At least with Mrs Howard there was a clear answer.

'Knock on the door, Anne. Let's see if Grandpa wants to play with us.'

The door swung open, revealing a middle-aged couple sitting hunched over a table, cutting paper shapes. The man had a square, weathered face. A grey periwig rose from his scalp in twin peaks and descended to his chest. His eyes were intent on the scissors, making delicate snips.

'Grandpa!' The children flung away from Caroline and ran toward him with arms outstretched.

He jumped and discarded his scissors. 'Annie! Fretzchen!'

'Fred,' Caroline corrected, under her breath.

Frederick clambered onto his grandfather's lap and played with the lace at his neck. Little Anne was content merely to stand by his side and let him stroke her hair like a spoilt cat. Caroline felt a throb of resentment on her husband's behalf. How could Georg Ludwig lavish love upon his grandchildren, yet never spare his son a kind word?

The Elector's mistress, Melusine, smiled and cleared the table of its sharp objects. She had high, slender eyebrows and a good nose, but she was no beauty. Her stomacher lay flat against her chest and the ruffles on her sleeves gaped around skinny elbows. She looked as insubstantial as a reed, but Caroline knew better. Melusine Schulenburg was not so easy to break.

'How pleased I am to see you, Father.' Caroline curtsied low, giving him a tantalising glimpse of her cleavage. It never hurt to remind the old goat of her beauty. 'May we sit with you a while?'

His smile melted into suspicion. 'What do you want?'

'*Want?*' Caroline pressed a palm to her chest. 'Must I want something, to sit with my own family?'

Fred squealed, forcing his grandfather to jiggle his knees and make him bounce. A familiar jealousy nagged at Caroline's core; Fred didn't smile like that for her. He never had.

'Caroline, you are no fool. Do not treat me like one.'

Very well. If he wanted to speak frankly, he would find her a match for him. She turned to Melusine. 'Madame Schulenburg, would you be good enough to play with my children for a moment? I have some business with the Elector.'

It was clear from the glint in her eye that Melusine would rather stay and listen, but she had more sense than to object. Her wiry figure wound around the table. 'Of course.'

Caroline watched them retreat to the corner; little Anne, balanced on Melusine's jutting hip and Fred, holding her hand. His legs were so thin in their white stockings. He stumbled – a reminder of the rickets that had blighted his infancy. Worry hovered about her for a moment, mingled with something akin to shame. Three daughters and one sickly son: a poor show. She needed another heir. Much as it scoured her to admit it, Fred might not last.

'Do sit.' As she did, the Elector spread his hands. 'Well?'

'No doubt your mother has spoken to you about The Honourable Mrs Howard, the English lady?'

He inclined his head. 'A new pet. How charming for you both.'

'I wish to keep her.'

Georg Ludwig shrugged. 'What stops you? I have no objections.'

'Ah! But I cannot keep the goose without the gander. Surely you see that.'

'There is a *Mr* Howard?'

'Naturally.' Caroline looked him in the eye. The trick was not to ask, but demand – to speak as if she had no doubt of his compliance. 'I want you to employ him.'

Georg Ludwig chuckled. He made a steeple out of his hands and leant his nose against it. 'You do, do you? A man from nowhere. Someone I have never seen in the course of my life.'

'Yes. Only a token role. I'm not asking for any honours.'

'You are asking enough. Do you not think this Mr Howard, husband of your *Freundin*, would be better suited elsewhere? Say, in George's household?'

She had him now. Caroline raised her eyebrows. 'Quite. But George cannot afford to take on any more staff with the allowance you grant him. After all, you didn't increase it when we married, or when the children were born . . . If I wanted him to employ Mr Howard, I would have to come here with another question . . . One I think you would rather I did not ask.'

The shutters came down on his face. Astonishing, what the mention of money could do. He would rather stretch his own resources, employ half of Hanover, than raise his son's allowance by a crown.

Caroline smiled sweetly and fluttered her lashes. 'Can I hope you will think upon it? It would save much . . . unpleasantness.'

He looked like he had swallowed lemon rind. 'I will think on it,' he said grudgingly.

1714 – 1715

CHAPTER FIVE

⤳ Herrenhausen ⤳

Stormclouds gathered, each one a chunk of granite. Behind them the sun burnt fiercely, chiselling away at the edges. Henrietta quickened her step. The foliage beside her glowed, astonishingly bright against the sky. Everything augured torrential rain, but Sophia showed no signs of turning back inside. She headed her gaggle of ladies like a general with his soldiers, striding along and barking orders to the gardeners.

Caroline walked by Henrietta's side, a pretty baby with a dusting of brown hair nestled in her bosom. Her third daughter, Carrie. As Henrietta peered into the chubby infant face, her heart seized up with grief. Henry had not been a plump baby like this, luxuriating in folds of silk. She had wasted the magic of his early days worrying whether she would be able to feed him, protect him from the hands of his father. She would never get those days back.

'You said you had a child too, Mrs Howard. A boy. How old is he?'

She could not repress a sigh. 'Seven years and five months, Your Highness. Just a month older than the Prince Frederick.'

Caroline moved the baby onto her shoulder and rubbed her back. The child's wet lips parted in a cough. 'Well educated?'

'Not as well as I would wish. You see, there have not been . . . My circumstances . . . '

'Ah. That *is* a shame. If he had a little learning, I could have invited him here to play with my Fred. You must miss him very much.'

They paused to watch the children chasing around the flower-beds. They were frisky, like animals before a downpour. Anne's lace cap bobbed up and down, roses and ribbons fluttering in the breeze. Fred shrieked, a painfully high-pitched sound, as he tried to grasp her skirts. What but dumb luck had put this boy in the position of a prince and Henrietta's in the gutter? Yet Frederick did not look any healthier than Henry. He was pale and struggled to clop about in the special boots made to straighten his rickety legs.

Caroline edged closer, her taffeta gown pressing against Henrietta's forearm. 'Come, I will tell you a secret in exchange for yours, Mrs Howard. Fred . . . Fred is slow.' Her eyes hovered on the little boy, running around with his sister. 'Slow to learn, slow to walk. I worry for him. This is not a world that favours the sluggish.'

Rain splattered on the paving stones. As they walked on, the drops accelerated, forcing Henrietta to hitch up her skirts. Baby Carrie moaned. Soon the air was thick with the smell of damp turf. Fretful ladies guided Sophia away from the path and under the cover of trees.

The sky flashed. Frederick, Anne and little Emily flew toward Caroline and buried their faces in her skirts. Thunder rumbled, deep-throated like a threatening dog. The baby wailed. Henrietta reached out and took her into her arms, while Caroline soothed the elder children. Drips fell from the brim of her hat and joined the quickly forming puddles.

Another blast of light, accompanied by a scream. Henrietta jumped; the sound was not a lady-like squeal, but a moan of agony. Her eyes darted to the tree, just as Sophia sank to her knees in the wet grass beneath.

'No. Oh, God, no.' Caroline jerked free from her children and sprinted across the lawn, skirts trailing in the mud and pearls dropping from her hair.

Henrietta's slick arms shook. 'Hush, now. Hush.' She gathered the children around her, trying to conceal her own fear. She watched as Caroline skidded beside the Dowager Electress and encircled the elder woman with her arms. The body tilted toward her, heavy and lifeless.

Caroline's wail of grief travelled across the gardens. Her blonde hair hung limp against the back of her ruined gown. She was no longer a royal wonder but an abject thing, grovelling in the mud and howling her pain.

'What's happened to Great-Grandma? What's happened to Mama?' Frederick's voice was high and scared.

Henrietta could not look at him. She was remembering her own grief, the old wound that suddenly opened up fresh and seeping. 'She has lost another mother.'

~ ~

Black crepe covered the walls. Despite the blue sky and birds chirping outside, Herrenhausen was locked in an eternal night; its clocks stopped, windows shuttered, mirrors and portraits turned to face the walls. Courtiers stood motionless, transformed from peacocks into crows. It was just like Henrietta's childhood. She remembered it well: the weight of melancholy and the numb days that followed a death.

Mr Gay, the man Henrietta had met on her first day, sat beside

41

her. He leaned to speak into her ear. 'They say it was a stroke. You were there. Did it look like one?'

She lifted her shoulders. 'I don't know. I was not close enough to see.'

Caroline sat taut as a bowstring, her yellow hair dimmed under swathes of gauze. George was beside her, pale and drooping with red-rimmed eyes. Henrietta felt a pang of tenderness, almost maternal, toward him. Where was the stroppy soldier prince now? She would not have thought, a few weeks before, that he was capable of such feeling. Yet all the while, underneath, there was this.

A distant clopping broke the silence. Caroline frowned as the sound grew louder. Soon, it was unmistakable: a horse at gallop.

Caroline put her hand upon George's and clasped it until her knuckles turned white. 'My love.'

'What? What now?'

She stood with a rustle of silk. Instinctively, Henrietta went to her side. 'There is a messenger. For some foolish reason, I fear he is from England.' Caroline glared at the closed door. 'Tell me I am wrong, Mrs Howard.' Rapid steps sounded in the hall, leather boots slapping upon parquet. Someone shouted.

'I wish I could, Your Highness.'

Caroline closed her eyes and massaged the bridge of her nose. There were purple stains on her eyelids. 'It could not be. Not now. It is too cruel.'

'I will go outside,' she said. 'I will find out who the messenger is.'

Caroline nodded. The gauze in her hair fluttered. 'Thank you.'

Henrietta slipped through the door and closed it softly behind her. She walked as if in a trance. This was a mere formality. She knew in her heart what had happened – it only needed the power of words.

No courtiers lounged against the walls now, no flowers decorated the pier tables. Feet skittered up and down on distant staircases and frantic bumping came from somewhere inside the walls. Henrietta made her way to the Elector's apartments. Every-thing was in confusion. Four pages clustered together outside Georg Ludwig's bedroom, gesturing with their hands as they spoke in hurried whispers.

'You can't wake him up!'

'Why not?'

'He'll be furious. He does not wish to be disturbed.'

'Not even for this? For the love of God, man – !'

Henrietta seized a loitering page by the arm. 'What is it?' she hissed.

'It's the English Queen Anne, madam.' Henrietta closed her eyes, knowing what would follow. 'She's – she's dead.'

The words scraped like a pair of talons. Poor Sophia, snuffed out on the verge of realising her dream. 'They have not told the Elector – I mean, the King – yet?'

He nodded over her shoulder. 'Looks like they're about to.'

A dark-haired man tiptoed toward the bedchamber, sweating profusely. He closed his eyes and winced as he rapped against the door. A snort came from within. 'Your . . .' The man hesitated, unsure how to address Georg Ludwig. 'I – I humbly beg permission to enter, my Elector.'

Silence. Taking a deep breath, he pushed the door open and went in. Henrietta craned forward. She had no chance of overhear-ing with her bad ear, but she wanted to catch something, some part of this momentous occasion to store in her memory. The dark-haired page reappeared at the door and shut it behind him.

One of the other pages threw up his hands in exasperation. 'What are you doing? Why didn't you tell him?'

'I did.'

'And?'

The man blinked. 'He grunted at me. Then he rolled over and went back to sleep.'

Henrietta felt hollow with a sense of injustice. Why did fortune always favour those who did not deserve it? Sophia would have given her eye teeth for an hour, an instant with the title of queen. And now she was cold in the grave while her son, an ungrateful man, took her dream and snorted at it.

∾ ∾

Caroline watched raindrops chasing down the window, her head pressed against the glass. She had longed for this moment: the day when her house finally became a great monarchy. She had plotted, planned and dreamed – but it was an empty victory, without Sophia.

Poor Sophia. Georg Ludwig did not want her crown. He wanted to live out his days at the hunting lodge, Gohrde, with his mistress and their bastard daughters. There was nothing of pomp or majesty about him. He would rule without a Queen Consort and there would not be another Queen of England until . . . Caroline herself. She hung her head, ashamed to take Sophia's deserts.

The door banged open. She jumped round as George's wig slammed into a portrait and sent the frame crashing to the ground. 'He's ruined everything!'

She regarded the pile of curled horsehair and glass littering her carpet. Another victim of George's rages. 'What has your father done now?'

George paced the floor. Rage warped his face into a red, sweaty mess. 'Damn it – don't ask me.'

She folded her hands in her lap. He must want to tell her, or he would not have come. 'Whatever the Elector – the King – has done, we'll find a way to make it right. He is grieving. He is not in his right mind.'

'He's a damned fool!' It took every effort not to flinch as the blast of his voice hit her with beads of spittle. He snatched a cushion from her sofa and pounded it with his fist.

'My love? What can I do?'

George bit his lip. 'Didn't you tell me that Queen Anne overthrew her father to take the throne?'

This was dangerous talk. Had it really come to that? 'She helped her sister to do it,' she said carefully. 'But surely that is not an example we would want to set our little Fred?'

To her astonishment, he stopped dead. His shoulders trembled beneath his brown silk coat.

Something hard lodged at the back of her mouth, leaking out the bitter taste of fear. Fred – it was Fred's name that had made him cry. 'George?'

In two strides he was at her side, seizing her hands. 'Oh, how can I tell you?' Tears coursed down his flushed cheeks. 'The King – he says we will set out for England at once.'

'Yes, that is sensible. You, the King and Melusine must go now. The children and I will follow when Carrie's cough is better.'

'*You* may follow. But not all of the children. Not Fred.'

Her heart constricted. 'Why not?'

He shut his eyelids, letting out a fresh stream of tears. 'Because Fred must stay here, to rule Hanover. He will not come to England.'

The room swirled. She grasped George's hands, afraid she would topple from the window seat. 'No. No! He's only seven years old!'

'I was not much older when the King took my mother away. He did not hesitate to lock her in a castle, far from me.'

'You are mistaken. You must be. He means Fred will stay for a little while, to represent the family, and follow in a few months.' George hung his head and said nothing. His silence made her panic more than any words could. 'Then none of us will go to England!' she wailed. 'We will all stay here, together, and the King can go with Melusine.' It would be a wrench to give up her English dreams, but nothing like leaving Fred behind. 'I will not let Georg Ludwig tear our family apart.'

Colour rose into George's cheeks. 'I told him that. But he's a knave, a damned mangy dog, and now he is King . . .' He released her hands and clapped his palms to his cropped hair. 'No one can stop him. No one *will*. Everything belongs to him, even our children.'

'The children are *mine*,' she returned fiercely. 'I bled and screamed and fought to bring them into this world.'

'I told him you and I would stay here,' he said in a tight voice. 'Stay as a family with Fred and the girls. But that is no better. The King is determined to separate us. He says that if we stay, he will summon the girls to live with him in England.'

Caroline gasped. She saw a chessboard, the pieces in checkmate. There was no room for manoeuvre. She could choose either England without Fred, or Hanover without her daughters. Oh, the King had played his game well. 'Let me understand you rightly. You are telling me I can either lose one child, or three?'

'That is the sum of it.'

Holland

Waves slapped and sucked at the shore. Sweating men heaved the last trunks onto the ship as it creaked like a baby's bassinet. Most of the court had already boarded, but Henrietta stayed with Caroline. Someone had to support her. The princess's skin was pale as milk curds and her eyelids fluttered constantly.

Charles stood beside them, awkward in his black jacket and knee-length waistcoat. He was grey round the gills, trembling from the lack of alcohol. Thanks to Caroline, he was engaged to work in the King's household. Henrietta could not imagine how he would conduct himself, or stay sober long enough to perform his role, but at least now they had a chance.

Salt breeze whipped the curls around her neck. Her hair was

growing again, thick and wavy. She inhaled the grainy air and listened to the birds calling above. Just a few days at sea and she would be home, with Henry back in her arms. She had so much to tell him – months and months of stories – she didn't know where she would start.

'Are we going, then?' Charles grumbled.

'In a moment. Have pity, Charles. She does not know when she will see her son again.'

Caroline knelt on the damp wood and put one hand on each of Frederick's shoulders. His little face was grave, far older than its years. 'You are a good boy, Fred. A brave boy. I know that you can do this.'

'I will not cry, Mama. I promise.' His piping voice was faint in the wind.

Caroline stroked his cheek. 'There's a dear. Your great-uncle Ernst will take care of you.'

'And I'll be allowed to come and visit soon, won't I?'

Caroline's features were moulded into an encouraging mask, but they shook with the effort. 'Of course. I'm sure your grandfather . . .' She did not finish.

'Do not worry, Mama. I'm looking forward to being in charge. I will do everything you taught me.'

Tears pricked Henrietta's eyes. What must Caroline be feeling? She recalled her parting with Henry; how the pain had threatened to split her in two.

'Make the people love you, Fred. That is the way to win power and keep it.'

'I know, Mama.'

Now it was Caroline's voice that came out needy and high-pitched. 'You will not forget me, will you?'

He shook his head, making his wig bob. 'You are being silly.'

With a lunge, Caroline clapped Fred into her arms. The King's

47

brother, Ernst, was there when she released him and placed a protective hand on the boy's back.

'I will care for him as my own. You have my word.'

She nodded. Heavily, she rose to her feet and backed away, but her eyes did not leave her boy's face.

He waved. 'Have a safe journey, Mama. Give my love to Grandpa.'

Caroline groped at her hat and cast the veil down. Turning on her heel, she seized baby Carrie from the nursemaid's arms and stalked over to the ship.

'Finally!' Charles blew out his breath. 'Right, then. Are we off?'

Henrietta glared at him. She often wondered if there was something wrong with him – if he had been born entirely devoid of feeling. Shaking her head, she picked up her skirts and dashed after Caroline.

CHAPTER SIX

✃ *London* ✄

Caroline stepped off the royal yacht. As her feet landed on solid English soil, a roar filled the cool air around her. The crowd was immense, swamping her view. She looked up and smiled, coaxing Carrie to wave her tiny hand. Though her heart was broken after leaving Fred, shattered pieces of it glowed. She was Princess of Wales now. This was her country and its people cheered for her. Surely that was worth some sacrifice?

Emily and Anne tottered down the gangway, their cheeks rosy from the cold. The people applauded. Of course, they were not used to a royal nursery after a line of barren Stuart Queens. Caroline pushed her advantage and took Anne's hand in her own.

George weaved through the low mist gathering about the river, carrying a walking cane in his right hand. He made a lunge for them with his free arm like a drowning man, squeezing her and Carrie tight against him. 'You had a good journey?' he asked. 'You left Fred in health?'

Caroline swallowed. She would not make his distress worse by letting him see her own. 'He bore it like a prince.'

'Good.'

The nursemaid came for the children. As the warm bundle of Carrie was taken away, Caroline suddenly felt cold. She laced her arm through George's. 'You look tired, my love. How has it been?'

He hesitated. 'I'll tell you later. Come to the carriage.'

They followed the guards through the swarming crowd toward a state coach. Eight bay horses gleamed beneath a golden harness. Her pulse raced in anticipation of a triumphal entry into London. *Princess of Wales.* She had imagined this moment so many times and now it was here. She must not fail. Clinging to George's arm, she drew strength from its stability and waved to the people.

It was only as the steps were put up and the footman was closing the door that she heard a dissonant voice call out. 'Why didn't you bring King James with you?'

Before she had time to turn round, the carriage jerked into motion.

George snarled opposite her. 'Insolent dogs.'

She looked from him to the waving masses outside. *King James?* 'Do they not accept your father? Are there still some who favour Queen Anne's brother?'

George leant both hands on the top of his cane. 'Some? Many. The King's accession is by no means secure. It has already sparked riots.'

Blood drained out of her face. 'But James is a Catholic. They do not want a Catholic.'

'They do not know *what* they want,' George scoffed. 'It is as you always said: we have to win them over. Do not fret.'

How could she do anything else when Sophia's dream and her family's safety were at stake? She closed her eyes and let the rocking motion of the carriage soothe her. 'Tell me more. What do people say?'

He heaved a harsh sigh. 'Some think that before her death, Queen Anne was racked with guilt over her brother. Others say she was on the point of changing the succession.'

'Well, she did *not*,' Caroline snapped. 'God, in His wisdom, took her before she could do such a preposterous thing.' No sooner had the words left her mouth than an object collided with the window. She shrieked, expecting the glass to crack, but it only showed a long smear. 'What was that?'

'The base mongrels!' George's hand flew to the glass, ready to push it down, but she grabbed him.

'George, what *was* it?'

'A bloody turnip!' he growled. 'These damned English think Hanoverians only eat turnips.'

She nearly laughed at the absurdity. She had credited the English with more sense than this.

George's hand squirmed in her palm. 'Let me put down the window and give the dogs a lashing.'

'No! They must see we are impervious to it. We do not grapple over insults in the street like commoners. We are royalty. We rise above.'

He scowled. 'Well, I suppose you are right. There are more people cheering than there are slinging turnips.'

'Exactly.' Undaunted, Caroline pushed her face up to the window and bestowed a dazzling smile on her new subjects. 'We will have much to grow accustomed to. We must do it with grace.' She looked at him, folding his arms and sulking like a boy. 'Oh, for goodness sake, George! Wipe that frown off your face. Smile and wave. That is what they want from you.'

He obeyed with a wooden action. 'I have smiled myself silly these past few weeks. I had to smile for two. You should have seen my father on the journey into London. He did not even twitch his lips.'

Caroline rolled her eyes, torn between amusement and frustration. 'Can he not pretend to be glad? Not even to save his own head?'

George met her eyes. 'He is pushing English people out of their

51

places to fill them with Hanoverians. The people laugh at him and his old mistress. He does not have the glamour or the skill to capture them.' His look turned beseeching. 'I want the English to love me. But the King makes my job difficult.'

She arched her brows. 'Does he? Or does he make it easier?'

'What do you mean?'

A plan formed rapidly in her head; one of dazzling drawing rooms and a sparkling, affable princess who would take the country by storm. She would serve the King right for taking her boy; she would snatch something from him. 'If the King does not have their hearts, then they remain vacant. Free to woo.'

George grinned back at her. There was something devilish in his ruddy features. 'And I know just the lady to woo them.'

Coronation day dawned crisp and bright. October sunlight sparkled onto fountains flowing with wine and ale. Women leant from their casements to scatter petals on the road, and their floral scent mingled pleasantly with the tang of alcohol. Flags hung from every balcony, slapping gently in the breeze. Londoners came out in droves. Luckily, they were in a carnival mood and not one of rebellion.

From her shelter in the cool splendour of Westminster Abbey, Caroline heard pealing bells, trumpets and drums. But she could not concentrate on the joyful cacophony with Anne beside her, rapping her knuckles against the arms of her chair. The child was a fidget. Her chubby legs swung over the edge of the seat, her little satin slippers far from the ground.

'Stop it,' she hissed. 'People are watching you.'

'It is dull in here,' Anne whined. 'When will the show start?'

'The *ceremony* will begin when the procession is finished.

Grandpa and Papa are making their progress through the streets.'

Light fell through the stainglass windows, casting rainbow puddles on the flags. It chafed to know the pageant was going on outside, without her. This was the grand day for Caroline's house, the one she and Sophia had dreamed of together, but she had no taste of the glory.

'Why aren't *we* progressing through the streets?' asked Anne.

'Because, my love, there is no queen.'

Georg Ludwig's mistress, Melusine, stiffened beside her. Caroline felt for the woman; having to play the role of consort in all but name. This accession was a victory for the men: the women simply suffered, whether through lack of title or separation from their offspring.

'Aren't the English women strange?' she whispered, keen to change the topic. 'They hold their heads down and always look like they are in a fright.'

Melusine smirked. Her eyes travelled over the cluster of English beauties, with their pale complexions and passive faces. 'Self-righteous, too. They tell me they show their breeding in titles and manners, not by sticking out their bosoms.'

'In such cases,' said Caroline, adjusting the frills that set off her own magnificent cleavage, 'I believe there is not much bosom to speak of.'

A sudden blast of trumpets interrupted their laughter. The congregation rose to their feet as Georg Ludwig paced down the aisle, dragging an enormous crimson train in his wake. Although he had men to carry it and help bear the weight, beads of perspiration stood out on his forehead. Diamonds encrusted the gold circlet on his head, each of them throwing out a shower of glitter. An anthem soared up, sweet and holy, toward Heaven.

'Mama, Mama,' Anne tugged on her skirts. 'When I'm older, will I be Queen of England?'

Caroline looked down into the bright face with its peachy skin and eager blue eyes. She did not have the heart to say *no*. She tried to imagine her little Fred as a grown man, taking the crown for his own, his dazzling smile in place of Georg Ludwig's forced grin. The picture would not come. 'Who knows, my love? You may be queen of something.'

'I'll do anything to be a queen.'

Caroline's heart twisted with the memory of Sophia. She closed her eyes and exhaled, listening to the Latin words proclaiming Georg Ludwig as King. They had done it. Sophia's vision was realised and the House of Hanover was on the throne. Caroline only prayed that from somewhere above, her dear friend could see it.

St James's Palace was a maze of crazy, smoky rooms, oppressive to Henrietta's spirits. The Tudor brick walls were no longer red and cheerful but a dull, charred brown. It stank, too. Houses from Pall Mall encroached upon the palace walls, pressing in the sounds and smells of common people. The Hanoverians who came over with the court were appalled. Henrietta could not blame them; after seeing Herrenhausen, it felt absurd to present St James's as the seat of princely glory.

But as the carriage bearing the Suffolk arms drew up in Whalebone Court, all the smoke and dirt fell away. The palace was transfigured, because now it contained her most precious treasure. She charged across the cobbles, dodging sedan chairs, to be ready with open arms when Henry clamoured down the steps.

'Henry! Oh, my love!' She did not stop to look in his face but wrapped herself around him. His head came up to her chest now. She buried her nose in his sandy hair, wetting it with her tears. It smelt different; powdery and clean.

'You're hurting me!'

She released him instantly. 'I'm sorry.' She peered down into his grave little face and took it in both hands. The sight rubbed her raw. So changed! Less childish, with softer cheekbones and darker brows than she recalled. After a year of good feeding, his eyes looked proportioned, not like the huge orbs of an owl. 'Oh, it is so good to see you!'

'I'm tired. The roads were abominable. May I go and lie down?'

'Of course.' Proudly, she took his gloved hand and drew him through the palace to the servant's quarters. He stared with a pensive expression at all the unusual sights of the court; the tapestries, the vases, the German entourage with their strange fashions. She hoped everyone saw her walking past with her handsome son, almost a little gentleman.

He stopped abruptly on the threshold of their apartments. Henrietta pulled up short, nearly bumping into him.

'We live *here*? It's horrible!' His lip curled back as he took in the peeling wallpaper and fingers of damp stretching up to the ceiling. She had tried to cover the missing window panes, but the sacking came free and whooshed across the room in a gust of black coal-smoke.

'That will be fixed soon,' she assured him.

Scratching came from the wainscoting. She followed Henry's eyes to the pile of droppings in the corner. 'Do not worry about that, either. The Royal Rat Catcher is doing his rounds.'

Henry's nose crinkled, making his expression as handsomely cruel as his father's.

She sighed. 'It does not matter. We're together again – that's what's important.'

He shook his head and flopped down on the floor.

Something had happened to Henrietta's boy in the year of her absence. He had grown – but she had expected that. What she had not foreseen was his maturity. He hadn't run to greet her or called out *Mama*. He had become a little man – and she had missed it all. She stood, lost, watching him toy with the silver buckles on his shoes. A year was a long time, especially to a child. How could she explain that she had left only for him – to give him a future?

'I am sorry you had to stay behind. Now we have places at court, everything will be well. I'll never leave you again.'

Henry turned up his face. His eyes were hot, angry beads. 'Why did you come back? I was happy at Audley End. It was clean and there was good food. I wish you had left me there.'

She rocked back on her heels. 'We could not . . . Your uncle . . . '

'My uncle says a boy should be given to men when he is seven.' Resentment spiked his voice. 'He should be put under governors and have nothing more to do with women.'

Henrietta's rage rose to meet his. 'You are *mine*. Ours. We will have you with us and be a family. It is not your uncle's concern.'

'I like my uncle. And my aunt. It's decent in their home.' He gestured around the tiny living-space. 'This demeans us. We are of the house of Suffolk – Papa and I. Should we live like rats?'

She took a step back. Was this really her boy, her own flesh and blood? Yet all he said was true. Had she not thought the same things a thousand times before? 'It's better than Beak Street,' she tried. 'Is it not?'

Charles slammed into the room, the tails of his coat flapping behind him. He stopped to ruffle Henry's hair before striding to the wash basin. 'Still no water?' he complained. 'In God's name! It's bad enough we have to share a chamber pot!'

Henry's sharp glare of *I told you so* was more than Henrietta could bear. She leant a hand against the wall. It struck her how very alike Charles and Henry were. Wherever she looked, the same steely blue gaze tethered her to the spot. Fear slipped down her spine. Charles had taken everything from her life – he could not, he *would not* get her boy too.

'I must say, Hetty, I thought you'd do better than this.'

56

'Give me time.' She pressed her hands against her eyes. 'That's all I ask – time.' Somewhere in the distance, a clock sang the hour. Its chimes were echoed by the Crow of the Court, ringing his bell and hollering. 'I have to go.' She seized her lace cap and jammed it over her hair. 'Princess Caroline will be expecting me.'

Turning sideways, she pushed her skirts through the narrow doorway and charged down the corridors to Caroline's apartments.

As she shuffled into the princess's chambers there was a chorus of titters. A coven of ladies-in-waiting stared at her with faces hard as flint; their eyebrows curved in disdain, their nostrils flared.

'You are late.' Henrietta ducked her head beneath the scrutiny of the Duchess of St. Albans, the Mistress of the Robes and most important woman in the room. She knew better than to make an excuse. In some ways, a life of service was very like a life with Charles: silence was the best policy. 'Nothing to say for yourself?' The Duchess flicked a curl over her shoulder. 'Very well. You will hold the basin.'

Voices came from the next room. Water sloshed and then the door opened, emitting a cloud of citrus steam. Caroline emerged with skin as pink as a raw trout. Swathes of linen covered her body, a little transparent where the water had soaked through. Henrietta's stomach dropped. She did not realise she had missed the whole bath. She fetched a basin of water and brought it before her royal mistress. Nerves made her hands tremble, casting ripples across the water. It was different, serving Caroline in England; there was more pomp and ceremony.

Caroline took a sponge and cleaned her teeth with a high-pitched, squeaking sound. Henrietta ran her tongue around her own gums. They felt filmy and rough. She cursed herself for not taking more care over her appearance. With Henry's arrival imminent, she hadn't thought of anything else. Now she saw how dark her skin looked next to Caroline's and the way her fingernails were tipped with black. She adjusted her hand on the side of the bowl.

Caroline leant forward and spat out the debris of last night's supper. Henrietta carried the dirtied water away, making the crumbs and shards of chicken bounce with her quick step, and fetched a clean bowl for Caroline to wash her face.

'Your boy has arrived, Mrs Howard?' the princess asked as she dipped a washcloth into the basin.

'Yes, Your Highness.'

'I envy you.' Caroline closed her eyes and dabbed at her temples. 'Is he much grown?'

Henrietta swallowed. She would not be foolish and cry before the whole household. 'Almost beyond my recognition.'

Caroline let the cloth drop into the water. 'What, in just a year?'

'I am afraid so, Your Highness.' She could not meet Caroline's beseeching look. She knew that if she did, part of her own agony would be mirrored there. She handed the princess a dry cloth and sped away with the sullied water.

Her next task was to lay out the underclothes while the chaplain read prayers. Helping her was a newly appointed Woman of the Bedchamber, Mrs Clayton. She had a short face and pert brown eyes. She surveyed the royal linen as if it belonged to her.

'My goodness, the princess is very gracious to you, Mrs Howard.' Shaking her head, she picked up the shift Henrietta had spread out and laid it again. 'Anyone would think you were old friends.' Henrietta detected a note of warning in the artificial, high voice. Already, she felt that this woman disliked her.

'The princess is very kind to me,' she said, putting down a pair of brocade stays and taking care not to squash the rosettes. 'I have known her some time. We came over from Herrenhausen together.'

Mrs Clayton puckered her mouth as if she had swallowed bitter aloes. 'Did you, indeed? Well, I am sure you must be the favourite amongst us. Anyone else would get a scold for being late.' She watched Henrietta place a quilted petticoat beside the other clothes. 'Now tell me, which of these items do I hand to the princess first?'

'*You* do not hand them to the princess, madam. Our position is not high enough. We simply pass the clothes to the Ladies of the Bedchamber.'

A little mole beside Mrs Clayton's top lip gave her smirk the air of fashion. 'Nonsense! Perhaps your birth does not entitle you, Mrs Howard, but I can assure you – '

'Birth has nothing to do with it,' Henrietta hissed. The rhythmic drone of the chaplain's voice masked her words from the princess. 'Your role is Woman of the Bedchamber. I would advise you to learn it, madam.'

'Oh, I see.' Mrs Clayton cocked one brown eyebrow. She picked up the petticoat. 'You don't want anyone to take your place. Well, I will fasten on her jewellery. I *know* I am allowed to do that.'

'It is usually me – '

She balled the petticoat in her hands and thrust it at Henrietta. 'You are not the only woman who has to make her way in this world, Mrs Howard.'

'Come now, Mrs Clayton.' A voice sounded behind Henrietta. She turned to see a startlingly pretty girl with chocolate hair and huge grey eyes smiling at her. 'No one is pissing into their bourdaloue for fear of you. Do your job and play nicely with Mrs Howard.'

Mrs Clayton snatched the shift from the bed. Her lips trembled with suppressed rage. 'I will hand the underclothes to the ladies-in-waiting. Mrs Howard, I suggest you take this impertinent Maid of Honour and teach her to mind her tongue.'

Holding back a smile, Henrietta put her hands on the girl's shoulder and steered her away. The other Maids of Honour lounged in the corner; bright, smooth-skinned girls still bearing the curves of late childhood. There could not be a face among them more than seventeen years old. They made Henrietta feel ancient.

Depositing the girl on a sofa, she patted her arm. 'There now, you stay here out of trouble. It was sweet of you to come to my defence, Miss – ?'

'Lepell.' She gave a dazzling grin. 'Molly. I've been longing to speak to you – and so has Mary.' She gestured to a girl in grey-blue satin standing by the window. A large, unlined forehead and a rose-bud mouth gave her an expression of serenity.

Henrietta was taken aback. 'And why would I interest you, Miss Lepell?'

Molly indicated that she should take the seat beside her. Henrietta sat gingerly on the edge, ashamed to be idle while the peeresses worked so hard. They sweated as they fastened silver hooks and heaved crimson whalebone hoops onto Caroline. The room was sweltering. Sharp notes of orange blossom hung in the air and made it difficult to breathe.

'Far be it from me,' said Molly, 'to tell you about your own job. I am sure you know that the Women of the Bedchamber supervise the Maids of Honour.' She rolled her eyes. 'As if we needed to be watched like children!'

Henrietta bit back another smile. If she was the mother of this chit – and she was nearly old enough to be – she wouldn't let her out of her sight. 'Actually, I was not aware of that duty, Miss Lepell. I am new to court life.'

Molly patted her hand; a quick, sympathetic gesture that told her not to worry. Her palms were so soft they were like watered silk. 'Well, you know now. Mary and I wanted to ask you – to entreat you – to be our guardian. You have such a kind face, I am sure you must be a good soul.' Henrietta felt herself blush. Her sisters had been like this girl at sixteen; honest and free with their affection. Trusting, open, not yet realising that death was close on their heels. 'Mrs Clayton has been watching over us so far. She's *horrible*. Isn't she, Mary?'

Mary nodded. She opened her dainty mouth to speak, but at that moment Mrs Purcell blasted Caroline's hair with the powder blowers. Fine, white dust filled the air and made everyone cough. Only Caroline was safe, her royal mouth protected with a conical mask.

They remained silent until Caroline's buttery locks were curls of snow. Mrs Clayton pranced forward immediately to fasten on the jewellery.

'You see.' Mary nodded. 'She is all out for what she can get. She would betray any of our mistakes and secrets to the princess in an instant. We would rather be under your protection, Mrs Howard.'

Their young, imploring faces awoke something dormant within her. All the maternal caresses Henry had repulsed tingled in her fingertips. These girls needed her. Little more than children, they had been taken from their mothers and thrown into a dangerous court.

She darted a glance at Caroline. Her face disappeared under a wash of white paint. Ladies stuck small black patches over her smallpox scars, perfecting her artificial beauty. There was no denying it; she was a princess, not a friend. And if Henrietta was to survive in this place, she needed friends.

She nodded. 'Of course. Of course I will take responsibility for you.'

Impulsively, Molly embraced her. She clung to the girl's slender shoulders and inhaled her perfume. The sweet scent brought back a thousand memories. She had been this age, this tender and fragile, when the last of her elder siblings had died. Cast upon the world alone, responsible for the little ones. With no one to guide her, she had married Charles.

It would not be the same with these girls, she vowed. There would be someone there to take care of them.

CHAPTER SEVEN

⤳ *London* ⤲

A pale lemon sun broke over the horizon and winked on damp cobbles. May heat sucked the April moisture from the air as if it had never been there. Before the clocks struck ten, a backdrop of cloudless blue filled the gaps between the buildings. Night soil men shambled away with their carts, replaced by lavender girls and women with baskets of fruit on their heads. Housewives hurried home with pies fresh from the pastry chef. Every window sported either a banner or a candle, ready to illuminate for celebrations in the evening. In just a day, spring had come.

Molly Lepell, Mary Bellenden and Miss Howe trotted along merrily arm-in-arm before Henrietta and her son. The pavement was still muddy from the showers, so they wore pattens to raise their shoes above the dirt. Henrietta was not accustomed to the contraptions. She found it difficult to walk whilst holding onto her skirt and Henry at the same time.

'Must we visit the shops for ribbon? Surely there are servants who can fetch it?' he whined.

Molly laughed and fell back to walk alongside them. 'Yes, little sir, but that's no fun. How could we stay inside on such a day?'

Henry looked with distaste at the knife grinder and a cluster of women balancing babies on their hips. 'You need not stay inside. It would be proper for ladies to take the air in the gardens.'

Did he not recall the part of London where he used to live? How could he sneer at these streets, in such good repair? Henrietta shook his shoulder. 'Come, now. Be of good cheer. This is the King's birthday and should be celebrated. Tonight will be the most splendid drawing room of the year, and I shall let you pick some new gloves.'

He brightened. 'Can we afford new gloves, nowadays?'

She blushed, hoping Molly had not heard. With the ringing in her ear, it was hard to tell how loud people were speaking. She kept her voice low. 'With my salary and the interest from my dowry, I can buy you a few trifles for this special occasion.'

'I will look like a gentleman! Wait until I show Papa my new things.'

She gripped him tighter than she intended. 'No. Don't tell Papa.'

They rounded a corner and faced a crumbling old church, its stone yellow with age. The spire rose up past the trees to wispy clouds above.

Henry cocked his head. 'Why are they ringing the bells?'

'That will be for the King's birthday, of course!' Molly told him.

Henrietta strained her ears, closing her eyes to listen. Had she really grown so deaf? She struggled with speech, but surely a loud noise like a church bell . . . ? Yes. She found it; a low clang that did not have a rhythm but jerked wildly, until it culminated in one almighty crash.

Her eyes snapped open. Molly had her hands clamped to her ears but Henry was pointing at the church. 'I saw it! I saw the bell fall from the tower!'

Shrieks rippled out from the church in a frenzied evensong.

People skittered away; for a moment it truly seemed they had unleashed the hounds of hell. Henrietta pulled Henry against her but she could not move; her feet were rooted to the spot.

Mary stared, mouth ajar. 'What in God's name . . .?'

Suddenly, a bevy of men tumbled out. Sunlight gleamed upon the large, horn-handled knives in their fists. As Henrietta took in the white cockades pinned to their jackets and the turnips, ill balanced upon their hats, she understood: the King's enemies had cut the bell-ropes. They would not honour his birthday, because they did not recognise him as the true sovereign.

'We need to leave,' she said. 'Now.'

Mary, Molly and Miss Howe turned and tottered back the way they had come. Henrietta could not mince; not with a son to protect. She kicked off her pattens and scooped Henry up. He was heavy, but somehow she found the strength to run.

'I can walk!' he cried. 'Don't carry me like a baby!'

'They are bad men who hate the King. They will hurt us.'

Henry craned over her shoulder. 'They're smashing windows and pulling down banners. Can't we stay to watch?'

'No! It is too dangerous.' Henrietta weaved around carthorses. The streets were clogged; she was forced to trot along in the kennel, destroying her brocade shoes. Her arms burnt from the weight of her son, but she had to keep going . . .

'I suppose I won't get my new gloves now, will I?'

Frost crept down her shoulders. Always focusing on the goods, the money. An eerie echo of Charles. She tightened her grip and made him cry out. 'No', she gasped. 'You won't get your damned gloves.'

~ ~

From then on the ladies took the air in the gardens, hiding behind ordered parterres and flanks of spiky yew. Hawthorn in the park beyond clogged the air with its overpowering scent, reminiscent of rotting flesh. Henrietta walked beside Caroline, while the Maids of Honour grouped close together like a fleet of battleships in their wide panniers.

'Mrs Howard, your husband works in the King's bedchamber. Has he heard anything about these terrible uprisings?'

Blossom fluttered past them as Henrietta tried to remember what Charles had said. It was seldom she got any sense out of him. 'He heard the King may call in Dutch troops to protect his rights. His Majesty was alarmed that Oxford turned out in favour of James Stuart.'

Clouds scudded in the brisk wind, shifting shadows over the grass. 'Yes, I heard that Oxford is full of white roses.' Caroline tapped her chin. 'How do we challenge this Stuart flower? What do our supporters wear?'

'Tin warming pans, madam. To remind all that James Stuart is only a changeling, smuggled into the birthing chamber in a warming pan.' Actually, Henrietta did not believe a newborn baby would fit into a warming pan, but she was ready to support the theory if it kept Georg Ludwig on the throne.

'Yet still people flock to this pretender.' Caroline trailed her fingers along the side of a clipped hedge. 'Why is that, do you think?'

It was a mixture of Georg Ludwig's foreign policy and his foreign blood. But how could she explain that to Caroline without offending her? Henrietta looked off into the distance, where the clouds swooped in low. Wispy grey stalactites told her it was raining somewhere close by. 'His Majesty does not have your tact, madam. He is not – *gifted* – with people. You knew at once that it would please your subjects to employ English ladies in your household.'

'Whereas the King favours his loyal Hanoverians.'

'Precisely.' Henrietta pressed her lips together, afraid of saying too much. But the words tingled on the edge of her tongue, demanding release. 'Then there is this business with the Baltic. He has sent English ships on a Hanoverian mission. It does not seem quite . . . sensible.'

Caroline frowned. 'No. Sometimes I wonder, Mrs Howard, if the King has any sense left at all.'

CHAPTER EIGHT

⌁ St James's Palace ⌁

Bitter wind howled past the windows, splattering raindrops on the glass. Frost turned the contents of chamber pots into yellow ice overnight. St James's had plenty of chimneys but they smoked, filling the air with a smutty fog.

Caroline flapped a fan before her face to dispel the choking fumes as she and George paced round the ineptly named Paradise Court. The Maids of Honour ran behind in high spirits. She had promised them a game of Blind Man's Buff – the perfect opportunity for flirtation. They whispered and twittered at her back, anticipating stolen caresses and sneaky kisses.

George squeezed her hand. 'What will you say to him?'

'I will think of something. First, I need to establish if it is true.'

Colour flooded his cheeks. 'It *is* true,' he insisted. 'I told you, I had it from Melusine herself.'

She caressed his palm with her thumb. 'Of course. I'm sorry, I do not doubt you. I just struggle to believe anyone could be so foolish.'

'Even my father?'

Caroline tried to laugh, but the smoke made her cough.

George's brows knitted in concern. 'You are sure you don't want me to come with you?'

'No.' His presence would only raise the King's hackles. She needed Georg Ludwig soft and malleable. 'You start the game. You need to be seen in the midst of them. You'll keep the English on our side, even if the King cannot.'

'I do nothing but praise the English,' he complained. 'I tell them they are the handsomest, best, kindest people in the world.'

'Keep doing it. You cannot flatter them enough.'

She dropped her husband a meek curtsey, belied by the twinkle in her eyes. She could sense he would come to her bed tonight. Her thighs tensed deliciously at the thought. But first, there was this ordeal to get through.

'Until later, my dear.' Caroline waved away the ladies, who moved to follow her. 'Stay with the prince. Mrs Howard, be so kind as to teach him the game.'

Henrietta glowed. Caroline watched her slot beside George before she turned and walked away. The giggles and whispers disintegrated as she wound her way toward the King's inner sanctum. Her mules clacked against the floor. Outside, the wind screamed like a soul in torment. Caroline peered through the misty windows as she walked, seeing nothing but a swirl of hail. The Thames would be frozen solid.

Guards stood stiff as pike-staffs, staring blindly ahead, and let her pass. But as she neared the King's closet, one of his gentlemen scurried up to her.

'Your Royal Highness. A pleasure.'

'Is the King with a minister?'

'I – I do not believe so, Your Highness. Allow me to check if he is receiving.'

She put on her haughtiest tone. 'He will see *me*.'

'Of course, but allow me – '

'I will not be turned away.'

The gentleman faltered. Caroline could see the scales in his mind, weighing her and Georg Ludwig against one another. She fixed her eyes on his face until he buckled. 'Please, come through.'

Georg Ludwig's closet was a haven of tranquillity. A pile of documents sat on his desk, illuminated by the clear light of beeswax candles. An apple log crackled softly in the grate. Peering down the end of his nose, the King seized sheet after sheet of paper, signed his name and designated them to a fresh stack.

'Your Majesty.'

He looked up. 'Daughter. To what do I owe this pleasure?' He darted a hard glance at the hapless Gentleman of the Presence, who ducked out the door and shut it behind him.

'Palace walls speak. They have whispered to me.'

'About what?'

She did not answer him straight away. Curiosity got the better of her. Upside-down, she tried to decipher the documents on his desk, but they were poorly scribed.

'Caroline?'

'Do you want me to translate them for you?' she offered. 'You really should try to understand them before you sign them.'

His mouth clamped shut like a steel trap. His poor English was a sore subject.

'You know what people say,' she continued. 'They think the Ministry does everything and you nothing.'

Georg Ludwig snorted. 'And that is all the thanks I get for the pains I take!'

Caroline wished she had held her tongue. Putting him in a bad mood was the last thing she needed. 'Forgive me. I only meant to help.'

'You may help by keeping your prying nose out of it. Now, why are you here?' He leaned back in his chair and assessed her.

Caroline forced her lips into the semblance of a smile. 'People – foolish people – say that you plan to return to Hanover.'

'And so?'

'Such rumours injure your reputation. The English begin to say you do not like their country, that you are Hanoverian through and through. I want your direct authority to contradict them.'

Georg Ludwig ran a hand down the length of his face. 'You can tell them I do not hate England. I would have hoped you could do *that* without asking me first. But you must stay silent regarding Hanover. I will visit Herrenhausen in the summer.'

The sheer idiocy of his scheme took her breath away. At a time when disaffected subjects were rising in the north, he planned to slip away on a holiday? 'You cannot mean it.'

'I do.'

Discretion abandoned her. Caroline planted both palms on the desk with a bang and leant forward. 'Are you mad? To leave now! The Pretender has set sail!'

He turned his nose up at the mention of Queen Anne's brother. 'My ships are searching for him now. There is nothing to fear. We defeated the rebels at Preston and Sheriffmuir. I have men I can trust.'

But were there enough to hold firm? The coalition of Jacobites in France and Scotland left England skewered between them like a hunk of meat.

'You cannot just abandon the country! Do you not see that you are giving James Stuart the perfect opportunity to win your people over?'

Georg Ludwig made a steeple of his hands. 'We are talking of summer. It is barely Christmas. The Pretender will be back in France with his tail between his legs long before I go.' His insipid calm made Caroline's blood boil. This was the future of their house they were talking about – George's throne, Frederick's throne. Sophia's legacy. It was not a thing to toy with.

'Still, I do not consider it wise – '

'You should not consider it at all.' He stood suddenly. 'It is not your concern. You are a woman and you are not on the throne.'

Her hands trembled with rage, so she balled them into fists. 'While you are in Hanover – my Fred – '

'I daresay I will call on little Fretzchen, yes.'

Her mouth quivered. 'And bring him back?'

'Certainly not.' He threw his arms out in exasperation. 'You would have me cast everything on England, would you not? You should know the value of making a hedge when you bet. I cannot just desert my people in Hanover.'

So her little boy was nothing but a piece on a chessboard, placed strategically in case another fell. Caroline's stays pressed hard against her heaving chest. 'I will not argue with you about this. You had my thoughts when you made me leave Fred behind. They are unchanged. But if you must go, will you at least take a message? A present? Something to let him know I am thinking of him?'

Georg Ludwig bent over his papers, shuffling them into neat piles. She could not see his face. 'I have done speaking with you,' he declared. 'I have business to attend to.'

Like magic, the door creaked open. Empty rooms yawned before her. Caroline looked back at her father-in-law, but all he revealed was the powdered top of his periwig.

'You will leave me. Now.'

Blinded by tears and frustration, she pushed past the guards and sped away.

~ ~

A sickly dawn seeped through the window and puddled on the floor. Henrietta had not slept for more than an hour. Cold crept into her very marrow, despite Charles's hot body beside her. But it wasn't her numb toes or chattering teeth that kept her awake: it was Henry. Her senses stretched, trying to hear the sounds she had loved so well before her ear was injured; a turn of his head on the pillow, his gently rasping breath, a murmur in his dream. It was impossible to consider being wrenched from him again – but that was what Charles proposed.

She shifted her feet, seeking relief from the chilblains erupting on her skin. The bed creaked. She turned and felt a thud of horror as her heel connected with the warmth of Charles's flesh.

He woke with a jolt. 'Huh?' She squeezed her eyes shut, praying he would doze off again. But Charles lashed his arms out. 'Ugh. What's going on?'

'Nothing. Go back to sleep.'

He grunted and massaged his temples. 'Damn it, I can't. What time is it?'

'It wants an hour before we rise.'

Charles groaned.

Henrietta turned to look at him. Suddenly, the question that had plagued her all night slipped out. 'Why, Charles? Why take Henry with you?'

It took a moment for his sleep-dazed faculties to whirr into motion. 'What now?'

She clasped the cuff of his nightshirt with supplicating fingers. 'Do not take him to Hanover when you follow the King in summer. Leave him here.'

'Blast your eyes woman! Didn't I tell you last night? He's spent enough years tied to your apron strings. High time he learned how to be a man.'

But not a man like you. 'I do not. . .' She stopped on the verge of blurting out criticism. 'I think – '

'Nobody cares what you think, Hetty. The boy wants to go and be with men. There's an end of it.'

Henrietta threw off the blankets and flung herself out of bed. Her breath was mist in the bitter air. She went to the washstand, but there was no usable water – her ewer had lumps of ice bobbing on the surface. Sighing, she heaved her day gown over her shift and tied an apron around her waist. With an income of her own, she had a modest wardrobe now. She was always quick to invest the money in tangible items before Charles could gamble it away.

Her chestnut hair fell in ringlets to the base of her neck. As she swept it up and secured it with a ribbon, she thought that she heard a rumble in the corridor. She tilted her head, trying to make out the sound with her good ear.

Henry stirred. 'Mama? What is it?'

She petted his tousled head. 'I am not sure, my sweet. I will go and see.'

Taking a rush-light, Henrietta shuffled into the gloomy passage. No one was about, yet voices echoed somewhere deep within the labyrinth. Shielding the light with her hand, she negotiated her way past an abandoned mop and bucket, someone's lost shoe and an empty bottle. Her skirts whispered against the wall. The palace was unearthly at this hour, its eeriness heightened by rolling grey mist outside the windows.

As she turned the corner, her heart stopped. A white shape floated into view, gliding straight toward her. Frozen to the spot, she gasped, extinguishing her rush-light.

'Mrs Howard!' She shrieked as someone grabbed her arm. 'Good Lord! What's the matter with you? Did you not hear me calling?'

Henrietta blinked. As her terror subsided, images slid into place. The white shape was no ghost – merely a linen nightgown with an untied robe flying around it. 'Mary! Mary Bellenden. You startled me. I did not hear you. I – '

Mary pressed her fingers to Henrietta's lips. 'Hush, it doesn't matter. I came to get you as soon as I found out. What do you think? We are all terribly frightened.'

Henrietta could not respond to such a strange question. Absent-mindedly, she caught up the sides of Mary's robe and secured them with the tapes.

Mary laughed, stretching her pretty neck. 'Oh, Mrs Howard, you are priceless. The Pretender lands at Peterhead and all you can worry about is my modesty!'

Henrietta's hands dropped. The news fizzled inside her for a moment, too hot to grasp. 'Queen Anne's brother is here? In England?'

'In Scotland! God bless you, did you not know already? Everyone is up and talking about it.' She seized Henrietta's sleeve and pulled her back through the corridors. 'Ormonde and Bolingbroke are fled to France, and my Lord Oxford will go to the Tower! The Tories are demolished – every one of them suspected of being a closet Jacobite!'

Henrietta's thoughts hummed. From what she had heard, James Stuart was not a conciliating man. He believed in his divine right and his religion. If he got his throne back, he would forbid Protestant worship in his country. She swallowed on a dry throat. 'Mary . . . What if the Pretender has friends in England? What if he succeeds? What will happen to us?'

Mary stopped walking. 'I don't know.' Looking at Henrietta, she shivered. Her face lost its usual composure. 'I really do not know.'

～ ～

Caroline watched from a raised dais as the weak horses stumbled past. Soldiers dragged at their bridles, pulling them and their riders through the streets toward the Tower. Defeated rebel leaders sat slumped in the saddles, their hands bound. Musket smoke stained their wasted faces, but their eyes were alive with hate.

For all her differences with Georg Ludwig, she had to admire his skill in quashing this rebellion. No panic had disturbed his cool demeanour, not when James Stuart entered Dundee or when he built a court at Perth. The Pretender's army had been woefully mismanaged. After defeats in the north of England, most supporters melted away like Highland mist. By the time the Duke of Argyll reached Perth to attack him, the Pretender had fled back to France like a whipped cur, leaving these unfortunate rebels to reap what he had sown.

Jeers rang through the crowd as soldiers led the defeated men past. A common man ran out before the procession, waving a mocking warming pan. One of the rebels spat at him.

Suddenly Caroline was glad for the black velvet mask that shielded her face. 'How many will die?' she whispered.

George's jaw set. 'A few dozen officers. Only six rebel peers will lose their heads.'

Bubbles rose up inside her belly. She felt nauseous. Either it was the idea of blood, or her suspicions were correct: she was with child again. She did not like to think of bringing a little one into such a violent world. 'The King has elected to be merciful?'

George eyed the nervous horses clopping by. Sweat patched their saddlecloths. 'He has been merciful to these traitors. But what about my friend Argyll? He should have been made Commander in Chief after his heroic actions. But the King honours Lord Cadogan instead!'

She pursed her lips. 'Was Argyll not vigilant? Did he not take enough prisoners?'

'Pah! He is Scottish. It's only natural he should be a little tender of capturing his own people. No, Argyll's only crime is being my Groom of the Stole. This is a slight on me.'

She sighed. Whatever the King did, George would find a way to make it about himself. 'I am not feeling well. Would you mind if I sat in the carriage?'

George scoffed. 'Are you such an old girl? You only have to stand, there is nothing trying in that! Watch them to the end.' He looked at her and his expression changed. 'Unless . . . Is it . . .?'

'A child. I think so.' She pressed his hand. 'I must go and rest. It could be a son for us.'

A grin broke through his stormy countenance. 'Of course.'

With her guards, Caroline pushed through the crowd. Hundreds of filthy faces swarmed around her; the toothless, the whores out for a cheap show. Her nausea swelled. She stumbled over her skirts. Her hoop felt as though it was weighted with lead.

'Your Highness!'

She looked down and started in shock. A dishevelled woman knelt on her train, grasping at her ermine cape with bony hands. She was dressed entirely in black.

'A petition! Your Royal Highness! A petition for my husband.'

Caroline waved the guards off. The woman was hysterical – no danger to anyone but herself.

'My husband,' the woman repeated. 'They are to kill my husband!' Her wet mouth gaped in an expression like a scream. 'Please, you must stop it!'

She brandished a piece of torn paper. Caroline took it and glanced at the writing. Swirling words throbbed off the page to the beat of a military drum. *Execution*. She imagined a scaffold covered in black and an axe, winking in the cold February light. Here were the human faces behind the traitors; the lives smashed apart. It was not so easy to kill after looking into their empty eyes. Why should this woman suffer for her husband's politics? A turn of the dice, a twist of fate and it could be Caroline in her place.

She drew herself up. Grief and rage would not make the people less lethal. It was only kindness that could break the lion's tooth. 'The King will read your petition. I will put it into his hands myself.'

The woman seized the hem of Caroline's gown. Lifting it from the street, she kissed the material, caring nothing for the mud. 'God bless you, madam!'

Despite her kind words, Caroline shivered. The ermine edging her cloak trailed in a puddle of icy water. That snowy white fur was the mark of royalty, of Georg Ludwig's authority. But soon it would be speckled with more than stray black dots. Come execution day, it would be stained with blood.

1716 – 1717

CHAPTER NINE

∽ *St James's Palace* ∽

Caroline sat awkwardly in the King's presence. He did not usually invite her and George to meetings with his ministers. He had told them privately of the new Septennial Act, which would allow his parliament to sit for seven years rather than three. What was he plotting now? She studied his jowly face for a clue but his expression gave nothing away.

He wet his lips. 'In July I shall go to Hanover, as I initially intended. My son will remain as Guardian of the Realm.'

A stunned silence met his words.

'Guardian of the Realm?' George's indignation broke forth in a splutter. 'What do you mean?'

'Just that.'

'Not Regent?'

'No.' The King tapped his fingers against the table. 'There will be a Regency Council. You may settle small matters. Affairs of greater importance must be referred to me by messenger.'

Caroline held her breath. She felt George simmering beside her, ready to spill over.

'This is unheard of! Why, that is the same way you rule Hanover in your absence!' He gave a bitter gasp. 'I am not a mere Hanoverian deputy. I am the Prince of Wales.'

The King pulled his lips into a tight line. Oh, he was enjoying this, Caroline knew. 'Do not huff at me. This is no snub. My father made the same arrangements for me, when he left his realm.'

George bristled. 'Your father was not King of England! It is completely different.'

'Indeed, Your Majesty,' ventured Townshend, Secretary of State, 'there is no precedent . . . '

'I care nothing for precedent. These are my wishes.' A barbed glare told Townshend he should take more care with his tongue.

'And *my* wishes, I suppose, do not matter?' cried George.

The King turned his eyes on his son. 'You will be Guardian of the Realm. It is an honour. If it does not please you, I will summon your uncle from Hanover to play the role in your stead.'

Caroline felt the trap close, like metal jaws snapping shut over a fox. It was cruelly skilful.

George surged to his feet, scraping his chair's legs against the floorboards. Without a word, without a bow, he tore from the room, the curls of his peruke bouncing around his shoulders.

Caroline grimaced. A show of temper was not the way to beat such people. George, like his father, was incapable of the subtle arts: flattery, saying what he did not think, playing the underhand game. Apologising, she curtsied to the King and followed her husband. She found him sitting at the card table, fists balled on his knees. The colour in his face had faded from beetroot to a pale strawberry.

'The King wants me dead,' he declared.

'Come, now. That's too much.'

'He does! That's why he took Fred from us. He thinks he can bring our boy up to be his creature, then put him in my place.'

Caroline laced her hands over her belly. She was not showing yet – the new baby was no more than a whisper. She prayed it would be another boy; a son to plug the gap left in their hearts. She sat down beside George. Folding back the huge cuff of his coat, she found a hand and unravelled it to take within her own.

'I will give you another son. I swear it. A son we will keep safe. And Fred . . .' she sighed. 'Fred might have more sense than you think. He might not be easily persuaded.'

'My love,' he said softly, 'he is only eight years old.'

It had been a year now. The little features were growing dim in her memory, no matter how often she tried to conjure them. She wondered what she had missed, if she would still recognise him.

'Sometimes I fear the King does not want Fred to succeed him, either,' George murmured, his eyes on the card table. 'You know my mother's reputation. Maybe the King will say I am not his son at all. He might denounce me as a bastard, marry Melusine and put their damned daughters on the throne.'

Caroline tensed. It was not beyond the realms of possibility. 'We will not let that happen,' she promised. 'We will make the English people love us. It is as I told you. They want a war hero, not that shuffling, tiresome old man. They will support your claim.'

He cocked his head. 'You really think so?'

'I know so.' Caroline edged closer to him. 'And what better timing? The King is going to Hanover.' She grinned. 'He does not fear James Stuart will woo his subjects in his absence. But someone else just might . . .'

He turned, understanding igniting his blue eyes. He raised her hand to his lips and kissed it. 'You know, my darling, I believe they just might.'

Hampton Court

Henrietta leant back on her cushions. Oars slapped gently beneath the blare of French horns. The river slid by, a blue-green ribbon dotted with crystals. Mary and Molly sat beside her in the boat flapping their fans. It was an idyllic summer. Sunlight caressed the riverbanks, while drooping willows trailed their leaves in the glistening water. She would be happy reclining in her boat, if she could forget about that other ship, bearing her son across the sea.

Six months: that was the sentence. The King planned to stay in Hanover until Christmas. So many days, bereft of Henry. Knowing his care rested in Charles's feckless hands. How would she endure it?

'You are very quiet, Mrs Howard,' said Mary.

'As are you.' A dragonfly darted by. Henrietta focused on its turquoise shimmer, trying not to show her weakness. 'What are you thinking of?'

Mary pulled a grimace beneath her straw hat. 'I am worrying about money. Living at court is so expensive! There seems to be nothing but bills and more bills.'

It was a predicament with which Henrietta could sympathise; she knew what it was to have the yoke of debt upon her shoulders. She leant forward and brushed a fly away from Mary's hair. 'Would you like me to speak with your creditors? See if they can give you a little more time?'

Mary's dark eyebrows shot up. '*You*, my dear Mrs Howard? I cannot imagine you calling on such people!'

She smiled. Better not to tell Mary of the extensions she had gained for Charles by throwing herself at the feet of London's moneylenders. 'I can be very persuasive.'

Laughing, Mary batted her hand aside. 'La! Now I am sure you are teasing me! Enough of my troubles. What were *you* thinking of?'

Henrietta sighed. 'I was thinking of my family.'

'You miss your husband and your son.'

'My son,' said Henrietta with an impish grin. 'My husband – less.'

The girls' laughter rippled across the river. It was wonderful: at court, she could abuse her spouse all day long and no one took it as more than wit.

'You should have another child, Mrs Howard! A daughter you can keep!' At the sound of George's voice, she flicked her eyes to the state barge. It powered through the water, casting puddles of crimson and gold.

'But how could I guarantee the gender, Your Highness?' she called across the water. 'I might have another boy!'

'Surely it is worth the risk, for treasures such as those?' Caroline gestured to the vessel containing her daughters. Emily shrieked with glee, trying to skim her fingers in the water, while Anne and Carrie sat hand in hand, gazing into the river in search of fish.

Henrietta's heart lurched. She loved to watch the little girls running all topsy-turvy in their tiny imitations of adult gowns. The unruly curls bristling beneath their lace caps filled her with a pain so sweet, it was almost pleasure. But her fear and revulsion for Charles outweighed her desire. That animal spirit, roused in a passion . . . Not to mention the risk of pox . . . She shuddered, suddenly cold. 'I will try my best to follow the princess's immaculate example and produce a fine girl!' she lied.

George placed a protective hand on his wife's belly. 'There's no girl in here, Mrs Howard. A good, strong Hanoverian boy and no doubt about it!'

'Of course. How foolish of me!' Henrietta settled back and closed her eyes. The hot sun played in streaks of red and yellow on her eyelids, but still her misery would not let her be. She saw it again: Henry standing in the doorway, his trunks ready, a cap pulled over his sandy curls.

'Are you sure you want to go?' Her own voice, pathetic with need.

He had regarded her as if she was a simpleton. 'Of course I do! Hanover's the magical land, Mama. You told me about it yourself.'

If only she had known that fairy tale would come back to bite her.

CHAPTER TEN

∼ *Hampton Court* ∼

Nothing could prepare Caroline for the glory of Hampton Court. From the pitiable state of St James's, she had supposed all English palaces were inconvenient, mean buildings. But this sprawling complex of red brick and elegant baroque lines knocked St James's clean out of her head. Gardens swamped the walls – endless masterpieces of floral geometry. From windows laced with white plaster mouldings, she could gaze out upon Fountain Court and listen to its gentle music.

'All this work and you spend your time looking outside?'

Smiling, she turned back to George and the state bedroom they had created: the shining wood panelling and crystal chandeliers refracting summer light. In the centre of the room, a towering state bed soared up in a froth of crimson damask. Georg Ludwig would never have anything so fine; he would certainly not allow the elaborate dressing ceremonies George intended to perform.

Suddenly, the baby jolted her with a nauseating kick. She swayed, pulled by the weight of her silver brocade train.

George ran forward and put a hand out to steady her. 'What's this? Not fainting on me?'

Caroline plastered on a ready smile. She would be damned if she didn't see this through: their first reception. 'No, dear. Just the baby. He wriggles.'

George rubbed his hands together, looking pleased. 'You haven't been this ill with a pregnancy since Fred. Never had any trouble with the girls. It *must* be another boy.'

Of their own volition, Caroline's eyes sought the ceiling. Amidst the swirling clouds, cherubs and gods were portraits showing the Hanoverian line of succession: Georg Ludwig in an oval by the bed, George and Caroline facing each other across the room – and, by the window, Frederick. His likeness had been copied from the pictures she kept with her; hopelessly out of date. He still had the pixie features of a child. Not in real life. By now he would be stretching into a young man. It galled her to think of Georg Ludwig in Hanover, able to see what she could not.

A servant opened the door. 'The Duke of Argyll, Your Royal Highness.'

She slid a look at George. 'Argyll? I thought the King told you to dismiss him?'

His blue eyes gleamed. 'I have dismissed him as my Groom of the Stole. But that doesn't mean I cannot see him, does it?'

With astonishment, Caroline watched men file into the room across the polished floorboards. Every one was a Tory or a malcontent Whig – political thorns in Georg Ludwig's side. A heady, reckless feeling washed through her and forced out a giggle. 'Your father will be furious.'

'He certainly will! That will teach him. Guardian of the Realm indeed!'

Her spirit climbed, surging a little higher when she met the eyes of Georg Ludwig's portrait and imagined his outrage. 'You may have my son,' she whispered, 'but your people will belong to me.'

'I think everyone's enjoying themselves.'

Henrietta nodded, speechless. Gay was right. Who would have thought so many brilliant minds would trouble themselves to attend her little supper party? There was the poet Alexander Pope, his slender figure wrapped up in a flannel waistcoat and three pairs of stockings despite the heat. Beside him sat Lord Chesterfield – a short, ungainly man who showed black teeth when he smiled. And next . . . She frowned. The Duke of Newcastle was unmistakable from his tall, stocky frame. His high forehead pleated as he bent over and whispered to a man in a long black peruke.

'Mr Gay, who is that?'

He followed her gaze. His face went rigid. 'Count Bothmer. The King's favourite Hanoverian minister.'

In her apartment? Why was he not in Herrenhausen with the King? Uneasiness whispered up her back. 'Do we have spies in our midst?'

Bothmer darted shrewd glances about. She noticed he held a pencil in his hand and was scribbling down notes.

Gay grimaced. 'Most definitely. They will not like the way the prince and princess have courted the public. They will be telling tales to the King.'

'But how can they complain of a thing that has brought us all joy? This has been the best summer I can remember.' Dreamily, she recalled the activities: parading in the garden under the adoring gaze of the public; the afternoon parties on the river. There had been enough balls and masquerades to fill every day. Without Charles, she even had the freedom to throw these supper parties and laugh out loud, as if she were free.

'The prince and princess have certainly outdone themselves,' Gay agreed. 'And Caroline, so heavy with child! How does she manage it?'

She tried not to let her mind dwell on Caroline; the woman she loved and envied in confusing measures. What would it be like to have that voluptuous figure, the waist-length hair that glowed like spun gold? To be the centrepiece of this glorious season: Guinevere of Camelot. She sighed. The sight of George and Caroline in their splendour filled her with a yearning she could not explain.

Footsteps and a sharp rap at the door made her jump. The hubbub dimmed as all eyes turned to Henrietta. 'I wonder who this can be.'

She moved to the door and swung it back. A pair of bright eyes, azure blue, met hers. 'Your Royal Highness!'

George strutted into the silence, his boots squeaking. 'I heard you were having a little supper, Mrs Howard.'

Henrietta's cheeks flamed. She felt dizzy, as if she were drunk. 'Yes, Your Highness, but I did not expect . . . I am honoured you could join us.'

He smiled. 'A pleasure. But I see you have lots of learned, bookish people here. That doesn't bode well.' He winked. 'You are not going to try and teach me more English verbs, are you?'

She realised she was holding her breath. 'We have cards too, Your Highness. There will be some games later. I have no intention of boring my guests.'

'That is very good of you. But if you will oblige me, for the moment, I only wish to talk. Be so good as to give me the pleasure of your conversation.'

'Gladly.'

Glowing with a sense of honour, Henrietta indicated two chairs. George flicked up his coattails and perched on a seat. There was an elegance to his actions that caught her. His form was small, yet he always displayed it to advantage, whether charging through the woods on his horse or sitting down to dinner. That was court training, she supposed. He had been taught to fascinate from an early age.

'Last time I spoke to you, Mrs Howard, you were telling me about your father. Fought in the Battle of the Boyne, did you say?'

'He certainly did.' Henrietta arranged her skirts and prepared for an account of the battle. He had spoken of it before, but she did not mind. Charles never shared any of his war stories.

'Killed in action, was he? Your father?'

'Run through with a sword, sir,' she amended. Better to let him think the injury was sustained on a heroic campaign. She didn't like to admit her father had lost his life in a petty quarrel over an election with his neighbour.

'Ah, but a noble death – noble. A great battle to go in. Of course the genius of the Boyne wasn't just in the numbers. It was the training and the equipment that set King William apart. The flintlock musket . . . That doddering Pretender should have paid attention to history before trying Protestants again, eh?'

Henrietta gave an appreciative titter. She thought, with a flowering tenderness, how George would sit Frederick on his lap and talk to him about battles – if he were able to. It wasn't fair; a good father kept from his son, while Charles had Henry in an iron grip. An image rose unbidden: Charles dandling a whore on one knee, Henry on the other, forcing a bottle into the boy's mouth. She reeled in her seat, digging her fingernails into the heels of her hands.

'Mrs Howard? Are you quite well?' She looked up. George's eyebrows rose into his forehead, giving him an endearing expression of surprise.

'Yes, I thank you. I am just a little giddy.' She shook herself.

'Had a tad too much wine, have we?'

'Yes,' she repeated, breathless. 'Yes, sir, I believe I have.'

Caroline exhaled and slid into the rose-scented water. Her yellow shift stuck to her like a second skin. Henrietta took another ewer from the page and topped up the tub with a gust of steam.

'Flushed cheeks suit you, my good Mrs Howard.'

Henrietta smiled and dabbed the sweat on her forehead with a handkerchief. 'It's the hottest summer I have known.'

Caroline paddled her hand in the water. 'And the best?'

She hesitated. 'Yes, Your Highness. Excepting . . .' She began again. 'If my son were here, I would have nothing to wish for.'

Caroline sighed, sending ripples through the bath. 'Yes, of course. There is that. But otherwise?'

'The greatest and most splendid court England has ever seen,' Henrietta answered obediently.

They really had gone all out. Despite swelling ankles and the pain clamping her back, Caroline had given the English a spectacle of royal splendour they would never forget. 'I wish we did not have to return to St James's,' she confessed. 'Winter. Smoke. A gloomy King.'

Henrietta picked up the linen wraps and placed them on a stand before the fire. 'You are forgetting your baby,' she said. 'A prince for England.'

No, she wasn't forgetting. She was trying not to get her hopes up. What if it was another girl? Much as Caroline doted on her daughters, four females in a row would be a failure. She ran a hand over her stomach, slicking the shift against her skin until the nub of her belly button stood out. A whole future beneath her palm. If only she could peer through the layers of skin, blood and time and know its secrets.

'I have bathed long enough. Bring the towels.' Dripping, she pushed back her stool and stood. Everything moved. Pin-pricks glittered before her eyes. She tried to call out but her mouth was dry as old parchment. All at once, she fell. One arm flung out; she managed to catch the side of the tub as her knees slammed into its base. Henrietta jerked on her shoulder, calling something, but Caroline couldn't hear it; her ears were filled with rushing water. What was happening to her?

Hands snatched, pulling at the sopping shift and lifting her from the bath. Caroline closed her eyes to stop the images spinning. She felt the upholstery of an armchair connect with her back, then bands of warmth, tying her down. The scent of rose-water made her queasy; she opened her mouth to retch but the Duchess of Bolton stuffed it with medicinal gold-powder.

'Your Highness? Your Highness!'

She blinked, chasing away the dark shapes. Faces swam into view, features creased in alarm. 'I'm all right,' she gasped. 'No need to worry.' She inhaled, catching the foul whiff of a burnt feather. She leaned toward the fireplace and gagged, but nothing came out.

'You had a faint, Your Highness.' Henrietta was covered from head to toe in water, her dress clinging to the contours of her slim figure. 'It is not the baby coming, is it?'

Caroline shook her head, damp hair slapping against her neck. She put a hand either side of her belly to be sure she was safe. There was no blood – nothing to suggest any damage. 'These hot days and the compliments of the gallants,' she said shakily, trying to laugh it off. 'They make me swoon!'

Eager to allay her discomfort, the ladies took up the joke and giggled.

'And Mrs Howard's red cheeks, Your Highness?' Mary asked.

'Why Mary, what but a flirtation could produce those rosy hues?' The comforting swell of their laughter surrounded her, steadying her quaking heart. But burrowed somewhere deep within was a kernel of fear. Caroline watched the fire play, her head feeling as hot and light as one of the flames. This had never happened to her in a pregnancy before.

CHAPTER ELEVEN

St James's Palace

Caroline was drinking spiced chocolate when the pains came; gentle at first, building to a deep-rooted pull. That steely grip on her spine was unmistakable. Carefully, she lowered her cup and dabbed her lips with a napkin. 'George, I must retire.'

He dropped his cutlery with a clatter. 'My son?'

She nodded.

'My son!'

Anne threw her napkin across the table. 'I don't want a brother! Do not let him out, Mama.' Her rosebud lips set. 'If I have two brothers, I will *never* be queen.'

'You are not meant to be a queen, you stupid girl!' George clipped her round the ear. 'Make yourself useful – go and fetch Mama's ladies.'

Anne sped off, her little sisters toddling in her wake.

Gritting her teeth, Caroline wobbled to her feet and walked, unaided, to her chamber. Every time she gave birth, the ferocious pain took her by surprise. She just managed to reach the state bed before black dots drifted into her vision like flies. Baby number five. Surely it would be easier this time?

Although the child was ahead of schedule, most things were prepared. Henrietta fetched the linen and the hot water while Mrs Clayton unlaced Caroline's day gown and soft stays. As the weight left her taut body, she exhaled in relief. The skin of her belly was stretched tight as a drum. Taking an arm each, Henrietta and Mrs Clayton winched her into bed. Pain bloomed with every movement. Groaning, Caroline swung her legs round and the ladies covered them with crimson damask. Her eyes dwelt upon the gilt and walnut rail a few yards from her feet. Like an animal in a menagerie, she would give birth behind a fence. The whole court would see; gentlemen on one side, ladies on the other. Mortified, Caroline flung herself back on the bolster.

'*Hier gehen wir wieder.*'

She started to hear her native German. Looking up, she saw a familiar face: the midwife who had attended the birth of all her children. 'It's a relief to see you.' Caroline tried to smile, but it came out like a grimace.

The Duchess of St Albans pushed to the side of the bed. Peering down her nose at the German midwife, she whispered, 'Really, your Highness, is this – *person* – suitable for the task? She does not speak a word of English.'

A spasm of agony racked Caroline. What was the fool talking about? 'Her language does not signify,' she panted.

'How will we understand her directions?'

'Perhaps I could fetch Sir David Hamilton?' Miss Meadows suggested.

Lady Cowper clapped her hands. 'Hamilton! The very best!'

'A *male* midwife?' Caroline cried out in horror. 'Have you taken leave of your senses?' They seemed oblivious to her writhing and the liquid leaking from between her legs. The German midwife tried to shove through but the ladies formed an impenetrable barrier.

'It is usual practice to have a male midwife in England, Your

Highness,' the duchess went on. 'Don't you think you had better have Sir David Hamilton?'

'You do not want to know *what* I think right now, Your Grace. I will *not* have a male midwife. I have made my arrangements.' The pain was excruciating, requiring all her attention.

'But Your Highness . . .'

Only Henrietta noticed when her waters broke. She moved in with deft hands to change the linen and sponge Caroline's legs while the others bickered.

'Go back! Go back, you horrible creature, you're not wanted here.'

The midwife whimpered in German. '*Was? Warum moegt Ihr mich nicht?*'

'What is she prattling about, the nasty thing? Tell her only Sir David Hamilton is good enough to attend the princess.'

Driven to the end of her tether, Caroline shrieked. 'For God's sake, *someone* attend to me!'

A stunned silence fell. The ladies were chastened, but still not useful; they simply stared at her, straining against contractions. Henrietta sprang from the room. In a moment, she came back with George and Townshend.

Caroline had never been so pleased to see her husband. His eyes flashed blue like the centre of a flame. 'What the devil is going on here?' He pushed into the swarm of ladies with two powerful strides. 'Let the woman through or I'll throw you all out of the window!' They scattered with little shrieks.

Henrietta pulled the German midwife forward. 'Help her! *Helfen Sie ihr!*'

Caroline didn't have the breath to thank her.

Henrietta leaned down close to Caroline's ear. 'What do you need, Your Highness? Tell me and I will fetch it.'

Moisture poured down Caroline's neck. She shook her head, unable to speak.

'Boxram with wine and sugar,' Henrietta guessed. 'And something to bite on?'

Caroline nodded. She was overcome with gratitude for this one, useful servant. It was as she had suspected all along: wages bought a measure of loyalty, but kindness laid claim to part of the soul. A single act of kindness had purchased her Henrietta – a devoted vessel for life.

'Do not worry, Your Highness. All will be well.' She brushed her hands, still wet with amniotic fluid, upon her apron. Streaks of blood stood out, vivid against the white. She hesitated. 'All will be well.'

～ ～

Henrietta tiptoed back through the bowels of the palace. Twilight leant a sombre hue to the tapestries. Stitched eyes watched her as she moved onward, taking care to shut each door behind her with a soft click. The poor thing. So small, blue and helpless in her hands. All she had done was carry it to the chapel, yet still she felt ashamed; somehow responsible for its lack of breath. Her nerves were in tatters. Even the whisper of her skirts sounded too harsh, too loud. There had been a great cry, then a silence, and it seemed that silence should last forever. Like the hush in a church, it would be disrespectful to disturb it.

When she reached Caroline's dressing room, George was there. He sat hunched in a chair, wigless, holding his head in his hands. What could she possibly say?

'Mrs Howard.'

Henrietta dipped a curtsey.

'How is the princess?'

'Better,' she said gently. 'The shivering fit has stopped. They tell me she is out of danger.'

He nodded. His jaw worked as the Adam's apple slid up and down his throat.

'Would you like to come through with me and see her?'

'No. No.' He cleared his throat. 'I would only be in the way.'

Aching with pity, Henrietta perched on the edge of a sofa. 'The child is your loss too. You also need some comfort.'

'No. These things are to be expected. We should count ourselves lucky it has not happened before. More children will come.' It sounded like something learned by rote – not something he felt.

'All the same, you are allowed to be upset.'

George's mouth twisted. 'Am I? You think so?'

She wished she could reach out and take his hand, or rest his head on her shoulder. He was royal but he had a heart, just like anyone else. 'Who forbids you?'

He shook his head. 'It is hard to explain, Mrs Howard. All my life, I have been expected to carry on and forget. Forget I have a mother and a son kept from me.'

Henrietta's interest stirred at the mention of his mother, Sophia Dorothea. That poor, lustful princess, banished for trying to find the happiness her marriage denied her. 'It is not in human nature to forget such things,' she prompted.

'So I discover.' He drew in a sharp breath. 'When she – when my mother – was taken away, I cried. I grieved, like any little chap would. But that behaviour was not acceptable. I was mocked and bullied for it.'

Henrietta could almost see the frightened boy, about the age of her Henry, tears streaming down his face. 'Good Heavens. By whom?'

His eyes finally met hers; dull and bleak. 'By one who should have known better.'

The King. Georg Ludwig didn't strike her as a villain, yet some of his actions . . . She knew the turmoil of losing a parent at a young age. It felt like the world was crumbling around you and nothing was certain, nothing safe was left. She sighed. 'Shall I take a message to the princess, sir?'

He swallowed. 'Tell her I bless God for preserving my most precious jewel. Tell her the peace of my life depends upon knowing she is in good health.'

And this was the man she had thought crude, consumed by temper.

She wondered what it would be like to live as Caroline for a day, married to a devoted prince. To know her life was worth something to her husband. She rose and drifted to the door. All was deadly silent in Caroline's chamber. She placed a hand on the cold knob, bracing herself for more heart-wrenching scenes.

'Mrs Howard.'

She looked back over her shoulder. The muscles of George's face slackened and she saw the faint gleam of moisture on his cheek. 'Your Highness?'

'Thank you.'

Caroline's chamber was dark and still. The ladies sat mute, faces pinched with shock. Their painted lips drooped like ugly red scars. All the linen and bowls of bloody water had been removed, yet their scent lingered in the air.

Henrietta moved to the bed, hoping to be of assistance. Caroline's round face had swollen to twice its usual size. The skin was pale as whey, except around the eyes, where it burnt a ferocious scarlet.

'Mrs Howard.' Her voice rasped. 'You have a good heart, but I do not want you to use it now. You are, I think, also a woman of reason?'

'I hope so, Your Highness.'

'Then tell me honestly.' Caroline shut her eyes, the lashes flickering against her livid cheeks. 'Do not mince words. Was it my fault?'

'*Your* fault?' In her astonishment, she projected the words louder than she intended. The ladies shifted. 'How could it possibly – '

Caroline held up a hand. 'If you listen close enough, you can hear them already. The palace walls are whispering.' Henrietta strained her good ear, but only silence met her. 'The King's set will say I brought it on myself. I should have rested, taken care of my baby instead of gadding about Hampton Court.'

After all Caroline had suffered, did she really blame herself? 'These whispers are in your head, madam. No real creature could be so unkind, so unjust to you.'

'But scientifically, Mrs Howard.' She sounded impatient now. 'I must know. Did I push myself too hard?'

Mrs Clayton watched them with her basilisk stare.

'I believe, Your Highness, there are poor women who toil up until the moment their baby drops, yet many of their infants live.' She thought of Henry; how he refused to be pounded out by Charles's fists. A tenacious child, even then.

Caroline's eyes slid from side to side beneath their lids. 'That is true. That is a point well made. But the midwife – I was wrong there. I should have listened and summoned Hamilton.'

'You had no reason to doubt the woman who had served you faithfully before.'

'But her mind was addled. She was afraid the English would hang her. Oh, why did I not call Hamilton?'

'My dear madam, do not torture yourself. The birth was difficult. No midwife, no matter how qualified, could have brought your son through it alive.'

Fresh tears trickled down Caroline's face, seeping into the pillow. 'My *son*,' she whispered. 'My son.'

Henrietta's mouth filled with platitudes, bland as dry bread. 'You will have another.'

'But not that one.'

She hung her head. 'No, madam. Not that one.'

CHAPTER TWELVE

~ *St James's Palace* ~

Henrietta pulled the shawl around her shoulders, hopping from foot to foot to stave off the chill. The aimless, sultry days at Hampton Court seemed a distant memory. Winter had come with gnawing chills and fits of rain. The courtiers were solemn once more; standing to attention in carefully brushed jackets and pressed taffeta gowns, as they awaited the return of their King.

Hooves clacked through the silence. Henrietta craned her neck, trying to see. She cared little for Georg Ludwig, but travelling with him was something as welcome as a fire on this cold and dreary day: Henry. His little heart, beating beside hers, would thaw her icy hands and numb toes. She longed to catch a glimpse of his face, but as the carriage ground to a halt, periwig curls and hats obscured her view.

'The King!'

Henrietta swooped into a curtsey. Around her, the courtiers drooped like flowers before the restored majesty of their sovereign. Painful seconds ticked by while she held herself rigid. Where was the royal welcome, the gesture permitting them to stand? A muscle in her calf quivered. There was nothing; only footsteps pounding across stone. Astonished, she peeped up to see the King striding forward with thunder in his brow. He sailed past Caroline and George with a mere nod. Cringing behind, the sycophantic ministers Newcastle and Bothmer followed. Caroline blanched as they swept into the palace, her plump lips set in a scowl. Henrietta wobbled and abandoned her curtsey.

'Of all the toady, base things to do!' Molly's whisper blasted hot in her ear. 'They must have followed the King abroad.'

'After they had spent enough time at the Prince and Princess of Wales's court,' she pointed out.

Molly frowned. 'Enough time for what? You do not mean . . . ' Her grey eyes widened. 'You think they were *spying* on Prince George and Princess Caroline?'

'What else? The King does not trust his son.'

Suddenly the frost crystallised in Henrietta's lungs. She had the chilling apprehension she was about to be caught in the middle of a vicious row.

∼ ⌐

It was much later when Charles and Henry burst through the door of her apartments, dusty and stained from the road. Groaning, they heaved their trunks across the threshold before collapsing into chairs.

'God's blood!' Charles huffed. 'What a journey. Fetch me something to drink.'

Obediently, Henrietta produced the bottle of weak claret she had saved from the night before. Once the glass touched Charles's hands, she was free to run to her son. She did not expect Henry to hug her and shriek her name like he used to. Much as it hurt, he was growing up. But she was pleased when he smiled and allowed her to kiss his soft cheek. 'It is good to have you home. I have a thousand stories to tell you.'

'Thank you, Mother. I will tell you of our travels too.'

She bridled at the formal use of *Mother*. Where had Mama gone? Maybe she should ignore it. Time in the King's train may have taught him stately manners, and that was no bad thing.

'Jesus!' Charles took a swig from the bottle and pulled his lips away with a pop. 'Look at you, Hetty! You're all brown and coarse.'

She cast her eyes down. 'Still a little tanned, I suppose. It was a hot summer. We spent much time out of doors.'

'Well, at least you had some amusement,' Charles grinned. 'Last agreeable days you'll spend in a while. The King's got the arse-ache over your mistress's antics. Damned foolish of her, trying to undermine him.'

She rounded on him. 'The prince and princess did no such thing! Does the King resent them for trying to have a little fun? Is it not bad enough that he keeps their son from them?'

'Mother.' Henry's small features turned grave. 'You must not contradict Papa like that.'

Henrietta stared at him, lost for words. Indignation flew up in sparks, finally catching flame when Charles grinned and clapped Henry on the shoulder.

'You tell her, boy. Now, I need to go and take a piss.' He banged out of the room, leaving Henrietta alone with her son in the curdling silence.

Henry showed no consciousness of having wounded her. Brushing his hands together, he bent over his trunk and unpacked. She might have been miles away for all the heed he paid her.

'Henry?'

'Yes, Mother?' He didn't look up.

She stumbled toward him and seized his hands. Was this still her little boy? 'Henry – do you not remember all those times

Papa – ' Her voice thickened. 'When Papa hurt me? When you screamed for him to stop?'

His face turned dark. 'Of course I do.'

'Then how – *how* can you speak to me like that? Saying I must agree with and obey him?'

'It's for your own good,' he explained. 'You do not know your own interest.'

'What do you mean?'

Henry's gaze slid from hers. 'You are not a biddable wife. You provoke him. You do not know your place.'

It punched the breath from her. 'My *place*? What is my place? Do you think I deserved those beatings? The black eyes?' Frantically, she grabbed both sides of his head and tilted it up. 'Look at me! Do you?'

'I don't know. I was young. It might have been your fault.'

'*My* fault?'

He shrugged. 'If you obeyed him, he would stop.'

Henrietta dropped his face like a scalding pan and flung him away. This was worse than broken ribs, swollen lips and missing teeth. Her Henry, her ally, no longer battled alongside her.

'Now you are crying!' Henry heaved a sigh.

Henrietta cuffed her cheeks dry. Taking deep, shuddering breaths, she steadied herself. He was just a boy, too young to grasp a situation so complex. He would learn with age.

He sidled up to her, produced a rag of handkerchief and held it out. She took it dumbly. 'You see? You can't look after yourself. You are only a woman.' Henry shook his sandy head. 'Papa says women are just children of a larger size.'

'Papa says a lot of things,' she growled.

CHAPTER THIRTEEN

⁓ *St James's Palace* ⁓

A buzz ran around the palace. Caroline and George stumbled out of their rooms, still dazed from their afternoon nap. Crowds thronged the guard chamber, a mass of powdered curls and bobbing caps. Their excited whispers hissed against Caroline's ears but she could not make out a word. No one turned when she entered the room. Whatever the gossip was, it was all-absorbing. She looked for Mrs Howard or Mrs Clayton, but the people seemed to merge beneath the swords and shields hanging on the walls.

'If I am permitted, Your Royal Highness, I will tell you what the fuss is about.'

She jumped round. The Duke of Newcastle's hooked nose was poking an inch away from her cheek. She only hesitated for a moment. Annoying as she found the man, she needed information. 'You are permitted. Speak quickly.'

'The King has dismissed Lord Townshend.'

'What?' The word exploded from George.

'Dismissed him, and quite rightly too. He was speaking disrespectfully against the coalition with Denmark.'

Caroline winced. George himself had been railing against the same policy. Townshend was George's friend; he would not tolerate Newcastle's criticism of him. 'Hold your tongue, Your Grace,' she hissed. 'You do not know what you are speaking of. The coalition may help Hanover, but it is dragging the British into an expensive war they do not want.'

Newcastle stiffened. 'Do not presume to tell *me*, madam. I am privy to the King's councils, I understand these things better than a lady could ever – '

George cut him off. 'First Argyll, now this. It is all a slight against me. A slight for speaking against his damned treaties.' A muscle twitched in his jaw.

Caroline knew better than to touch him. Keeping her voice cool and soft, she said, 'He will have his little revenge, George. Our popularity in the summer was more than he could withstand. The best retaliations he can come up with are these petty tricks. It pleases him to think they vex us. Do not give him the satisfaction.'

'I wish he would give *me* satisfaction!' Spittle flew from his mouth as he hurled his wig at the door. 'If he was any other man, I'd take him out on the heath with a brace of pistols and have done with him.'

Heads turned. The buzz of conversation wavered until finally it dried into a pit of silence. Everyone watched them.

Quickly, Caroline took George's arm and steered him from the room. 'Hush now,' she whispered as she hurried him along the corridors back toward their bedchamber. 'It is futile to think of duels and pistols. The King does not have your spirit.' They turned a corner. 'He is old and his time is short. Your day will dawn. He hates the very thought of it. You are a living reminder that one day, he must die.'

'I wish he would do it soon.'

'And he will. All in good time.'

They reached their chamber door. George rested with one hand on the wood. 'I worry, Caroline,' he confessed. 'I worry about you and the children.'

She planted a kiss on his burning forehead. 'Why, dearest?'

'Because he takes the things I love. First Mama. Then Fred. Who next?'

Hampton Court

'God damn them, what's keeping them so long?' Charles's voice brayed in Henrietta's good ear.

She dabbed her forehead with a handkerchief. 'He is the King. He makes his own time.'

Footsteps beat on the path. The royal procession marched toward them, headed by the Yeoman of the Guard. Behind them came the dukes with their white wands of office, then the sergeants at arms, maces in hand. Henrietta took a step back as they passed. The sword of state sailed before her eyes, its massive golden hilt refracting shards of light across the courtyard into the fountain. Jewels nestled around the blade; venomous-looking emeralds and rubies like globs of blood. Knowing the King would follow the sword, she scrunched into a curt-sey, cramped against the other ladies' swaying panniers.

Georg Ludwig swanned by, grinning and nodding to his sub-jects. Gone was his usual morose face, the creased brow. Henrietta sensed the change was a deliberate one. Ever since the King heard of Caroline and George's fine summer at Hampton Court, he had tried to emulate them.

After His Majesty, the little princesses scuttled along with their parents bringing up the rear. Caroline, magnificent in pink bro-cade, clamped a palm either side of her belly. Henrietta sighed. It did not help her to see Caroline breeding again so quickly after her disappointment. Why should one woman have so much love, whilst Henrietta had none?

With her various duties, she hardly saw Henry, but when she did, he treated her with polite detachment. All his laughs and smiles were reserved for Charles. Father and son had forged a bond in Hanover and it did not weaken with the passing of time. Henrietta tried to join in with them, but she always missed the joke.

A sea of bodies heaved and pushed her forward into the chapel. Swept up in the crowd, she was separated from Charles and fell into a pew next to Molly Lepell. Her friend's painted lips twitched. 'Well, well. Bless me, what an excellent view we have.'

The chapel was a masterpiece of deep blue and gold. A thousand painted stars studded the azure ceiling, winking at Henrietta as she surveyed the arches and glittering pendants. Gilt made a hazy sheen in the wooden choir. 'Yes. The architecture is magnificent.'

Molly erupted into giggles and elbowed her. 'La! You teasing thing. I meant *that* view.' She nodded to where the gentlemen of the court sat, and tugged down on her bodice.

'Really! Molly!'

A hint of red grazed Molly's cheekbones. 'Well! It doesn't hurt, does it? My curves have grown mightily since last year, it would be a shame not to show them off.'

A slim young man watched them, one dainty leg crossed over the other. His blue suit reflected the colour of his large eyes, which dominated a face with features delicate as porcelain.

'If you are trying to catch Mr Hervey's attention, Molly, I think you have succeeded.'

The strawberry stain spread down Molly's cheeks to her neck. 'Who said I cared a fig about *him*?'

Mary Bellenden laughed. 'Yes, why stop there? Mr Hervey is not worth a groat when the Prince of Wales is looking for a mistress!'

'What – what did you say?'

Suddenly the organ blared. Molly pressed her lips close to Henrietta's ear. 'A mistress. Prince George wants one. Mary jokes about it, but she would never take him.'

Her thoughts whirled. Surely there was some mistake? 'But he loves his wife.'

Molly looked at her like she had sprouted an extra head. 'Lord, when did that ever stop a man? He's had mistresses before. In Hanover.'

'And the princess knows?'

'Of course! It does not bother her.'

She could not believe it. She had watched George adore Caroline for years. A mistress did not fit into that relationship – there was no space for her. 'I do not understand. Why now?'

Molly clicked her tongue in irritation. She had been bestowing her smile on a dark young gentleman. 'Isn't it obvious? His wife is swelling with child. She is being extra careful this time. She will not let him near her until it is born.'

Henrietta folded her hands on her lap and stared down at them. Now two women would get soft looks from those china-blue eyes, sweet words and princely devotion. There would be two women for her to envy until it hurt.

∽ ✑

Henrietta turned before the looking glass, making her peach skirts flare. Stripes of shimmering silver trimmed the hem of her masquerade gown. She twisted this way and that, watching the iridescent colours chase across her tissue apron. Back in the grime of Beak Street, she would have swooned to see a gown like this.

She pulled the laces of her silver bodice a little looser and poked another pin into the hat positioned on the side of her head, folded back to reveal a spray of flowers in her chestnut hair.

'Are you a shepherdess, Mother?' Henry asked, watching her every move.

'Yes.' She passed to the sideboard and picked up a black eye-mask, along with the letter hidden beneath it. 'Do you think I will do?'

He nodded. 'Very nice indeed.'

She beamed at him. That simple praise was the best she could expect from a ten-year-old boy.

The masquerade would start soon. She should not tarry, but she wanted to read the letter from her brother again. He was to be married, this very year. It seemed incredible that he had grown up so fast. She still remembered him stuttering his first words.

I wish you could join us for the ceremony Hetty, but I am sure that is impossible. Even if your royal mistress granted you permission, Charles would not let you travel without him. Will you think me very selfish if I tell you I cannot bear to have him there? He is still bitter he cannot touch your marriage portion, and he blames me for that. I would not want my bride exposed to unpleasant scenes.

Thoughtfully, she slipped on her peach and silver shoes. She was not offended by John's remarks; she too would avoid Charles, given the chance. But it seemed very hard that she was never to see her brother again because she was shackled to a beast. She had married young, hoping a connection with an Earl's son would rebuild the family fortune. How foolish she had been.

'What's Papa going as?'

She started – she had almost forgotten Henry was there. 'I do not know, love. He has not told me.' The clock chimed. She snapped on her mask, pushed the letter into her bosom and dashed to kiss Henry's cheek. 'I have to run. Sleep tight.' She hesitated, looking at his small, fragile limbs. Maternal worry never drained away, no matter how old he grew. 'It will be late before I'm back. Are you sure you will be all right?'

'What about Papa? Are you not waiting for him?'

She shrugged, sleeves glimmering like moonlight. 'He is not ready.'

'You should wait.'

Henrietta ruffled his hair, scattering it over his disapproving face. 'We are late. At least if I go now, we will not get into trouble.'

Henry groaned and put up his hands to straighten his curls. 'He will not like you dashing off, Mother. You know that, don't you?'

She tried to ignore the sudden constriction of her throat. 'Nonsense. A King overrules a husband. Now be a good boy. I will see you later.'

Blowing him another kiss, she pattered out in her heels. The last thing she saw before she closed the door behind her was Henry, pensively shaking his head.

Heat embraced her the moment she entered the gallery. A thousand characters flashed before her eyes; a jester, a highwayman, a sea-goddess. She peered through the small holes of her mask, trying to make out someone she knew. Everything was alive. With a dizzy thrill of abandon, she threw herself into the throng. Wax dripped from the chandeliers and sizzled as it hit the floor. Henrietta dodged around the molten pools, sweat pouring down her neck.

'Do you know me?' A Roman centurion bowed to her, his voice disguised. She didn't recognise his figure. He was rather short; the bristles on his helmet only came up to her hairline. Silver armour encased his broad chest.

'Not I, indeed. You have disguised yourself well.' She fluttered her fan before her face and ducked away from him.

Buzzing conversation overpowered the orchestra. Violinists plied their bows, but she could not make out the tune with her bad ear.

'Fair shepherdess!' A harlequin pranced beside her. Was it Lord Chesterfield? 'May I have the honour of fetching you some punch?'

'It would be gratefully received.'

While the harlequin scampered off, she moved to the open windows, eager for a breath of fresh air. The drapes barely stirred. Fountain Court lay dark and still below, rendering up the nutty scent of conifers.

'Ah, here is the person we must ask!' A tap on her shoulder forced her to turn round and meet the intent gaze of a highwayman. A woman dressed as Cleopatra stood at his side; from her wand-like figure, Henrietta guessed it was Molly Lepell.

Grinning, she held up her hands. 'Take what you must, sir! I am but a poor shepherdess, willing to give up her little purse.'

The highwayman put a hand to his scabbard. 'You are safe, madam, I want no fee from you.'

'We came to ask about your supper parties,' Cleopatra said. 'Will there be any, this summer? Do say there will.'

For an absurd moment, Henrietta mourned the failure of her disguise. Then the question slammed into her. *Supper parties.* Charles didn't know she had entertained in his absence. He must not find out. She darted a look over her shoulder. The centurion still hovered, his armour shimmering in the candlelight like a firework's silver rain. She could not see Charles in the throng, but her skin grew tender with the anticipation of bruises.

The harlequin returned with her drink. She took the glass in her hand; some of the liquid had slopped over the rim. 'Have they asked you yet? I do long for another supper party in Fountain Court.'

Henrietta gulped her punch. It was hot and too sweet, but the alcohol gave her senses the kick they needed. 'No. I am afraid there will be no suppers.'

'Surely one – just one? The whole court pines for it.'

The whole court? Were they talking of it so openly? 'I dare not – I must not.' She knocked back the rest of the punch and thrust her glass at the harlequin.

Bunching her skirts in her hand, Henrietta moved away from her companions and pushed through the crowd. Her eyes skittered over faces, seeking the grim countenance of her husband. Images swirled before her. The taste of punch clung to her mouth, fruity and sharp.

'Oh, cruel shepherdess! Will you not bestow one kind glance on me?' She jumped and saw the centurion, still on her heels. Without thinking, she extended her hand to him. He seized it and carried it to his lips. His popping blue eyes never left her face. Something in them was familiar . . .

'That is very kind,' he whispered. 'Very kind indeed.'

She stumbled back, colliding into a passing nymph. The German accent gave him away. The centurion was the prince. Mumbling her apologies, she flew to the door. A small, dark panelled room led off the Cartoon Gallery toward the King's Eating Room. She shut herself into it and slumped against the wall. Her glossy skirts slid until she was on the floor in a pool of grey and peach silk.

Her heart thumped. Had it really happened? Had the prince kissed her hand and looked at her with desire? She pushed the idea down, like a stubborn dress that would not fit in a trunk. It was no use. She saw it again: the brush of those cool lips against her heated knuckles, the soft look in those blue eyes. *Madness. Utter madness . . .* She wrenched the mask off her face and flung it away.

A step echoed on the wooden boards. She tensed, aware that her prone position made flight impossible. Through the shadows, she saw glinting, buckled shoes walking toward her. Her eyes slid up clocked stockings to claret breeches, a long black waistcoat spangled with silver and a frothing lace cravat. The man shrugged off his crimson jacket and let it fall to the floor like a puddle of blood. His mask was an elaborate Venetian style, flame-red with a long, cruel nose. Though it covered a third of his face, Henrietta recognised him. No disguise could transform her husband of eleven years.

'Henry told me you hurried off. He was suspicious. Damned boy's getting smarter than I am.'

He always was.

'So tell me, then. Who are you waiting for in this deserted room?'

Henrietta swallowed. 'No one. Why would I meet someone here?'

'You tell me. You charge off from our apartments, leaving me behind, a wild gleam in your eyes . . .'

'We were late,' she bleated.

'Late, for a masquerade ball!' The harsh sound of his voice reverberated back at her through the empty chamber. 'Tell me, Mrs Howard, why you felt the need to be punctual for a masquerade ball? Who would notice us enter that push of hot, sweaty courtiers? Who would look at the clock and tut? Who, if they did, would even recognise us in costume?'

Henrietta opened her mouth. A pathetic, breathy noise came out but she had nothing to say. She strained her failing ears, listening for a trace of laughter or music. If she called out, would anyone hear her?

Charles shook his head. 'You really do think I'm a mutton-brain, don't you?' To her horror, he slid his hand down to the scabbard on his hip. He did not unsheathe the blade but she could see its hilt, winking menacingly at her.

'No. No, of course not.' Her dry tongue stumbled over the words. '*I'm* the fool, Charles. You are right – I did not think. I thought we would be in trouble for being late. I see now that I was wrong. I am sorry. I should have waited for you.'

He paced closer. Hairs stood up on the back of her neck. 'You should have sought me out when you reached the gallery. Instead, you left me to see you, flirting with other men. Making a fool of me.'

'It's a masquerade,' she gabbled. 'Everyone flirts. It means nothing, Charles, nothing . . .' She gasped as he closed the gap between them and clamped a hand on her hat. He pressed down, leaning his weight onto the straw. Hot pain seared through her scalp. The material snapped and buckled, causing hat pins to scrape mercilessly along her skull.

'And then,' he continued, watching her writhe and squeal, 'I hear of supper parties. The great Mrs Howard's supper parties, where men of the court flock. You never thought fit to mention these to me. I wonder why?'

Henrietta panted, willing words to come. She could focus on nothing but the pain. Blood dribbled down her cheek and spotted the floor.

Giving one final shove, Charles released the hat. Relief made her giddy, toppling her straight forward into his legs. He bent and seized her shoulders, burrowing his fingers into her flesh. 'Supper parties,' he snarled. 'More like orgies, from the sound of it.'

'Don't be absurd!'

'Absurd?' He shook her, jolting her head back and forth. 'Me, absurd? When half the court tells me you spent these little *parties* making eyes at the Prince of Wales!'

His rabid face flashed as her head snapped from side to side. 'I – I,' Her voice shook. 'I sp-spoke t-to the p-prince. N-nothing m-m-more.'

All of a sudden, he dropped her. She fell to the floorboards with a thump, the flowers in her hair exploding in a cloud of petals.

'You expect me to believe that?' He laughed grimly. 'Always the actress. You were born for a courtier.'

Henrietta focused on his ankles and black shoes as they strode up and down the length of her body. She thought of a tiger survey-ing its prey, deciding where to bite.

'They say the prince wants a mistress. You thought yourself fit for the task, I daresay. Meant to cuckold me before the whole of London!' His foot flew toward her face. Pain shrieked through the delicate cartilage of her nose. She dug her nails into the boards and scuffled, but she couldn't get up. Every time she made progress, another kick sent her sprawling back on the floor. Stars danced before her eyes. She heard snaps and thunks, the sickly squelch of splitting skin. Then she heard nothing at all.

～⁀

Pain awoke her; searing through her limbs, scorching her face. The small chamber was silent and dark. For a moment she was confused. She had expected to see her old room at Beak Street. Gritting her teeth, she attempted to rise onto her knees. They buckled, useless, beneath her. She tried to call out. Her throat was tight and raw, producing nothing but a feeble moan. Gingerly, she turned her aching neck to assess the damage. Diaphanous material surrounded her. She put out a hand and fingered cool, slippery fragments. Her beautiful dress, cut to ribbons.

'Good God!' Feet pounded toward her, making her head ache. The guards?

She did not look up. Shame lit her from the inside. All that time trying to keep up appearances and now she was exposed – before the whole court. What would people say? She pressed her forehead back against the dusty floorboards. Perhaps some good would come of this. Maybe Caroline would expel Charles from court. But no, Caroline did not have the power; that was the King's remit. And the King was not one to pity disobedient wives. Henrietta remembered the queen locked up in a castle, never to see her children again. *Henry*. If Charles left, he would take Henry with him. Her trembling body steeled itself with sudden purpose. She could not let the guards find her. Charles must not be caught. Contorting her face into a determined snarl, Henrietta put one hand in front of the other and clawed her way across the floor.

'Stop! Madam, in Heaven's name!' Hands touched her gently.

She tried to wriggle away but exhaustion took over. 'Let me examine you. I can help. I am a physician. Dr Arbuthnot.'

She slumped, defeated. Through the mist of frustrated tears she saw a man with a weathered face and a pointed nose leaning over her. A grey wig flowed from beneath his hat to graze his chin. 'You must not . . . please, do not tell anyone.' Her mouth bubbled with blood.

'You have been assaulted, madam. How can I stay silent?'

With all her might, she gripped the shoulder of his jacket. Her eyes burnt into his. 'It was an accident. I fell.'

He looked at her ripped dress, the bruises, and her missing teeth. 'I do not believe that for an instant. But if I do not call for assistance, will you let me help you?'

Her neck hurt too much to nod. She simply closed her eyes and sighed. Gently, his arms laced under her legs and beneath her shoulders. She groaned as he lifted her. 'Go quickly, sir. I cannot, I *will* not let anyone see.'

CHAPTER FOURTEEN

～ St James's Palace ～

Caroline reclined against the bolsters of the state bed, sweat plastering curls to her forehead. This time, she was triumphant. The first Hanoverian prince born on English soil nestled in her arms. She gazed at his small, squashed face, so reminiscent of a pug puppy. He poked the tip of his tongue through a pair of bow lips. A fierce need to protect him closed like a fist around her heart. Her boy, her prince, at long last.

Courtiers gobbled down caudle, a traditional mixture for new mothers and their visitors. The scent of bread, eggs and sweet wine made Caroline's stomach heave. Luminous faces peered at her, eyes slipping over the bed frame and round the posts for one precious glance of their new prince. Some pressed so close to the rail that she feared it would break. George bounced around the visitors, a grin pinned from ear to ear. That handsome smile and the proud strut to his step made her own happiness complete.

Voices swelled, making the baby squirm. Caroline jiggled her elbow and settled him as the door clicked. Melusine swept into the room, still dressed in a travelling cloak. Her red wig looked windswept.

'Where's the King?' George barked.

'Still at Hampton Court. He will come presently.'

Brushing the false red curls from her face, Melusine bent down and crooned at the baby. His small hands fluttered. 'Ah, he is beautiful. Aren't you, little one? That is the one thing I never had,' she added sadly, 'a son.'

Instinctively, Caroline's arm tightened around his tiny body.

'We are calling him William.' George said stiffly. 'I have not announced it yet. The King must approve first.'

Melusine raised one pencil-thin eyebrow. 'I will inform the King of your choice. I do not foresee any objections.'

Caroline flicked her gaze from George to Melusine and back again, sensing the plush cushions transforming into a battlefield.

'And I have chosen godparents,' George announced.

'My, you have been busy.'

'Obviously, the King will be one. I want my uncle Ernst as another.'

Silk rustled as Melusine smoothed her skirts. 'That's quite natural, my dear. But there might be a problem.'

'Oh?'

'I will tell you in private.'

George turned to the company and flapped his hands. 'Leave us. Get out.'

Lady Bristol sighed. Reluctantly, they formed a shuffling line to exit. Mrs Clayton craned her neck, still trying to peep at the baby. Mrs Howard peered back over her shoulder before the guards shut the door. Her face was painted white as marble. Caroline narrowed her eyes. That was strange. Henrietta didn't usually wear cosmetics.

'Well?'

'You know your uncle has no heir.' Melusine perched on the side of the bed.

George lunged forward, grabbed her arm and hauled her to her feet. 'How dare you sit there?'

'George, I do not mind. She can sit where she likes. Keep your voice down, please.' Caroline gestured at their son, his face screwed up with displeasure.

'Well,' Melusine sniffed, 'there is no need to be uncivil. Like I said, your Uncle Ernst lacks a son. If he had a godson, do you not think he would leave land to him?'

'I should hope so!'

Melusine held up a finger. 'No. Do not wish for it. Your uncle must leave everything to Frederick. Otherwise the Hanoverian dominions will be carved up piecemeal.'

'And so?'

'All that your grandfather worked so hard for will be in jeopardy. Divided, Hanover might not qualify as an Electorate of the Holy Roman Empire. Your father would rather die than lose that Electoral cap.'

'A cap!' George flared. 'He has a King's crown, in God's name! Is our second son to starve for the sake of a bloody Electoral cap?'

'George.' Melusine's voice softened. 'Come, now. You know this is important. None of this is to spite you.'

He scoffed.

'It is *not*,' she insisted. 'The King's ministers pressure him. They say it is an English tradition to have the Lord Chamberlain as a godfather.'

All colour fled from George's face. Caroline wrapped a hand around her baby's ear; she feared the white heat of George's anger more than the red. 'What? The Lord Chamberlain? Why, that's the Duke of Newcastle! That knave, that dog, godfather to *my* son?'

'I know you do not care for Newcastle. But what can we do? These are not the King's wishes, but those of his ministers.' Melusine tilted her head to the side and gazed at him. 'George, the King has no wish to interfere with your son.'

In three swift strides he stood before Melusine and clamped his hand to her chin. 'You expect me to believe that? Just like he had no desire to interfere with Frederick? Do you know how long it is since I saw my boy?' Melusine tried to move her mouth. 'Four years and two months,' he spat.

'Do you want the weeks and days?' Caroline asked from the bed. 'For we have counted, I assure you.'

'Pah!' George released Melusine and turned his back on her. 'What do you know? You are the King's mouthpiece. And Fred . . . Fred's probably just the same by now.'

Melusine touched her throat. Her necklace hung at a strange angle and her wig had slipped to the back of her head. 'I will – I will tell the King of your *concerns*.' Without another word, she left the room. Caroline watched her go through the door with a pang of apprehension.

'George. My love.' She held out a hand and beckoned him.

He kicked off his shoes and crawled up beside her on the bed, seizing her hand and holding it to his face. 'I know. I was too rash.' He deflated, wrinkling the fine silk of his waistcoat. 'I couldn't help it.'

'My darling, I understand. You know I do. But we have to be clever. We have to make amends.'

'Amends? *He* is in the wrong!'

'Yes. But he blames us for our summer at Hampton Court. He wants us to grovel – and we must. We must keep on good terms.' She met his mutinous glare. 'For the girls. For this little fellow.' She angled the baby to stare straight into George's face. If she had to manipulate his love for the children to keep the peace, so be it. Royalty came at a price.

'What I said about Fred. That just came out. It is not true.' He raised his swimming eyes. 'Is it?'

Something sharp as a thistle lodged in her throat, stretching out prickly roots to her chest. 'No. No, Fred will always be ours.'

Caroline could not postpone the Christening. Her wishes did not signify to the English. They did not care that the boy was hers; pushed out from the depth of her pain. In the ministers' eyes, he was property of the state. Custom forced her to remain in the bed throughout the ceremony, holding her child in the crook of her arm. She bunched the covers tight in her spare fist to hide her swelling anger.

The Duke of Newcastle strutted in, full of his own importance. Thrusting up his chin and twirling his cane, he bowed to George, Caroline, and then her ladies. 'If I am permitted . . . The King sent me ahead with a message. There has been a slight – amendment – in the name.'

The mattress tilted beneath her. '*Amendment?*' she echoed. 'What kind of amendment can be made to William?'

Newcastle's lip curled. Oh, he was enjoying this. 'Really, the child should be named after his godfather the King. Georg.'

'We do not choose to call him Georg.'

'No, indeed. That is why His Majesty, in his great condescension, suggested a compromise. George William.'

Caroline's gaze locked with George's; a tunnel of fury. Newcastle and the King had them bent over a barrel. Surrounded by courtiers and clergymen, they could not object. In the only act of defiance she had left, she planted a fierce kiss in the centre of her baby's forehead, the rose-hip from her lips staining his skin.

'This is *my* son,' George growled. 'I would expect to be consulted before now.'

Newcastle flashed a row of teeth. 'It is the King's decision. Consultation is not required.'

Trumpet blasts drowned out George's next words. The baby screeched as the pages called, 'The King, the King!'

George bowed, rigid as a ramrod. He gripped his hat so hard that the rim bent.

The ceremony passed in a blur. Caroline was glad of her position in the state bed – she merely had to lay and watch. But poor George had to swallow his bile and play the part of a happy father. His taut shoulders quaked. Whenever he looked at the King, there was a tick in the corner of his eye.

At last, at last, it was over. The Holy Cross sealed her little boy with a name that was not his own. Caroline held up her arms to take him back, but the nursemaid whisked him away. The courtiers milled and dispersed. George escorted the King from the room, a ghastly smile pinned to his face. Caroline leant forward, straining to hear what passed between them. She could not make it out.

The Duke of Newcastle seemed in no mood to leave the scene of his triumph. He came up to her bedside, a smile spread beneath his hooked nose. 'I think that went off rather well, Your Royal Highness. And after all, George is a much finer name than William. William is not to my taste.'

'It is my brother's name,' she said. 'And we did not think to consult *your* opinion in this matter, Your Grace.'

Before Newcastle could reply, George marched back into the room, his face set in a scowl. In a flash, he seized Newcastle and pinned him against the wall.

The duke's eyes popped. His mouth moved like a landed carp. 'P-please, Your Royal Highness . . .'

George's accent took on the thick choler of its native German. He slid between languages, too furious to get a foothold in either. '*Schurke! Gauner!* Blasted rascal! *Ich werde dich finden,* expose you before the whole court! Oh yes, I will find you out!'

Newcastle whimpered. His wig, trapped against the wall, arched up over his scalp. Caroline smirked. She would not be surprised to see a damp patch appear on the front of Newcastle's breeches.

'You are a disgrace! This is the last time you ever cross me. I will not forget it.' George shoved Newcastle again, making his skull crack painfully against the wall. Then he dropped him and walked away. 'Get out,' he snarled over his shoulder. 'You are beneath my anger.'

Newcastle groped on the floor for his hat, trembling. As soon as his fingers closed around the brim he sped out through the door without closing it behind him.

Evening fell in a veil of cold black silk. Wraiths of cloud drifted in the sky, obscuring the moon and stars. Henrietta curled her index finger tight around the loop of her candleholder and pressed on. She was not well enough to carry out her duties; Dr Arbuthnot had made that clear. But she ached for company – the witty remarks, the Maids of Honour with their mischievous dimples. If she peered through the points of iridescent light before her eyes, she could see them: fine courtiers, resplendent in lace and diamonds; Caroline and George, the perfect couple with a bonny baby and three squealing girls running around their knees. She aimed for the mirage. Oh, she hated her own life, but to gaze upon them . . .

Her muscles were like iron, stiff and unyielding. She tottered off balance, fluttering the candle flame. With one hand against the wall, she righted herself and kept on walking. A metallic scent rose from the ceruse coating her bruised face. Her mouth was still swollen and her gums chafed on the false ivory teeth that plugged the gaps that Charles had made. She prayed the threatening migraine would hold off. Any more time spent abed, pleading illness, was bound to cause suspicion.

A scrape of metal made her jump. She pulled up short. The sharp curve of a halberd gleamed an inch away from her nose. 'No passage here, madam.'

'But – why? Why am I shut out?'

'Not just you, Mrs Howard. No one's to pass. King's orders.'

She didn't understand. She had come so far, in agony, and now . . . 'I need – I need to see the Princess of Wales.' She grappled with her words between gusts of pain, struggling with her false teeth. 'Tell me why I cannot go to my mistress.'

The Yeomen exchanged a glance. 'You won't find the prince and princess here, Mrs Howard. Only the little-uns.'

What did it mean? Her head was full of sand and sharp, pointed seashells. She swayed.

'Steady on, madam. I'll fetch Dr Arbuthnot, shall I?'

'No! Take me to the princess. That is all I ask of you.'

'But I can't!'

'Why? For God's sake, have some pity.'

'Because she ain't here. Halfway to Lord Grantham's now, I shouldn't wonder.'

Henrietta stared at him.

'Lord, don't you know? The King's turfed them out.'

Her knees turned to water. She stumbled back and collided with the skirting board. 'What are you talking about?'

'Some scuffle over the baby's Christening. They're out on a limb and the little mites stuck behind.'

Henrietta fumbled across the wall to a window. Ferns of frost decorated the glass. Wind moaned as it sailed through the streets. 'He threw them out?' she cried in disbelief. 'Threw them out in this weather?'

The Yeomen nodded. 'Sad times, madam. You should've seen the princess carrying on, fainting and sobbing, fit to break her heart.'

Henrietta jerked up, galvanised by the image. Caroline needed her. 'Where did you say they were gone?'

'Lord Grantham's, down Dover Street. But madam . . .'

Henrietta did not stay to hear the end. Kicking off her heels she scooped up her skirts and pelted down the corridors, shooting out into the Great Courtyard. Freezing air cut through her like a blade. Cold cobbles burnt her feet, but she didn't pause. By the light of the smoking braziers, she pushed on past the guard and through the palace gates.

⌒ ⌒

The princess was reduced to dumb, animal grief. Tears ravaged her face; she clutched and tore her golden curls until they resembled matted straw. Her feet wobbled and gave way, unable to support her.

Henrietta worked her way past Mrs Clayton and Mrs Titch-burne. Her lungs stung from running. She gripped Caroline's fur cloak and used all her strength to hold her mistress upright, even though her bruised muscles screamed in protest.

'Oh, my dear Mrs Howard!' The white oval of Molly Lepell's face loomed out of the shadows. 'I knew you would make it.'

Caroline reached out and grabbed Henrietta's arm. 'They took him, Howard. Took another one. Straight from my arms. He – he –' She did not finish the sentence. Her hand went slack on Henrietta's arm and she plunged, threatening to spill onto the pavement. People surged around her; Henrietta's weak fingertips lost their grip on Caroline's cloak and the princess disappeared in a cloud of fluttering, crying ladies.

Henrietta fell back, suddenly sapped of strength. Two strong hands gripped her shoulders and held her. 'Careful, Mrs Howard.' The voice warmed her chill skin. She recognised it instantly: George.

His eyes were the only living things in his face; liquid and lapis blue. Red rings puffed up like a pair of hideous spectacles around them. He looked beyond crying now. Beyond everything.

'Your Highness – '

'Where are your shoes?'

Henrietta looked down at her blue toes. There was no pain; they were like slabs of ice. 'I left them behind. There was no time, I had to run . . .'

'You have no belongings with you,' he observed.

The others carried baskets, sacks and trunks. She had not thought. Instinct forced her to run to Caroline and George just as she came to them five years ago: with nothing but the clothes she stood up in. 'No. I just came.'

George laced his fingers with hers. She froze, breathless at the intimate gesture. 'God bless you, Mrs Howard. You are all heart.'

Before she could respond, his hand withdrew, leaving hers cold and empty. All at once she noticed the biting air and drizzling rain, slicking her dress to her arms.

'Thank God you're here. I thought we would never get word to you.' A slim arm linked through hers. It was Mary Bellenden. She swept Henrietta with a glance. 'Christ above, look at the state of you!'

'What happened, Mary? I do not understand it. One minute Prince Georgie was being christened and now – this.'

Mary fixed her with a strange look. 'Didn't your husband tell you anything? He works in the King's bedchamber, does he not?'

Shame made Henrietta cast her face down. 'We are not . . . we are not close.' She wondered if Mary would see the bruises flowering on her face.

'That explains it. We wondered which side you would choose.'

Choose? How could anyone question her loyalty to Caroline, the woman who had transformed her world? She shivered and wormed her way under the folds of Mary's cloak. 'Please explain. I do not know anything.' Her breath turned to mist in the air and lingered between them for a moment. When it evaporated, Mary looked old and sad.

'Well, you heard the to-do at the Christening, didn't you? The Prince and the Duke of Newcastle at each other like fishwives.'

'I was unwell. I may have – I may have heard them argue.'

Mary scoffed and untied the lacings at her throat. Throwing back her hood, she opened her cape and encased Henrietta in the damp wool. 'You would have heard them if you were on the moon! He deserved it too, that odious duke, pushing his way into the ceremony. But he got his revenge.'

'It was him? He did this?'

'He said the prince had challenged him to a duel! Put on a right show, pretended to be scared out of his wits. The prince insists he did not issue the challenge. He says the duke is making up tales. If you ask my opinion, the King has been waiting for something like this. He saw an opportunity to quarrel and took it.'

Massaging the stinging lobe of her ear, she mulled over Mary's words. From her life with Charles, she knew the slightest thing could kindle a bad temper. But it had always been George, not the King, who struck her as the petulant one. 'And the children?'

Mary shook her head. 'Give thanks to God that you missed the parting, Mrs Howard. It was dreadful. Princess Anne clung onto her mother's train like a wild cat.'

It beggared belief. 'What about the baby?'

'Oh!' The breath left Mary in a cloud of steam. 'Do not speak of it, Mrs Howard. I cannot bear to think of the poor dear. And the princess too, still weak from child-bed! I will never forgive the King. I do not care if they spike my head outside the Tower for saying it.'

They stumbled on. The ladies' metal pattens rang through the night. Only Henrietta heaved her unwilling feet through the puddles and refuse. Exhaustion, both physical and emotional, took hold.

Finally, the iron railings of Lord Grantham's house came into view. She put out a hand and sagged against the cool metal, spotted with rust. 'I'll – I'll see the princess to bed,' she gasped. 'I am not fit for any more. Mary, would you lend me enough coin to hire a sedan? I left everything at St James's.' A crease appeared between

Mary's brows. 'Oh, Mary, I'm sorry. I forgot about your bills. Do not worry, I will see if Molly . . . '

'No. It is not that.' Mary fixed her with a look that made her quail. 'Lord, you really don't know anything, do you?'

Dread crept up to her chin, splashing into her mouth. 'Then tell me.'

Mary closed her eyes. 'Look around you. Do you see the Duchess of St Albans? Lady Cowper?' She did not wait for Henrietta to answer. 'It was a choice. The King or the prince and princess. Some ladies have stayed behind so their husbands can keep their positions. The King will not let them serve both courts.'

'What are you saying?'

'You have made your decision without knowing it.' Mary's arm came round her waist, ready to hold her up. 'Now you are out of St James's Palace, they will not let you back in.'

CHAPTER FIFTEEN

∾ *Dover Street* ∾

Caroline snatched the letter from the messenger's hands and cracked apart the royal seal, scattering wax over her lap. She knew the King would relent eventually. What kind of man kept his son and daughter-in-law away from their own children? She snapped the paper open.

Words floated off the page and stung her like a swarm of bees. She read them again and again, sure there must be a mistake. No – it was true. The King offered her poison, wrapped in a sweetmeat.

'What does it say, Your Highness?' Mary Bellenden fixed her with curious eyes. 'Are we going back to St James's?'

'No.' Caroline said shortly. 'We are not.' She folded the letter away and tucked it in the pockets around her waist. Fury gripped her throat and nearly squeezed the breath from her. The King granted her the chance to see her children – if she dropped all contact with George! What was his plan? To bring poor George to his knees? Caroline remembered the words he had whispered in anguish: *the King takes everyone I love from me*. Well, he would not take her.

Carrie's doleful little face and Georgie's chubby limbs teased at the corners of her mind, but she pushed them away. That was what the King wanted: to play on her emotions. Georg Ludwig knew if he got Caroline back in the palace, it would increase his popularity. The Londoners would not pity George then – they would think him a reprobate, cast aside by his father and wife alike. She drummed her fingers against the arms of her chair. God, she had to think, but how could she when her brain was tangled? What would Sophia do?

Henrietta stood by the fire. Her skin, always pale, was ash-grey. The flames did nothing to warm it – they only cast eerie shadows. A crumpled piece of paper rustled against her skirts as she made a fist, balling it tighter and tighter.

'Mrs Howard,' Caroline said softly. 'Have you received a letter too?'

She did not lift her eyes from the flames. 'Yes. It is from my husband.'

'He wants you back,' Caroline guessed.

Henrietta inclined her head.

'That's preposterous!' cried Mr Gay, brandishing a newspaper. 'Look, it says it right here in the *Gazette*! No one who pays court to the Prince and Princess of Wales will be admitted into St James's Palace.'

Henrietta swivelled round, the fire's orange glare reflected in her pupils. 'Oh, he has a dispensation,' she said bitterly. 'He has the King's approval to haul me back.'

Caroline leapt to her feet. She pushed as close to Henrietta as her hooped gown would allow. 'Will you go? I could use a pair of eyes within the King's household.'

Henrietta squirmed. As the lace at her elbow moved, Caroline glimpsed a yellow-grey patch of skin. How many other bruises were hidden under the folds of that gown? 'He'll – ' Henrietta half-choked. She dropped her voice to a whisper only Caroline could hear. 'Charles will kill me if I return. He really will. I know it.'

'There now, calm yourself, child.' She glanced around. Mrs Clayton was watching them intently, but no one could overhear their hushed words. 'Surely you exaggerate. How could he kill you, in the King's palace? How would he explain it?'

'Would he even have to?'

She deliberated. Once again, she thought of George's mother and that secret lover who disappeared from Herrenhausen. 'Perhaps not. Perhaps you are safer here.'

∼ ⌒

A slim, golden vial. Henrietta turned it in her hands, making the contents glow. Funny, how it was always her hair that suffered. First she cut it to ribbons to buy Henry a future and now . . . She was a woman alone. There was nothing for it. The old Henrietta Howard must die.

She passed to the basin and picked up a jug. Water slopped into the bowl. When it was full she knelt, twisted up her hair and plunged it into the cold water. Her scalp tingled. She ran her fingers through the heavy tresses, soaking every last strand, washing the past away.

She was doing the right thing. It made sense to stay with Caroline. She had thought about it over and over, through the sleepless nights pressed up against Mrs Clayton and Mrs Titchburne in their tiny bed. She would work hard and save. She would deny herself, do whatever it took. And then, when she had the funds, she would snatch Henry from his school and run.

Flicking droplets from her hand, she reached into her pocket and clutched a piece of paper: the last letter from Charles. Its language was so gross and abusive she wanted her damp fingers to blur the ink and blot out every trace of him. He might threaten her with the law, he might invoke the name of the King, but she would be his victim no more. Once she had reduced the letter to a limp, peeling rag, she flung it into the fire. She washed the ink from her hand and uncorked the little vial. At once, the sharp scent of horse urine brought tears to her eyes. She drenched her hair from root to tip, bleaching the chestnut curls Charles had dragged her along by. Gold glowed back at her from inside the basin. No more would she envy the buttery tumble of Caroline's hair. She would have her own tresses, blonde as winter sunshine. She took a pinch of saffron from a twist of paper and massaged it through to take away the smell. That done, she wrapped her hair in the linen towels she had set warming before the fire. With a second jug, she rinsed her stinging hands. Water slid across her wedding band, forcing a glint from the dull metal. Henrietta stared at it for an instant. Then she plucked it from her finger and tossed it into the flames. She took up a poker and pushed the ring deep into the glowing embers. She expected to feel something: sorrow, glee, or at least spite. There was nothing.

Suddenly she heard a high-pitched wail, followed by a jangle and clunks. It seemed to be coming from downstairs. She shot to the door and looked out as Mary Bellenden stomped up the steps. A bright red stain suffused her face. The crescents of her breasts heaved, fit to burst out of her stays. Henrietta nipped out of the closet, seized Mary's wrist, pulled her inside and shut the door. 'What is happening?' As the words left her lips, a roar came from below. Something smashed.

Mary yelped and collapsed into her arms. 'Oh, Mrs Howard, it was horrible! Just horrible!'

Finding a stool, Henrietta perched Mary upon it. From her pockets she produced some smelling salts and waved them under Mary's nose. 'Hush, now. Tell me what happened.'

Mary hid her face in her hands. 'Lord, I hope I haven't done for myself. Listen to him, down there! He is so angry!'

'The prince?'

'Yes.' Mary squealed. 'He wants me to be his mistress.'

The words slid through Henrietta like a corked wine. She felt queasy and knelt down. 'No. Surely you are mistaken. He flirts with all the maids. He just pushed you a little too far.'

Mary shook her head, making her earrings swing. 'He wants me,' she whispered. 'I heard him talking to the princess about it. He lies there, next to her in bed, and tells her the strategies he's employed to win me over! I heard him complain that I always cross my arms against him.'

'What?' Henrietta's head lurched with the heat and the stench of horse urine. 'And what does the princess say?'

Mary crept closer, her breath hot in Henrietta's ear. 'She *encourages* him. I was by the door when she spoke to Mrs Clayton – they didn't know I was there. She said she does not mind him taking a mistress any more than she minds him going to the close stool.'

They stared at one another, their painted lips hanging open. Henrietta raised her hands to the warm linen on her head and pressed it against her scalp. 'This cannot be true,' she said. 'It defies all sense. He might have wanted a mistress when the princess was pregnant, but why now?'

'Male pride. People say Caroline rules him. He thinks that if he has a mistress, he'll look stronger.'

Henrietta's eyes expanded. 'He *told* you this?'

Mary nodded, looking down at her lap and wringing the folds of her gown. 'In so many words. And just now he was sitting, counting coins in front of me! As if to say he knows I am in debt and will pay it off if I . . . ' She choked on a sob. 'A shabby trick. I told him I couldn't bear it and if he sat clunking his money together any longer I would leave the room. But he kept on.'

'So what did you do?'

'Oh, Mrs Howard! I was so angry, I yanked the purse from his hand and chucked it at the wall!'

'You never did!'

'I did. And I would do it again.' She jutted her chin. 'Only – what if I lose my place?'

Henrietta put out her hands and clasped Mary's. The finger on her left hand felt strange and naked without the wedding ring. 'You won't. Princess Caroline will hardly throw you out for refusing to sleep with her husband.' She assessed the girl sitting before her, heaving for breath, turning pink and white in quick succession. Was there something else, beneath this show of offended virtue? Mary was hardly a prude. 'Mary . . . Forgive me for asking. But why? Why did you turn him down?'

The lobes of Mary's ears burnt strawberry red. 'Do you think I would hand my virtue away so easily?'

'Of course not.' She squeezed Mary's hands. 'I am sorry if I offended you. But many maids would jump at the opportunity.'

'So they might. But I . . . I am in love.'

'In love?'

'Hush!' Mary snatched away a hand and pressed it to Henrietta's lips. 'You must not say a word. I do not know if the gentleman feels the same way. I only know he never *will* if I go to bed with the prince. What saint of a man would endure the shame of marrying a royal mistress?'

What man indeed? Something shifted in Henrietta's brain, like a seed dislodging the soil to push out a green shoot. She could not make out what it would grow to be yet, but it unnerved her. Standing, she passed to the fire and unwrapped her hair. As she hung her head upside down, she saw golden highlights blooming. She seized a comb and tidied the tangled mess, counting in her head. A hundred strokes to make it gleam like a newly minted coin.

Mary watched her. 'Blonde, like Caroline,' she observed. 'That's one way to show your allegiance.'

Without replying, Henrietta tugged on the comb. An excess of energy bubbled up inside her – she needed to be doing something, moving quickly.

'No wedding band, either,' Mary observed.

Henrietta gritted her teeth, aware she was blushing. 'I want to forget the past. You think the prince's temper is bad, but you do not know my husband.'

There was a pause, with only the crackle of the dying fire and the whoosh of Henrietta's comb to fill the silence. Suddenly, Mary spoke. 'Take care.'

Henrietta whirled round, comb in mid-air. Mary regarded her solemnly. 'Whatever do you mean?'

Mary looked down at her feet, stretching them inside her brocade shoes. 'Nothing,' she mumbled. 'Just – take care of yourself.'

Silently, Henrietta turned back to the fire and continued to comb her hair.

~ ~

Caroline knew something was wrong the moment she awoke. Thick clouds blocked out the sun and sent a splatter of rain against the windows. It felt more like the middle of the night than a late January morning, but she rose and allowed the women to dress her as usual.

She stared at herself in the mirror. Her face sagged into folds of sorrow. Her eyes were no longer the bright blue of a summer sky but cool, indigo chips. Losing the children had sucked the life from her like the juice from an orange. Standing up to the King's bullying was the right thing to do, she had no doubt about that, but it was a hard path to tread. Sometimes, she felt she walked it alone. George never unburdened his aching heart. Now he was chasing Maids of Honour and pouting when he could not get them into bed. She tried to kindle some jealousy, but she could feel nothing. Life without her little ones was like a walking death. Let George do what he would – she would get them back. Somehow.

Nothing would go right; her hair fell limp, her dress was too tight and the makeup failed to cover her smallpox scars. She spat into the basin Mrs Howard held out, but her mouth still tasted bitter. Yes, something was wrong.

Deep inside, she was ready for the smack of hooves in the courtyard before they came. Each harsh sound struck a chord within her, and it was a tune she recognised. In a trance-like state she stood, pushed her gaggle of ladies aside and drifted down the stairs. She had no thoughts, no feelings. She was prepared for bad news, and it had come. The only thing to do now was face it.

Bareheaded, she went down the steps of the front porch into chilling rain. A steaming horse tossed its head and snorted as its rider conversed rapidly with an equerry, Wentworth. Both men froze when they saw her.

'What is it?' she demanded. She took in the roll of parchment in Wentworth's leather glove, its surface spotted with rain. The royal seal and ribbons hung limp. Probably another document from the King, pressing for their signatures. There had been many over the last few months. First, he had urged them to sign the guardianship of their children over to him. Next, he demanded forty-thousand pounds to subsidise Fred's education. Caroline had agreed, providing Fred was allowed to come and finish his studies in England. After that answer, the King fell strangely silent.

'Your Highness,' Wentworth came to her and knelt in a puddle, proffering up the letter. 'Your Highness, I think you had better go inside to read it.'

She fixed her eyes on his damp, pale face. Water gathered in the corners of his hat and trickled down over the brim. 'Why?'

'It's – it is your son.'

'Fred?'

'Not Prince Frederick. Prince George William.'

Caroline swayed, putting out a hand to grip the slick iron railing outside the house. 'My baby?'

Wentworth hung his head, casting forth a stream of water to soak her hem. 'You need to read it, Your Highness.'

Caroline took the message. Her fingertips were numb and struggled to break the wax. Unfurling the parchment, she stared unseeing at the words, as rain fell and blotted them like tears. 'I cannot make it out,' she said. Her lower lip trembled and she hated herself for it.

Wentworth stood and gripped both her shoulders. The press of wet material against her skin made her shiver. 'The prince is ill,' he said. 'Gravely ill. You are summoned to Kensington.'

'No.'

'I assure you, it's the truth.'

Caroline looked at the foaming horse, the messenger tapping his whip against his thigh, and her cloudy thoughts crystallised. That feeling of foreboding all morning, a mother's sixth sense; it was all leading to this. 'Dear God. I'll fetch my husband.' She turned but Wentworth seized her wrist in his wet glove. It was as well he did, for her knees were liquid, like the rain puddling on the streets and dribbling from the eaves.

'No, madam. Just you.' Her mouth flew open, ready with a hot retort, but he interrupted her. 'Please, Your Highness. There is not a second to lose. Every moment you argue is a moment gone forever. Do you understand?'

She did. She saw the truth in his eyes and it filled her with despair. 'My boy,' she whispered, 'Sir, give me your horse.'

'I ordered the carriage before you came out.' As Wentworth spoke the vehicle rounded the corner, water dripping from its harness.

Caroline stumbled forward, putting out a hand to touch the

horse. Its flank was smooth and shiny as a black mirror, its tail spotted with diamonds of rain. 'My boy,' she repeated.

They bundled her inside – she didn't know how. She sprawled across the seat, groping and gasping like a drowning woman as the driver swished his whip and the vehicle lurched forward, creaking and splashing through the streets. How could this be happening? Her baby, her *liebchen*. All she could see was his face on the day they had parted; scrunched up and bawling to return to her arms.

Scenery rolled by in a blur. She pushed her cheek deep into the velvet upholstery, seeking comfort in its soft touch. By the time the wheels churned over the muddy roads of Hyde Park, she could barely breathe. *Gravely ill.* She searched the words over for cracks, feeling with persistent fingers for a flaw. She had survived grave illnesses – smallpox and pneumonia. Wasn't there a chance, just a slim chance, that Georgie would rally?

They slowed outside a square, redbrick building with slate tiles and urns decorating the roof. Before the vehicle fully stopped, Caroline unlatched the door and jumped out. She fell hard on her knees, coating her mantua in dirt and gravel. Heedless of the calling servants, she hauled herself up on grazed hands and pushed past the guards. She had to keep moving before she dropped. Already dark shapes fluttered around her eyes, like the wings of a black butterfly. The palace was in disarray; scaffolding covered the staircase and the air cloyed with the scent of paste and wet paint. Was this a place to bring a sick child? She glimpsed a wall, stained green at the corners with damp. Shuddering, she pressed on. She had no idea where she was going. She took step after step, her mules clicking on the floor, mimicking a tiny heartbeat.

As she rounded a corner, she saw Melusine speeding toward her. She wore no wig and no cosmetics. 'Thank God you are here!' She wrapped an arm round Caroline's shoulders and pushed her on with surprising strength. 'He's this way, Caroline, this way.'

At the threshold, Caroline heard a weak moan. She flew forward, her skirts flaring around her ankles, and skidded to the bedside on her knees. Her tiny boy lay on a wad of mattresses, covered in green brocade. He looked so small, so helpless as he retched and coughed. Caroline slid her arms around his thin, hot body. He had the bulging blue eyes of his father and they stared into hers intently. 'It's all right, my precious. Mama's here now.'

He wriggled, nestling his flushed cheek against her arm. Caroline choked on a sob. She would not show him worry or fear. She would be strong for him, and his last moments would see her smiling and confident. She sang to him; a song she remembered her own mother crooning at her bedside. Georgie punctured the tune every few minutes with his rasping, pathetic cough. Melusine's daughters hovered in the background, but Caroline took no notice of them. She focused on her son, drinking in every feature; his tuft of golden hair, the chin with a miniscule dimple. He stared at her with glassy eyes, little wet lips forming a circle to cough. It seemed as if he too was gathering information, trying to impress her face on his young mind so he could take it with him to the next world.

'There now, my pretty one.' She stroked his burning forehead. His eyelashes flickered at her touch.

Suddenly, his head twitched, then his arms. Little tremors rippled through the bedclothes, until his whole body contorted and arched from the mattress. His eyes rolled back into his head. Caroline bit hard on her lip to suppress a scream – she would be damned if the last sound he heard was a cry of pain – but she couldn't stop the tears. She gripped her son tight in her arms. She was like a peasant fighting for a greased pig; she would not let go, not when his little fist caught her mouth, nor when his head snapped up to hit her nose. Melusine and her girls sobbed softly from the corner.

'What's happening?' Caroline demanded. 'Where's the doctor? Dear God, will nobody help me?'

'This has happened before,' Melusine whispered. 'Every hour or so. The doctor says he can do nothing.'

Squeezing her eyes shut, Caroline rocked with the rhythm of Georgie's fit. 'Mama loves you so much, Georgie.' With a sigh, he fell limp.

Caroline did not know how long she held him. She heard Melusine call her name, but no one dared come near and unlace her arms. She held him until the warmth seeped out of his tiny body, until the light failed and the room plunged into darkness. Someone entered to light candles. Caroline could not stand the merry cheer of their orange glow. She looked at the bobbing flame beside her, a dancing spot of light, so fragile, so easily snuffed out. She puffed her cheeks and blew. The flame dissolved, leaving a feeble stream of smoke. She watched the grey line as it wound its way upward and melted away, like the spirit of her poor, poor son.

Henrietta closed the book softly and clasped it to her chest. Carefully, she wormed her way down the bed and hopped off the end without waking George. Her stories always lulled him to sleep, but not Caroline. The princess lay, hands clasped over her chest like a stone effigy in Westminster Abbey, her bloodshot eyes fixed on the ceiling.

Chickenpox had struck the royal couple within days of their little boy's death. In the confines of Dover Street, they no longer had separate bedrooms, so they stayed cooped up in one stifling sick chamber, sour with camphor and vinegar. But while George fretted and scratched, swearing at his spots, Caroline fell under the disease calmly, like a red enchantment. She made no comment on the itchy mounds bubbling beneath her skin, or sounds of relief when Mrs Clayton applied soothing camomile.

Henrietta placed the book on a shelf and turned to see if she could help Mrs Clayton mop Caroline's brow. But as she put her hands on the basin, ready to take it out and fetch fresh water, they were slapped away. She moved to the foot of the bed instead and watched George snore into his pillow. She liked his face better without the swamping wig.

'Listen to him.' Caroline hissed. 'How can he sleep so soundly?'

Mrs Clayton opened her mouth, but Henrietta spoke first. 'Emotions affect us all in different ways. Some they exhaust, others they . . . ' She trailed off, reaching for an adequate word.

'Torture,' Caroline supplied.

Henrietta bowed her head.

'I wonder his conscience does not keep him awake. If he had not quarrelled with Newcastle –'

'The baby still would have died.' The words were out before Henrietta could stop them.

'So they say.'

Henrietta smoothed the coverlet at Caroline's feet. 'I apologise. I did not mean to speak so bluntly. Only, I did not like to hear you accuse your husband. When we lose one we love, it is natural to cast blame. But we cannot let misery turn us against those closest to us.' She took a breath. 'The autopsy showed an excess of water on the brain and a polyp on the heart. Little Georgie was never destined for a long life.' She felt heartless mentioning scientific details, yet she knew they would appeal to the logical part of Caroline's mind.

'But the King! If the bone-headed King hadn't taken him to that draughty palace –'

'He may have had a few more days,' Henrietta conceded. 'That is all.'

Caroline's throat worked convulsively. It was terrible to stare at the emotions chasing across her face, but somehow Henrietta could not look away.

'Mrs Clayton, stop that.' Caroline put up a spotted hand and batted her aside. 'You may leave. I want to speak with Mrs Howard alone.' Lifting her nose, Mrs Clayton flung the wet rag into the bowl and strode off. She administered a deft pinch to Henrietta's shoulder as she passed. 'You always speak the truth to me, Howard. I have to say, I am not fond of you for it right now.'

Henrietta regarded her sadly. 'I'm sorry to cause you pain, madam. But I know whom you really blame, and until you admit it there will be no peace for you.'

A tear slid down Caroline's cheek. She winced as it met a blistering spot. 'Did I do the wrong thing? Should I have gone to the children when the King invited me? Those extra days I might have had . . . I failed my son.'

'You did the right thing for your husband.'

Caroline closed her eyes. 'Oh, my husband! Sometimes I lie here and think I'll strangle him while he sleeps. I know it is not his fault – not really. But I am not sure I will ever forgive him.'

'*You* made the choice,' Henrietta reminded her softly. 'The prince would have understood if you left him for the children. He would let you go even now, if you asked.'

Caroline's eyelids snapped open. 'And let the King win! After all he has done to us! Never.'

Henrietta shrugged. It was a hopeless situation, ringed with pride as hard as iron on all sides.

'Oh, Mrs Howard! Why can I not keep a son? Just one?'

'You are not alone in that, madam.'

Caroline looked up at her. Impulsively, she reached out and squeezed Henrietta's hand. 'No. No, of course I'm not.'

1718 – 1719

CHAPTER SIXTEEN

⤳ *Richmond Lodge* ⤲

Glorious sunshine blazed over Richmond Green, bringing the foliage to life. Caroline preferred the landscape of her new home to the geometric, ordered patterns of St James's privy gardens; it was free and natural. A lawn stretched down from the elm tree toward the glittering river. She imagined Emily rolling down that bank, coating her dress with sweet-smelling grass stains, and Anne chasing butterflies with a net. She stepped away from the window and sighed. Nearly six months since little Georgie's death, yet still she pictured him waddling, stiff-legged, holding his sister's fingers as he learnt how to stand.

She sat heavily on the sofa. The new baby pressed against her pelvis and sent a shock of pain through her spine. She was sick of this pregnancy – she could never get comfortable. As if the heat was not bad enough, her child was intent on sprawling across her at impossible angles.

A tap on the door. 'Lord Townshend and Sir Robert Walpole, Your Highness.'

She screwed on a smile as the two men shuffled into the room. Townshend she knew of old, but his brother-in-law Sir Robert Walpole was a new sight. She studied the man, trying to get the measure of him. His appearance was not appealing. He was a man of enormous girth, ruddy-faced with thick lips and a pair of eyebrows like black caterpillars wiggling across his forehead.

After Townshend's fall from power, Walpole had resigned his own post as Chancellor of the Exchequer. But now the King had made himself unpopular with an Act to limit the creation of peers. He was courting both Walpole and Townshend in the hope they would bring disaffected Whigs back on to his side. Caroline was determined: she would win these two politicians before Georg Ludwig could.

'Please be seated, gentlemen.' Townshend cast a wary glance at the skirting-board before flicking up the tails of his coat and obeying. Caroline laughed. 'I can assure you the rats are all gone now. Our man was most thorough.'

Townshend removed his hat and ran the brim through his fingers. 'I am glad to hear it, Your Highness. A terrible thing. Had an infestation myself, years back. Hard blighters to get rid of.'

Caroline pursed her lips. 'It is a misfortune we have become accustomed to. When one is thrown out of one's own palaces and has to purchase others – what is it you English say? Beggars cannot be choosers?'

'Yes, that is the phrase.' Townshend looked uncomfortable. 'Though – I believe – did not the King say you could stay at Hampton Court, while he is in Hanover? Perhaps I am mistaken.'

'A little mistaken.' Caroline bit back the bile rising in her throat. 'He said *I* could stay. Not my husband. Just as my husband was not permitted to visit his dying son.'

Townshend plaited his fingers together. 'Ah. I see.'

'Our summer residence will be here and in winter we will live in Leicester House. The King may have taken away our homes but he cannot stop my husband's allowance without Parliament's consent. We will buy our own palaces.'

'And may I ask what our role is to be in these palaces?' Walpole asked. 'Perhaps Your Highness wants to be a Whig hostess now?'

Caroline smirked. 'Whig, Tory – is there a difference, these days? I know your party is divided amongst itself. I know you, Sir Robert, make suggestions that do not fit in with the philosophy of the Whigs at all.'

He inclined his head.

Caroline adjusted a cushion behind her. 'It strikes me that these are the actions of a man who likes to keep one foot in each camp. This is a strategy I admire.'

'I do not believe your husband admires it, or me.'

She spread her hands. 'And you see where this has led him. But this is not a matter of admiration, it is one of trust. And there is one thing I can always trust a politician to do.'

'What is that, pray?'

'To look after his own interests.' Caroline saw a gleam in Walpole's large, dark eyes. They understood one another. 'Sometimes you have the King's favour; sometimes not. It is wise to try and win it. But then . . .' She left a tantalising pause. 'The King is old. Nearly sixty. What happens when – God forbid – he leaves us? Would my husband want to keep his father's relics in the Cabinet?'

'No. Not unless,' Townshend said slowly, 'he owed them an obligation. Some favour from before he came to power.'

'Precisely.'

A thoughtful silence descended. Outside, the sun shifted. A branch's shadow waved across the floor.

Walpole clapped his hands together. 'My dear madam, I know what it is you desire. You want your children back. And I can say with confidence that I can get them for you.'

Caroline's self-control wavered. Like a foolish woman, she was ready to fling her arms around the neck of any man who suggested the return of her daughters. But she took a deep breath and focused on the fine strokes of a painting, hanging directly above Walpole's head. 'What makes you so sure you can bring my girls back to me?'

Townshend cleared his throat. 'Wait. Things are progressing slowly. I understand the King has granted permission for you to visit your daughters once a week?'

She glared at him. 'Do you think that will be enough? Once a week, with their damned governess hovering over us all the time? He has our heirs in his keeping and uses them to humiliate us. Even now, while he is in Hanover, he forbids me from holding levees or drawing rooms. Our *children*, all younger than ten, are given the honour on my behalf. How do you think that makes me look?'

Walpole leant forward. 'You will get them back, madam, if you can only keep control of your emotions. I think you shall. But the prince . . . Forgive me, Your Highness, but father and son are both stubborn as mules. I believe you realise, madam, that you are the only one who can bring them together again.'

The baby fluttered inside Caroline. A ray of light dropped through the window and bathed the back of her aching neck. He was right; she had always known. It was all up to her. She had to be a great monarch, even if George let her down. 'I need help,' she admitted. 'This is a double-pronged attack. I can work on the prince but . . . I cannot do it on my own.'

Walpole's grin changed into a full-mouthed smile. 'You are not alone, madam.' He exchanged a look with Townshend. 'We will get your daughters back. I guarantee it.'

'And in return?'

He shrugged his broad shoulders. 'The influence of the queen. When she comes into her own.'

Caroline put out her hand. She was glad to see it rock-steady.

'Gentlemen. I believe we have an agreement.'

~ ~

Clods of mud flew through the air as the horses charged on. A gust of wind drew out strands of hair from beneath Henrietta's hat to whip behind her. She felt like a girl again. She hadn't ridden since the summer she was eight years old, charging around Cawston Heath on a pony. But the body did not forget. The reins sat naturally in her hands and she found the rhythm of her gelding's stride. It was only the lopsided sense of balance and burning sensation in her muscles that reminded her how much time had passed.

Her horse was a gleaming bay with a mane and tail as black as pitch. They called him Dandy. He was a sweet goer, very gentle. As Molly Lepell galloped up beside them on a skittish grey, rather too close for comfort, he merely snorted and held his pace.

'Lord,' cried Molly, 'haven't they caught the stag yet?'

'No,' Henrietta called above the thunder of hooves. 'They take longer than foxes. But you know the prince. Only a stag will do for him.'

'Venison for dinner again, then! A shame we are too far back here to see the kill.'

Henrietta did not reply. It was nothing for the Maids of Honour to watch an animal in pain; they had never been the ones pinned down, at the mercy of bared teeth.

Dandy gathered himself and leapt over a hedge. His hooves sent up a shower of leaves. Henrietta giggled as she was pelted with foliage. It was good to laugh and feel her lungs burn with something other than pain. Life without Charles was even better than she had imagined. It had been a summer of cloudless skies and drowsy insects. Even her body was renewed, as if it remembered the health she had enjoyed as a single woman. The scars hardly showed on her skin now; they were faint ghosts of the past.

She took the reins in one hand and swept leaves from her face and hat. She wondered if Henry rode now, if he had any opportunity to practise at the King's dull court. He was all she regretted. But the plan kept her steady. She would find a way to raise money – she had done it before. Enough for a passage to the colonies. When the heaving ocean held Charles at bay, they would start a new life, just the two of them. Safe.

As she cantered past the river, birds swooped down to fill their beaks with water. Henrietta was watching them when a deep bay in the woods made her jump. Dandy jinked to the side. She caught her breath as he tripped and lurched, forcing her to drive her fingers into his mane and grip the pommel of the saddle with her knee. Molly and her horse shot forward, out of sight.

'Easy, now.' Henrietta pulled back on the reins and brought Dandy to a halt. He was standing strangely with one hoof on point. In a tangle of skirts she managed to dismount and run a hand down his hot foreleg. He flinched. 'Poor fellow, you've pulled something.' She patted his neck and spoke softly to him. 'I'll get you back to the stables, shall I?' She removed her hat and wiped the sweat from her brow. Over in the distance, Caroline's carriage stood beneath a tree with the window rolled down. The princess never participated in the hunt, but watched from afar. Only today, there were gentlemen on horseback beside her coach, leaning in and talking to her. What could that mean?

Henrietta clicked her tongue and Dandy obediently limped after her. Swallows wheeled in the sky and birch trees shivered beside the water as they walked. She went slowly, allowing for Dandy's injury. She did not notice the pound of returning hooves until a shout greeted her.

'Mrs Howard!'

Dandy tossed his head as another, steaming horse pulled up at his side. The Prince of Wales sat in the saddle, sweaty and beaming.

She dropped into a curtsey. 'Oh, do forgive me, Your Highness, I did not see you there.'

'No trouble, I hope?'

'My horse is a little lame.' She gestured to his hobbling gate. 'I want to get a cold compress on it as soon as possible.'

George swung down from his horse in one fluid movement. 'Poor chap!' He felt around the leg for damage while his own mount cropped grass. 'No – nothing sinister there. A bit of rest is all he needs. But let one of the grooms take him back. You should not trouble yourself.'

Other riders returned from the hunt, keeping a respectful distance. They watched Henrietta and George with curiosity. A lady leant sideways in her saddle to whisper to her companion, while one man stood up in his stirrups, straining to hear the conversation.

Heat flushed into her face. 'I do not mind, sir. I like to care for him.'

George fisted his hands on his hips and considered her. 'Aye. That is like you.'

She tugged on her earlobe and looked down. His mud-splattered boots stood close to hers. She smelt the hunt on him: sweat, leather and the faintest tang of blood.

'You look well,' he commented. 'Happy. Are you?'

Henrietta bobbed him a curtsey. 'I am always happy to serve you, Your Highness, and the Princess of Wales.'

He grinned and shook his head. 'Of course, of course. You are the perfect courtier.' His face suddenly turned grave. 'I fear, Mrs Howard, that you may not have seen me in the best light of late. I was sorry to have you present when the princess and I had our little . . . disagreements.'

She almost laughed. His anger was louder than Charles's, but it was less malicious. The royal couple's arguments were mild by her standards. 'Please, do not mention it. I understand perfectly. This pregnancy is hard on Her Highness – the baby sits so far back on her spine. She cannot get comfortable. These little – *irritations* – are bound to occur.'

'Always practical, Mrs Howard. Always thoughtful.' She inclined her head at the compliment. 'Now answer my question honestly, not like a damned courtier: are you happy here? Do you regret your choice?'

She coloured, a little ashamed. 'I *am* happy.'

'You'll be starting your supper parties again, I suppose?'

'I will, sir. And as always, you are welcome to honour us with your presence.'

He clapped his gloved hands together. 'Happen I will, happen I will.'

'There is only one thing, I regret sir,' she ventured. 'My son. I do not suppose you ever hear word of him?'

George shook his head. 'No. Getting information about my own children is hard enough. Do you not write to him?'

'All the time.' Henrietta cleared her throat. 'He never replies. I do not suppose he is allowed to.'

George sighed. Suddenly mindful of his horse, he jerked its head up and began to lead it, signalling Henrietta to do likewise. 'I wish I could solve your problem, Mrs Howard. Truly, I do. I may not be one of these simpering puppies, but I do have a heart, I assure you.'

'No one doubts it, sir. Least of all me.' Her eyes travelled over to Caroline's carriage. She glimpsed the white circle of the princess's face, surrounded by golden curls. 'Your Highness understands, far better than many here, how difficult it is for a woman who has nothing to mother.'

He followed her gaze and his lips drooped. 'Ah, yes. That I do, Mrs Howard.'

~ ~

A harsh, white light scorched through the curtains. The windows were open but no breeze came through. Thick heat licked against Caroline's skin and made her clammy. It was like living in a bowl of soup.

As she adjusted her sticky thighs on the edge of her seat, the baby turned somersaults within her. Perhaps he sensed her nerves; sensed that the course of his future would be determined by this meeting. Everything depended on George's reception of Walpole.

He leant back in his chair and ran his eyes over their visitor. Walpole returned his gaze levelly. 'Your Royal Highness. It is an honour to be here. Thank you for granting me an audience.'

George indicated a wing chair. 'Do sit. My wife seems to be under the impression that you can help us.'

'I hope I can.'

'I struggle to see how that's possible. You are not in the King's government.'

'Not at present,' Walpole amended. 'But the King needs both me and my brother-in-law to stand beside him. To be blunt, he needs the support of the people we influence. And to get us he may be willing to grant certain . . . concessions.'

Caroline's heart beat so loud in her ears, she was afraid that George would hear it. Everything within her willed him to be reasonable – to listen to Walpole's proposals, at least. He rubbed his chin. 'The princess will have told you that we want our daughters back. That is true. But it is not the only consideration. Since leaving the palaces, life has been – expensive.'

Walpole looked around the room, as if costing up the silk walls and crystal chandeliers. 'Yes, of course. I imagine it will not be long before you find yourself in debt.'

'You imagine correctly.'

'Now there, sir, I can certainly help you.' Walpole sat forward eagerly. 'Have you heard of a venture called the South Sea Company? It trades on the Spanish coast of America, and won a large portion of our national debt. It's a scheme sure to make money.'

Caroline's mouth was as dry as flint. It was far, far too hot. Sweat slicked her cap to her hairline. She longed for a gasp of cool air to clear her head and think. She must keep control of the conversation; she couldn't let it bolt. 'Your scheme sounds like a gamble, sir. We need our money safe, to provide for the girls.'

Walpole grinned. His teeth were small and uneven. 'What in life is not a gamble? Besides, you would not need to invest much. The owners will gift you stock in return for your support.'

She groaned, too hot for manners. Would stock return her daughters? Could money bring back a dead boy? This was not why she had enlisted Walpole's help. 'My main concern is – '

George stopped her with a raised hand. 'Caroline, please. Let the man speak.'

'But –' She gulped in a breath. Suddenly, her chest constricted. She could not inflate her lungs; there were chains coiled about her. She slumped sideways in her seat.

George leapt up. 'There now, you have distressed yourself. Mrs Howard! Sir Robert, be good enough to ring that bell for Mrs Howard.'

Through hazy eyes, Caroline saw Henrietta dash into the room. The scent of her lavender perfume made the baby squirm in her stomach. 'Your Royal Highness, are you unwell? It is the heat.' Henrietta's cool hands pressed on Caroline's forehead. 'The heat is most fatiguing.'

'I am well,' Caroline wheezed. 'A little swoon. I will be restored if you fetch my fan.'

'Absolutely not,' George ruled. The sides of his eyes crinkled in concern. 'My dear, we do not require your presence in this matter. You should be upstairs resting.'

Thwarted ambition rattled inside her. Damn her body, damn the wriggling child, to fail her at a moment like this! She needed to stay in the room. Who else would act as mediator? Who would ensure the focus remained on her girls and not money?

Walpole looked at her, supine in Henrietta's arms, and knit his black brows together. 'I am sure Her Royal Highness has a strong constitution. With a fan and a little water, perhaps she might remain?'

George pushed out his chin. 'No. I forbid it. One cannot be too careful with a child on the way.'

Caroline gaped, looking from George to Walpole and back again. She had arranged this meeting. Surely George could not cast her out?

'Well sir, you know best.'

～ ↘

Henrietta's apartments buzzed with company. She threw her doors open to the courtiers and they came in droves. She spied new guests amongst the usual followers: Sir Spencer Compton, speaker of the House of Commons, and the Duke of Argyll. It made her uneasy to see these Tories flocking to her rooms when Caroline was seducing the Whigs. She did not want to be accused of encouraging those who worked against her mistress.

Sweating, she opened another window onto the sweet-scented night air. No breeze cooled her burning skin. This summer was an unrelenting furnace of heat.

'Oh, Mrs Howard, how cruel you are to stand there by the shade of night.'

Henrietta turned to the elderly Lord Peterborough, who had sneaked up at her side. She gave him a carefully proportioned smile. He had a habit of making absurd declarations of love that, while amusing, were starting to grate. 'You only shine the brighter against the stars and moon.'

She laughed. 'It is not difficult tonight, my lord. I see no stars and only the faintest ghost of a moon. Look at all the clouds. I think we are in for stormy weather.'

Peterborough leant against the windowsill with her. 'Ah, but with your angel wings, you will rise up against such tempests.'

Henrietta rolled her eyes. 'My dear Lord Peterborough, if you wish to pay me a compliment, you have only to tell me I am a very fine woman, and I will thank you for it. You know I have no patience with the ridiculous cant of love.'

'These sound,' he said archly, 'like words from a woman who has never been in love.'

It hit a nerve. Charles had been a hasty infatuation, more an image of her own making than a real man. She had never truly been in love. A sad admission for a woman of nearly thirty. She shrugged it aside, unwilling to let Peterborough see her discomposure. 'My lord,' she went on, 'I believe a person truly distressed by his emotions would express them naturally. Similes and affected expressions do not suggest real passion.'

Sauciness flickered in the old lord's eyes. 'If you give me leave, I will report your preferences to an exalted acquaintance of mine. It would save him much trouble.'

Henrietta caught his meaning at once. Ever since George singled her out on that hunting trip, tongues had wagged. 'Be careful what you say, Lord Peterborough.' She flung away from the window and pressed back into the crowd. Was that the reason courtiers flocked to her rooms? Did they have their eyes on her as the next royal mistress? Grabbing a tankard of ale, she took a fortifying sip. Her whole frame trembled. She thought of George; his short but upright figure, the soft eyes, the full lips. An attraction was there – it always had been. Henrietta recalled how awkward and clumsy she had felt that first night they met. When she had managed to please him by showing an interest in his conversation, her heart had soared like a dove . . . A dove. The image jolted her back to reality. There was another memory, more precious than any George could inspire: Caroline finding her by the dove-cote. Repulsed by her own treachery, Henrietta wiped at her forehead with a handkerchief. If only she could blot the traitorous thoughts away as easily.

Beneath the rattling dice and chinking glasses came a knock at the door. Henrietta's servant, Daniel, let in a royal page carrying a box. 'Mrs Howard. Something for Mrs Howard.'

Everyone looked around.

'Oh!' Molly squealed. 'How exciting!'

Sly glances passed between the ladies.

'Who is it from?' asked Henrietta.

The page shrugged as he set the box down on the floor. 'Don't say. Ain't no note on it. I just got summoned to the stables and told to take this to Mrs Howard.'

Henrietta's curiosity grew. Now she considered the box, it seemed to move. Noises came from within, but she could not distinguish them amidst the excited chatter. She swapped a look with Molly. It was irresistible; as one, they crouched, skirts pooling around them, and levered the lid. A flurry of black, white and tan exploded into Henrietta's lap. Amongst the straw spilling onto her skirts, she felt fur wriggling in her fingers. When a warm, wet lick touched her chin she realised what was leaping about her: puppies. She giggled, falling back and letting them jump over her.

'Oh, Mrs Howard, they're beautiful! Look at them!'

One was all brown, a shade lighter than Henrietta's natural hair colour. He had a domed forehead and crazy little twitching ears, which were neither up nor down. The other puppy was a girl, black and white like a domino, all melting eyes and silky fur. They bounced on Henrietta, coating her face in kisses and disordering her cap. She laughed until her belly hurt.

'Goodness me!' Mary Bellenden pushed through, flapping her

fan. 'What little darlings. Who do you think would send them?'

Henrietta shrugged. For a moment, she did not care. 'The page said there was no note. Maybe the princess sent them? I admired her little dog aloud the other week.'

'Or Mr Gay,' Molly put in. 'He's away from court at the moment; he might have thought you needed a reminder of him.'

There were a thousand possibilities. She had written to her brother John recently; perhaps one of his bitches had pupped. Or – did she dare hope – had Henry smuggled them away from a litter in the King's stables? Was there a chance that, forbidden to write, he sent her a gesture of affection the only way he could?

Henrietta handed the bitch to Molly and the dog to Mary then stood to brush her skirts. 'You had better take this box back, there is no room for it here,' she told the page.

'Yes, madam.'

She bent and helped him pick up the lid, ready to secure it back in place. Just then, a scrap of paper caught her eye, buried amongst the straw. Her hand shot out and grabbed it. The page raised his eyebrows – he had seen her quick gesture. Henrietta shook her head at him. He winked and together they put the lid back on the box.

When the page was gone, Henrietta scooped the brown puppy under one arm and used him to conceal her precious scrap of paper. She longed to be alone and read it. Everywhere she turned there were faces, laughing and shouting. Not even the window was free – Lord Peterborough still lounged there, casting calves-eyes at her. 'Oh puppy, puppy,' she murmured. 'What will I do?'

It was unbearable. She couldn't wait – it would be two o'clock in the morning before her guests left. The puppy whimpered and nuzzled under her head. He writhed, as if he was uncomfortable. *Of course!*

Henrietta seized her black and white puppy from Molly with her free arm. 'I'll just be a moment,' she gabbled. 'I think they need to relieve themselves. I do not want them making water in my rooms.' She sped from the door like a woman possessed, plunging herself into the dark gardens.

She ran until the light glowing in her chamber melted to a yellow smear. Her chest relaxed; although the air was muggy, it was easier to breathe without the heavy scents of perfume and food. She plonked her puppies down on the grass, where they waddled about. The little black and white one circled and squatted. 'You're a good girl,' she cooed.

The piece of paper was creased and stained with her sweat. She smoothed it out as best she could, squinting. The stars were dull and the moon was a mere fingernail of white behind rags of cloud. It was hard to read, but she was sure she didn't recognise the writing – slapdash letters, slanting lines. It could not be Henry. Her heart sank and her knees went with it, depositing her in a puddle of silk on the lawn. She so wanted it to be from him. She stared at the paper, as if she could change the writing by sheer will-power. When her eyes adjusted to the darkness, she made out shapes. An *S*. The word *to*. Then, as the moon sailed out from beneath a cloud, she saw the whole sentence. Everything froze around her.

Something to mother. G.

CHAPTER SEVENTEEN

⌁ *Leicester House* ⌁

The new London residence was a spacious, two-storey building on the north side of Leicester Fields. A gatehouse and courtyard guarded it from the dirt of the streets, but there was no escaping the smells: horse dung, sweating bodies and vegetable peelings.

Caroline peered out through misty windows and watched the people dashing to and fro, using the square as a shortcut to Charing Cross or the Haymarket. Heavy clouds glowered over them, threatening a summer shower. The pressure in the air made her temples throb, but that was nothing compared to the pain of her anticipation.

Walpole stood before George with his hands joined behind his back. His feet were splayed, as if braced for an attack. He always brought his news straight to George; for the sake of male pride, she had to pretend she was nothing, a mere observer with no interest. So after she had gazed from the window, she turned back and adjusted the knotting work on her lap. Though her fingers moved, her concentration on the pair was complete. Men might bridle her tongue, but they could not stop her ears.

'I have informed the King that you are anxious to submit yourself.'

She darted an upward glance. George crossed his arms. '*Submit*? Pah, I suppose such terms are necessary for the booby's pride. What did he say?'

'His Majesty declares he will only receive you back in the palaces if you are bound hand and foot.' It was as well that Walpole was standing, for he managed to dodge the book that hurtled toward him and made a dent in the wall.

'The villain! The base knave!'

Disappointment drained her like a leech. After all this time Georg Ludwig was still obstinate. *He* had taken their children, *he* had provoked the quarrel that led to Georgie's death. What right had he to resent *them*?

George snatched a breath. 'So he will not pay any of my debts? Not one?'

'On the contrary,' said Walpole. 'I have concentrated my efforts on that point.'

Caroline fumbled with the knotting shuttle. What about her girls? They were the crux of all this.

George eyed Walpole warily. The curls of his wig fell forward, partially shading his red face. 'And what does the *wise* King say on that subject?'

Walpole pulled a bundle of paper from his pocket. 'I am certain we will come to an agreement soon. But in the meantime, here is a gift for you.'

'From His Majesty?'

Walpole did not answer the question but moved his lips silently, counting as he shuffled the pieces of paper. 'Additional stock in the South Sea. Have you seen how it is rising? Upon my word, you will be rich as Jews!'

Eagerly, George started forward and swiped the certificates from his hand. He turned them over with a rapacity that made Caroline wince. 'How much is there?' she asked.

'Enough.' Pocketing the hoard, George started toward the door. 'I will be back presently,' he called over his shoulder. 'I want to put this in safe-keeping before the King changes his mind.'

His footsteps pattered down the corridor, leaving Caroline and Walpole alone. Rain dripped down the chimney and made the fire hiss.

She picked up the purse she was knotting and laid it aside in her workbasket. 'You speak much of money, Sir Robert. Very little of my children. Do not forget who employed you in the first place.'

He grimaced. 'Did you go to the King's mistress as we discussed?'

'Yes, I have begged Melusine, to no avail. I will try again. She will hear nothing but complaints until my girls are returned to me.'

'I suppose we could try the law courts. But at present, your husband will not authorise the expense.'

She inhaled, drawing herself up. 'What if *I* authorise it?'

'I imagine you could only do that if the prince was somehow preoccupied. Busy enough to overlook his accounts.'

Caroline raked her mind for ideas. George loved numbers; the perfect tallies of his ledger. He only failed to heed them when at war . . . or in love. Her stomach wallowed with misgiving. 'Nonsense. I am sure that, between us, we could persuade him – '

His large forehead crinkled. 'Then we had better do it soon. I am serving two masters as well as yourself, madam. They may come to an agreement in spite of me.'

'Whatever do you mean?'

'I did not mention it while the prince was present, but the King has implied that he will pay off your debts . . . if you yield a certain point to him.'

Her throat tightened. 'Not . . .'

He nodded. 'The princesses.'

Her sense of injustice swelled until she thought she would burst.

She had imagined England as an enlightened country with a monarchy balanced by Parliament. Now she realised that the crown held ultimate sway. It had the power to separate a mother from her children with no just cause. 'It does not matter what the King offers,' she said hoarsely. 'George would never sell his children. No amount of money will make him concede them.'

Walpole's furry black eyebrows lifted. 'Are you sure of that, madam?'

Richmond Lodge

Caroline tilted her parasol, shielding her eyes from the sun as it slipped down the horizon leaving streaks of crimson and coral in its wake. Muggy air filled her lungs with each breath. The baby fluttered inside her, as if he knew what she meant to do. As if he could stop her.

Horses thundered past in a swirl of dust, racing to the end of the track. She had smiled at them until she thought her face would break with the effort. Finally, the courtiers cheered and a chestnut mare with white socks passed the post. As the air cleared, Henrietta appeared slowly from a cloud of brown powder, her cheeks flushed with excitement. Deep blue flowers in her cap set off her blonde hair and sparkling eyes.

Envy flared in Caroline's chest, but the task still had to be done. She had made the decision in cool logic. The time for sentiment was dead. Everything had died, it seemed to her, the moment Georgie pushed his last breath through tiny blue lips.

Gritting her teeth, she waddled over to Henrietta and placed a hand on her arm. 'Take a turn with me, won't you?'

Wariness flashed in Henrietta's eyes. *Yes, you may well look sheepish, Mrs Howard. You know all too well what attention you have attracted.* Perhaps she wouldn't be adverse, after all. Caroline could not decide if that pleased or sickened her.

Henrietta pulled on two leashes wound round her hand. Her little dogs trotted after her, pink tongues lolling.

Caroline smiled at them. 'Have you named your dogs yet?'

'The brown one is Fop. My black and white one, Marquise.'

'Good names. And you still have no idea who sent them?'

Blushing, Henrietta shook her head.

'*I* do.'

'You do?' Henrietta stumbled, her foot caught in a clod of grass. 'Pray, tell me. Who?'

Caroline sighed and rested her parasol on her shoulder. 'Oh, Mrs Howard, we could go on playing this game all evening, couldn't we? But it is too hot and I'm not in the mood. You know, as well as I do, that the prince sent you those dogs.'

Henrietta remained silent, chewing the inside of her cheek. Such meek behaviour only validated Caroline's choice: Henrietta must be the one.

'My husband, Mrs Howard, tells me everything. I mean *everything*. You cannot imagine. In the past, he has taken mistresses and recalled every encounter in sickening detail. He talks of his conquests as if I should rejoice in them.'

Henrietta's eyes expanded, two pools of pewter grey. 'However do you bear it?'

Caroline did not know. Even now she felt a lump of coal in her belly, emitting choking smoke. 'I will not pretend it is easy. But princes will be princes, kings will be kings.' A breeze shivered through the willows. One duck took alarm and skittered off with a splash. Caroline sucked in a breath. She couldn't believe she was about to sully her tongue with these words. 'Mrs Howard, it occurs to me that you may be due for a promotion.'

'A – a promotion?'

Caroline itched to pinch her. Surely she was not so naive? 'The prince may come to you with a rota of extra duties. I would recommend that – I would *wish* you – to accept them.'

Henrietta scooped up Marquise. 'You cannot mean it,' she whispered.

For an instant Caroline was tempted to say *no*, of course she did not mean it. She wanted to clap her parasol shut, point the end at Henrietta's chest and tell her to stay away from her husband. But that was how a Billingsgate fishwife behaved – not a Princess of Wales. 'He will offer the post to someone. I cannot stop that. Far better someone I trust, someone discreet. Besides,' Caroline looked to where Walpole and Townshend whispered in the shade of an elm, 'I have my own reasons for wishing George – *distracted* – at present.'

To her surprise, tears spilled from Henrietta's eyes onto Marquise's black and white fur. 'I cannot do it. Not to you.'

She grunted in annoyance. This was hard enough. Did Henrietta want her to fall on her knees and beg? 'I did you a good turn. Now it is your chance to repay me.'

'I hope I am not ungrateful, but . . . '

'Believe me, it is quite a burden entertaining the prince all day. Won't you help me, my good Howard? I am sure you will. The prince has attended your supper parties. Tell me, how many times have you heard his Oudenarde story?'

'About nine.'

She snorted. 'So few?'

War raged beneath the mask of Henrietta's face. Caroline remained silent and let it play out, hoping something would emerge in her favour. She shuddered to think of a giddy Maid of Honour like Mary Bellenden with the role of *maîtresse-en-titre*. Most women would try to wield power and influence politics – Henrietta would never dare.

In the distance, a rider dismounted from a sweating black gelding. The festivities were drawing to a close – there wasn't much time. Guilt and anger were the only prods to use now. 'Really, Mrs

Howard, I did not expect this. I am sure your delicacy does you credit, in some circles, but not with me. At my own risk, I have supported you. It was in my power, any hour of the day, to let you drop through my fingers. I ask you one *speculative* favour – for who knows if the offer will ever be made? – and I find you stubborn. Yes, stubborn. You know the projects I work upon could restore us to our children. I had least expected – I had least *deserved* – such treatment from you.'

Henrietta stepped back, gasping. Her lips moved, unable to find purchase, until she caught at one word. 'Charles.'

Caroline had expected this. It was her ace. 'Yes, I thought you might say that. Not that Mr Howard retains any moral right to your fidelity, but legally I suppose he does.' She leant forward slowly, extending a hand to toy with Marquise's ear. 'My dear Howard, I will reunite the two courts. I do not care if it kills me – I will do it. I will turn over houses, move mountains, to get my girls back.'

Henrietta gestured to Caroline's burgeoning stomach. 'This baby will be yours to keep – the King will not take it away.'

'Oh, fie! Do you think I will forget my other children? Have I forgotten Frederick? Do you forget Henry, with these pups running around?'

Miserably, Henrietta shook her head.

'No.' Caroline moved her face closer to Henrietta's, until her breath stirred the strands of hair hanging beside her ears. 'Now when the courts come together, Mr Howard will try to claim you. Hurt you. But what could he do if you were under the prince's express protection? Under my protection?'

Henrietta turned an anguished gaze upon her. 'Are you saying that if I refuse, I will not be granted such protection?'

Caroline grinned and backed away, one hand held up, the other twirling her parasol. 'I am saying nothing, Mrs Howard. It is all speculation, my dear, speculation like a card game. But you may hold a winning hand. A new position, with luxuries and protection. No power,' she added in a harsh undertone, 'no political power at all. But benefits. Let the notion play about that great mind of yours.'

She turned and staggered back toward the lodge, taking racking breaths. She had done it – she had set the wheels in motion – and taken two large scoops out of her own heart. Her husband and her friend. Mrs Howard would never look at her the same way, no matter what happened. Caroline bit her lip. A necessary sacrifice. All must bow, all must fade before the chance of getting her daughters back.

∽ ⤳

Henrietta sat beside the empty grate with a tankard of ale in her hand. She couldn't put her thoughts in a straight line. Letters spilled on the table before her, illuminated by a dying candle. Good news and bad; her brother John told her she was an aunt, while the black-edged paper from Charles's brother announced that the Earl of Suffolk had died. She wondered fleetingly if Charles would receive an inheritance. If he did, he might abandon Henry and disappear for months on end to squander it. She remembered the times Charles had deserted her in their early marriage. They were the only pleasant memories of him she had.

She slugged down her ale and stood to close the window. The air was humid, a damp breath on her cheek. She drew the curtains, shutting out the patch of grass churned by racing hooves – the very spot where her own emotions had been pounded finer than dust. She slumped back in her chair, massaging her temples. The whole episode carried the mist of unreality. Surely she had imagined the serpentine slide of Caroline's eyes, the veiled threat in her words?

Caroline had changed since little Georgie's death. She had always possessed a hard core, but recent pressures had turned it from coal to adamantine. After five years of acquaintance, Henrietta still wasn't sure she understood the royal woman. As for what she suggested . . . Henrietta squirmed from the idea and poured a large measure of ale. She gulped it, relieved to feel alcohol tingle through her. She picked up the jug and poured again. She was not repulsed by George; far from it. But it was one thing to sit, admiring his fine profile and imagine planting a kiss on his strained forehead – quite another to actually do it. This was Caroline's *husband*; nothing could change that. But wouldn't it be sweet revenge to cuckold Charles, to taste the physical delights the Maids of Honour giggled about?

She put her lips to the tankard and took another swig. It went down too fast and made her retch. Her hands shook as she hushed the leaping dogs and wiped her mouth on her apron. There would be money in this opportunity. Money to save for a life with Henry. What was holding her back? Nobody cared for her. Every family member was either dead or estranged. But George . . . She pictured the soft crinkles beside his eyes when he smiled, and her heart seemed to unravel within her. Becoming his mistress would be a slice, a tiny slither of happiness. Why did she not seize it with both hands and devour it?

Just as the clock chimed seven, the latch clicked. Henrietta leapt to her feet, sending the puppies skittering. All at once, the ale hit her like a wave; she grasped the back of a chair to stay upright. With a creak the door swung open, revealing a short, broad silhouette. Her pulse thundered. She did not need the light of the guttering candle to see it was George. He stepped in and closed the door behind him. Shakily, she performed her curtsey. Surely Caroline had not told him of their conversation?

'Mrs Howard. Pray, forgive the intrusion.' He beamed as the puppies rushed up to him, tails wagging. The expression made his face all too handsome. 'I have often been here of an evening and found you with Miss Lepell and Miss Bellenden.'

'Yes,' she breathed. 'But tonight, Your Highness, you find me all alone.'

He looked at the vacant chair opposite her. 'May I sit?'

She cursed her lack of decorum. 'Oh yes, please do.' She busied herself with pouring ale, slopping liquid over the side of the jug with her nervous hands. 'You do not need *my* invitation, sir.'

He laughed and sat down. Crossing his legs, he accepted a tankard of ale. 'You think not? I was a little less mannered with your friend Mary Bellenden and suffered for it.' He paused. 'I suppose she told you about storming out on me?'

She could not look at him. 'She did, sir.'

Thoughtfully, he swirled the ale around his tankard. 'Well, I have learnt my lesson. Then again,' his voice dropped to a husky whisper, 'you do not seem like the storming type.'

Henrietta swallowed. 'No, sir.' Without waiting for his permission, she sat. Her legs would not support her a moment longer. She gripped her tankard with both hands.

'You are quiet, my dear Mrs Howard. Are you afraid of me?' His eyes, burning blue as lapis, darkened.

She tried to laugh, but only a squeak emerged. 'Truly, I think I am a little afraid of you tonight.'

'And why is that?'

Because tonight I am permitted to see you as a man, not a prince. Tonight I have your wife's permission to unleash my secret thoughts. 'Perhaps the weather. It is close – stormy, I think. Makes horses and women flighty.' She smiled, though her lips hurt with the effort. George's lingering gaze travelled down to her mouth. Her heart hammered. She couldn't understand what she was feeling; she was simply frozen, awaiting her fate like a pheasant at the end of a gun. 'Sir . . .'

Gently, he reached out and slotted his fingers through hers. Her skin tingled beneath his. It had been an age since a man had touched her kindly. Her body yearned for human contact, the feeling of warm flesh that told her she was not alone. And here was George, looking tenderly upon her, his bare hand encasing hers. Deliberately slow, he raised it to his lips. The kiss jolted through her. She closed her eyes. George let her hand drop and rose from the table. She heard his footsteps as if they were far away. She felt like she was floating – a dandelion seed wafting on the breeze. Whatever was going to happen next, she was powerless to stop it.

His hands cupped her face. Obedient to their soft pressure, she stood. She was ashamed at how readily her loins melted and a deep, urgent craving took root in the pit of her belly. It had been so long . . . When his lips came, they were warm and laced with ale. Henrietta drank him in, responding to his need. These were not the biting kisses of her cruel husband. These made her giddy, made her reach out and put her arms around his waist. She relaxed into him with a sigh of pleasure. This was no longer Caroline's husband – it wasn't even George – it was just comforting warmth and a feeling of safety.

Henrietta barely noticed him move her to the bed. She pulled her skirts up readily, eyes still closed. This was the natural progression of the sweet, intoxicating dance they were locked in. He fumbled with his breeches. When he entered her, she gasped and clutched at his back. It mesmerised her; the slide of heated skin, the caresses, and the soft kisses perfectly placed. She had not realised it could be like this. Her heart beat in her stomach, thick and fast. Little ripples of pleasure took her by surprise as they grew and surged. She was liquid beneath him, yielding to his expert touch, gasping against his lips. Another second and bliss exploded within her, dotting the back of her eyelids with stars.

So that was it: what she had never felt with Charles. Only now did she realise how cheated she had been. Weariness took hold. Before memory could resurface, before she could cogitate what she had done, Henrietta gave into sleep's pull, her arms wrapped tight about her prince.

CHAPTER EIGHTEEN

～ *Richmond Lodge* ～

It had happened. Caroline sensed it almost the moment Henrietta walked into the dressing room. The way she carried herself was subtly different; lighter, more fluid. Her features were soft and dreamy, her cheeks flushed as if by rouge. She looked as content as a well-fed cat. She would do; George was always a satisfying lover.

The muscles in Caroline's shoulders locked. The image rose unbidden: the pair together, naked, caught in an embrace. She drove her fingernails into her palms to stop from screaming.

Henrietta knelt before her with a basin of water, her grey eyes studiously averted. Caroline's stomach turned. She had wanted this, she reminded herself. She had commanded it. Sometimes it was not a blessing to be obeyed. Picking up the sponge, she began to clean her teeth. She doubted she would be able to wash the bitter taste from her mouth.

Her emotions were spreading, expanding until they pressed against the papered walls. She couldn't show weakness now. She had to focus on the task at hand: a deal with Walpole and the King. Her girls. She tried to conjure their faces on the surface of the water before her, but all that looked back were her own red-rimmed eyes. She spat into the bowl, showering Henrietta's hands with the finest spray of her contempt. It was not fair or reasonable to hate the woman, but it helped.

~ ~

Henrietta lay sprawled on her new silk coverlet, fingering the delicate embroidery. Crimson curtains framed the stormy landscape outside her window; rain lashing the trees and a sky dark as night. She sank deeper into the mattress and sighed. The new bed clothes were soft, but they stung her with remorse. She was a fallen woman now. Wicked, unchaste. Yet how could she be otherwise? It was the only way to stay in employment. The only way to save. Was it really a sin, if she was obeying an order? Doing the best for her child? Her mind said no, but it could not persuade her heart.

Beeswax candles, housed in golden sconces, shone upon Mary Bellenden, Molly Lepell, Mr Gay, Lord Chesterfield and Mr Pope as they explored all her new acquisitions. She was embarrassed to have her friends here, exclaiming over the wages of her debauchery.

'Pure mahogany!' Gay exclaimed, rapping his knuckles on her desk. 'Look at the gleam on it.'

Henrietta chuckled grimly, remembering her years in Beak Street; fighting against hunger and misery, darning the same stocking again and again until the material fell away. Rush lights, stinking tallow candles and flea bites. How far she had come.

'Goodness!' cried Molly. 'So many letters on your desk.' She picked them up, whistling as she saw the seals. 'Some of England's greatest families.'

Shame seeped through her. You didn't visit the chamber pot in this court without society hearing of it. How galling to think of her most intimate moments, broadcast amongst the nation's aristocracy.

The whore Howard, the topic over pipes and brandy in every stately home. 'Oh yes. They all come cringing to me now. They think I can do them the most miraculous favours.'

Pope cocked an eyebrow. 'And can you?'

A flash of lightening shot past the window. Wind howled down the chimney, stirring ash in the grate.

'If I could,' said Henrietta, 'my dear friend Gay would have a place at court. You would be earls – no, dukes! Then I would grant Molly and Mary outrageous dowries so they could marry Mr Hervey and Colonel Campbell.'

They all smiled at the thought. Henrietta saw ambition flit through her friends' eyes. But at least these trusted few knew the limits of her role. George had taken a mistress to show he was not under Caroline's paw. He would not be ruled by Henrietta. But he could pay her. And if she continued to invest in the South Sea Company, who knew what might happen? She might really make enough money to whisk Henry away from his school and live alone with him in secret. The very thought made her heart thrill.

Mary plopped down on the foot of the bed, her eyes wide. 'You have not told the prince, have you? That I love Colonel Campbell?'

'Of course not!'

Thunder grumbled outside. Tree branches groaned and creaked as the wind rattled Henrietta's windows.

'Sounds nasty,' Lightening washed over Chesterfield's face. 'Well, at least the prince cannot make us hunt tomorrow.'

Bad weather would mean George prowling around, frustrated. She raked her mind for subjects to cheer him – perhaps she would ask if he knew of any battles fought in fierce rain. Yes, that would do nicely.

Gay peered through the curtains, springing back when a shower of hail hit the glass. 'God above, those clouds!'

Henrietta propped herself up on one elbow. It looked like the end of days outside; horizontal rain and formidable walls of cloud. She shivered. 'Oh, pull the curtains. I'll ring for some wine.' As she moved, there was an explosion of sound. Molly and Mary fell to their knees screaming. Powder and plaster chips dropped from the ceiling onto their dark hair. Leaping up, Henrietta dashed to the window beside Gay. A flaming tree branch slammed into the grass outside. There was a terrible groan of wood, like the moaning timbers of a ship, and then the elm tree hurtled toward them, its base splintering to pieces.

'Get down!' Gay pushed her to the ground. Henrietta huddled in his arms, shrieking as glass cracked. Terrified screams echoed above her head.

'We're all right.' Lord Chesterfield's voice. 'Do not be afraid. You can get up.'

Warily, Henrietta lifted her head from Gay's shoulder and surveyed the room. A thick white mist coated her friends, but they were unscathed. No glass was missing from her window panes. Her ears rang and moaned. Cautiously, she eyed the ceiling. A large crack ran across it.

'It will hold,' Pope said, seeing her glance. 'Praise be to God! How that tree missed us, I will never know.' His thin, fragile frame trembled. Henrietta wanted to sit him by a fire and fetch him a drink, but something troubled her. Then she realised: the muffled wail was not tinnitus inside her ears; it was an actual sound.

'Upstairs,' she cried. 'It's hit them upstairs.'

Molly covered her mouth with her hand. 'The princess.'

As one, the three women stumbled to their feet and flew from the room. Henrietta tried to dust herself down, but the powder was everywhere, making her choke. Her trembling legs tripped and faltered on the stairs as the screams grew louder. They burst into the princess's room and gasped. Glass littered the floor, glimmering weirdly in the half-light. The elm had thrust its singed branches through the window and halfway across the room. The curtain pole fell at a slant, its damask drapes torn to ribbons. Candles steamed, their flames extinguished by the wind and rain that beat onto the carpet.

Mary tensed beside her. 'Blood.'

Shards of glass covered the ladies who chanced to be near the window when the tree fell. They raved, beside themselves, plucking at the wounds on their arms.

'Go to the linen cupboard,' Henrietta said quickly. 'Tear up some bandages.'

Mary put a shaking hand on her shoulder. 'No. There.'

Caroline curled on the bed, howling in pain. Her petticoats, her quilt and the floor beneath her bed were bathed red. *The baby*. They dashed forward to help her, but it was too late. After a shock like that, nothing could be done for the child.

Mary and Molly got Caroline on her back and dosed her with opiates while Henrietta and Mrs Clayton mopped up. Another small corpse, blue-red and tangled, lay sprawled in a pool of gore. Determination set in Henrietta like a thick clay. The red substance was sticky and hot on her bare hands but she couldn't let herself think about what she was doing. She would get through this horrific chore for Caroline. Mrs Clayton took the body out of the room, leaving only mess and liquid for Henrietta. A tangy, animal scent rose up from the fluid. Her throat worked convulsively, pushing down her gorge.

When they were done, Henrietta rinsed her hands in a basin. A crimson stain floated from her fingers and swirled in the water. Another poor child, obliterated from existence.

Under her directions, ladies dodged around the tree and blocked the broken window with oilskin. Someone lit a fire to keep the princess warm, while others changed her bed linen and skirts.

Caroline barely moved as they fussed around her, turning her this way and that. Henrietta only hoped it was the medicine, carrying her off to a weighted sleep, and not the paralysis of grief. They could not protect her from the truth of what had happened, but she deserved a few hours of oblivious slumber.

'Could you see?' Henrietta asked Mrs Clayton. 'Was it another boy?'

She shook her head. 'I could not tell.'

Caroline stirred. She stretched out a hand, crusted with dried blood. Instinctively, Henrietta moved forward to take her accustomed place: kneeling beside her mistress. 'Mrs Clayton.'

Henrietta swayed as if she had been slapped.

'Mrs Clayton. Come to me.' Smug, even in this terrible scene, Mrs Clayton shoved her aside and went to Caroline.

She stood stunned. *She* had issued the sensible orders, *she* had been Caroline's mainstay through every other tragedy – not Mrs Clayton. She flexed her fingers by her sides and they felt empty, like she had lost her grip on something infinitely precious. Caroline did not look at her again.

She left the room, understanding all too well. Things had changed. The woman who slept with the prince was no comfort to the princess when she lost his baby. She was not a beloved friend now. She was the one who had to go and tell George.

1720

CHAPTER NINETEEN

⌐ *Leicester House* ⌐

The clock ticked, every second a needle in Caroline's skin. Purgatory would be better than this. Anything but the weighted silence of her courtiers and the strange hush in the square outside. Surely, after three years, the King would accept George's olive branch? How long could he hold a grudge? Her thoughts stretched down the winding streets to St James's Palace, tracking George's sedan chair. She saw his large cuffs, embroidered with gold thread, and the flaps on his pockets. In the left-hand side was the speech she had laboured over all night. She made a steeple of her hands and rested her aching head against it. *Please God, let it work.* Today would tell if her years of hard graft had paid off. She had wooed Walpole and Townshend, persuaded George to copy letters and distracted him with a mistress. She had spent hours on her knees – sometimes to Melusine, sometimes to God. What if it was all in vain?

Outside the window, April weather mocked her, brazenly cheerful and bright. Fragile blossom grew on the trees and daffodils peeked out of the earth.

Henrietta hovered at her side, equally tense. It gave Caroline a strange sense of relief to know that, whatever happened, she would not face the burden of George's temper alone. 'Mrs Howard, tell me your thoughts. Will the King and the prince be reconciled? Or do you think my husband's pride will stand in his way?'

Courtiers looked around, intent on the exchange between princess and mistress.

'I hope not, Your Highness. He loves you and your daughters very much. He will do anything to reunite you.'

A perfect, gentle answer as always. Caroline was not appeased.

Noise outside catapulted her to her feet. She dashed to the window, thrust Miss Meadows from the cushioned seat and gripped it with both hands. About thirty men ran into the square, whooping for joy. A lad amongst them tossed his cap into the air. 'I do not believe it.'

Yeomen of the Guard tramped into Leicester Square. Sandwiched between the point and the vanguard was George's sedan, its leather flaps pulled back from the windows. His face was flushed, pink and smiling behind the glass. Caroline's knees gave way. 'It is the prince,' she gasped. 'The King has restored his guard.'

Without waiting for her signal, the courtiers hooted and spilled from the door. Caroline turned to the deserted room. Only Mrs Howard remained, her expression unreadable. 'You have done it, Your Highness. They are reconciled.'

Caroline blinked. She had pushed long and hard against the same unyielding wall until it became her life's focus. Now it lay in rubble, she felt lost. 'My girls . . . ' she started. But then it came to her in a flash of joy: she would regain more than just her children. George and Henrietta would be at her command once more. Now peace was secure, there would be no need for Henrietta to whore herself.

When the sides of George's sedan opened back on their hinges, Lord Chesterfield and Mr Gay lifted him aloft and carried him back to the house.

Caroline pushed forward to claim his trembling hands as they set him down on his feet. 'What happened?'

His eyes glowed with tears. 'I hardly know. I knelt to him and I said what you told me to say …' His voice caught. 'The King went pale. He could not speak.'

'He didn't speak at all?'

'He said something about my conduct, and then I came back with all this honour. We are to attend the next drawing room.'

Caroline gasped. 'We can go to court? Our girls will be there?'

George nodded, his lower lip quivering. 'Yes, my love. They will be there for us to see.'

Heedless of the crowd, she kissed him full on the mouth. 'Are we moving back in to the palaces? Can we leave now?'

George draped his arms around her shoulders and eased her head down onto his chest. 'I do not know. Let's see what happens at the drawing room. It is too much to think about now. What are you always telling me?'

'These things take time,' she recited, her lips moving against his silk waistcoat. 'We must be patient.'

He planted a kiss on the top of her head. 'Precisely.'

She nuzzled into him. After spinning so long on the wrong axis, her world stood straight again. Its shattered pieces were slotting back into place.

∼ ∽

Anticipation crackled in the air. Henrietta choked on a thick cloud of perfume. The Maids of Honour tittered and scolded their servants, demanding more rouge, darker eyebrows, more patches. A real drawing room at last, a chance to recapture their old beaux. They had ordered the finest court mantuas, sparing no expense. A rainbow of sumptuous material sparkled all around the room. But for Henrietta, every happy notion receded before one dark phantom: Charles. He would be there, smiling his seductive smile, convincing everyone he was nothing but a respectable, wronged husband.

She touched her hair, stiff with sugar water and pomade. Beneath the flowers were white scars, burnt into her scalp at the masquerade. Charles would punish her for leaving him. She was not sure if he knew about her affair with George yet, but if he did . . . She swallowed. She was a dead woman.

The maid powdered Henrietta's alabaster face. Next, she painted her lips, bringing colour to her lifeless frown. The courtesan peering out from the mirror did not look like plain Henrietta Howard. Another patch, another tweak to the eyebrows and she saw what she had become: *maîtresse-en-titre*. She had worked hard and risen far to become a leading lady of the court, but she did not feel invincible. Beneath it all, she was every bit as frightened as the girl who had cowered in the corner at Beak Street, begging her husband not to hurt her.

Now she was mistress to the Prince of Wales, her wardrobe brimmed with treasures. She wore a duck-egg blue mantua, shot through with gold spangles. Her petticoat was cream, embroidered with flowers and cherubs. A froth of lace sat at the back of her head, while cool pearls hung against her throat. She gripped the handle of her fan and gritted her teeth. It was time to go.

The April night was mild, a welcome relief after the press of heated bodies preparing upstairs. As Henrietta descended the palace steps into the courtyard, Caroline climbed into her sedan chair. She looked every inch a princess, resplendent in soft pink satin. Henrietta followed her with tiny, mincing steps, constricted by her gown.

By the flickering light of a flambeaux, she folded her panniers until they looped at her sides like an insect's wings, and tilted her head back to protect her curls. When she was ready, the sedan men closed the doors and slammed the roof shut. She fought a surge of panic as they hoisted her up and carried her into the night.

Caroline's chair swayed before her, surrounded by a cluster of guards. Their uniforms flared blood red in the torchlight. By the time they reached the gatehouse of St James's, crowds had gathered on both sides of the road. Eager faces pressed against Henrietta's window, desperate for a glimpse of a famous courtier. Unable to give the smile they craved, she let down the leather curtain with a slap.

A crescendo of noise signalled her arrival in Whalebone Court. She sucked in breath as her chair bumped down and the sides fell back, releasing her from captivity. The air failed to refresh her; it was tainted with smoke from the braziers and horse dung. She staggered to her feet, unfolding her panniers and smoothing her mantua over them.

The courtyard teemed with activity. People looked strange with white-painted faces and powder dulling their hair. The night was dark, casting shadows that leapt and shrank. Flames shimmered on jewels as fresh ladies alighted on the cobbles. Everyone aimed for the palace, but it was impossible to move more than one footstep at a time. Boys dashed to and fro with lamps; sedan chairs weaved from all directions. Inch by inch, Henrietta nudged her way toward the portico.

Just before she reached the staircase, Gay emerged from the crowd in a suit of silver and dark blue. She grabbed at his arm, reassured by his masculine scent of pepper and cedar wood. 'For God's sake Mr Gay, stay with me.'

His eyebrows climbed. 'Of course I will.'

He helped her up the steps. Anchored by his steady arm, she could look around. Lord Chesterfield walked up ahead with Molly on one arm and Mary on the other. The girls glided beside him as if on wheels. They moved through the guard room, the presence chamber and the privy chamber, penetrating ever deeper into the beating heart of the court. Finally, the door to the great drawing room opened and Henrietta closed her eyes, trusting Gay to guide her across the threshold. People pressed against her, jostling, squeezing. Behind, she heard a thump and a shriek as someone fell down under the relentless stream of heels. A tall gentleman shouted his apologies over his shoulder.

'It is all right,' Gay laid his hand upon hers. 'I do not see your husband. The King and his court are not here yet.'

Henrietta cracked open her eyelids. He was right. Only Leicester House courtiers crushed together, beneath the grave figures on the tapestries. Their faces whirled. It was hot, so very hot . . . She snapped open her fan and waved it.

In the corner, Caroline chatted to her ladies. She made fluttering gestures with her hands. George stood beside her with a false smile nailed to his face. Poor thing, he was wound tight, ready to snap at any moment. This was not him; the counterfeit charm, the grovelling, the pretence. He would sooner fight a round of fisticuffs with his father and have done with it. Henrietta itched to lay her hand upon his arm and offer some reassurance, but she knew it was impossible.

The Maids of Honour dropped their voices to a silky whisper. A latch clicked, an inner door opened, and the King entered, his head held high. Behind him came Melusine and the three little princesses – much grown since Henrietta had last seen them.

Perfectly rehearsed, the girls lined up before their parents. Caroline gasped and stepped forward, but the King moved his head ever so slightly to the side. Her face flickered as she saw the denial written there. Trembling, she offered a curtsey. The little girls returned it with heartbreaking formality.

Silence stretched. Henrietta stared at the King's lips, willing him to speak. He merely nodded at George and Caroline, then turned away. His favourites clustered round him, elbowing others aside for attention. They swept him, Melusine and the girls to the opposite side of the drawing room.

Henrietta turned to Gay, distraught. He offered her a bewildered shrug. It did not look like a reconciliation at all – simply permission to share the same room.

Molly stood on tip-toes, trying to catch a glimpse of the King. 'Look at that!' she whispered. 'He will not speak to them!'

'Do you see Colonel Campbell?' Mary asked. 'Or Mr Hervey?'

'Yes! Over there, by the door.'

'Then let us go to them. If the royals won't make it up, *we* may as well have some fun this evening.'

Henrietta grabbed Mary's sleeve. 'Be cautious. You know the prince does not like to see you with other men. Do not flirt too openly, or your colonel will take the blame.'

Mary leant forward to press her lips against Henrietta's good ear. The scent of rosemary drifted from her skin. 'Mrs Howard, I am going to marry him,' she whispered. 'You must not tell a soul.'

Henrietta fell back, stunned. Marrying without permission would send George into a frenzy of rage. Did Mary not realise she was playing with fire? 'I would counsel you against such a rash step.'

Mary's painted lips grinned. 'Oh, la. It is the greatest adventure. And Molly is going to marry Mr Hervey, before his horrid mother can stop them.' She fluttered her eyelashes, so pretty and girlish. So full of hope. 'Please swear you will keep our secret?'

What could she possibly say? Too much resistance would only push her further down the wrong path. She gripped Mary's hand. 'I cannot stop you. I believe Campbell is a good man. But be sure, Mary. Think. Do not let me see you tied to a spouse in haste. Do not let me see you throw your freedom away. Especially when it will prevent you coming back to court.'

Mary kissed her. 'We are both certain, my dearest. These men are worth the sacrifice. They are nothing like your beastly husband.'

But Charles had not arrived in her life in the shape of a monster. He had come dressed as a lamb. She opened her mouth to tell Mary, but her slender fingers slipped away and she was gone in a cloud of lemony herbs.

Shaking, Henrietta leant on Gay and took a turn about the room. She was fraught with premonition. She had not seen Charles enter, but after Mary's words she felt him; a contaminating presence, wafting sour threats.

'You have your sword, don't you?' she asked Gay.

He looked to the dress scabbard at his side. 'This? In Heaven's name, Henrietta, what do you fear?'

She shook her head. Lord Chesterfield arrived beside them. 'What a to-do, eh?' He dabbed at the sweat on his face with a hand-kerchief. 'It's frosty as January between the royals.'

'I can feel it,' Gay said. 'Why won't the King talk to the prince and princess?'

'In his mind, he's done no wrong. It is all their fault.'

Poor George. However would she comfort him? As for Caroline, this would destroy her. She had worked so hard . . .

'Well now, look at this.' It was him. Charles. That dread voice froze the marrow in Henrietta's bones. 'Why am I not surprised to find my wife sandwiched between two gentlemen?' He stalked toward them, a *chapeau bras* hat clamped beneath his elbow.

'Mr Howard.' Gay bowed, lips pressed together.

Charles's eyebrow lifted, sinuous as the whipping tale of a snake. 'This is one big reunion of happy families, is it not?'

Henrietta could not move. Every barbed word she had rehearsed fled in terror. Obeying the habit of a lifetime, she performed a curtsey and asked, in a quaking voice, after Charles's health.

He smiled his slow, treacherous smile. 'As you see I am surviving, despite my misfortunes.'

He was running to fat; his belly protruded from beneath his waistcoat, stretching the watered grey silk. 'I am glad to hear it, sir.'

Charles let his gaze slither over Gay and Chesterfield. 'Perhaps the stories I hear of your rise in favour are true. You seem to have your own little guard. But as for the other tales . . . ' He whistled. 'They would make your hair stand on end. It's a good thing you can come back to court and live with me, Hetty. Show all the gossips you are a virtuous wife.'

Horror seized every muscle. *Live with him again?* 'Nothing is finalised yet, Mr Howard,' she said in a rush, 'I do not have permission to leave the princess . . . We do not know what will happen.'

'You should have seen Henry's face when he heard about you and the prince. I never saw a lad turn so pale.'

Henrietta snapped her fan shut, trying to conceal the tremor in her hands. 'Henry will be pleased with me when I explain I am saving for his future. When I tell him about the stocks in the Mississippi venture and – '

Charles clicked his tongue. 'Well, like you say, my dear, nothing has been decided . . . If you cannot live with me yet, you cannot see Henry.'

Her pulse beat thick in her throat. 'Yes I can. My son can come and visit me.'

He shook his head with a mock expression of regret. 'I do not think so. You see, unless you return to the family home, you will have no admittance to *my* son.'

Gay's arm came up under her elbow, ready to support her as she swayed. 'But . . . '

'Do not distress yourself, Hetty. It's not personal. I must think of Henry's welfare, his reputation. He could hardly associate with a runaway mother, could he?'

'He is my flesh and blood. He –'

'Oh hush, hush. Save your breath.' He put a clammy finger to her lips. She recoiled at his touch. 'This is not *my* doing. I am advised in my actions by the King himself. He and I think alike on these matters.'

She stared at him. 'The King?'

'Yes. He takes rather a hard line with disobedient wives.'

Her mind ricocheted back to Herrenhausen and the stories of George's mother. She remembered George, particularly emotional one night, confiding that he had not seen her face since he was nine years old.

Charles grinned, backing off. 'I bid you a good evening.'

It was too hot. She could not breathe. Tapestries, laughing girls and sparkling waistcoats danced before her eyes. Chesterfield's strong arm came around her waist. There were no chairs in the drawing room. They propped her against a wall, rough with fibres of ancient tapestry. Gay snatched the fan from her hand and wafted it before her face, but it only blew back the same reeking air.

'Take her out, you fools.' Caroline's voice came tinny and far away. 'Before people gossip.'

For an instant, the haze cleared and Henrietta met Caroline's eyes. They were empty and soulless.

'I wish you better, Mrs Howard,' she said stiffly. 'It seems neither of us have obtained what we wanted from this night.'

CHAPTER TWENTY

～ St James's Palace ～

Caroline pressed a vinegar-soaked sponge to her mouth, gagging as its acidity filled her lungs. She had not been in the private chambers of this palace for years, but she remembered every twist and turn.

How degrading to be reduced to the condition of visitor in her previous home. Visitor to her own girls – for Georg Ludwig insisted that they would remain under his care. Well, he could not stop her this summer, far away in Hanover. She would sleep under the same roof as poor Anne. Not even the royal guard would tear her away.

They reached the end of the corridor and entered a stifling chamber. Sickly light trickled into the room, illuminating the bed in a yellow-green glow. Anne lay submerged beneath a tangle of sheets, writhing and moaning.

Mrs Clayton hopped from foot to foot in angst. 'Your Royal Highness – the danger – '

'I am in no danger,' Caroline snapped, her words muffled by the sponge. 'I've come through this disease and so has my husband.' She approached the bed. Anne's breath rasped, trying to squeeze its way through her swollen mouth. A burning rash covered her skin and liquid-filled pustules obscured her eyes. Her girl, her beautiful girl . . . She barely recognised her.

'Mama? Is that you?'

'Yes *liebchen*, it's me.' Caroline sat and picked up a damp cloth to swab Anne's forehead.

'I can't see properly,' Anne murmured.

'No. You will not be able to, for a while. It passes. Do not be afraid.'

'You sound like you're far away.'

Caroline moved the sponge aside, freeing her lips, but the putrid stink made her gag and cover them again. 'I am close by,' she said, reassuring Anne with another touch of the cloth. As it passed over the skin a pustule burst, emitting a reeking yellow stream.

'What is it?' Anne tossed her head on the pillow. 'Is it smallpox?'

'Don't try to talk. It hurts the scabs on your lips.'

'Will I die?'

Caroline squeezed the sponge in her hand so hard that vinegar dribbled out. 'No,' she said firmly. 'I will not let you die. I am the Princess of Wales and I will not allow it. Do you hear?'

Anne's lips moved but only released a string of unintelligible gibber. The fever was taking hold again. Caroline motioned for Mrs Clayton to take over the swabbing and strode to the doctor.

'What have you given her?' she demanded.

The doctor bowed his head. 'All that I can. We must wait for the crisis to pass. She has been bled, and taken an emetic to make her vomit – '

'To what avail? This is not an illness that requires a lowering treatment, doctor. You do not throw it up or bleed it out. The pus must carry the infection away, do you not see?'

The corner of his mouth twitched. Men always smirked when she offered them scientific opinions. Frustration bubbled hot inside her head. Didn't he know she dined with the best minds of the age, Sir Isaac Newton amongst them? 'With all due respect, madam – '

'Dear God!' Caroline glanced back to the bed, where Anne thrashed and threw the sheets from her body. 'Is she wearing a flannel shirt?'

'To make her sweat, madam. The sooner we can bring about a pitch of the fever – '

Caroline dropped her sponge and gesticulated to Mrs Clayton. 'Get it off her! Get it off her! And get that damned fool out of the room!' Together, Caroline and Mrs Clayton turned Anne over and yanked the sweat-soaked flannel from her body. Every gland was swollen, every inch of skin swamped by the red stain.

'Mama?'

'I'm still here, dearest.'

Lady Wortley Montagu bent close to Caroline's ear. 'I have seen something curious for this in my travels. They say if you lance the pus and put it in a nutshell, you can use it to prevent others getting the illness.'

'My other children, you mean?'

Lady Wortley Montagu nodded. 'What they do is dip a needle in the pus and then prick the healthy child in their thighs and arms until they bleed.' Caroline screwed up her face in horror. 'Each jab turns into a boil and breaks. The child is a little unwell but they never catch the pox.'

'And you have proof of this?'

'My son underwent the procedure. It could be tried here.'

The creamy, sickly scent of pus was overpowering. Caroline fished on the floor for her sponge. 'Yes. But I will not test anything on my children. It must be proven first.'

'Mama.' Anne's thick voice rose again. 'If I do not die – '

'You *won't* die.'

' – will I be terribly ugly?'

Her chest constricted. Anne would never be ugly to her, but the ravages of this disease were well known. 'Are you grown so vain, since you left me?' She tried to sound cheerful. 'I've had smallpox, and so has your father. Are we ugly?'

Anne grimaced and shifted on the stained bed. 'If I'm ugly, a foreign prince will never want to marry me.'

'Of course they will. You are a Princess of England and you have a dowry fatter than Madame Kielmansegg.' The ghost of a smile appeared on Anne's bloated face. 'Enough of this nonsense. Your grandfather has turned you into a milksop. You will fight the small-pox, Anne, and you'll live to be a queen. Come on, say it.'

'I'll live to be a queen,' Anne gasped.

Caroline nodded her approval before pacing away from the sickbed. Surely the Almighty would not snatch another child from her arms? She had seen many perish from this ravenous disease: her father, her step-father and his mistress. But Anne was stronger than them. She would pull through. She had to.

A muffled knock at the door disturbed her thoughts. The servant opened it a crack.

'Sir Robert Walpole for you, Your Royal Highness. Will you come down to him?'

'Walpole!' she exclaimed. 'What in God's name . . . Does he not know this is a place of sickness?'

'Said he'd take his chances, madam.'

Tempting as it was to send Walpole a snub, she knew he wouldn't come this far for nothing. The last she had heard, he was down in Norfolk, hiding from George's wrath. She straightened her skirts. 'I'll come. Mrs Clayton, you will fetch me immediately if there is any change to the princess's condition. Do you understand?'

'Of course, madam.'

Caroline tramped down the stairs, torn between annoyance and curiosity. Walpole met her with his self-satisfied smile and corpulent bow. There was an excited gleam in his eye, a deeper flush to his apple-red cheeks.

'Be quick. My daughter is gravely ill.'

'I am sorry to hear that, Your Highness. But what I have to say is more important.'

Caroline raised her eyebrows.

'It *is*,' he insisted. 'London is falling apart, although you have probably not heard, cocooned in here.'

Uneasiness crept over her like a chill. 'Then sit and tell me.'

He bounced down on the sofa. 'You remember a while ago I told you to invest some capital in the South Sea Company?'

'Yes.'

'You may write it off – that money is lost.'

She snorted. 'Thank Heaven it was only a small sum. That is more bad advice I have received from you.'

'Oh no, no.' Walpole shook a chubby finger. 'Stay with me, dear madam. I've had an unaccountable stroke of luck. If I can hold this out . . . ' He took a breath. 'My future is made, and your prestige heightened by your association with me.'

She viewed him sceptically. 'Pray, tell me how.'

'The Bank of England was always a Whig institution, the South Sea more Tory. I played on both sides. I dabbled a little in the South Sea but I called for their stock to be fixed.'

'What do you mean, fixed?'

'The Bank of England has a fixed ratio for its annuities. The South Sea Company was free to vary the annuity – create a surplus.'

Caroline bit her lip. She didn't pretend to be an expert on finance. 'So the South Sea Company was all built on confidence? Its stock free to rise above its market value.'

'Precisely. And Lord, how it rose! I sold my stocks long ago and made a tidy sum. I am not on the South Sea books now. I look like a Bank of England man, through and through.'

'And this is important why?'

'Because the South Sea Company has failed!' He clapped his hands together, making her jump. 'If you didn't have your shutters down and straw muffling the noise from the street, you would hear hysteria. The stock is dropping like a rock. I have been in crisis meetings with the Bank of England trying to save it, but I tell you it won't work.'

'So many will be bankrupt?'

His eyes sparkled. 'Hundreds. There will be riots. One of the directors has already taken poison. Another has been shot at in the street.'

Caroline put a hand to her throat. 'God Almighty. The King is in Hanover.'

'Yes. This will reflect very badly on the King indeed. Both he and his mistress have large holdings in the South Sea. He'll have to return to England. Otherwise, the Pretender will make a move for the crown, while the country's in turmoil.'

'What shall we do?'

Walpole grinned. 'Nothing. I'm going back to Norfolk and you will stay here to nurse your child.'

'You're going back to Norfolk?' she repeated, incredulous.

'Yes. I'll wait for them to summon me – and they will. Townshend and I will swoop in and look like we have saved the country. The King and his mistress will be unspeakably grateful.'

'Giving you power.'

He nodded.

Caroline did not trust him. He was an able man, but all he had given her was a humiliating truce with the King and limited access to her girls. Meanwhile, he and Townshend had wormed their way back into the King's government. Whose side were they really on? 'Tell me, Sir Robert, will you now have enough power to negotiate the return of my children?'

He flashed her an enigmatic smile. 'We shall see. We shall see.'

Leicester House

Without warning, George burst into Henrietta's apartments, his coattails swinging to the beat of his stride. She jumped, dropping her book.

'George?'

Tension gripped his jaw. The whites of his eyes flared like a spooked horse. Instinctively, she glanced at the clock on the mantle. Quarter past two. Something must be seriously wrong to break his precious routine.

He seized her hands in a painful grasp. 'I don't know what to do, Hetty.'

'What is it?' Her thoughts flew to Mary and Molly. They must have eloped already.

He gave a strangled laugh. '*What is it?* Have you not heard the clamour outside?'

He led her out of her apartment into the corridor. A frantic lady dashed past wringing her hands. Another stood at the head of the stairs, weeping onto a gentleman's shoulder. Henrietta peered over the balustrade and saw men gesturing furiously to one another. One in a green coat was slumped with his head against the wall.

'Damned Walpole again. God strike me if I don't string him up the moment I am king.'

She clutched his arm. The wild faces of the other courtiers frightened her. 'I don't understand . . . what has Walpole done?'

'The man is a snake. He was trying to make me exchange my daughters for more stock in this blasted South Sea Company. I bet he knew where it was heading!'

The world seemed to slow around her. She shivered inside, her hopes fragile as glass. 'There is a problem with the South Sea Company?'

'You really did not know? Did you hold stock?'

Did was a telling word. She swallowed through a raw throat. 'Yes.'

'My dear, it is all lost. Every penny.'

She went giddy. Blinking back her tears, she gripped onto George's lapels and tried to stay upright. *Henry*. She would not carry him away now. She had failed him. The pain of that was more intense than giving birth; like something had ruptured within.

With a supreme effort, she shook herself and tried to focus on George. 'There must be mayhem,' she croaked. 'Nearly everyone I know held stock in that company.'

He tightened his hold on her shoulder. His fingers were hot through the muslin of her gown. 'Yes. And the King is away. I must take control of this.' He leant in to whisper in her good ear. 'I can face down scores of soldiers on horseback. Give me a cannon and I will fire it. But I have to admit, Hetty, this frightens me. People are taking their own lives.'

Just then, somebody screamed. Henrietta shuddered. 'What will you do?'

'I have received plenty of advice. Bribe the army to protect me or hire foreign troops to take charge of the city.' He gave a rueful grin. 'One particularly sanguine chap thought we should all resign and return to Hanover. I have entreated my father to come back. I never thought I would do *that*.' He released her and ran a hand across his brow. 'In the meantime I must start an investigation and see justice served. God knows, I could use some support. Will you come downstairs with me?' He offered his arm.

Henrietta hesitated. What would Caroline say? 'The princess . . .'

A muscle quivered in his jaw. 'My daughter Anne is sick. The princess refuses to leave her.'

She laid her hand on his forearm. He needed her. *Her.* She could not be there for Henry, but she could help George. He was all she had left now. 'Then I must fill her place. Today I will be the princess's deputy.'

1721

CHAPTER TWENTY-ONE

✧ *St James's Palace* ✧

It would be hard to imagine a more dismal new year. Chaos in the streets, despairing businesses and calls for the royal family to resign. Every day brought fresh news of a suicide or a stress-induced death. Even poor Stanhope had fallen prey to a fit, leaving a crater in the ministry. The King had decided to fill it with the hefty lump of Walpole.

Henrietta surveyed the collection of depressed courtiers moping around the drawing room. No new gowns and hardly any diamonds. They had thought themselves floating on a bubble that could never burst – but it had, leaving behind a sticky, black residue.

The weather did what it could to add to the gloom. Mist rose from the river, obscuring the park, and joined with smoke lowering down from the chimneys. The only good news was that Princess Anne had recovered from her grave illness. Nonetheless, smallpox had ravaged her face, leaving deep pits.

Henrietta sighed and adjusted her necklace. The South Sea and

Mississippi had taught her to dream, but now it was time to wake up. She would not have enough money to set up home with Henry now. He would be of age by the time she could rebuild her savings. Who knew what poison Charles would have poured into his ear by then?

She tried not to dwell on her misfortunes. She knew that, compared to others, her financial losses were not material. She'd heard of aristocratic dynasties ruined, men stripped of fifty-thousand pounds. But it felt like the South Sea had taken away her hope, along with her money. It had torn Henry from her arms all over again.

She walked over to where Dr Arbuthnot stood with his friends, Bolingbroke and Pulteney. Lord Bolingbroke was a jowly man with full lips, recently returned to grace from the Pretender's court. Between him and Walpole there simmered immense distrust. Pulteney had hawkish eyes and dark, menacing brows that belied his good humour. This trio of men were Henrietta's main companions at present. Pope had removed to a country villa in Twickenham for his health, though he visited occasionally. Mary and Molly were married. Barely a comment had passed on their disappearance from court. That was the only consolation of the South Sea; its uproar had reduced two elopements from scandal to mere tittle-tattle.

'Gentlemen.' She curtsied, receiving their bows in return. 'This is the King's first drawing room since the disaster. How do you expect him to look?'

The public were baying for blood. Investigations carried on apace, but the man in charge of the South Sea subscription book had whisked himself off to the Continent and couldn't be traced.

Pulteney grimaced. 'He'll brazen it out. From what I understand, Walpole and Townshend have solved all his problems.'

'Surely that's not possible?'

'Of course not. But the King believes they have, and that's what matters.' Pulteney's eyes glittered fiercely. 'The Whigs have their feet firmly under the table. It will be Walpole all the way now, you mark my words. The King thinks he can turn stones into gold.'

George would certainly not be happy about that. She pressed a hand to her bosom and felt paper shift beneath her stays. He had written her a love letter – her very first. She wasn't one for drivel, but he expressed himself well: manly and straightforward. He was so thankful for her assistance during the crisis. Sometimes she could almost pretend . . . But no. He loved Caroline. He would always love Caroline more than her. It was Caroline who carried his child once again. It was useless to indulge in fantasy.

Feet stamped in the halls. An inner door opened and the King sailed in. Henrietta drooped into a curtsey but kept her eyes raised; she wanted to see this. Georg Ludwig carried himself admirably, without a trace of strain. Tension had scored Melusine, though; her slender face was pinched.

'My son.' The King nodded curtly to George. Then, turning to Caroline, 'Ah, daughter-in-law. I have a gift for you, all the way from Hanover.'

Caroline started forward. Hope flitted over her face. She clearly expected a letter from Fred. 'For me, Your Majesty? How kind.'

'It is something sure to please you.' The King clicked his fingers. 'Fetch the boy.'

Henrietta's heart skipped a beat. Caroline reached out and grasped the lace at George's cuff. *The boy?* Could it be – had he bought Fred back after so long? The door opened once more as the court held its breath. What happiness this would bring. It had been six, almost seven years . . .

A furious yowl rent the air. Something scampered through the door on all fours, a mass of bushy brown fur – or was it hair? Ladies near the door gasped and jumped back. Yes, it *was* a boy, but hardly recognisable; hideously dirty, dressed in green with red stockings. He roamed around like a dog, spouting gibberish. Green eyes peered out of his grubby face. A rancid, animal smell seeped out of him and reached across the room to scratch Henrietta's throat.

The King laughed and clapped his hands. Seeming to recognise that noise, the boy hurtled toward him. 'What do you think, eh? Found him wandering the forest. Doesn't speak a word of any language. God only knows how he survived. Must have been suckled by a she-wolf.'

For a moment, Caroline's mask slipped. But her muscles flickered quickly, transforming her look of bereavement into one of pity. 'Poor creature,' she said, bending down to inspect the boy. 'He must be confused.' Warily, he sidled over to her. A sparkle on the hem of her gown caught his eye and he reached out, stroking it.

'I know you like curious things and odd people,' the King continued. 'He will be your pet – but not for a while. I'm having too much fun playing with him. You should see him gnaw on twigs!'

The courtiers tittered, succumbing to curiosity, and edged closer.

'His name is Peter,' said the King. 'I named him. It should say it on his collar. Damn it, where's his collar?'

An unwilling servant crept forward to clasp the iron band about Peter's neck. He scurried away as Peter emitted a low growl. Henrietta felt ill. Was it some kind of cruel joke? This monstrous thing, to replace the children the King had stolen?

'Surely it is not necessary to chain him?' Caroline remonstrated. As she spoke, Peter reached up and snatched the glove from her hand. She gave a little cry.

The King laughed. 'You see? He's a nifty fellow. Best keep him shackled for the moment. We'll teach him. It will be our mission.'

Peter inspected the glove, looking to Caroline's hand and back again. Murmuring, he tried to cram the white lace on his own paw but only succeeded in ripping it.

'Who do you expect to care for him?' George barked. 'He's filthy and wild. It's not for the princess to clean up after such a – creature.' He wrinkled his nose as a dark patch appeared on Peter's breeches.

The King cast his eyes around. With horror, Henrietta saw them settle on her little group by the fire. 'Dr Arbuthnot. Come forward, sir.' The doctor shuffled out of the ranks. 'Who better than a physician to take him in charge?' The King offered Dr Arbuthnot the chain. Reluctantly, he took it, and thanked the King for honouring him.

This was a pointed slight on the Tories – on all Henrietta's companions. Instinctively, her eyes flicked to George. Oh yes, he felt the King's snub; it was scratched into his brow, flaming in the rash on his neck.

'What a kind gift, Your Majesty,' Caroline put in her silver tongue. 'We offer you our thanks.'

George made the bow required of him with a rigid back. While he faced the floor, malicious satisfaction gleamed in the King's eye.

∿ ∽

Caroline leant over the crib, her heart in her mouth. Beneath the dimity curtains and embroidered coverlets, her new baby slept sound as an angel. Her fingers itched to reach out and touch him; stroke the downy head, trace the miniscule fingernails one more time. He was here at last: her William.

'A fine boy.' Pride lit George's eyes. He spoke in a whisper, careful not to wake the child.

'I don't think we have ever had a prettier baby.'

'Pretty? *Handsome*, you mean. I'll make a splendid soldier of him.'

Caroline grinned at the ludicrous image of her tiny boy trussed up in a military uniform. 'He must not be exposed to danger. He's too precious.' She looked cautiously at her husband. 'The King hasn't . . . The King has not made any demands?'

He shook his head. 'This one's ours. Ours to keep.'

Relief embraced her. Finally, her arms were full. William would go everywhere with her, be everything to her. All her thwarted affection was finally let loose on one little bundle of wrinkled skin and wispy hair.

'Yes, little lad.' George pulled down the blanket and peeked at William's face. 'An English prince, aren't you? Born on English soil and you will be trained as an English soldier. We'll make you someone worthy to sit on the throne, just you see if we don't.'

A flutter started in Caroline's chest. 'The throne belongs to Fred.'

Their eyes locked over the cradle. 'Aye. Of course.'

Caroline gazed back down at the baby, so full of possibility. Right now he could be anything, do anything, whereas Fred's character would be set. She did not even know what it was. 'Do you know,' she whispered, 'when I think of the future and try to picture Fred as a king . . . I just cannot see it. I can form no image. It's all black. What do you think that means?'

'It means you're being sentimental and foolish. Of course you cannot imagine it. You do not remember what he looks like.'

She glanced at the ladies clustered in the corner, out of earshot. William had caught them in his spell too. Mrs Howard stood on tiptoe, yearning for a glimpse. Caroline sighed, her breath stirring William's fluffy hair. She always felt vaguely guilty when she considered Mrs Howard. She did not mean to treat the woman harshly, but how could she help it? When she saw that pale skin and waif-like figure she imagined her husband lusting after it, petting it. At thirty-eight, a survivor of eight pregnancies, Caroline's curves were slipping to fat. She could bear the thought of George sleeping with other women, but preferring them? Never.

And why was it he still visited Henrietta's apartments? The affair was meant to last a summer. George usually tired of them after that. But this was dragging on, turning into something like true affection. And in his usual crass way, George kept her informed of every conquest, filling her head with horrific images. She only had herself to blame. She threw out her rage but it only bounced back at her. Henrietta did not absorb it. She just stood there with her big doe eyes, the picture of wronged innocence. It was insufferable.

Gently, Caroline extended her index finger and stroked William's pudgy cheek. Since coming to England she had managed to skew every relationship in her life with conflicting emotions. Not this one. William would be different. She would simply love him with all she was worth, whatever he did.

'I fear for Fred.' George's voice came low and rough like gravel, stirring her from her thoughts.

'Why?'

'Messages from Hanover. People in the King's train I pay to watch and report back.' George stared down at his new-born son, as if to preserve the image of him innocent and unspoilt. 'Fred is his grandfather's heir through and through. The King always intended this. To raise a rival for me.'

'No. It can't be true. Fred – '

'– will barely remember us. And I have this note from his tutor.' George reached inside his pocket and fished out a letter. 'Just read that.'

She did not want him to pass the letter over William; it seemed an evil omen. Instead, she came round to George's side of the cradle and took the note from his hand. A line jumped out from the page and smacked her. *The most vicious nature and false heart that ever man had.* A lump rose to her throat. *Nor are his vices the vices of a gentleman, but the mean base tricks of a knavish footman.* Caroline dropped the paper. 'No. No, that's not about my Fred.'

'I'm afraid it is.'

Her legs grew weak. She stumbled into the cradle, waking William and making him bawl.

The ladies moved in. Mrs Clayton put her arm around Caroline's shoulders and guided her to a chair while the nurse scooped up William.

'No – no,' Caroline said disjointedly. 'Do not take him away.' Henrietta waved smelling salts at her nose. Another lady doused her temples with rosewater. The onslaught of scents only served to make her queasy. Everything around her was moving fast, spinning. . .

George shifted uncomfortably. 'I've said too much. I will go and visit Anne, see how she's doing.' He moved away with rapid steps. Caroline wanted to hit him. He could brave an onslaught of enemy soldiers, but faced with a screaming baby and a weeping wife he was helpless.

She put her head between her knees to drive off the giddiness. William's cries cut through to the bone. She winced, feeling her own hurt and fury echoed in his wails. Fred, so very bad! It could not be true. The tutor didn't know what he was talking about.

As her eyes roamed the carpet, she glimpsed a flash of white. Her heart thumped. The note – she had dropped the note. Her son's shame lay open on the floor for all to see. She couldn't bear it. Even if she had to crawl, she would snatch it up. Shoving Henrietta aside, she made a lunge for the paper, caught it and tucked it under a flounce of her sleeve. 'Leave me, leave me,' she murmured, shooing the women away. 'You're making me dizzy. Get some water if you want to be useful, then leave me in peace.' A door closed and William's sobs retreated into the distance. Henrietta came forward with the water and put it to her lips. She drank a shaky sip. 'I'm easily overcome,' Caroline explained, feeling like a fool. 'The birth has left me weak.'

The note in her sleeve teased her, calling her name in seductive tones. She had only read two sentences. There might be others of a softer construction, offering extenuating circumstances. Her ladies were too far away to see now . . . She hesitated. She should burn the letter and never look at it again. But there was some dreadful compulsion, an invisible force drawing her toward it. Unable to contain herself she pulled the paper down, took a breath and then read.

It was George's writing, not the tutor's. And now she inspected the paper closely, she realised it was not one scrap but a whole folded sheet: a letter. She had not dropped this. It belonged to someone else. Vague words jumped out at her, but none of them mentioned Fred. Bewildered, she ran her eyes over the salutation. *My dearest Hetty.* It was a love letter. George was writing Henrietta love letters, now?

'Mrs Howard.' She managed to make the name sound like an insult.

Henrietta stepped forward, confusion etched in her forehead. Caroline beckoned her with one finger. She leant in close, wafting a cloud of lavender perfume. 'How can I be of assistance? Would you like some more water?'

Damn the woman; always so kind, so perfect. Why couldn't she give Caroline one reasonable cause to hate her? This was what George held onto for comfort, these were the wide grey eyes that soothed him when the cares of the world grew too heavy. Once, they had calmed Caroline too. She thrust the letter at Henrietta's chest. The cup of water sloshed and spilt onto her dress. 'Take better care of your secrets in future, Mrs Howard.'

Leicester House

Henrietta lay with her cheek nestled against George's bare chest. The soft, wiry hairs growing there seemed to rub her raw. A single tear ran down her nose onto his skin.

He started. 'What? Crying? What is it with you women?' He

threw his head back against the pillow. 'All you do is cry at me.'

Henrietta swiped her cheek. 'I'm sorry, I did not mean to.'

'What ails you? Are you ill?'

She shook her head, scared of trying his patience. 'I'm being foolish. It's just . . .' Her exhalation caught on a sob. 'The princess has a son. Molly has a son. I . . . I do not have my son.' It took all her self-control not to cry again.

'You do not have Henry because you left him,' he pointed out.

'I was in fear of my life! And when I ran from St James's, I didn't know . . . I did not know I couldn't go back.'

'So you want to return and live with your husband?'

She threw her arm across his stomach and clung on to him. 'No, no. Anything but that. I just miss my son.'

'You could have had a son with me by now,' he said brusquely. 'But you insist on using these blasted herbs and sheep guts.'

Sometimes he was so stupid. 'Can you see the princess tolerating a little by-blow running round her palaces? And what about Charles? You do not know him. If he found out I had another man's child, he'd hunt it down and dash its brains against the wall.'

He choked on something between amusement and shock. 'Is he really that bad?'

'You have no idea.' Henrietta climbed out of bed and stumbled to her writing desk. Groping amongst the papers, she found the letters from Charles and her brother John. She pulled off Charles's Howard seal and tossed it into the fire before sitting down beside George. He propped himself up on the bolster. 'Look at these. When the Earl of Suffolk died, he left Charles Audley End House and his brother Edward the title.'

George frowned, scanning the page. 'On the condition that Charles pays his brother one thousand, two hundred pounds a year from the rents, it says.'

'Yes. Perfectly reasonable. But rather than running a good estate and putting some money aside, Charles has decided to sue my brother.'

'*Your* brother? What has he to do with this?'

'My brother has charge of my dowry. Our uncle tied the money up in the marriage contract to keep it safe from Charles. He had better judgement than I! Charles is suing to get his hands on it and pay off his brother. My entire four thousand, and legal costs! This will ruin poor John.'

George peered down the end of his nose at Charles's letter. 'These insulting terms he addresses you by! Are these usual?'

Henrietta scoffed. 'These? These are polite. Practically affectionate. These are my *billet-doux* from my spouse.' Now she had George's attention, she wanted to spill her past before him. Shame was nothing compared to the acid rising inside her, demanding release. Every venomous thought, every agony of her life; she wanted to press them deep into him like a seal until he felt her pain. 'Didn't you see the scars?' she cried, pulling up her nightgown. 'That one on my thigh. And there, on the sole of my foot, where he pressed it against the grate until all the skin peeled off. What about my four ivory teeth?' Wildly, she flicked her hair back and pointed at her scalp. 'These! Look at these! In St James's Palace, at the masquerade. Do you remember, when you dressed as the centurion and then . . .' Emotion bubbled up and hampered her voice. 'The blood,' she spluttered. 'You wouldn't believe the blood.'

George sat staring at her. Never before had she seen him lost for words. Silently, he wrapped his arms around her and pulled her back against him. 'I did not realise. Caroline intimated, but . . . I didn't realise.'

'I did not tell her everything,' Henrietta mumbled. 'I was too ashamed.'

He stroked the back of her head. 'And no one could help you. The law would have little quarrel with Charles until it was too late.'

She looked up at him, beseeching. 'Do you understand now

why I left my Henry? I had no choice. I didn't want to leave my son any more than your mother wanted to leave you.'

He stiffened beneath her. Henrietta cursed herself. She had said too much. But to her surprise, George's face crumpled. 'It is not fair, keeping a little boy apart from his Mama.'

'No. It isn't. I worry Henry will forget me. He never writes.'

He kissed her forehead. 'A boy never forgets his mother, Henrietta.'

She only hoped that was true.

1722 – 1726

CHAPTER TWENTY-TWO

⌁ *Leicester House* ⌁

Caroline's correspondence lay in piles on her desk, organised into rows. George would approve; it was like battle formation. And what a dreary fight it was; nothing but bad news, dismal letters begging for places and pensions she was unable to give. She peered out of the window, mottled with London grime. The court's summer trip to Richmond could not come soon enough.

Only William's constant mumble kept her spirits up. The nursemaid walked him round the room as Caroline worked. She massaged her eyes and read on. Lord Bristol's eldest son, Carr Hervey, was dead. That left Caroline's old Maid of Honour, Molly, and her husband as the new Lady and Lord Hervey. Caroline shelved that letter somewhere in the middle. A particularly troublesome piece, requiring a reply of condolence and congratulation.

'Bring William here,' she told the nursemaid. He grinned at her, all gums. Caroline cooed and chucked him under his dimpled chin. Such a darling child. She ran her hand down his chest, under his shawl and stopped. 'What's this?' She picked up a yellow ribbon between her index finger and thumb. It ran diagonally from William's shoulder across his torso.

'The yellow sash of Hanover, Your Royal Highness. The prince says he always wears it on the battlefield.'

Caroline laughed. 'Oh, William. Let us hope you have a taste for blood and swords. Your father will never forgive you if you do not.' He was more interested in grasping the pearls in Caroline's hair. 'You're still dosing him with syrup of violets and sweet almond each day?'

The nursemaid nodded.

'Good. He seems to thrive on it.'

Abandoning the pearls, William turned his attention to Caroline's desk. One letter had a flourish of red ribbons. He caught at it, pulling the letter into the air and scattering paper. The nursemaid gasped. 'Oh, you naughty little prince! I'm so sorry, Your Highness.'

Her system was ruined. 'Well,' she said, prising the letter from William's pudgy hand, 'you have broken through my defences and dashed my strategy. I'll be sure to tell Papa.' She ran her eyes over the sheet he had snatched. Dread dropped into her stomach like a ball of lead. 'You may take him back to the nursery now. Send for Mrs Howard on your way up.'

The nursemaid nodded and scurried off. Caroline sat back down and put her head in her hands. God, this was going to be dreadful. There was no good way to break the news contained in that letter.

A soft rap came at the door. Caroline straightened, tidying her hair. 'Enter.'

Mrs Howard slipped in, eyes downcast, and curtsied. A new ruby cross hung at her neck. Another gift from George, no doubt. 'You have been causing me trouble, Mrs Howard.'

Henrietta held her curtsey. 'Indeed, Your Royal Highness? I am grieved to hear it.'

Caroline waved a hand. 'Sit, sit. God knows you'll need to.'

214

All vestige of colour drained from Henrietta's cheeks. She took her chair, respectfully perching on the edge with hands clasped in her lap.

'You do not look well, Mrs Howard.' Caroline snapped her fingers at a page. 'Some wine?'

'Yes – thank you, madam.'

Caroline took a glass from the page and drew a long draught of wine before setting it on her desk. Henrietta accepted hers, but only ventured a sip.

'I am afraid what I have to say is not pleasant. If I could put off telling you, I would. But these things are best over with quickly.'

Henrietta's shoulders trembled.

'I received this from your husband.' Caroline tossed a letter onto her desk. 'He demands you retire from my employment. Apparently the King himself has ordered it. He is set on getting you back to St James's.'

Henrietta viewed the letter like a serpent in the grass. 'You won't – you are not going to send me away, are you? If the King demands it?'

'Only if the King orders me directly. I do not answer to such men as your husband. You belong to my household and that's that.'

'Thank you. God bless you, madam.'

Caroline bent her head over the paperwork. Pity and envy wrestled within her. How did the woman manage it? So cursedly sweet and proper. It was enough to set your teeth on edge. Henrietta was the one in the wrong. She bedded a married man, yet it was Caroline who felt like the brute.

'I have a trickier letter, however, which I must reply to.' She produced the paper William had grabbed. 'From the Archbishop of Canterbury.'

'What has *he* to do with me?'

Caroline tapped the paper. It was easier to stare at the swirls and flourishes than Henrietta's stricken face. 'He warns me that your presence is a danger to my honour. He thinks your damnable husband will go through the courts to get you back and bring a writ to my house.'

'A writ?'

'To seize you, Howard.' Henrietta flinched and slopped wine down her dress. 'Yes, I know – highly distressing. The Archbishop urges me to get rid of you before such a scene can take place.' She met Henrietta's gaze. Memories of her own mother floated to the surface: her blank, hopeless face; the bruises that burned purple in the centre and faded to a jaundiced yellow.

'I will write to the Archbishop,' she said softly. 'I will assure him that, should you ever *wish* to return to your husband, I will willingly release you. But I do not see that happening anytime soon.'

Henrietta shook her head, blonde ringlets shivering beside her ears. 'I do not understand. What is Charles thinking? He said he never wanted to see me again!'

Caroline picked up her wine and swirled the red liquid around her glass. 'Could it be a ploy to get money from my husband? He knows you have become somewhat – precious – of late.' It sickened her to see Henrietta blush like a maiden. Suddenly she did not feel so charitable. 'You must hope it is that, Howard. For if your husband wins money at a cockfight and takes his grievances to court . . . Do you remember what the law courts said when I tried to claim my children back?'

'Yes,' Henrietta mumbled. 'That the King had an absolute right to them.'

'Mr Howard also has a right to your person, however ill deserved. It is his property.' She sighed. 'I will do what I can to keep you in my service. And I am sure the prince will also offer you his – *protection*. But you must be aware of your situation. Our power only goes so far. Your husband's right is greater than ours. If he gets a writ and takes you . . .' Caroline put her wine on the desk, staring deep into the cup at the crimson reflection of her face.

'You can do nothing,' Henrietta said.

~ ~

Madam

You seem to labour under the misapprehension that I have not received your letters. Let me correct you: every note of yours has reached my hand. No filial command tied my pen – I did not respond, because I chose not to. However, the base insinuations cast at my father's door compel me, against my resolution, to break my silence.

You must comprehend how impossible it is for me to address a person who I am conscious commands the duty and respect of a mother, yet has forsaken the family home and lends her name to a species of gossip it would demean me to repeat.

You speak of my father's ungentle hands. I own, it once distressed me to see him chastise you, but I believe there was a necessity for it. Your behaviour, once out of his supervision, seems to prove this.

Given these circumstances, madam, I beg you to desist in a correspondence that can only be painful to you and your dutiful son,

Henry Howard

Henrietta's head throbbed. A migraine crept over her like a dark mist, fluttering behind her eyes and pinching at her temples. She could not let the paper go – it might be the last thing she ever received from her son.

'I'm sorry, Henrietta. Truly, I am.' George plucked at the gold braiding on his coat. 'I wish there was something I could do.'

It took all her restraint not to lash out. If she had not given herself to him, perhaps Henry would still respect her. But no; it was not George's fault – not really. The blame lay with Charles. With *her* for marrying Charles in the first place. 'I know you cannot change my son's mind,' she said in a trembling voice. 'But what about the warrant Charles writes of? Surely you have some power to . . .' She trailed off before his hopeless expression.

'I have none, my dear. Whatever has been between us, you belong to him. If he finds you with that writ, he can take you.'

Her heart quailed. 'Well, I hope he kills me! He might as well, for all you seem to care!'

She burst from the room, her black gown flapping around her ankles. It felt like she waded through mud. Every limb was heavy as she repeated the words to herself again and again: *how could I have let this happen?* Her boy, her only comfort in the days of poverty, declared her enemy! Oh, why, why did she ever leave him?

She turned on her heel, not knowing where she went. Who could help her? Not Caroline; she had made that clear. She floundered in the hallways, first going one direction, then turning and trying another. Gay, her most trusted friend, was away from court. The Maids of Honour were too young to be of any use. Who could she talk to? Lord Chesterfield? Her new Tory friends? She withered at the thought of explaining her shameful situation to them.

She remembered the day they had carried her father home after his duel, run through the stomach with a blade. She had watched crimson gore spurting from the wound with a fascinated horror, wondering how it felt to be impaled. Well, now she knew.

Turning again, she came up short against a lady she had never seen before. 'Forgive me,' she muttered and swerved to the side, but before she could take another step a hand fastened on her sleeve and pulled her back. Henrietta glared at the lady. Some ten years her senior, she had small, friendly features, squashed close together. Her stylish blue dress was patterned with gold, and she wore pearls at her throat. 'I said that I am sorry, madam. Pray, let me pass.'

'Truly, I cannot. You look most unwell.'

Her strength began to crumble beneath the gaze of kind eyes. 'I need to – I need – '

'You need to sit down and have a strong, sweet cup of tea, that's what you need.' An arm encircled her shoulders.

'Please, I do not wish the servants to see me.'

'Come in here, then.' The lady directed her to a lumber room. A strange, soupy light engulfed them, highlighting dust motes dancing in the air. Everything was covered in white Holland sheets. The lady pushed Henrietta onto a chaise and took a chair opposite, releasing the citrus scent of the rosemary packed within.

'I – I do not know you, madam.'

'No. I am just visiting court at present. My name is Elizabeth Germain. You may call me Lady Betty.' She extended a hand.

Henrietta still held Henry's crumpled letter. Casting it on her skirts, she managed to return the handshake. Goodness knew what Lady Betty thought of her. 'I am Henrietta Howard.'

'I know.'

She winced. 'My infamy goes before me.'

'I did not mean that. Now, get your breath my dear, then you can tell me what's wrong.'

She yearned to tell someone, but perhaps not this kind stranger. What did Lady Betty really want, after all? 'Forgive me, but as I said, I don't know you. Gossip in a court . . . '

Lady Betty smiled. 'I'm sure your caution does you credit, but you have nothing to fear from me. I only wish to be of assistance. Or at least comfort.'

Henrietta stared at the ball of paper on her lap, recalling its jagged words. 'Really, madam, I do not believe you *can* console me unless you know what it is to lose a child.'

Lady Betty surveyed her black gown and bowed her head. 'I have lost three,' she said softly. 'A husband as well. You are in good company.'

Henrietta's head snapped up. She saw Lady Betty's eyes and felt churlish for her own self-pity. 'Oh, not this.' She tugged at her sleeve. 'He has not died, praise Heaven. And yet . . . Forgive me, I think I could bear it better if he *had* died, still loving me.' Tears came at last; great wracking sobs torn from her chest. She put a hand over her mouth, as if she could push them back in.

Lady Betty handed her a handkerchief. 'You deceive yourself, my dear. You would not be able to support a son's death. Love can be regained, but life . . . ' She shook her head. 'Now tell me all.'

She struggled, desperately trying to repair her defences. But it was no use. She was too weak and the tears stung her head. The barrier of her discretion cracked and gave way. To the stranger with soft eyes, she confided things she had barely let herself think about: her marriage to Charles from the first shocking blow to her near death at the masquerade; her decision to stay at Leicester House; the money she had saved for Henry before the South Sea Bubble; the letters to Caroline. Lady Betty retained her composure. She did not swoon, nor was there exaggerated horror in her looks. Henrietta blessed her for it.

'Now Henry writes to say he hates me,' Henrietta finished. 'I should never have left him. I see that now.'

'We all make rash decisions in fear. Besides, children are easily deceived. What he believes now he may, with reason, recant in later life. How old is he?'

'Sixteen.'

'A headstrong age. Too apt to see things in black and white.'

'But even if he does change his mind, I will not live to see it.' Henrietta's voice caught on a bubble of tears. 'My husband has a warrant from the Lord Chief Justice. It gives him the right to seize me wherever he finds me.'

'Then he must *not* find you. Surely the guards around the palace are sufficient to keep him out?'

'Until next week. Then we move to Richmond.' Henrietta shuddered. In her mind's eye she saw the carriage for the Women of the Bedchamber, far from Caroline's vehicle and its guards. She saw Charles swoop out of the crowd like a bird of prey and cling on to the side. In the commotion, he would yank the door open and pull her tumbling into the dust. The women wouldn't have the strength to help her. Mrs Clayton would probably give her a push.

Lady Betty turned pale, as if she too saw the nightmare. 'I have moved with courts before. It is a very public affair. Crowds lining the streets, endless bustle. Easy to target a single coach. What if you rode separately from the Women of the Bedchamber? Where he does not expect you?'

'Where? Protocol would not allow me to move. And if you think the prince or princess would let me ride in their carriage, you are highly mistaken.'

'I did not mean that,' Lady Betty shook her head, making her lace lappets swing. 'I mean *separately*. Not with the official progress. You could set out hours before.' She tapped her chin with her fingers. 'I have friends here: Lord Argyll and Lord Ilay. Do you know them?'

'Yes – but –' Henrietta paused. How to explain? She didn't want to tell them about her shambolic marriage. 'They are not aware of my circumstances.'

'Leave it to me. I will arrange it with them. We will get you to safety.'

Henrietta stared at her; this pale woman with her motherly air and brisk resolution. Where had she come from? Her unexpected kindness caught her off guard, like a drop of rain on a summer's day. Was it a trick? A spy from Charles? 'Why? Why would you help me?'

Lady Betty patted her hand. 'How could I hear your story and let you suffer? Did you expect me to wash my hands of you?'

Henrietta nodded. That's what Caroline had done, what Henry had done. It was the courtier's code: drop a hot coal before it sends your career up in cinders.

'Poor girl. That's all you have ever known.'

∼ ∽

Dawn had barely grazed the horizon when the carriage arrived. Its lamps floated in the dark like protective sprites, revealing a shadowy driver and a man with a loaded blunderbuss at his side. Henrietta scurried the few steps from door to door, every sense painfully alert. With her hood pulled up over her face, she let Lord Ilay guide her into the carriage. Lady Betty followed with a confident stride.

Even when the brothers Lord Argyll and Lord Ilay sat on the squabs, their swords glinting in the waking gleams of daylight, Henrietta did not feel safe. She hunched, trying to make herself as small as possible. Argyll rapped on the roof with his cane and the carriage jerked into motion. She squeezed her eyes shut, hoping she would not vomit. She couldn't dispel the image of Charles clinging to the bottom of the carriage, waiting to pounce. Suddenly she could hear with frightful clarity. Every noise made her tremble; the clop of hooves, the creak of upholstery and the first birds of the day calling to their mates.

Lady Betty thrust a vial of smelling salts into her face. 'Keep alert. You may need your wits about you.'

'There's nothing to fear,' Ilay countered. 'If I know Howard, he'll still be abed half-soused this time of the morning.'

'We will be at my house in Petersham before you know it,' Argyll said. 'You can stay as long as you like. My wife will take good care of you.'

'You have all been very kind to me.' Her own voice sounded far away.

'And so has the princess.' Lady Betty patted her hands. 'She's excused you from your duties until it's safe to resume them.' An owl screeched. Henrietta jumped and clung to Lady Betty's arm. 'Hush, hush now. Look, the sun is rising.'

Henrietta could not bear to see the honey-coloured sky or the lower orders shuffling out of their homes, ready to begin a long day's work. Any one of them could be Charles in disguise. 'For God's sake close the curtains,' she hissed.

'I faced down a Jacobite uprising,' Argyll reminded her. 'Your husband is no challenge to me. He will not get near you.'

The rest of the journey passed in a blur. All Henrietta could do was keep her eyes open and focus on her breathing. She did not register a single feature of the house at Petersham or the kind ministrations of Lady Argyll. She was vaguely aware that the men had carried her from the carriage to the parlour and onto a day bed. She didn't stir until the doughy scent of warm bread drifted from the kitchen. Henry's cheeks had that same fresh, yeasty fragrance when he was a boy. Not now. He was a young man, probably splashed with cedar wood cologne. Or worse, the alcohol and tobacco stench of his father.

A maid placed a roll and a dish of tea beside her. Steam wafted into the air as the liquid cooled and daylight crept across the parlour, finally engulfing Henrietta in a pool of summer heat. She did not take off her cape – she didn't dare move. She focused on the patterned china, finding a strange comfort in the blue and white swirls. A clock on the mantle chimed. Hours passed. She had no idea what time it was when she finally moved, stiff in her joints, and went to the window. Summer bloomed in all its glory. The last of the blossom lay scattered on the ground in a carpet of white and pink. Cotton clouds adorned a sky of perfect blue. Henrietta pushed her face against the glass. Even the window panes were hot. The scene failed to cheer her. She did not fit into the happy world outside; pale with stress, draped from head to foot in black. She pulled away but the imprint of her face remained on the glass; a misty death mask. She stared at it until it faded into oblivion.

CHAPTER TWENTY-THREE

↶ Petersham ↷

Dusk cloaked the garden. An unearthly calm spread beneath the trees, scented with violet and peony. Leaves whispered above Henrietta and her dogs as they walked in the growing darkness. It was a blessing to be out in the fresh air again. Marquise trotted under the hedges with her nose to the dirt. Fop kept a steady pace behind. Now and then he gazed back over his shoulder to check Henrietta was still there.

She did not feel completely safe outside, but a year of hiding in the shadows was enough. She needed to stop cowering from Charles and start to live. She had taken so much time away from her duties at court that she feared her position would be usurped. Her power was fading. George was looking elsewhere for his pleasure. Since her departure, Caroline had given birth to another daughter, Mary, and showed signs of breeding yet again. There was nothing for it. She would have to muster all her courage and return, whatever the risk. If she lost her place at court, she would be back where she started: poor, dependant on charity. And there was only so long her welcome at Petersham would last.

'Mrs Howard.' A male voice made her shriek. She whirled round and saw a man dressed all in black except for his shirt and stock, which glowed in the dull light. He had a satchel tucked under one arm and held a scroll of paper. Fop growled from the depths of his throat.

'Sir?'

'Do not be alarmed, madam. I hoped to find you alone. I am sent by the prince.'

'Oh.'

He reached into his pocket and gave her a parcel wrapped in linen. 'These are jewels. You will find gilt plate in your apartments when you return to court.'

She took the package in her hands, bewildered. It felt heavy. 'For me? To what do I owe – '

The man interrupted her. 'Please, madam. You must read these.' Opening his satchel, he thrust documents into her hands. She squinted, but could barely make out a word in the twilight. 'Eleven thousand, five hundred pounds in the stocks,' he explained, seeing her difficulty. 'And a shipload of mahogany.'

Henrietta stared at him. 'I'm sorry, I have a little difficulty with my hearing. I thought you said eleven thousand – '

'– and five hundred pounds. That is correct, madam.'

The figure bounced about her mind, too enormous for comprehension. 'Why, that's enough to build a house! And mahogany? Does the prince intend . . .' Her thoughts solidified. He was doing it. Her short-tempered, unromantic prince had not forgotten her; he was opening her cage. She remembered his expression as he spoke of his mother and understood. 'God, if my husband ever finds – '

He cleared his throat. 'You will also see, when you have time to inspect the documents madam, certain clauses.' He recited, '*These are gifts with which Charles Howard shall not have anything to do. They are for Henrietta Howard to use or dispose of as she pleases as if she was sole and unmarried. Any premises to be purchased with these gifts will be for the sole and separate use and benefit of Henrietta Howard alone.'*

'He cannot touch them.' She trembled, overcome. 'You really mean it?' Catching her glee, Marquise jumped up and planted her muddy paws on her skirt.

'I mean it. I shall leave these with you, madam.' He bowed his head. 'I bid you goodnight, Mrs Howard.' With a quiet tread he disappeared back into the shadows and the garden's fragrant embrace.

Henrietta sank to her knees. She clutched the documents to her heart as the dogs tumbled about her. 'We are safe,' she whispered to them. 'The prince has given us security. We will be free.' Fop and Marquise regarded her with melting eyes. As the gloom deepened around them, a breeze cooled the trails of happy tears on her cheeks. 'We will be free,' she repeated, trying to believe it. A woman with property of her own. It was the rarest breed of creature; some said, against nature. But George had done it. He had broken all convention for her. 'We will be free.'

∼ ⌣

Henrietta pushed past Gay and Pope with a tray of macaroons in her hands. She dodged around Dr Arbuthnot and Peter, the wild boy, who was chained to the door handle. The sight of the poor boy and his confused, animal eyes confirmed her resolution. If she did not take this step with the money George had given her, she would be forever like Peter: bound.

Chesterfield and Lady Betty stood before the table; she set down her offering in front of them. 'Come, everyone, gather round and eat. I have some exciting news.' They all regarded her. She felt a little breathless. When she spoke her plan out loud, it would sound recklessly bold. 'My good Lord Ilay has just purchased eleven and a half acres of land on my behalf. It is at Marble Hill in Twickenham – near to you, Mr Pope.'

Her friends exchanged glances.

'Whatever will you do with it?' Chesterfield asked, his large head tilted.

Hope clutched her throat, turning her voice to a whisper. 'Build.'

'A house?'

'Yes.' Passing to the sideboard, she opened a drawer and gathered the plans together. 'Look, here are the designs. Lord Argyll engaged a man to draw them for me.' She spread them across the table, covering the macaroons. Here it was all just paper and pencil lines, but she could imagine her villa rising up from the ground in blazing white stucco. Somewhere to call her own. She had never been mistress of a real household – just a hole in Beak Street. She remembered her mother, shining like a beacon as the elegant hostess of Blickling Hall. Her chest clenched with longing.

'Palladian style,' Gay observed. 'Very modern.'

'Very fine indeed,' said Pope. 'And not far from me, you say?'

Henrietta smiled. 'We will be neighbours. Only two hours by barge from court.'

'I can help you plan the gardens.'

'I hate to say it, but someone has to.' Lord Chesterfield pursed his lips. Reaching under the plan, he picked up a sweetmeat and tossed it to Peter. 'You cannot live there. Not without palace guards posted outside. Your husband will come and seize you instantly.'

Henrietta watched Peter fall on the food and devour it with snorts. 'I know,' she said tightly. 'Not now. But I'm planning for the future. You can all enjoy it while I'm still at court and one day . . . ' She shrugged. 'I am five and thirty. Charles is fourteen years my senior and he lives a lifestyle that would knock up a Titan. He will not survive forever.'

Lady Betty wrinkled her nose. 'You have good reason to hate him, my love, but sitting and waiting for his death . . . That's a bit ghoulish, don't you think?'

'Perhaps, but it's practical. Do you believe, Dr Arbuthnot, that I am likely to outlive Mr Howard?'

Dr Arbuthnot leant both hands on his cane and blew out his breath. 'Who can say? I should hope so, dear madam. But these pains in your head. . . I don't like them at all.'

She recoiled. 'You do not understand. This house has to be built. It does not even matter if I never live there; it's what the house represents.'

Lord Chesterfield tapped the plans. They showed a fine square villa, completely symmetrical, fronted by three columns. The grey slate roof came to a point with a weathercock on top, buttressed by a chimney either side. On one front there was a great fresco decorated with urns, while on the north side a perron staircase formed the focal point, sweeping up from both directions to gain entrance to the first floor. 'I do not mean to discourage you. I am only afraid your husband will claim whatever you construct.'

'Charles cannot touch it. The prince specified in the legal terms that Charles has no right to the money, or what I spend it on.'

Pope viewed her critically. His grave eyes and mouth loomed out from his slender face. 'I do not suppose the princess knows her husband gave you these funds. Best she does not find out.'

Henrietta nodded. Cold fingers of fear ran across her neck. 'No. Best she does not. Especially in her present condition.'

St James's Palace

Caroline seethed as she sat at the card table, turning her mother-of-pearl game counters over in her fingers. Outside, the sun set in ribbons of gold and salmon. It was the last night before she went into confinement – a time for games, celebration and dances – but she felt only anger.

How convenient, that Henrietta should conquer her fears just in time to fill the place left vacant by the retiring princess. How strange, that it coincided with George authorising a huge amount of unspecified expenses. They thought her a fool, but she knew exactly what had happened.

George drummed his knuckles on the green baize, waiting for her to place a card. It was impossible. Rage glowed hot, making the suits and colours swim before her eyes. She saw only one card: the Queen of Hearts. Who ruled George's heart now? Was it still her? Was she still mistress of her own court?

'Are you ever going to play?' he demanded.

She put her cards down and sighed. 'Forgive me, my dear. I am tired. The baby . . . '

He nodded. 'Never mind. I have already won a hundred pounds.'

She tried to smile back, but merely bared her teeth. He would need to win more than one hundred pounds to keep up with his mistress's demands. 'Indeed! How fortunate.'

As the light outside faded, the bobbing flames of the candles picked out gold thread in ladies' mantuas and diamonds laced around slender necks. She glanced over the glistening female court-iers, wondering why George did not simply pick another woman to amuse himself while she was lying-in. What was it that bound him to Henrietta?

'I received a letter from Mrs Howard,' she said, as carelessly as she could, 'advising me she would return to her position. I half expected her tonight. Has no one seen her?'

He waved one hand as he picked up some cards with the other. 'Oh, she arrived a few hours ago. Her head troubles her. She remains below stairs.'

At least she had the decency to stay out of Caroline's sight.

Sweat ran down her back. Perhaps it was the baby – perhaps

she was not being reasonable. But she could not see why Henrietta troubled to return to court at all. If George had given her money, surely she could pay that damned Howard off? Or at least find other friends to protect her? There was no need to come back here like a loathsome scavenger and take Caroline's husband while she was locked in child-bed, unable to stop it.

She massaged her tired eyes. She would bide her time for now, but she knew what she must do. There *was* only one thing to do with a leech that would not let go: you had to burn it off.

CHAPTER TWENTY-FOUR

⌒ *Leicester House* ⌒

'Mama, I'm uncomfortable. I want to sit down.'

Caroline bit back a retort. Anne did not know the meaning of *uncomfortable*.

Ever since the birth of her latest daughter, Louisa, there had been a pit of fire in her belly. It tugged hard when she moved, stealing her breath. When she probed her stomach she found a small lump, painful to the touch. Even the pressure of stays was unbearable.

'I know you are uncomfortable.' She shifted herself in the bed. 'I *intend* you to be uncomfortable. Emily told me you kept your lady-in-waiting reading until the poor thing fell asleep on her feet. You'll have a taste of your own medicine.'

Anne flipped the pages of the book in a huff. 'Emily is a tittle-tattle.'

'She is. But you must serve your penance.' In truth it soothed Caroline to hear her daughter's voice. Visits from the girls were always too short – in no time their grandfather would be calling them back again, stealing their sweet looks and youthful giggles.

She had missed so much of Anne's life. Now the girl was reaching a marriageable age – she would be sent abroad, out of reach. Caroline was jealous for every moment, every word she had left.

She must have slipped in to a doze, for when George came into the room she started awake, sending a bullet of pain through her belly. She grimaced but did not say anything. She hadn't told George about the problem. He was impatient with illness, and the injury would probably go away of its own accord.

'Papa! Thank God,' cried Anne. 'Can I sit down now? Please?'

Caroline's brain turned, trying to remember what had happened before she fell asleep. 'Erm – yes. Sit over there.' Anne made an exaggerated show of falling back in the chair and resting her legs. Caroline looked to George. His face was furrowed in thought. 'Have you been to the nursery?' she asked.

'Hmmm? No. It is but a daughter.'

'A daughter I laboured long and hard to give to you. And she's pretty. Even little William leant down and kissed her.'

'It's about William I've come.' George plonked himself on the end of her bed, bouncing the mattress and sending ripples of agony through her. 'His nurse said you were going to stick him with a pin! What is she rattling on about?'

'Do you remember the smallpox vaccination I told you of? The one Lady Wortley Montagu suggested?'

He returned a blank look. 'Vaguely. Some scientific nonsense.'

'Life-saving nonsense. All our tests worked. The doctor's going to administer it to Emily and Carrie this week. William will be next.'

He gripped her fingers. 'Lord, do you remember when you had smallpox? I was sure you would die.'

'Alas for you, I did not,' she teased. 'And now none of our children will either. I have even sent someone to Herrenhausen to inoculate Fred.'

He dropped her hand, leaving it to fall heavy at her side.

'You needn't have bothered with that.'

Caroline bit back a sharp response. Fred was a wound that could never be stitched. She liked to talk of him and think of him – anything to keep him present and amongst them. But for reasons she could not comprehend, George had cut him off like a limb with gangrene. 'Fred is still our son.'

'Is he? In name, perhaps. We have not seen him in – how long?'

'Ten years.'

'Ten years! His character will be formed, and all under the King's direction. It would be a blessing for smallpox to carry him off and leave William as the heir.'

'George!' She jerked up, gasping at the agony that exploded in her stomach. 'Can you . . . Can you really wish that on your son?'

'You have to admit it would be better. The English take to William, a prince born on their soil. What will they make of Fred?'

The politician and the queen inside Caroline conceded, but the mother could not. She held out hope, however obscure, that Fred would return to them untainted, full of love and merit. 'Fred . . . Well, I suppose they will treat Fred as they treated us. We were not born here, were we?'

'It seems to me Fred is perfect to rule Hanover,' George went on. 'He's German through and through, and they love him out there. Would it not make sense to divide the inheritance? Make Fred heir to Hanover and William heir to Britain?'

Caroline looked at Anne, sprawled across the chair opposite. It didn't do to voice these opinions in front of their elder daughters. One never knew what tales they would take back to the King.

'That would be for the King to decide,' she said carefully. 'Or for you to consider, once you are king yourself.' But it was a sensible plan. The idea of William on the throne sent a surge of pride through her unlike anything she had ever known. He was every inch her son; quick to learn, precocious in wit and ready to laugh. She thought of

Fred at age three and realised what a chasm lay between the two boys and her feelings for them. 'It does seem unjust though. Fred has been raised to expect the British throne. It would be cruel to take it away.'

'Pah!'

'I'll tell you what *is* cruel,' Anne put in. 'It's cruel that these boys get to rule when I would be much better at everything.'

'Well, if you weren't so snappish and marked with the pox, maybe someone important would take you for a wife,' George barked.

Anne pouted, flicking her golden curls back from her face. 'I want to get married. Why haven't you arranged it yet?

'It is not in our hands, my love,' Caroline explained wearily. Exhaustion permeated her. She wished they would leave her alone to sleep. Always with their petty quarrels and short tempers. Was she the only member of the family with a thread of patience? 'It's for the King to decide.'

George surged to his feet. Blood rushed to his face. 'Oh yes! Everything is for the King to decide!' He strode out the door and slammed it behind him, making the gilt frame shake.

Somewhere far above, in the nursery quarters, Caroline heard the thin thread of Louisa's cry. Tired as she was, she managed to give Anne a wry grin. 'Are you sure you want to get married?'

Twickenham

Henrietta gripped the edge of the barge. Trepidation and excitement meshed within her until she thought she would swoon. She had not ventured out openly like this since Charles secured the warrant to seize her.

Water plashed against the oars as they progressed downstream, pushed up against wherries and scullers. A group of men spotted her and hollered the usual lewd appreciation bestowed on a prince's mistress. She ducked behind Lady Betty's straw hat, her pulse hammering. When they called her name, she expected Charles to emerge from the stinking water like a sea serpent and drag her under.

'Take courage,' said Lady Betty. Her words were muffled by the scented handkerchief over her nose.

Henrietta did not use anything to save her own nostrils. The sour, pungent scent of the river was the only thing holding off her giddiness, kicking her senses like a bottle of smelling salts.

She could not see clearly at first – it was too busy, too crowded and her emotions blinkered her eyes. But gradually, the traffic thinned. Her breath levelled. A pale spot in the distance came closer, and materialised into a villa: white, tall and symmetrical, fronted by a colonnade. Grass spotted with daisies sloped down to the river, where Pope waited by the steps.

The barge jerked as they docked. Water licked up the sides of the bank, making it muddy and slippery. Pope offered his slender arm to help Henrietta climb out of the boat. She did not know if she could stand. She wobbled, uncertain on her legs, clinging to him for dear life. When she gained the shore, her shoes sank with a soft squelching sound.

'Come, Mrs Howard. This will be your home one day. I will keep you safe here.'

Gingerly, she opened her eyes and tilted her face to the sky. Clouds shifted. The sun burst out in jagged patches, illuminating spots of turf.

So this was Twickenham: the scene of her future happiness. She could almost feel the heartbeat of her own land close by, pure and untainted. Such a perfect spot; full of green shade, sparkling water and the most elegant villas.

Pope smiled. 'Do you like what you see?'

'Very much.'

'Good. Now, come inside. I have a particular friend I would

like you to meet.' With Henrietta on one arm and Lady Betty on the other, Pope picked his way up the slick incline, toward his shining villa.

It was not a palace. It had none of the grandeur of Hampton Court or the antique stateliness of St James's, but Henrietta liked it better for that. There was more real taste and comfort than she had seen in a house before. Once through the doors, they climbed a stone staircase to the piano noble, a floor of grand receiving rooms. They passed through a pair of double-doors, inlaid with gilt, to a sumptuous chamber. A grey marble fireplace formed the centrepiece, clicking as it burned apple wood. The walls were a pale sage green and displayed framed scenes from the *Iliad*. The company were already assembled at small tables beneath chandeliers.

Henrietta instantly recognised the ungainly Lord Chesterfield and Mr Pulteney, with his severe brows. But there was another man there beside them. He had an impish face and gently curving lips. He was a stranger, yet somehow he felt familiar . . .

He turned his head and caught her watching him. Blushing, she slid her glance to the corner. The sight there was safer: a shrunken old lady, sat smothered in shawls. She must be Pope's mother.

'I have an introduction to make,' Pope said.

'Oh no, my dear.' Lady Betty pushed in front, a glove raised to silence him. 'The pleasure of this introduction is mine. Mrs Howard, may I present one of my brothers, The Honourable Mr George Berkeley?'

So that was why she recognised him. He made her a stiff bow, relying on one leg, and she detected a resemblance to Lady Betty lurking in his slender features.

'What a pleasure to meet you, Mr Berkeley. I'm delighted to meet any relation of Lady Betty's. Why have we not been introduced before?'

He emerged from his bow, dark eyes glistening. 'I am one of those embarrassing relatives a family tries to hide, Mrs Howard. I used to be a Whig and your friends will not forgive me.'

He really was rather handsome. His wig was sensibly powdered and shorter than the court styles, sitting naturally on his head like real hair. Coupled with his light brown suit and slender figure, it gave him a pleasing appearance. Something in his smile made her flustered and ashamed of herself at the same time.

'Well,' said Pulteney, 'Mr Berkeley's past politics do not matter. We have talked you round to the winning side at last, haven't we?'

'Victorious or not, it is my side now. I am not a man to change my loyalties lightly. I have made up my mind, and here I plant my feet.'

Could he really be a politician with this constancy, this sense of honour? Henrietta doubted there was a single man in the House of Commons or Lords who would speak thus and mean it. Yet Berkeley seemed to be in earnest.

'But look,' said Pope. 'Our refreshments are here.'

They all sat down as servants presented dishes of steaming coffee. With a blend of pleasure and dread, Henrietta found her place was next to her new acquaintance, Mr Berkeley. He smiled and pulled out her chair. She sat, a nervous grin pinned to her face, and let him push her in. She could not think of what to say to him. Every word flew clean out of her head. Oh why, why did they sit her there? It was beyond her power. She had been out of society for too long to strike up conversation with a stranger.

Mr Berkeley took his own seat and looked at her expectantly. She shrank from his gaze. He was Lady Betty's brother – she desperately wanted to befriend him. Yet her mouth was dry, useless, like a shrivelled leaf. She leant over her saucer and inhaled the sweet cinnamon and nutty scents of her coffee. Anything not to look directly at him.

'Just a word of warning.' Berkeley's whisper made her jump. 'The coffee here is little better than brown water. Put on your best face and swallow it down. Yesterday I had to tip some of mine in the fire and feed the rest to the dog.'

Before she could reply, Pulteney sidled over, bringing a cloud of musk with him. Henrietta coughed and took a sip of coffee to ease her throat. Berkeley was right – it was foul – and she felt him looking at her, trying not to laugh.

'Forgive me, Mrs Howard, but I cannot wait for coffee to finish before I speak to you.' Pulteney's intense eyes bored into hers. 'What have you heard since your return to court? Are we Tories in favour with the prince?'

She swallowed her coffee, barely concealing a wince. 'Really my lord, how should I know?' Talking politics made her feel like she was being smothered. There was nowhere in politics she could tread safely, for fear of upsetting either George or Caroline; all she could do was tiptoe over the ice and hope it didn't crack.

'Well – obviously – you hear the prince in *unguarded* moments.'

The hideous coffee rose in her throat. Why did he have to say such things in front of Lady Betty's brother? A man she had just met! What must he think, when Pulteney addressed her in this way?

She lowered her eyes to the coffee and saw her painted face reflected in the dark liquid. For the first time, she was truly ashamed of her position. Lady Betty's brother would not be surprised by Pulteney's words, she realised. He must know – everybody knew what she was.

'I have been absent from court for some time,' she said quietly. 'From what I gather, the prince means to name Sir Spencer Compton as his First Minister when he comes to his throne.'

Pulteney whooped. She took another sip of coffee, not even noticing the bitter taste this time. From the tail of her eye, she saw Berkeley regarding her with interest.

'Thank you, Mrs Howard. It gives me such comfort to think we could be in power with the next reign. To know that the prince sees our merit.'

She sighed. 'But who knows what the prince will think from

one day to the next? The princess is still very thick with Walpole and Lord Hervey.'

Berkeley leant forward on the table. Still she could not look at him. 'Do you really think the princess will have a say in politics?' he asked softly. 'She is a clever woman, an admirable woman, but from what I have heard, the prince will not let her govern.'

Let her govern! She would like to see anyone stop Caroline, once her mind was made up. 'Oh, you do not understand, Mr Berkeley. The princess is the sharpest woman I know. She manages the prince in *such* a way. She agrees with his opinions, then nudges him toward her own by inches and degrees. He doesn't realise it is happening. I have no doubt the Tories will come in when the new reign begins, for the prince hates all ministers associated with his father – but they may not retain power for long. Any slip, and the princess will take advantage of it.'

'But why cannot *you* persuade the prince?' asked Pulteney. 'You have watched the princess for years. Why can't you use her methods to push for the Tories?'

A warning bell clanged in her head. This was beneath her – humiliating. She tried to shut him down with a tight voice. 'The prince rarely speaks to me of politics.'

'You could try. What have you to lose?'

Everything. It amazed her that they did not understand.

Of course she could persuade – she had done it thousands of times before under the assumed name of Mrs Smith. She had convinced Charles's creditors to give him lower repayments, more time. But she did not want to go back to those tricks.

'My mistress was raised to manipulate powerful men. It is in her blood. Whereas I … '

'You must get what you can,' Pulteney cut in. His brows, usually so stern, had softened. 'You know the way of this world, Mrs Howard. Nothing is safe. The Whigs are not the only ones who may find themselves out of favour when the prince becomes king.'

Fear slammed into her. She grappled with it, a quiver of arguments ready. George would never abandon her. He might be changeable, but he was not heartless. He would not cast her out with nothing. Except . . . She frowned. He had already given her so much. Material to build a house, that she could keep safe from Charles. Independence. Slowly, her brain absorbed the chilling possibility. All this wealth, this land – perhaps it was not an incentive to return to court, a little secret between them. Perhaps it was a grant to pay her off. One his wife knew about only too well.

Pulteney saw the change in her face. He leant down over her, enveloping her in the scent of musk and clean linen. 'Time may be short, Mrs Howard. Let us make the most of what we have left.'

She stared into the coffee, trying to gather herself. So many eyes were trained upon her that she could almost feel them, burrowing into her skin. 'What would you have me do?'

Richmond

Dandelion seeds wafted on the breeze as Henrietta and George walked, arm-in-arm, beside the river. Gnats gathered above the water in a cloud. The swans were building a nest of reeds ready for their cygnets. They shook their tails in the water, spraying out crystal drops.

This was nature: to prepare a shelter for the times ahead. To pluck whatever resources were at hand and bend them, with a determined beak, to your purpose. The swans did not blush from what they must do. Neither would she.

'So, you are building a house?'

She jumped, her attention snatched back to George. 'Yes. With your generous gift. I cannot thank you enough.' She squeezed his arm. 'I have never had a place of my very own. I cannot tell you what it means to me.'

He took her hand from his arm and kissed it. 'A small price to pay, for you. I only wish I could see that dog Howard's face when he realises he can't touch a thing I have given you!'

The breeze rattled in the trees and set Henrietta shivering with them. She did not want to imagine Charles's rage, or who would bear the brunt of it.

'Where is your house?' George asked.

'At Twickenham. I went to inspect the foundations only last week.'

She hesitated over her next words. She knew, deep in her heart, that Pulteney was right; she had to push her advantage while she was in the ascendant. It would not be long before Caroline recovered from her fits of illness and took back full possession of George and his opinions.

And to tell the truth, a bitter part of her wanted to thwart Caroline's political plans. She remembered her face on the dreadful day Charles's letter had arrived; passive, staring into a glass of wine. Unwilling to help. The image hardened her resolution

She screwed her eyes shut and forced out the sentence. 'I happened to meet Mr Pulteney there.'

'Oh?'

'Yes. He told me a tale that I feel obliged to . . . I hate a tittle-tattle, but really this is something that – '

'Tell me.'

She put a hand to her throat. 'It concerns Sir Robert Walpole. Perhaps I should not speak ill of him, for I know the princess – '

He cut over her again. 'I have told the princess what I think of Walpole.'

'Mr Pulteney told me some shocking things that Sir Robert said when he negotiated for you with the King.' A dandelion seed floated between them. Henrietta followed it with her eyes, avoiding George's intense stare. She had started now. She was compelled to go on.

'What did he say?'

'Please don't be angry. Remember, these are not my words.'

'That is duly noted, my dear.'

She licked her lips. 'When Mr Pulteney asked Sir Robert what he had managed to obtain for you, he gave a very impertinent answer. He said that you were to go to court again and have your drums and guards. He said that this was more than you deserved – and that if he had to do the deal again, he would not ask for so much.'

George dug the end of his cane into the dirt. A muscle ticked in his jaw 'You did right to tell me of this. I thank you for your loyalty.'

Guilty delight squeezed her like a new pair of stays. She had done it. In a few words, she had picked apart Caroline's carefully woven tapestry.

It was not just petty revenge – it was the right thing to do. Walpole was too powerful. With a seven year parliament and his corrupt practice of buying up boroughs, he was not truly representing the British people. While she had some influence left at this court, she must work against him. It was in her power to help her country.

They were silent for a while. George slashed the grass with his cane as they walked. Finally, he spoke. 'Very soon, my son William will be made Duke of Cumberland. My father is creating Knights of the Bath at the same time. He has allowed me to put some names forward. Perhaps you will help me consider who I will honour?'

She clutched his arm tighter. Never before had he offered something like this. She had been a convenience, a friend, not an equal partner. But this . . . It was like being a real royal mistress.

Finally, she could realise the dream that had foundered when she married Charles: she could make the Hobarts of Blickling Hall great once more.

'A gentleman to honour as a Knight of the Bath? Well, I am sure that I can think of someone.'

CHAPTER TWENTY-FIVE

⤳ *St James's Palace* ⤶

Henrietta ran about her apartments in a frenzy of excitement, checking that everything was in order. The dogs yipped and got under her feet. She slipped a circle of lace under a vase, arranged the flowers and then straightened a plate on her display of porcelain. After fluffing the cushions on the sofa, she adjusted the lemonade jug and a tray of sweetmeats on the table. She hadn't been this nervous since her arrival at Herrenhausen. It was the first time she had seen her brother John since the early years of her marriage.

The door handle turned. As Henrietta held her breath, her servant Daniel ushered in a young couple with two children. Her eyes filled with proud tears. John had the same chestnut hair as her father. A red sash over his chest and a gleaming star at his throat proudly proclaimed him a Knight Companion. He held his wife's arm in one hand, while the other clutched a white wand of office. If only her parents were there to see this moment!

'Oh, John! It's so good to see you.' She flew to him.

He gave her a smacking kiss on the cheek and pushed her back

245

to see her face. 'Hetty! How can I ever thank you? You are a good sister to me.'

'Do not thank me! It was not all my doing. I'm sure you earned it on your own merit.'

He laughed. 'Flatterer! The King only chose thirty-five men for this honour. He wouldn't have thought of me, without you.'

John's wife cleared her throat. She was a fine-boned woman with dark eyes that glimmered out of a pallid face.

Henrietta offered her hand. 'You must be Judith. How wonderful to finally meet you. What a pretty wife my brother has!'

Judith returned a thin smile, merely brushing Henrietta's fingers with her cold hand. 'You are very kind, madam. John has spoken of you many times.'

Henrietta dipped her head, understanding Judith's reserve very well. What had she expected? To other women, she was a whore. Judith knew exactly what Henrietta had done to get John this privilege.

'Dog! Doggy!' A high voice fractured the tension.

It was a little boy, petting Fop with heavy hands. Her breath caught. He could only be two years old, with his toddling legs and big smiles. His sister was much older, perhaps about seven.

'Oh! These are your little ones.'

John beamed. 'Yes, you get to see them at last. Come on, you two – meet your Aunty Hetty.'

Suddenly bashful, the girl curtsied and twisted her fingers together while John announced her as Dorothy. Dark curls framed the perfect oval of her face.

'Oh, but John,' Henrietta said, 'she's the image of Mama.'

'Yes. And this little chap is Jack.' The boy stared at her as John put a hand on his back and coaxed him into a bow. It was a lovely age – she remembered Henry at this sweet period.

Jack straightened up, pointed at Fop and proudly announced, 'Dog.'

'Yes, I have two dogs. You may play with them all you wish. And do go over to the table. There is lemonade, and some sweetmeats – unless there is something else you prefer? Judith, perhaps I can fetch you some wine or ale?'

'Wine, please. Thank you.'

Dorothy and Jack scrambled over to the table and plunged their fingers into the treats. After filling her mouth and wiping a sticky hand on her skirt, Dorothy took the jug and poured her brother a drink with great care.

Henrietta fetched wine for the adults, unable to believe the sight of a happy family in her apartments. 'They really are beautiful children.' She nodded to Judith, keen to thaw the ice. 'A credit to you, my lady.'

Judith smiled, but it flickered on her face. Henrietta knew what she was thinking: loose morals might be contagious. She didn't want to expose her daughter to the prince's mistress. There was no way Henrietta could explain the chain of events that had led her to this shameful position – especially to a stranger.

'What of your own boy?' John asked in a low voice. 'I wish I could see my nephew.'

Henrietta's throat closed up. 'They tell me he studies at Magdalene College, in Cambridge. He will travel to an academy in Paris next year.'

'Where do you suppose your worthless husband got the money for that?'

She dropped down onto the sofa, suddenly weary. 'He must have won at the gaming table.'

Judith darted a look at her children, as if this reference to vice would taint them. 'Will you not visit your son, while he is at College?' she asked. 'It seems a perfect opportunity to see him without Mr Howard being present.' With a little more kindness, she added, 'From what John tells me, he's a beastly fellow. He's certainly put us to a great deal of inconvenience and expense.'

Henrietta sighed. Judith was the perfect model of a wife, dressed prettily in green velvet with a modest fichu covering her cleavage. Her large cap of spotted lace gave her an eminently respectable, maternal air. Perhaps if Henrietta had married the right man, she would be like that herself. 'I cannot travel to Cambridge – I dare not. Charles has a warrant to seize me. So far he hasn't made any attempts, but if he heard of my journey he would be sure to follow me, or wait at one of the stages on the way back.'

'Oh. I see.' Judith grew a shade paler.

Henrietta held her gaze, willing her to feel her pain. 'Beside which, I don't think Henry wants to see me. He listens to those who speak ill of me. I suppose I am an embarrassment to him.'

Judith tensed. 'It is a very difficult situation.'

'Why would anyone speak ill of you, Aunty Hetty?' Dorothy sat at the table with her dark head tilted to the side. The depth of her brown gaze told Henrietta she had been listening for some time.

'Do not be so impertinent, Dorothy,' Judith cried.

'Oh, no, it's quite all right.' Henrietta adjusted her position on the sofa. What could she say? She didn't know how to address this tiny apparition of her mother, or explain her sordid circumstances without distressing the child. She took a breath. 'Some people do not like me, Dorothy, because I am the prince's friend.'

Dorothy sipped her lemonade as she considered this. 'That doesn't make sense. Being friends is a good thing. Why would it be wrong to be someone's friend?'

'Well, my dear, some people are jealous,' she said carefully. 'They wish the prince liked them as much as he likes me. As for the others . . . they do not approve. They do not think he is the type of person I should be friends with.'

'Mama told me I should not be friends with the butcher's boy. She said he wasn't appropriate.'

Henrietta smiled indulgently. 'So you understand.'

Dorothy pulled off a morsel of sweetmeat and fed it to Marquise. Her brother was already under the table, rolling about with Fop. 'Don't worry, Aunty Hetty. *I* will be your friend. And so will Jack.'

He looked up at his name, smiling. 'Jack,' he repeated.

Henrietta dabbed her eyes with her handkerchief as John and Judith laughed. 'God bless you for that, sweetheart.'

Caroline hovered, torn between the company that pleaded for amusement and the husband who so needed her. For once, his bad mood was not a burden she could foist off on to Mrs Howard. This responsibility was hers, and hers alone.

George leant on the window frame with his forehead pressed against the glass. His breath made mist and obscured the view of the courtyard below. Lights shifted beneath the haze; lamps moving in the darkness as sedan chairs were set down for the King and Melusine.

How was Caroline supposed to buoy his spirits when her own were at nil? The small nub that had appeared on her stomach after Louisa's birth was now a hard mass that caused her persistent pain. She felt its presence constantly as it chafed against her stomacher, a flesh bubble of agony.

George heaved a broken sigh. She walked over and placed a hand on his shoulder. Together, they peered through the misted glass and watched the King's sedan lumber off into the night.

'How often does my father go to the theatre? He hides in here like some damned rabbit in a warren and then, on the one day he should court solitude . . .' Tears made his eyes sparkle like blue crystal.

'He is doing this on purpose to distress you. Do not let him succeed. We will keep your mother's memory in our own way.'

His face crumpled. 'Why did she have to die, Caroline? Why now?'

She placed her arm around his shoulders. Her stomach twanged with the movement. She had no answers for him; only the comfort of her touch. How woefully inadequate it was.

'If my mother had lived until I was king . . . ' He closed his eyes and exhaled. 'I meant to set her free. You know I did. She could have come to England in honour, I would have made her Regent of Hanover.'

'It was not meant to be.'

'But why?'

'I don't know.' She sighed. 'Dear heart, I have been through this pain. I understand the wild thoughts that fly through your head. But asking questions that can never be answered will do you no good. Don't try to make sense of it. It is a cruel blow. Allow yourself to suffer under it, then you can start to heal.'

'You do *not* know this pain,' he muttered, his jaw clenched. 'You were allowed to mourn, you were allowed to say goodbye. My loss is not even acknowledged. I am forbidden to dress in black.' He shook his head. 'The whole court goes on, without even a day of mourning. How can he treat her so? Even in death, she receives no pity.'

Caroline swallowed, choked by his emotion. He had not seen this woman in thirty-four years, yet still she broke his heart. Did Fred lean out of his window like this, longing for her?

It did not make the least bit of difference if he did; her son would soon have another woman to replace her. The King was determined to marry Fred to his Prussian cousin the next time he visited Hanover. Never mind that the Prussian King was a violent brute whom George had hated since birth. Like everything else in Fred's life, his parents had no part in his marriage.

'I cannot even remember what she looked like. I keep trying to see her, but I can't. The King insisted on putting the portraits away so many years ago . . . But I recall her smell.' His voice cracked. 'Jasmine and bergamot. What troubles me most is that she didn't know I loved her. She must have sat in that castle and thought I was my father's child through and through, raised to hate her. I wanted to tell her I never changed. But now I will not get the chance.'

'She knew,' Caroline said with conviction. Images of Fred filled her mind; his chubby baby face, his first wobbly steps, the first time he had said her name. Surely he must still feel something for her?

'She couldn't have known. My father saw to that.'

Caroline pinched his chin between her fingers and tilted his head to look at the inky sky. Through the November frost, dozens of tiny stars burnt fierce and bright. 'If she didn't know it living, George, she knows it now. She sees you.'

He blinked, studying the twinkling dots. 'And yet I still cannot see *her*.' He thought for a moment. His mouth twisted. 'People say she prophesied the King would die within a year of her. Do you think she sees him too? That she glares down on him, ill-wishing him?'

Caroline thought of Fred's face when she had left him. 'Let us hope so.'

1727

CHAPTER TWENTY-SIX

∽ *Richmond Lodge* ∼

Bumps in the anteroom stirred Caroline from her sleep. She groaned and turned over, wincing as the strange nub on her belly caught in the tangled sheets. She felt listless, plagued by constant headaches. Even now, during her afternoon rest with George, she couldn't escape the sun; it burnt behind the heavy curtains, filling the room with a muted glow. The frosty spring had given way to a scorching summer – one the King was missing, on another jaunt to Hanover. By the time he came back, winter would be advancing and Fred would be a married man. She shuddered. It didn't bear thinking about.

Thumps came from outside. She closed her eyes and tried to ignore them. Impossible – now there were voices, one male and one female, passing a rapid exchange. Something was going on.

'George, wake up.' She nudged him, making him snort. He didn't open his eyes. 'George!'

'Ugh?'

A hesitant tap at the door. She stared at the polished wood. The knock came again, forceful this time.

George lifted his head. 'What the devil?'

Carefully, she swung her legs over the side of the bed and pulled on a robe. She walked to the door with a strange, excited dread.

'Send them away,' George spluttered, turning his pillow over and nestling down again. 'Damned fools.'

Caroline opened the door a fraction. The Duchess of Dorset stood before her with an expression of shock. 'What is it?' Caroline hissed.

'May I come in, Your Highness?'

'The prince is not dressed. Can it wait?'

The duchess shrugged, her face creased in confusion. 'I don't know, Your Highness. I don't think so.'

'For God's sake!' George's voice blared from the bed. 'What do you want, woman? How dare you disturb our rest?'

'It isn't *me*, Your Highness! It's Sir Robert Walpole.'

'Walpole!' George sat upright in bed, his nightcap hanging from his ear. 'What the bloody hell does Walpole want?'

Caroline cleared her throat. 'What message did he give you, exactly, Your Grace?'

'Only that it was desperately important, and he needed the prince to come out and see him at once.'

'I won't dance to his tune!' George bawled.

Caroline held up a hand. She was growing more uneasy by the minute. 'A moment, George. Think. Walpole is not a stupid man. He wouldn't risk your wrath for a trifle.'

'I don't go running to his call. He can wait – I'll talk to him later.'

She looked at him, trying to convey the dread that pushed up and clogged her throat. 'I know he would not act this way unless . . . It is gravely serious, George. I can tell. Please see him.'

George scowled. '*Now?*'

'Please. If I am mistaken, you can kick him out on his ear.'

He held her gaze for a moment, pulling the taut thread in their battle of wills. When she didn't blink, he threw back the covers. 'Very well. He has one minute.' George yanked on his breeches and stuffed his shirt down inside them, not bothering to button himself up. Throwing a red coat over his shoulders, he shambled to the door.

'Thank you.' She planted a kiss on his face as he passed. He followed the Duchess of Dorset and shut the door behind him.

Caroline was suddenly alone in the mellow light. She looked at the bed, all scrunched sheets and lopsided pillows, and wondered if she should climb back in. What else was there to do until he returned?

The silence hummed. Around her, the air smelt foul with sweat and sleep. She pressed one ear to the smooth wooden door. Very faintly, she heard the rumble of a male voice. George or Walpole? She wasn't sure. Wringing her hands, she crept back to the bed and slumped down on its soft mattress. Something was coming, hurtling toward her, but she had no idea what it was – or how to protect herself from it.

'That is a lie!' George's shout rang through the corridors. Somewhere in the lodge, a dog barked.

Caroline closed her eyes and curled her fingers into her palms. Her heart pounded in time with George's footsteps as he raced back to her. The door flew open, slamming against the wall. George looked half-wild.

'What is it? George. What did Walpole say?'

Blinking, he met her gaze. 'He says – he says the King is dead.'

Something unlocked inside her. It was as if she had been holding a lead weight for many years and now it had lifted. She tried to find grief. There was none. Every dark emotion disintegrated beneath a blinding wash of light. 'No . . . The King is not dead. *You* are the King.'

George staggered and gripped the bedpost. 'And you are the Queen.'

At last. 'I am the Queen.' She felt herself swelling, transforming to fit the role she had aspired to for so long. She shook herself. It was not decent to celebrate straight away. 'Did Sir Robert say how the King . . . ?'

A crease appeared between George's brows. 'A stroke, like Grandmamma. One on the road, another in Osnabruck.'

Unsteadily, Caroline rose and went to him. 'Are you sad?'

'Perhaps. No. I'm not sad that he is gone. Only sad that he was not – that circumstances were not – different.' He looked around the room, lost. 'What do we do first?'

She wanted to talk to him of a hundred things; the children, sending for Fred, the funeral, the move to the royal palaces. Where to begin? They had planned for this their whole lives, yet it did not seem real. 'Government must continue. What did you tell Walpole?'

George's jaw set. 'I told him to take his orders from Sir Spencer Compton.'

Images of herself and George on the throne scattered, chased away by a bolt of jealousy. 'Compton? Compton will be your First Minister?'

'Yes.' He disengaged himself from her arms. 'I always intended it.'

Did he? Or did Henrietta Howard plant the thought in his susceptible mind? 'I do not recall you telling me that.'

'No? Well, I am telling you now.'

Henrietta, always Henrietta, lurking in the background. Caroline could tolerate many things, but an interference with politics was not one of them. This was *her* husband, her throne and her government. She wouldn't let Henrietta ruin it like a bumbling puppy, desperate to please her Tory friends.

George read her silence. 'You do not approve of my minister?'

She had to be careful. Criticising his choice would only make him cling to it; she had to change his opinion by inches, by hair-breadths. 'On the contrary, I think selecting him is a wise move. Why would we want ministers who served your father?'

'Precisely.'

She pulled her long plait over her shoulder and began to untie it. 'A bold move, too. It shows people we are not afraid for our inheritance. We are secure – we don't believe, as many say, that every Tory is a closet Jacobite.'

George sat down on the bed. 'Do people really think that? Who could believe that the Tories want James Stuart on the throne instead of the King – I mean, instead of me?'

'People will believe anything.' Her fingers worked to separate the strands of her blonde hair, threaded with silver. 'It does not matter. You are setting the standards for your reign: trust and loyalty. You favour men who are loyal to you, not those famous for their abilities.'

'You do not think Compton has ability?'

She offered an airy shrug. Her hair unwound as she moved, spilling free over her shoulders. 'Really, how should I know? He is untried. But he's a good man and he pleases you. That is enough to win my esteem.'

'It's a good choice,' he said, more to himself than to her. 'The right one. He has been recommended to me.'

By Henrietta, no doubt. England would not get far with Compton at the head of her ship. It was all very well for a mistress to play games and win places for friends; she did not have to rule the kingdom. Walpole was the best, and by God Caroline would only have the best working for her. She smiled sweetly. 'You are the King now, my love. You make your own decisions.'

Leicester Fields

Crowds thronged the courtyard of Leicester House. Henrietta

257

stood, packed in tight amongst the sea of people, craning her neck for a better view. A fierce summer sun blazed over her. Dressed, like the other courtiers, from head to toe in black, she was sweltering.

Lady Betty wafted an ostrich feather fan in her face. 'Can you see anything?'

'A little.' Caroline and George waved from the doorway. Henrietta barely recognised them as the people she had served for thirteen years. Now the couple had come into their own, a transformation was working its way through them. The prince and princess had gone into Richmond Lodge like a chrysalis and emerged as King and Queen.

Her eyes lingered on George's stocky figure. A blue sash and star draped across his torso. King. Would a king still want her? Or would the inevitable shake-up of the royal household see her displaced? She had not been with him since the news arrived from Hanover – he had not visited her. Despite the heat, her skin turned cold. Marble Hill was not built yet. If George chose a new mistress, there would be nowhere to hide.

Lady Betty elbowed her. 'Look, the elder princesses! The Queen will be so happy to have her family reunited.'

Anne, Emily and Carrie drooped, sober-faced beside their new governess.

'Poor girls,' said Henrietta. 'They truly seemed to love their grandfather.' She wondered what he was like, the princesses' version of Georg Ludwig. Had they seen a different side to the stern, haughty man?

Lady Betty's brother, Mr Berkeley, hobbled up beside them, tousled from making his way through the crowd. 'If the princesses loved the late king, they were the only ones,' he observed. 'This is no day of mourning.' He frowned on the smiling, hungry faces. Everyone was jostling for a place in the throng and a position of power. They wore black, in concession to Georg Ludwig's demise, but that was all. There was no oppression of spirits.

'I cannot blame George and Caroline for their happiness,' Henrietta admitted. 'They had reason enough to dislike the late king. But the courtiers . . . ' She fell silent as a huzzah went up. So many people, so much noise. It was not decent.

'Do not startle yourself, Mrs Howard.' Berkeley's slender features turned down. 'Vultures always make a ruckus when they feed.'

Henrietta found she couldn't meet his earnest eyes. There was something so direct in his gaze that it threw her off kilter.

'We must not judge their joy too harshly!' Lady Betty shouted above the hubbub. 'We also profit by the change.'

Or did they? Charles would be out of a job. There was no chance George and Caroline would transfer him to their court. He would need money – and that always meant trouble for Henrietta.

'My position has not been confirmed,' she said, remembering Mr Pulteney's words. If Caroline was to oust her, surely now would be the time? 'I will not celebrate yet. But the Tory party certainly has much to rejoice over.'

Berkeley grinned, accentuating the dimple in his chin. 'Do not think we are ignorant of what we owe to you, Mrs Howard. Everyone knows you persuaded the new King to take Spencer Compton as his First Minister.'

Blaring sunlight hit the back of her head. 'In truth, I hardly mentioned it to the prince – I mean, the King. Sir Spencer owes it entirely to his own merit.'

Lady Betty glanced over the crowd and laughed. 'Either way, his predecessor is in disgrace. See over there!' She pointed. 'Sir Robert Walpole and Lord Hervey look frightfully foolish. How the mighty have fallen!'

Henrietta followed her eyes to the far side of the courtyard. It was the only place where people were not packed cheek by jowl. Three figures stood alone, while others gave them a wide berth: this week's social pariahs. Sir Robert Walpole scowled, looking like a comic villain from the theatre with his dark brows drawn into a single line. Delicate, handsome Lord Hervey bore the degradation differently. His thin figure sagged, bowed by pressure, but his eyes were alight with defiance. Despite appearances, he would not be beaten easily. And there, at his side . . .

'Why,' Henrietta breathed, 'it is Molly!' Her friend, now Lady Hervey, was so changed. The pretty, carefree girl had become a smart society lady, with her hair drawn up under an elaborate cap and cosmetics covering her face. Jewels twinkled at her throat. Beneath her fine lutestring gown, cut in the latest fashion, her figure was plumper than it used to be – no doubt the effect of many pregnancies. Henrietta's heart twisted. 'Molly!' she called, waving her arm.

Molly turned. Her face lit up, making her girlish again. Whispering hurriedly to her husband, she pushed through the crowd and made a dash for Henrietta. It was not hard for her to pass. Courtiers fell away, knowing her husband was out of favour. They drew up their skirts and shuffled aside, as if even brushing hems with her could taint them.

Before Henrietta knew it, she was in her friend's arms, kissing her and inhaling the scent of her perfume. 'Look at you, little Molly! My dear, you are a woman all at once. You make me feel old.'

Molly clasped Henrietta's hands, pressing jewelled rings into her flesh. '*Old!*' She scoffed. 'You look lovelier than ever!' All of a sudden, her grey eyes filled. 'It is so good to see you. You have no idea how much I need a friend.'

'Then meet two of *my* friends.' Henrietta said kindly, turning to her companions. 'Lady Hervey, may I present Lady Elizabeth Germaine and The Honourable Mr Berkeley?' They made their reverences with stiff legs and with wary eyes. 'You must not think I will abandon you, dear Molly, because I am a Tory now. I would never let matters of party come before friendship.' She nodded over to where Walpole and Lord Hervey still held their ground, bereft of company. 'It's ridiculous. The King may not like Walpole, but there is no reason to avoid him.'

Powder shifted on Molly's skin as her expression changed. 'I don't mind about Walpole,' she confided. 'I always hated him. But my husband . . . Poor Hervey. He does so want a position at court worthy of his talents.'

Henrietta nodded her sympathy. 'So does Mr Gay.'

'Oh yes, dear Gay! How does he?'

'Well, I thank you – and I hope he will be better. Surely, now Caroline and George have come into their own, they will reward him for years of unpaid service? There must be a place for him.'

'I do hope so. If anyone can persuade them to employ him, it is you.'

Henrietta coloured, realising Berkeley was listening. She dreaded to think what a figure she cut in his eyes. He probably thought she asked a favour for every inch she lifted her skirt. 'No, not I. My opinions mean nothing. If they did, I would speak up for Lord Hervey. But I am going to leave his case in the best hands: those of the Queen.'

Lady Betty raised her brows. 'The Queen still favours Walpole and Hervey? I struggle to believe that. After all the false promises he made her!'

'The Queen does not hold grudges unless they are useful. Believe me, I know her.'

'Well, I will tell Lord Hervey of your hopes, dear Hetty,' said Molly. 'But for the moment I think Sir Spencer Compton is quite secure.'

'You've lived in a court. You know nothing is secure. Even I am not secure.'

Berkeley shifted his weight on his cane. Involuntarily, she glanced in his direction.

He was still watching her. Watching with those big brown eyes, so soulful they belonged in the face of a spaniel. He pitied her – she saw it now. He did not consider her a slut. She was below that: she was an object of his compassion.

'I am sure you are valued at court just as much as you are valued amongst your friends, Mrs Howard,' he said gently.

She quivered, unable to bear his scrutiny. Angry words she could withstand, but kindness . . . It pushed her dangerously close to tears. 'Sir, you know nothing of the matter.'

It came out more savage than she intended. She wished her words back at once, but it was too late.

Molly squeezed her arm. 'Well, none of us know the court as well as you, my dear. If there is any one amongst us sure to make their fortune by this new reign, it is you. You have a place with both the King and the Queen!'

And that, Henrietta thought, was precisely the problem.

~ ~

When George finally visited, he took her by surprise. Without knocking, he surged through the door and strode to the fireplace. Kneeling beside the hearth, he piled more wood onto the dwindling flames.

Henrietta pulled out her pocket-watch and tapped the dial. Half-past six. It was still ticking, she had not forgotten to wind it. Her heart dropped as she realised something terrible must be afoot. This was a man who numbered his underwear for the days of the week; he would not break his routine by half an hour if he were not distracted.

She knelt awkwardly beside him, her skirts pooling around her. Orange flecks jumped in the grate like luminous fleas. 'George? What are you doing?'

He lay a wad of paper on the fire and used a poker to shove it into the blue heart of the flame. 'Better to do it here,' he muttered. 'No one will think to inspect the ashes in *your* grate.'

A tongue of fire darted and wrapped around the paper. It blackened and smoked at the edges. With a soft hiss, the red seal that bound the pile melted and dribbled between the logs. Henrietta would know that seal anywhere. It was the late king's. She put a hand on his shoulder, terrified. 'George, what is that? What are you burning?'

He gave a devilish grin and winked at her.

'Dear God, is that . . . Is that your father's Will?'

He pushed to his feet and dusted off his hands. 'God rot him. Thought he could marry my children into Prussia, did he? Planned to have me kidnapped and carried off to America? I hope he sees this from wherever he is. I hope he learns how it feels to have your wishes swept aside with the evening's cinders.'

She gaped at him. Her eyes kept returning to the fire, where the paper had become a charred heap. 'But George . . .'

'Don't say it's disgraceful. He did exactly the same thing to my mother's Will. Serves him right.'

Shakily, she climbed to her feet. 'I am not blaming you. I am simply concerned. This is a legal document with many ramifications. What if you are discovered? What if there is another copy?'

He pursed his lips, suddenly sober. 'There *is* another copy. The damned Duke of Wolfenbittel has it. I shall have to tread carefully with him.'

Henrietta turned cold. 'I thought Melusine was staying with the duke? Surely she, of all people, will fight to get this Will proved?'

'I will handle Melusine. I am King now. I can do whatever I want.' He seized her and groped hungrily for her mouth with his own. His lips were warm. He still smelt of smoke from the fire.

She broke the kiss, suddenly shy of him. 'And do you still want *me*, Your Majesty? Now that you are King?'

'Of course I do.'

She sighed and relaxed her cheek into the embroidery on his

waistcoat. For now, she was safe. But how long before Caroline changed his mind?

'Then I am the most fortunate of women. I expect many positions will change. What of my dear friend Mr Gay? Will he finally have a place?'

'Oh yes, I will find Gay a place. And what about brother John? Do you think he would like Treasurer of the Chamber?'

The room seemed to flip. She snapped up her head to search his face. George smiled back at her broadly. 'You would do that? You would give my brother such a great station?'

'Of course.'

When she kissed him again, her whole heart was in her mouth. 'Sir, you cannot imagine how happy you make me.'

His eyes darkened with desire. Wrapping one arm around her waist, he began to tug her toward the bed. 'Talking of your friends . . . Are you intimate with a family named Berkeley?'

Her stomach swooped. She recognised the threat in his voice. 'With – with a lady of the family. She is no longer a Berkeley but Lady Elizabeth Germaine. With the men I have no more than a passing acquaintance.'

'Hmm.' He ran his hand over her hair and unpinned her lace cap. 'See that it stays that way. It was Admiral Berkeley, Lady Germaine's brother, who offered to spirit me away for my father. Impudent wretch! I will not look upon that family with a kind eye.'

She swallowed. Something inside her screamed at the idea of giving up her friends; Lady Betty's maternal tenderness, Berkeley's soft voice and brown eyes. But what choice did she have? They could offer her nothing compared with George. He would make John Treasurer of the Chamber! Just imagining the pride on her parents' faces hardened her resolution.

'Then, Your Majesty, neither will I.'

CHAPTER TWENTY-SEVEN

～ *Kensington Palace* ～

Caroline was anxious about moving to Kensington, the palace that had swallowed Georgie's life in its damp embrace. But the redbrick building with its decorative urns and endless gardens was a different place to the building site she remembered. When she ran through the corridors nine years before, they had been full of scaffolding. Now the decorations were complete. The King's apartments were splendid, swimming with frescoes and gilt. Unfortunately, she and George spent most of their time in the modest Council Chamber. It was a shadowy room, papered in sage green with heavy mahogany furniture against the walls. Here they thrashed out the business of their government, sweating like blacksmiths over an anvil as they forged a new reign. But there was one question that was never resolved.

'When will we send for Fred?' Caroline stood, twisting the folds of her dusky purple gown, while George sat before the desk, scanning a scroll of paper. Already he was showing the strain of kingship; the skin was tight around his forehead and dark stains sat beneath his eyes. 'Do you attend to me, Your Majesty? I deserve the honour of your attention.'

He peered at her over the top of his scroll. 'I am busy.'

'You need only say one word. Just one, and Fred can come home.'

'Fred has business in Hanover. He cannot just leave. I will send for him presently.'

'But before our coronation,' she insisted. 'How can we be crowned without our heir present?'

George threw down the scroll with a snap. 'For God's sake, woman. Why can you not understand?'

A chink in the armour. Caroline pounced on it, moving round the desk to caress his tight shoulders. 'How can I understand if you do not talk to me?' she cooed. 'You don't even try to explain.'

He sighed. 'You do not believe me when I tell you Fred is my father's creature. I don't know whether I should curse you as a blockhead or bless you as a dear heart for that.' He hung his head, letting the curls of his wig spill over the desk. 'But even supposing . . . Even if my father has not raised my son to be a thorn in my side . . .'

'He hasn't,' she assured him, leaning down to press her cheek against his. It was rough with stubble. 'Fred is ours.'

'Suppose you are right. Does that mean he is not a threat to me? Look at me, Caroline.' He held out his fingers, showing how age had marked them. 'I am forty-four years old. I am not a dashing young prince now.'

'You always will be to me.' She took one of his hands in her own and squeezed. 'Forty-four is not *very* old.'

Chuckles came from deep in his throat. 'Not for you my love; you still shine on. But think of it. Fred is twenty. People will look at him and say *there goes the future*. He will make me look like a relic.'

'A man in his prime,' she corrected. 'Fred will seem nothing but a boy beside you.'

George shook his head. 'Since I came to England, I have spent every second fighting. It was always me against my father.' He turned to look up into her face, his expression infinitely weary. 'I want some time to be free and enjoy my position. Can you not give me that? Just a few months without a rival?'

Her heart clenched. She knew what it was to live alongside a younger specimen. 'I understand,' she murmured. 'A few months. Then Fred must come.'

George blew out his breath and picked up his scroll again.

'What are you reading?'

'My accession speech. Compton has just finished it.'

'Lord, no wonder you look so glum.'

His lip curled. 'Actually, he's done a very good job. You underestimate him.'

Intrigued, Caroline read over his shoulder. Her brow furrowed. It *was* a good speech. 'This is rather different from his usual style.' Yet something in the turn of phrase and the formation of sentences was familiar to her. Not like Compton, but like someone she knew. Who had he tried to imitate?

George smirked. 'You see? He's risen to the occasion. There is only this one paragraph here that I want changed.' He indicated with his finger.

'Yes, I agree. That is not quite of a piece with the rest.'

He nodded to a servant standing by the door. 'Go and fetch Sir Spencer Compton. I'll have him alter it now while the Queen is by.'

As the man sped away, Caroline read the lines again. They bothered her. Who did they remind her of? Compton had received help with this speech, she was sure. Not once in his career as Speaker for the House of Commons had he shown a glimmer of promise. Now, this.

The door opened and Compton was announced. His cringing manner of slinking into the room only heightened Caroline's suspicion. He had a long, dull-witted face with a fat chin and a nose turned up at the end. His eyes were shallow, like a cow's, staring passively out from beneath a frizzy auburn wig.

'Your Majesty. You asked to see me?'

'I did. Come closer, man. It's my speech. You see this paragraph, here? It needs amending.'

Compton's face blanched. His thick lips stuttered. 'Am-Amending, Your Majesty?'

'Yes. Damn it, don't look so frightened. You can do a little amendment, can't you? I don't like this phrase.'

Compton came to George's side and blinked at the speech. 'I – er, yes. Of course. But I would have to take it away and think about it.'

The first flush of anger stained George's cheeks. 'Take it away? You can think about it here, man. I am not going to hurry you. Give me a new draft of this one paragraph and I can approve or deny it immediately. It will save a great deal of toing and froing.'

He trembled. 'I am not sure I . . . You understand, I want this to be my best possible work. I find it easier to think in private.'

Caroline put in her voice, velvety soft. 'Indeed, you must, Sir Spencer. This is quite superior to anything I saw you write before. Did it take a very long time?'

Her compliments seemed to make him more uncomfortable. 'Thank you, Your Majesty. I don't recall how long it took. I was . . . deep in concentration.' He turned a ring over on his finger. 'You cannot be too careful with a King's speech. One change can alter the entire interpretation.'

She stared at him, knowing she could break him. How could George not see through this fool? Her eyes narrowed. 'You wish to consult some of your colleagues, perhaps?'

'It would be wise, madam.'

'For God's sake!' George hit the paper with his fingers. 'It's a paragraph. I don't want a whole new speech. Surely you can sit here and change a paragraph without a bevy of attendants? A First Minister has to think on his feet, you know. He cannot go scuttling back to his followers for help every five minutes.'

That was it. The pieces slotted into place. Caroline remembered exactly where she had seen this style before. 'My love,' she said sweetly, fixing Compton to the spot with her eyes, 'do not worry yourself. I believe Sir Spencer only wishes to consult one man: Sir Robert Walpole.'

The chamber fell deadly silent. Compton froze, not looking at either of them. George sized his minister up, incredulity and anger dawning on his face. 'Walpole? Do not tell me you went to him.'

Suddenly, Compton burst into a flood of tears. Caroline turned her head away to hide her laughter. She had never seen anything so ludicrous.

'Walpole wrote the whole thing!' Compton wailed. 'I couldn't do it. I – I'm not c-capable of this off-office!'

George's face was a picture, full of outraged disappointment. 'Pull yourself together, Compton! Stop blubbering like an idiot.'

'S-sorry, Your Majesty.'

Pushing back his chair with a scrape, George stood and paced the room. A muscle flickered at his temple. 'You've made me look like a damned blockhead!' he shouted. 'I trusted you. You told me you could do this.' His fingers strayed to the lace cuff of his sleeve, worrying the ruffles. 'I cannot go back on my word. I can't start a rule by doing that. Oh, this is a fine mess you have gotten me into, Compton.'

'Perhaps Sir Spencer will have the goodness to resign,' Caroline suggested. 'It may cause a little embarrassment, but surely he would rather endure that than force his King to retract his word of honour?'

Compton nodded, his wig bobbing. 'Oh yes! Yes, Your Majesty, do let me resign. I'll do it with pleasure.'

'Far better to step down than be dismissed,' she agreed.

'But it leaves me without a First Minister!'

She braided her fingers together. Best not to suggest Walpole now, while he was still angry. She would get word to him and advise him to push his advantage. It would not take long. She smiled. She could feel everything coming together perfectly. 'I am sure we will find someone, my dear.'

~ ~

It was all going hideously wrong. Henrietta shook her head at Gay, struggling to find words. 'I cannot believe it. Are you sure – are you absolutely sure that's what the King said?'

Gay nodded. 'Oh yes. Gentleman Usher to Princess Louisa. He spoke as if I should be glad of it.'

'I do not understand. He promised me you would have a place worthy of your talents. After thirteen years of service, with no wage at all . . . this is the best he can offer?'

Gay grimaced. 'It isn't your fault. I am of humble birth. I should never have expected more.' He pulled his lips into a bitter grin. 'Well, I wanted a place at court, did I not? At least I can say I was offered one.'

She reached out and squeezed his hand. She felt awful. She tried to ignite her anger at George but it would not kindle. Deep down, she knew this wasn't his doing: it was Caroline's. 'Let me speak with him again.'

'No. I have *some* pride left. I will not have you beg on my behalf.'

'But where will you go? What will you do?'

He shrugged. 'The Duchess of Queensbury has invited me to stay with her. It is an honour and I enjoy her company.' He fought his features into a hopeful look. 'There will be more time to write, in the country. Happen this will work out for the best.'

'You will leave me,' she said quietly. Gay had always been there. The idea of him leaving court, never to come back, sent her into a spasm of panic. Kensington would be awful without him. Her apartments in Clock Court were devoid of cheer; three feet underground, damp and unwholesome. She could not display any of her fine paintings or her blue and white porcelain for fear they would mould. Even now, in the corner, she saw a crop of tiny mushrooms.

'We will only be parted until Marble Hill is built. We can meet there.'

'If Charles does not snatch me away first.'

Gay groaned. 'I am sorry, Henrietta. I do not have a choice. If I stay here I will be laughed at. Is that what you want?'

Guilt pricked her. 'Of course not. I'm sorry. This has just been a terrible day.' She walked over to the desk and touched the letter again – black-edged, cold as the grave. Her brother's wife, Judith, was dead. She could barely take it in. When Judith visited at St James's Palace she had been well, full of life. There had been no hint of the doom stretching over her.

Gay hung his head. 'Oh, yes. Of course. I forgot about your sister-in-law. Those poor children, without a mother.'

Her heart squeezed. She knew how they felt. 'The little boy, Jack. He's barely three. And my poor brother! He has led such a hard life.'

He rubbed her shoulder. 'Invite him and the children to stay with you,' he said softly. 'It would do you all a world of good.'

The clock chimed. It was a quarter to seven.

'The King will be here soon,' she observed. God knew, she wasn't in the mood for his antics today. Perhaps he would be kind when he found out about Judith's death. She could never tell. Sometimes George was a comfort – but not one she could rely on. Not like Gay.

He nodded. 'I will leave you. I have packing to do.'

'Gay . . . ' Sorrow made her breathe in great gulps. The air tasted of fungus; a horrible, mouldering flavour. 'You will come and see me before you leave, won't you?'

His face softened. 'Of course I will. I'll miss you more than anyone.'

After Gay left, she sat and read the letter about Judith again. Once more, the world was changing around her. The children . . . They needed a woman to watch over them. She might have lost her own, darling boy, but here was a second chance. If she couldn't be a mother, she would be an aunt. The very best aunt that ever was. She thought of Dorothy and Jack as she had last seen them, sitting at her table drinking lemonade. Her heart flared with a protective flame. They were her future now.

The door slammed open. She jumped to her feet and curtsied before George.

'Well? What have you to say for yourself?'

She held her stooped position. 'On what topic, Your Majesty?'

He scoffed. 'Don't play the innocent with me. There is only one subject going around the court today and you know it.'

'I have not been out amongst the court, Your Majesty. My sister-in-law – '

He cut across her. 'That abominable puppy Compton! I never saw a man more inept. His failure makes *me* look like a dolt. I'm having to do a thing I said I never would, and get bloody Walpole in office.' He wiped a hand over his perspiring face. 'He's the only one with a glimmer of ability who can promise me a decent Civil List.'

Henrietta's mind worked fast. George never explained the whole story; he just ploughed in half-way through and expected her to catch up. 'What did Compton do?'

'He got Walpole to write my entire accession speech! Couldn't change even a single paragraph without running back to his master for instructions. And *this* is the man you would have me put at the helm of my country!'

Why had Compton done such a foolish thing? There were enough Tory men about to help him with writing speeches. 'I never

272

pretended to be a judge of politics, Your Majesty. I only tell you which men have good hearts, and will serve you loyally.'

He removed his hat and kicked it across the room. Fop dodged out the way with a squeal. 'There is your problem! What politician ever got along with a good, loyal heart? Pah! You judge like a baby.' He stalked about the room. 'I don't know why I'm surprised. I should have known you were a lousy judge of character the moment I met your husband.'

Henrietta flinched. Anger and hurt bubbled beneath her stomacher, but she could not let them show. If she dared to fling angry words back at him, she would be out on her heel, with Charles lurking like a wolf in a fairy-tale, waiting to gobble her up. 'I was very young when I married Mr Howard,' she said carefully. 'I should hope my understanding has improved since seventeen years of age. But I see you no longer trust me. I have some explanation now for your treatment of Mr Gay.'

'Oh, Gay!' He strode across the room, coattails swinging, to the fireplace. Flames leapt and dipped in the grate. 'A thankless fellow! After all these years begging for a place, he turns it down!'

'Gentleman usher to a three-year-old girl? A man of his talent? It was an insult.'

George grabbed the iron poker and thrust it between the gleaming coals, sending up flakes of ash. 'Many men would give their right arm for such a place. At least your friend Molly Lepell has a little more wit – or her husband does. Lord Hervey's just accepted a place under the Queen. That's what you wanted, was it not? Him in employment? Though I don't suppose you'll thank me for that either.'

Henrietta took a steadying breath. The musty air only made her feel ill. Was she being ungrateful? After all was said and done, she was just a mistress. George had never led her to believe she would receive anything for her trouble except protection from Charles.

'Speaking of thanks, how is your house at Marble Hill? Is it built yet?'

'Is that your wish now?' Her voice compressed into a sob. 'For me to go and live there?'

'No, of course not.' George did not look at her. 'Damned Howard is still prowling out there with his warrant.'

'Is that the only reason? You only want me to stay so my husband doesn't kill me?'

George sighed. He looked weary; tired of women and their tender feelings. 'Be sensible, Henrietta. You know I have an affection for you. Do not try to make it into something else.'

His words winded her. Not love; still not love. They were all the same: Charles, Henry, Caroline, George. Demanding all, then tossing her aside with the dregs of their coffee. Her slippery fingers could keep hold of no one; not even a friend like Gay. 'You need not worry. I know you do not love me. I have known that all along. I am merely a convenience.'

He blustered. 'Hetty! You speak wildly. Haven't I been kind? Have I not looked after you?'

He had. He had provided for her needs. But he would never understand why that wasn't enough. 'Yes, Your Majesty. I am much obliged to you.'

George screwed up his face as if trying to make out a complicated sum. 'Good.' He nodded briskly. 'See you behave yourself then, and don't suggest any more blockheads for my government. Do not suggest anything at all.'

'As you wish, Your Majesty.'

'I will talk to you when you are in a more agreeable mood.' He cast a deprecating glance around her apartments. 'Wait for my boy to summon you to my rooms. I do not want to spend any more time in this dank place.'

Rage throbbed again, forcing words from her. 'You could always move me to better apartments.'

'What did I just say about suggestions?' Shaking his head, he turned and left her with the mould and mushrooms.

CHAPTER TWENTY-EIGHT

↶ *Westminster* ↷

Caroline's time had come at last. At Georg Ludwig's coronation, she and Anne had waited inside the cool of Westminster Abbey, excluded from the pomp and glory. Not today. October sunlight washed over them, glittering on their diamonds and blinding the spectators. Caroline walked slowly on the raised gangway that stretched down to the Abbey doors, crushing herbs beneath her feet. She had thought she would feel nervous, with so many eyes fixed upon her, but she did not. She sparkled like water. This was where she belonged. For once her mind was clear; she had truly come to life for the first time.

The weight of her jewelled dress was immense, straining her legs and rubbing painfully against the nub on her stomach, yet she found she could bear it. People blinked as she paced just in front of the gold canopy with its jingling bells – her radiance was too much for them. They could not touch her, could not look at her; she burned white hot like a star. The Bishops of London and Winchester were at her side and her three eldest daughters bore her train. The girls were cloaked in purple with silver circlets on their heads. All those years she had spent pining for them and now they were here, wrapped up like gifts.

Henrietta was in pleasing subjection, branded in the scarlet robes of a mistress. Though she looked comely, with the silver edging to her dress and her bleached hair streaming over her shoulders, she paled into insignificance beside Caroline. The kettle drums, the choir boys, and the shower of petals were all for the Queen alone.

George made a comic spectacle, parading from the other direction. He hid beneath his canopy from the unseasonable heat. Now and then his crimson cap, lined with royal ermine, slipped and covered his eyes. Caroline repressed a smile. Though he was far away, she saw his lips forming cross words. He would be as fretful as a toddler by the time he reached the Abbey. It was *her* the people looked to for dignity and splendour. The sceptre and ivory rod sat easily in her hands. Finally, she was home. If Fred were there, she would have nothing left to wish for.

Shade was a welcome relief as she entered the Abbey at George's side and inhaled its cool scent. It was hard to see, after the blazing sun. Anthems soared around her; the rousing strains of Mr Handel's new anthem, *Zadok the Priest*. Caroline closed her eyes. A kind of sacred trance took hold of her as the ceremony progressed. She felt herself changing, transforming into an anointed queen. People no longer viewed the monarch as a demi-god, but surely there was something heavenly flowing down from above and working its way through her veins. *Look at me, Sophia. Mock me now, Georg Ludwig.* Their dead hands rested on her shoulders, smelling of the crypt. She shrugged them off and took her oath. It was hers now – the throne, the children, the country – all hers.

Holding the orb and sceptre, George knelt at the altar to receive his crown. The instant it touched his head, trumpets blasted out a fanfare. Their joyous sound travelled through the Abbey, reverberating around the stone walls. A dim pop in the distance told of the guns saluting from the park and the Tower. Sweet voices rose in a *Te Deum*. Caroline watched as the peers drew out their coronets from beneath robes of crimson and green silk. She was the only one waiting for her head to be covered. Her brow, still wet with anointing oil, tingled in anticipation.

Flanked by her women, she made her way to the altar. Henrietta removed her velvet cap with gentle hands. How light she felt, how insubstantial, until the metallic weight of the crown pushed through her coif. She closed her eyes, exhaling. The climactic moment was everything she dreamt it would be. Henrietta and Mrs Clayton pinned the crown into place. It was fixed now – immovable. Nothing but death could take it from her.

Images danced on the back of Caroline's eyelids. She was locked in an endless whirl around Westminster Hall, reliving her Coronation Banquet. She still saw gilded branches and their glowing candles illuminating the hall; she smelt the thick scent of meat before her on a golden platter. There were the pyramids of fruit, and the triumphal arches with statues of her and George. She felt she was sitting on the dais once more, watching the King's Champion ride in on his steed.

Her dreams were so vivid that she didn't notice the noise at first. Shouts in the courtyard sounded like her cheering subjects; the banging doors were fireworks exploding in the night sky. Only when she heard the name, roared out with blood-chilling ferocity, did she start up in bed, her heart pounding. 'Henrietta!'

She froze, trying to make sense of it. For a moment, she flattered herself it was her imagination. But then the cry came again, dreadful in its wrath. 'Henrietta!' The voice was not George's. Footsteps pounded closer and closer . . .

Springing from the bed, Caroline threw on a wrap and dove behind the thick damask curtains. It felt safe there, cocooned in darkness. With a trembling hand, she drew a bolt on the shutter and eased it open a crack. Wet leaves clung to the window, hampering her view. She stood on tiptoe. Outside, the moon's pearly light illuminated the courtyard. Guards ran toward the entrance of the palace, an unearthly sheen on their halberds. They were too far away to help.

Suddenly, the door to her bedroom crashed open. Footsteps clopped around and a chair smacked against the floor as the intruder struggled in the gloom. She hunkered down in the window seat, trying to make herself small. If this man should find her alone, undressed . . .

'Bloody woman, flitted off like a damned coward.'

His words hit a tender nerve of pride. What was she doing? A grown woman, Queen of England, hiding behind curtains? She should not fear subjects – they should be afraid of her.

Barely considering what she did, she put out a hand and parted the curtains. A beam of moonlight fell upon an unshaven face, blotchy in complexion. Greasy hair straggled from beneath the man's beaten hat down to his shoulders. His eyes were bloodshot, ravenous. Familiar . . . Her heart shivered as she placed the man in her memory. 'Mr Howard. What is your business here?'

It was satisfying to see him jump at her voice. 'I am here to retrieve my property. I will have my wife leave your service and return to me at once.' His breath stank of alcohol.

Caroline edged, ever so slightly, to her right. The door to her dressing room was at the far end of the chamber, unblocked. If she could creep her way toward it, she could cut him off from the rest of the palace. 'I have no intention of parting with your wife, Howard.'

He glowered. 'Then I'll keep moving through. Find the King, see what he has to say.'

Her head swam with terror. A fight would break out. But it was not the idea of Howard and George grappling that scared her; it was the idea of him stumbling across Henrietta. Caroline drew herself up. Who would have thought? After all her envy and spite, she still cared for her erstwhile friend. She could not let this beast seize and devour Henrietta. She had to stop him.

She took another step toward her dressing room. 'The King will give you no answer. He'll tell you it is not his business to interfere with my servants.' Her movement betrayed her. Howard glanced at the door.

'I *will* get her. You cannot stop me. She's mine.' He gathered himself, ready to pounce.

'Do it if you dare,' she growled.

At the instant Howard leapt, the door burst open. Guards swarmed round him in a flurry of red. Their shouts and the jangle of metal drowned out his screams. He fought against the burly guards, straining toward the dressing room. He would never get there. Henrietta was safe.

'Are you hurt, Your Majesty?' a guard asked.

Caroline raised her chin and shook her head. 'No. The fellow would not dare to hurt me.'

'Shall I fetch the King?'

'I see no reason to trouble him. Just make sure you dispose of this villain. Then post a sentry outside Mrs Howard's room.'

The guard nodded. Kicking and yelling, Howard was dragged from the room.

Caroline stood with shaking legs, breathing fast as she listened to the tramp of boots retreating into the distance. At last, all was still. For a moment, she thought she would faint from the shock. But then she forced her feet into motion. She ran through the corridors, careless of her appearance. She didn't stop until she was in Henrietta's apartment, beside her bed. She picked up a candle and lit its wick in the embers of the fire. How peaceful Henrietta looked in sleep. Without worry to pinch it, her face was smooth and white as alabaster. The deep grey eyes were hidden by a sweep of lashes, twitching occasionally beneath the lids.

'Mrs Howard,' Caroline said softly. 'Mrs Howard, I need to speak with you.' She touched her arm.

Henrietta stirred. Blinking, she stared at Caroline as if she were the fragment of a dream. 'Your Majesty? Is it the King? Is he well?'

'He is perfectly well. It is *your* husband who brings me here.'

With a sharp intake of breath, Henrietta extinguished the candle. 'Charles? What has he done?'

Casting the smoking candle aside, Caroline sat on the bed. 'Your husband is currently being escorted from the palace by my guards. He broke into my room, seeking you.'

Henrietta clutched the bed-clothes. 'No!'

'I am afraid so. I come to warn you, my good Howard. You need to be prepared. I will try to help but . . . ' She shrugged. 'We have spoken of this before. The only material difference now is the King.' Henrietta blinked at her. 'Come, now. You know George. As he grows older, he is tetchy. He does not take kindly to things that cause him inconvenience or expense. I fear Mr Howard will cause him both.'

'No.' Henrietta shook her head, but trouble lit her eyes. 'He would not . . . cast me off?'

He would if Caroline told him to. She shook off the ungenerous thought. 'I doubt it. But be that as it may, you will need a security. Write to your boy in Paris. Tell him how his father shames the family. Surely by now he is of an age to understand, even to offer you some protection. Write him a letter and beg his return.'

Henrietta looked somewhere over Caroline's shoulder. 'I will,' she said softly. 'I will add it to the pile.'

Caroline followed the direction of her gaze to a stack of paper on the desk. Dipping the candle in the coals once more, she passed to inspect Henrietta's correspondence. A heap of un-opened letters met her eyes, every one dotted with tears. They were franked, but had been returned by the recipient without even a note. Not one wax seal was cracked.

'What about *your* boy?' Henrietta asked gently. 'They are of an age, our sons – but a month apart. Why have you not reclaimed him?'

It had been a long time since they had spoken confidentially. How Caroline yearned to unburden herself to someone who understood. She turned from the desk to face Henrietta. 'It seems Fred is still not mine to claim. The King decides.'

'Yes. Children only belong to us while they grow in our belly.' They fell silent. 'I could – I could ask George for you,' Henrietta put in tentatively. 'See if I can persuade him? I am sure he will listen to me.'

Rage took hold of her. She drew great, heaving breaths, stretching and hurting her stomach. Suddenly the light falling from the candle was not golden: it was pure red. This chit, persuade George? As if Caroline was incompetent, unloved! 'You will do well to mind your own business, Mrs Howard.'

With her heart pounding, Caroline swept from the room and slammed the door behind her. Her bare feet slapped against the floor as she stormed back to her bedchamber. Why had she bothered? Protecting Mrs Howard, indeed! She was her husband's whore, not a friend. It was weak and pathetic of her to make that mistake. She would never make it again.

Kensington Palace

Henrietta leant on Lord Chesterfield's arm, her head bowed against the wind, as they made their way back from the menagerie. Bleached leaves swirled around their feet and rattled on the paving stones. Her friends thought the air would do her good, but her migraine was worse than ever. She gleaned no joy from watching the tiger pace around its pen, or the tortoises with their wrinkles and slow, creeping gate. She felt sick – maybe from pain, or sorrow, or fear.

She could hardly tell the difference anymore. Before she stepped inside, she took one last look at the sky. It was a shock of vivid blue, fretted with bare branches. Even the heavens resembled a cage.

It was a relief to be out of the buffeting wind. In her absence, Lord Argyll had ordered a fire in every grate, making the room glow. Through the haze of smoke, the silhouettes of two more friends became clear: Mr Gay and Dr Arbuthnot.

Henrietta let go of Chesterfield and flung toward them. 'You came! Thank God.'

Gay embraced her. 'As if I could desert you at such a time.'

Dr Arbuthnot inspected her eyes and recommended some pills for her headaches. 'I wish you would reconsider that operation we spoke of. It may even help your hearing.'

'I will. But I am not equal to any procedure yet.' Henrietta closed her eyes, feeling pain throb beneath their lids. Whatever else she lacked, she had good friends. She must be grateful for that. They sat her down before the fire and pressed warm ale into her hands.

'I spoke with your brother John and your family's lawyer, Mr Welwood, as you asked me to,' Lord Argyll said. 'We have established that a divorce is far too expensive, even for a lady of your means. And as for the disgrace it would entail . . . I do not see the King responding well to it. He might even stop your allowance.'

Disappointment soured her mouth. Would she never be free of that villain? 'I expected you to say as much. But legal separation – surely I have some hope there?'

Lord Argyll studied the floor, his hands clasped. 'That would go through the church courts. We would have to prove adultery and life-threatening cruelty.'

'I can!' Henrietta flared up. The sudden burst of emotion and noise made her head swim. 'God knows, that's all I have had in my marriage!'

'But can you prove it?' Lord Argyll asked. 'Did anyone see?'

'No. I took great care that no one should.'

Everyone fell silent. The fires sizzled.

Henrietta shifted in her seat. Were they really telling her that she was tethered to Charles, even after his assault on Caroline? 'Is there no hope for me?'

Lord Argyll patted her hand. 'I did not say that. Welwood told me there is such a thing as a private deed of separation. A kind of informal divorce, if you will. Between you and your brother, it might be affordable.'

Grimacing against pain, Henrietta tried to think. 'What would that mean? Would Charles still have a claim on me?'

'Nothing beyond the terms written in the deed.'

'An agreement,' she muttered. 'Knowing Charles, that will not come cheap. If he even consents to sign it.'

Lord Argyll pursed his lips. 'There is one piece of good news for you. Do you remember your neighbours from Beak Street? Mrs Hall and Mrs Cell?'

Fragments of memory returned, sharp and jagged. Henrietta refused to let her mind wind back to that time; it was too dangerous there. 'I recognise the names. I think they looked after Henry when I went out to get work. Gave me dinner, sometimes.'

'They did. They are good women. We had difficulty finding them, since they knew you by the name of Mrs Smith.'

Henrietta snorted. She had forgotten her alias, assumed to avoid Charles's creditors. 'Yes, they would.'

'But they remembered you vividly. With pity.' Lord Argyll cleared his throat. 'Most people would have nothing to do with a case like this. You must know how these proceedings are frowned upon – even when the claim is honest. Women suing for separation are described as blasphemous troublemakers.'

Henrietta gave a lopsided grin. 'That's me, my lord. Wouldn't you agree?'

He patted her hand again, making the ale jig in her tankard. 'No one here thinks that. And neither do your neighbours. That's why they're willing to come forward and say a few words on your behalf. Testify to your good character.'

Lord Chesterfield bit his lower lip with stained teeth. 'The King will not like this. It's better than divorce, but he still will not approve.'

Henrietta downed a sip of ale. Nausea rose and pushed it back up in her throat. 'The King does not approve of anything I do lately,' she spluttered. 'In this I must please myself, not him.'

The door opened. Everyone looked up to see Daniel usher in Lady Betty and Mr Berkeley. Here was another thing George would not like. They took an immense risk visiting the palace after their brother the Admiral had been dismissed in such disgrace. Somewhere, in the fog of her misery, she felt a gleam of gratitude.

'Welcome, my dears.' She put out her hand to them. 'How brave of you to come! Forgive me for not rising to greet you, my head . . . '

Lady Betty clasped her fingers. 'No trouble at all, my love. You rest.'

Berkeley did not lean on a cane this evening. He looked unsure of his welcome. As his sister moved aside, he took up Henrietta's hand and pressed it briefly to his lips.

Embarrassment squirmed in her stomach. She had been so rude to him the last time they met, at Leicester House. 'It is good to see you without a stick, Mr Berkeley. I trust your gout is better?'

His dark eyes penetrated hers. 'It is, I thank you. But Mrs Howard, I would gladly have it back if it could spare you your pain.'

'Well, it cannot.'

Why was she so abrupt with him? She did not mean to be. Everything was so wretched, and she only made it worse. She wanted Berkeley's friendship, she even admired him, yet she brushed him off like a louse. It was instinct, she supposed. Self-preservation. Every time she trusted a man, he slid a knife between her ribs.

Dinner was announced. Gay offered her his arm and helped her hobble out to the table.

The scent of roast lark drifting from the kitchens made her queasy, but she would see the charade through. She had planned a fine spread for her friends, far superior to the offerings at her first supper parties so long ago. There was potted pork, pheasant with prune sauce, artichokes and pigeon pie.

She toyed with her food while chatter and the sound of chinking glasses buzzed around her. She cut her meat into tiny pieces, careful not to scrape the cutlery against her precious porcelain. Suddenly, she felt as if she was being watched. She raised her eyes from the plate. Berkeley stared back at her.

'I have been thinking, Mrs Howard, about your poor niece and nephew.' Berkeley dabbed at his mouth with a napkin. 'Your brother must struggle to care for them, without his wife by his side. Why do you not have them here?'

A hard lump rose in her throat at the memory of Dorothy and Jack. She would give much to see them again.

'I discussed the possibility when I met with Mrs Howard's brother,' Lord Argyll confessed. He took another sip of wine. 'He was very agreeable to it. As soon as this dreadful business with Mr Howard is finished, he means to send the little girl here.'

There it was again: hope, irrepressible this time. Dorothy, the little image of her beloved mother. Family. A future. If only she could be sure that the dream wouldn't recoil upon her like all the rest. She set down her knife and fork. 'I would like that of all things. I mean to sign Marble Hill over to Dorothy, once it is complete. She needs property of her own, a place she can be safe.' She sighed, struggling not to let it turn into a sob. 'Lord knows, I will never get there.'

'Do not despair,' Berkeley urged.

'If this deed of separation we plan comes through,' said Lord Argyll, 'you could – '

A hammer on the door made them all jump. Raised voices rang in the hallway. Before Henrietta could get to her feet, a rough-looking man burst into the room. He put his shabby hat in his hands and sketched them the briefest of bows. 'Missus Howard?'

Berkeley rose, scarlet with displeasure. 'Who the devil are you to ask?'

'A messenger from *Mister* Howard, I'll have you know.'

Henrietta fell back in her chair. Not again . . .

'No person here cares what Mr Howard has to say,' Berkeley told him. 'Take your business elsewhere.'

A sickening thought lodged within her. 'No, let him speak! Is it Henry? Is my son well?'

The impertinent messenger laughed. 'Lord, yes, it ain't about him. It's about the money.'

'What money?'

'Twelve 'undred pounds a year for the upkeep of Audley End House. Master don't have it and says you're to pay it. I'm to get your word before dinner.' His beady eyes travelled to the clock. 'Time presses, ma'am.'

Incredulity snatched her breath. She should not be surprised, but Charles always found new ways to astonish her with his impudence.

'Your master can pay it from his rents,' Berkeley shouted, 'like any other gentleman.' Then he grimaced. 'I forget myself. That term does not apply to your master.'

Despite everything, Henrietta glowed. She was pleased to have him so warmly on her side.

'My master don't even have four-'undred pounds a year,' the messenger protested. 'Thanks to his wife's brother, who snuck away her dowry.'

'When I lived with your master, I didn't have four-hundred *pence* a year,' Henrietta said. 'Yet I managed to feed myself and my child.'

Lord Argyll cleared his throat. 'Mrs Howard, if I may . . .'

She glared at the messenger. 'Leave us.'

'I'm not to go back without an answer.'

Berkeley hobbled at him, fist raised. 'You'll go back with a good hiding if you're not careful!'

Whimpering, the messenger scuttled from the room. Berkeley banged the door shut behind him.

Lord Argyll came swiftly to Henrietta's side. 'Please, Mrs Howard, consider this request. You must write to your husband.' She gaped at him. 'I know,' he said hurriedly, 'it is impertinent and grossly unfair to make you pay for the upkeep of *his* house. But dwell upon it. If you agree, Mr Howard may sign the deed of separation. Would this not be the perfect bait to force his hand?'

He was right. There was only one way to win Charles, and that was with money.

'I do not have it,' she gasped. 'I cannot afford that much. Not unless I tear down Marble Hill . . .' The very thought rubbed her raw with loss.

Lord Argyll coughed again. 'I do not mean to be indelicate but . . . Surely, the King might . . .'

Henrietta looked down, her cheeks scarlet. 'No! I cannot ask him for the money. He is not pleased with me, after the debacle with Compton.'

'What about the Queen?' Lady Betty said. 'Can we try her?'

Pride beat frantically in Henrietta's chest. Ask Caroline for another favour? She saw the maze at Herrenhausen, a twisted labyrinth of box hedge. She remembered the pure white doves at the centre and a young princess, touched with pity. That woman could not be dead. Years had scored lines into her face and fat had swamped the perfect figure, but surely, somewhere beneath all the majesty, there was that kind heart which had spoken to hers?

'Try the Queen then, Lord Argyll,' she whispered. 'Once again, she is my only hope.'

CHAPTER TWENTY-NINE

∼ *Kensington* ∼

It was coming up to Christmastide. The turnspits in the kitchen revolved and the air became thick with the scent of roasted fowl. The royal children spoke of nothing but the buttery taste of Christmas Pie and the games planned for Twelfth Night. Even Henrietta's musty apartments took on some cheer as frost sugared her crop of mushrooms. But it seemed the season of goodwill had not thawed Caroline's heart.

Men were bringing in evergreens to decorate the mantelpieces, leaving a carpet of leaves behind them. Maids of Honour dashed to and fro, squealing about the Yule log and speculating what Caroline would give them in their Christmas boxes. Henrietta was tempted to warn them: *do not expect much.* From the way Caroline spoke to Lord Argyll, one would think her on the verge of being seized for debtor's prison. Of course it was all flam. Caroline did not *want* to pay the additional money. She could not forgive, even to help Henrietta free herself of Charles for good.

Henrietta's head pounded in time with her footsteps. She had a lowering cold that tore up her throat, but she could not remain in bed. She had to get the money from somewhere, even if it meant angering George again. Men hauling slabs of meat passed her on their way to the kitchens. Blood stained their aprons in crimson streaks. She pictured the hogshead presented before the Christmas feast: staring, gaping, leathery with death. A shiver rippled through her. She could not let Charles keep his hold on her.

The Presence Chamber embraced her with the heat of a wood fire. She stopped beside the door and held out her hands to the flames dancing inside the grate. George did not notice her; he was absorbed with directing the placement of holly and mistletoe. She watched the decorating process for a while, aware that he would fly into a rage if the slightest twig was out of place. Finally, his eyes settled upon her. 'God's blood! What now?'

Henrietta twitched her head at the servants.

'Leave us,' he ordered. The men left their plants and made a quick retreat.

'Your Majesty.' She curtsied, feeling she would fall down with exhaustion. How to persuade and wheedle, when she felt so ill? 'I am sorry to trouble you.'

He plucked a sprig of mistletoe and began shredding the leaves with his fingers. 'Aye, you are nothing *but* trouble. They tell me now that you mean to divorce your husband! Do you have any idea of the noise that will cause?'

She wanted to make a quip about being hard of hearing, but it was not the time. Instead, she inched further into the room, keeping her eyes meekly trained on the floor. 'You of all people know why I have to do it. Your mother . . .'

'Do not bring my mother into this.'

'I beg your pardon. I only meant to say that I might be rid of my tormentor for very little expense. It is not a divorce, but a private separation I seek.' She peeped up at him. The mistletoe hung in green rags around his fingers now, with only the berries intact.

LAURA PURCELL

'This expense you speak of. I suppose it is one you want me to pay?'

'I did not *want* you to pay it. I am sensible of how much you have given me already. I asked my mistress first, but – '

'You did *what*?' He dropped the mistletoe and ground it under the heel of his shoe. It lay splayed across the wooden floor like an animal hit by a carriage wheel.

Her breath caught. 'I asked the Queen for an additional one thousand, two hundred pounds a year.'

His face turned liver purple. 'Blast your eyes, woman! I thought you were discreet, I thought you were delicate? How dare you expose my wife to your tawdry schemes?'

Henrietta cringed back toward the fire. Lord, how she longed for a soft bed warmed by a cinder pan. She was too ill to play this game. She could not pretend, even for George, that Caroline was a genteel lady who would be shocked by the scandal of separation. Caroline had acted no better than a bawd in a Covent Garden bagnio. Why shouldn't she cough up the ransom Charles demanded? 'I believe I am the Queen's servant. At least, that is what her man writes in the account book when I draw my wage. But I see that I was wrong to go to her. I should have trusted in your generosity first.'

He scoffed. Walking over to the throne that stood across from the fire, he flung himself down and crossed his legs. 'What makes you think I will agree if the Queen has already refused you?'

She closed her eyes briefly and swayed on her feet. Her pannier knocked against the fireplace. She did not want to take this route, but what choice did she have? 'I know that you are not ruled by the Queen. You make your own decisions.'

Suspicion darkened his brow. 'There is a difference between standing together on a point and being ruled by one's wife.'

She groped beneath her waist seam and pulled the crumpled paper from her pocket. For an instant, she was tempted to commit it to the fire. Then she remembered Caroline's hard words. 'That is not what your critics say.' She edged toward the throne and dropped the satirical poem on his lap. It said that he was nothing but a strutting, puppet King who let his wife reign. That if he wanted to have any influence, he would need to lock her up like his mother. She did not envy the poor servants who would have to clean up after he read this. 'You may wish to look at that paper before deciding whether to agree with the Queen. I shall be in my apartments awaiting your answer.'

Alight with shame and a strange thrill, she backed quickly out of the room and shut the door behind her.

~ ~

The air was damp and cold. Fine rain soaked through Caroline's hood and made the short curls at her temples flatten around her face. She inhaled the scent of earth as she watched her gardeners unrolling turf and scattering seed. Knocking things down and building them anew gave her a sense of control – as if she could command the very order of England's trees.

Of course, she could not. She could not even curb the pen of her former courtier, Mr Gay. How many of the carriages splashing through the muddy park toward town would be going to see his new satire, *The Beggar's Opera*? She wiggled her frozen toes inside her shoes and felt the familiar stab of gout. Reason urged her to protect what was left of her health and return inside, but she would rather brave the rain than George's current mood.

What folly she had committed in snubbing Gay! The written word was a powerful thing; she had always known that. But when Gay needed employment, spite had drowned all her reason. She had encouraged George to slight the man – and now there was this. A play that mocked Walpole and exposed the government as a hotbed of corruption, and that blasted, blasted poem . . .

Below the sharp wind, she heard hooves crunch across gravel.

Curious, she wandered away from the gardeners, dragging her gouty leg. A foaming horse skidded to a halt before the palace in a shower of stone. It steamed under the rain. Its rider, splattered with mud, flung from the saddle and darted past the guards.

Goose flesh crept up Caroline's arms. The sight of a messenger in haste always recalled the day of baby Georgie's death. She closed her eyes as rain sprinkled over her face. Surely not Fred?

Shaking, she limped back to her ladies. They looked miserably cold with their damp gowns plastered against their skin. 'Enough of this. I will go inside to the King and tell him how we progress.'

Lady Bristol sighed with relief. Only Mrs Clayton looked at Caroline askance. She had wit enough to realise George cared as little for gardens as he did for painting. She crept up to Caroline's side. 'Perhaps you feel unwell, Your Majesty? We will sit you beside the fire and warm you through. Then I will fetch you some of that cordial Colonel Negus makes.'

Dare she confess what she feared? No; she had grown too close to a servant before. 'I merely wish to speak with the King on a private matter.'

Pulling her skirts clear of the mud, she wound her way toward the palace and entered with her head held high. Every tendon ached with the effort of appearing calm. Rather than taking the mahogany steps up to her own apartments, she climbed the King's stone staircase with its iron balustrades. Her progress was slow. Her rasping breath and heavy footfalls echoed in the stairwell. From the walls, painted figures watched her struggle; the leading courtiers from Georg Ludwig's reign. She felt her dead father-in-law's shadow over her still. He had parted her from Fred. If anything happened to him before she had the chance to see him again . . .

George's voice carried from the King's Gallery. Reaching the top of the stairs, she turned right and pushed her burning muscles on. The gallery was long and high with white moulding and a pale wooden floor. In the gloom, its red damask walls looked dark as blood. The messenger's footsteps had left mud tracks leading to the fireplace where George leant, his hand to his forehead. Four courtiers clustered around him with pinched faces. The moment they saw her, they bowed.

Fear was a solid lump in her breast. She could not even acknowledge their courtesy. 'George?'

He flung away from the mantelpiece and whispered to Colonel Lome. Nodding, Lome waved a hand at the other men and they disappeared through the door toward the drawing room.

'George, for pity's sake, tell me what is wrong. Is it this Beggar's Opera again?'

'No. It is Fred.' She held herself tense, unable to breathe. 'He is coming home.'

Her knees buckled. As her panniers knocked against the wall, she put out a hand and touched the soft fabric to hold herself steady. 'But … but that is good news,' she gasped.

George snorted. 'You think so? Wait until I tell you why I have sent for him.'

She turned her eyes to the wind-dial above the fireplace and imagined a breeze carrying her son home. But the hand, linked to a vane on the roof, showed that the wind was in the East. 'Why?'

'I have intelligence from our envoy in Prussia. Fred plans to escape Hanover and elope with his cousin Wilhelmina.'

For a moment she was so relieved that Fred was safe that she didn't absorb what George said. But then she looked up into her husband's face and saw resentment there. Her foolish, foolish boy. He had done for himself. 'We left him alone too long,' she murmured. 'The young are so restless – '

'No!' George barked. Spittle foamed onto his lips. 'You will not defend him! This is wilful disobedience, contempt for my authority. I told you – I *told* you that he was my father's creature!'

She shivered. It had been Georg Ludwig's wish that Fred marry the Prussian princess. She had heard the girl was so violent in her temper that she fell into fits. How George's foe, the King of Prussia, would crow to saddle them with such a daughter-in-law. 'Are we in time to stop him?'

'To stop the marriage? Yes.' He drew his watch from his waistcoat pocket and swung it around on its chain. His face set. 'But for me and Fred . . . I fear it is far, far too late.'

1728

CHAPTER THIRTY

✦ St James's Palace ✦

Caroline emerged from her bath in a damp cloud of floral scents. She shivered as Mrs Clayton wrapped linen around her shoulders.

'You are glowing, Your Majesty. The news of the prince's imminent arrival makes you well again.'

Caroline did not contradict her. She hobbled out of the tub, wincing against pain in her feet. They were prickly, as if she trod on a carpet of fine needles.

Mrs Clayton guided her into the bedroom and sat her by the fire.

'Mrs Howard is still not here,' Caroline observed, holding her arm out for the ladies to dry. 'What is she about?'

Mrs Clayton smirked. 'Hiding, I expect. The mere sight of her makes the King explode.'

Caroline smiled. Contentment sat in her lap like a warm, satisfied cat. It served Henrietta right, after her shameless begging and underhand tricks. What did she mean by asking for more money? It was bad enough that Caroline had to keep George's slut under her own roof – she was not going to pay for the pleasure too.

The little witch must have thought she had won, with her evil rumours and poisonous poems, when George agreed to pay her thirty pieces of silver. But at what cost had she purchased them? She had proven herself worse than a bloodsucker, for at least leeches dropped off when they had drunk their fill. George would not forget this treachery.

'Shall I fetch the basin, Your Majesty?' Mrs Clayton asked.

'Not at all. We will wait for Mrs Howard. I particularly wish her to perform this duty.'

A clock ticked by the minutes. At last, Henrietta bustled in, flurried and discomposed. Her face was wrapped in a quantity of handkerchiefs, like a person with the toothache.

'Mrs Howard. You are late – again.'

She blushed and dropped into a curtsey. Without responding to the chide, she moved to the washstand and fetched a basin of water.

Caroline peered down and saw her own face reflected in the smooth liquid; smug and twinkling with humour. She had the upper hand at last. It was delicious.

'Kneel, please, Mrs Howard.'

Henrietta remained standing. Her fingers shook on the edge of the basin. Caroline blinked and tilted her head.

'Do I speak into your bad ear, Mrs Howard? I told you to kneel.'

Two red spots flared in Henrietta's cheeks. Her dull eyes ignited like lumps of coal. 'No, Your Majesty. I remain still merely from surprise. You have never requested this before.'

Caroline's lips stretched into a grin. She would enjoy this. She would have Henrietta know her place: on her knees before her queen. 'I find, however, from old records, that it is protocol in the English court. I would wish for things to be done properly.'

The ladies tittered. Henrietta wavered. For a second, her knees bent. Then her face changed and she stood tall. 'No. I will not do it.'

Caroline laughed. 'Now I am sure it is *I* who cannot hear aright. What did you say, my good Howard?'

'I won't do it.'

'Yes, dear Howard, I am sure you will. Indeed you will. You do not wish to displease me?'

Henrietta's features twitched with bottled rage. Calmly, Caroline held her gaze.

'I will not kneel, Your Majesty.' Henrietta thrust the basin, sloshing water, into Mrs Clayton's hands. 'I do not believe it is the correct form.'

Such pride, for a beggar! 'Fie, for shame! My little daughters never made such a display. Go, my good Howard, you are not yourself. Go, and we will talk of this another time.'

Trembling with anger, Henrietta turned and left the room. The moment the door shut, Caroline erupted in giggles. She took Mrs Clayton's hand.

'Oh, Clayton. Forgive me. That was too good.'

~ ~

'It cannot be true. Ask Lady Betty again.' Henrietta paced the room. After all she had done for Caroline! How dare she treat her like a worm, a chicken bone to be tossed from the window when gnawed clean?

'Calm yourself, my dear madam,' Dr Arbuthnot said. 'Will you not sit and take a dish of tea? This agitation does you no good, after your operation. You need to rest and recover.'

He was right. Agony seared along her jawline, making her dizzy. She slumped down in a wingchair and raised her hand to her forehead. A surgeon had bored a hole into her jaw to relieve the pressure on her ear, but so far she felt no benefit. The blisters Dr Arbuthnot administered did not help; nor did the gillyflower syrup, or the slices of onion she placed on her pillow. The only advice he had left was to shave her head. She could just imagine Caroline's glee if she did that.

Dr Arbuthnot stole over and laid a hand on her shoulder. 'You will have to kneel when holding the Queen's basin,' he said softly. 'Also when serving her at table. Lady Betty confirmed that Mrs Masham performed these ceremonies in Queen Anne's reign.'

Could she subject herself like a base reptile? Curtseying to the woman was bad enough; the thought of bending the knee to help her wash was insufferable. 'The Queen used to be my friend. Once, I would have knelt to her willingly.'

Dr Arbuthnot sighed. 'Indeed. But power can warp a person. Not everyone retains their sweetness like you, Mrs Howard.'

Memories flashed before her eyes: Caroline weeping; the remnants of her miscarried children; the fateful day at Richmond, when Caroline had asked her to become George's mistress. 'Does she not recall the kindness I have shown her? Shall all our goodwill turn to dust?'

Dr Arbuthnot glanced at the window as hooves clopped in the distance. 'You speak of her as an ordinary person. She is royalty. She sees your service as nothing more than her due, and your duty.'

She raised her head and looked Dr Arbuthnot in the eye. 'Did Lady Betty say what happens to a discarded mistress? I never stopped to think of it before.'

'You are not cast off yet. If I know the King, he will keep you for the pleasure of having someone to shout at.'

'My good fortune knows no bounds.'

A rap at the door. Before Daniel could open it, John burst into the room. He held his hat in one hand, a cane in the other. 'Hetty!'

'John! What are you doing here?' She fell into his embrace. He smelt of home; Norfolk air, the trees of Blickling Hall. Behind his coattails she saw her niece, Dorothy, offering a shy smile. Her heart hitched.

'Hetty, you will never guess. Look at this.' He produced a paper and pressed it into her hands. It was good quality; smooth and silken.

'What – what is it?'

John beamed. 'It's the deed of separation. That extra money from the King did it. You are free, Hetty.'

She blinked. The knowledge hovered over her mind like a mayfly on a pond; it hesitated before dipping beneath the surface. 'Free?'

John took the deed from her and read. '*Henceforth during their joint lives there shall be a total and absolute separation between them. Mr Howard must not by any means or pretence whatsoever claim, seize, retain or detain the said Mrs Howard.*' He looked up. 'See?'

Dorothy crept forward, twisting her hands together. 'I am allowed to stay with you now, Aunty. Now that my evil uncle cannot grab us.'

Their happy faces tilted. In another second, Henrietta sunk into her brother's arms and lost all consciousness.

～ ～

Nerves squirmed in Caroline's belly. She stood and paced by the window again, watching carriages scythe through the slush in the streets. Their bobbing lamps oozed light onto the melting snow, but she could not decipher the crests on the carriage doors. Anticipation half-blinded her. Fred was coming. Her firstborn, her son. Another instant, and they would breathe the same air.

She took a chair by the fire and smoothed out her taffeta skirts. She had chosen a deep royal blue, lustrous as a sapphire. One of the dogs sighed and flopped down on a leather cushion to her right. William scuttled over and stroked its silken ears. Caroline watched him, apprehension tying knots inside her chest. Perhaps she should not have William in the room. Fred would come to her apartments first; they had agreed. Now he would walk through the door and come face to face with his replacement. The boy they had petted and spoilt; the child they had loved so much that they had almost forgotten their firstborn. She rose in a rustle of taffeta and prowled around the room.

'You'll wear out the carpet, Mama.' William looked up at her, mischief glimmering in his face.

She pulled her lips into a false smile. 'I feel the cold, love. Walking keeps me warm.' Actually, walking shot arrows of pain through her legs and abdomen, but it was better than remaining still.

Would Fred like her? She had not stopped to ask herself the question before. Did nature prompt a child to love its parents, whatever its age? She had heard Fred enjoyed poetry, music and art. These were pleasures she could share with him, but they were unlikely to endear him to George. How would she manage to juggle the two of them?

The door creaked. Caroline wheeled round, every inch of her skin electrified.

'The Prince of Wales, Your Majesty.' A blast of bitter air swept across the threshold. In a flurry of sleet, a slim young man entered the room. He was small and delicately made, rather pretty, except for his long nose. Flakes of snow melted into his fine, fair hair, as blond as Caroline's own. He regarded her with wide, grey eyes like a cat.

He bowed. 'Your Majesty.' His voice rumbled from deep within his chest, shocking her with its masculinity. Mouse-coloured velvet clothed his slender figure, sparkling with silver embroidery and scarlet trimmings. Silk stockings highlighted his legs, bandy and skinny like Caroline remembered them. Wet patches crept up his ankles where he had walked through the snow.

'Fred?' Stupidly, she had hoped he would run to her like a child. But there was no recognition in the smooth, handsome face. He merely looked cold and tired. William crept up to her side. She grabbed his small hand. This boy was hers. He would not mutate as suddenly as Fred. 'How was your journey?'

Fred frowned. 'I am afraid it was terrible, Your Majesty. We were nearly lost on a marsh and then our carriage slipped off a dyke into deep water. It's a miracle no one was killed.'

Guilt needled her. If she had been more insistent, if she had persuaded George, he would have had a guard of honour. 'Goodness,' she said lamely. 'Do sit by the fire and warm yourself.'

He moved to the flames, spreading his hands. 'Our boat was almost swamped by ice flows.' His lower lip jutted, a ghost of his childhood pout. 'Then the roads were so bad, I had to alight at the Friary and walk here.'

'Sounds like an adventure!' William cried. 'Did anyone freeze? I heard a man froze solid on top of the mail coach last week and they had to chisel him off.'

Caroline took her boy's arm. 'Now, William, be patient. I have not even introduced you to your brother Frederick yet. Have some manners.'

Fred rubbed his eyes. He was clearly exhausted, but he flashed William a lazy smile. 'Oh, I don't mind, Your Majesty. Let the Duke of Cumberland sit by me and I'll tell him about my travels.' Crowing, William flew to his side.

Caroline watched her sons chatter in the firelight. She wanted to hold Fred's face up to a magnifier and examine every pore. His English was good – better than her own, for he had mastered the accent. Pride stirred within her and yet . . . The onslaught of emotion she had expected did not come. There were so many things she was supposed to feel, but did not. Time had skewed the natural order of things. After a lifetime of separation, Fred was just a strange young man.

'You regard me very intently, Your Majesty.'

Your Majesty again. *Mama* had faded with his childish, piping voice. 'Of course I do. It has been so long.' Nervously, she smiled. 'You are not as I remember you.'

'No,' he said. 'And you are not as I remember you.'

Her smile faltered on her lips. She had not thought of that: Fred, keeping a mental image of her. She feared he was disappointed by the changes he saw. She fiddled with the pendant at her neck, feeling large and ungainly under his gaze. 'Perhaps you would like to see your sisters? They have changed greatly. And you have not even met Mary or Louisa.'

'Yes, I would like that.' He stood, brushing down his breeches.

'Well then, follow me.' Caroline glided down the corridors, her sons in her wake. William's familiar trot echoed on the floorboards but Fred's step overpowered it, slow and strong. She was taut with nerves. After Fred's tomfoolery with the Prussian princess, he could not expect a particularly warm welcome from George.

They turned into the King's Presence Room, where the family were assembled. Anne was speaking but George held up his hand and stopped her as Caroline crossed the threshold. Sick with anxiety, she watched her husband cock his head to one side and assess Fred, as if he were searching him for a good slice of meat.

'Your Majesty, may I present the Prince of Wales?' To Caroline's horror, he returned Fred's courtly bow with a mere nod. She shivered as chills from the past wrapped their cold arms around her. It was like watching George with his own father.

'Well then, let me get a look at you. See what sort of fellow Georg Ludwig has made you into.'

Fred coloured as George stood and paced round him, inspecting him head to foot. 'I – I have every reason to be grateful for my grandfather's kind care of me,' he stuttered.

George grinned horribly. 'I'm sure you do.'

Anne scowled. She would be the last to welcome her brother. Up until now she had enjoyed the position of eldest child, but Fred's arrival would strip all her privileges away. To her, he was nothing but a usurping cuckoo. Carrie cringed, nervous as always. At the other side of the room, Emily sat with little Mary and Louisa. Leading strings hung from their shoulders. Their small faces were pale and stretched, terrified to see a stranger.

Lights flashed behind Caroline's eyes. It was not meant to be like this. She remembered a summer day at Herrenhausen, before the throne, before England. A tiny Fred rode on George's shoulders, shrieking and swinging a twig like a whip. Anne and Emily toddled behind them, eyes wide with adoration. Caroline's own laugh rang through the gardens as she sat watching. The image faded. Reality confronted her; stone-faced figures, speaking with cold formality. Their eyes were dull, bled of affection. It was not a family now.

1729 – 1731
CHAPTER THIRTY-ONE

✲ Marble Hill ✲

Henrietta's dream stood before her, complete and flawless. Marble Hill rose up in proud white stucco and cast its shadow over her companions: Dorothy, Gay, Pope, Lady Betty and Berkeley.

'Aunt Hetty, why are you crying?' She reached down and clasped Dorothy's hand. She did not want to ruin the moment with speech. She was content to listen to the men hollering from their barges and the clop of dray horses negotiating the tow path. Underneath all the noise flowed a note of birdsong, golden and sweet. Sound was pure here. Henrietta didn't struggle to catch a pitch or live in a world of muted voices. Perhaps Dr Arbuthnot's treatments had worked after all. 'Aunt Hetty?'

'I am happy, my love.' Her words came out in a sigh. She was like a girl in love; stunned, breathless. 'I suppose I never really thought it would happen.'

Dorothy tugged at the ribbons securing her hat. 'That's silly. You paid money for the house and you ordered it. Of course it was built.' Let her go on believing that. At ten years old, Dorothy would not understand that life could crush even the most reasonable plans.

Music rose from the river. Henrietta turned as a gilded barge drifted past, packed with courtiers. Ladies held up parasols to shield their delicate complexions from the sun.

'The yearly trip to Hampton Court.' Lady Betty eyed Henrietta askance. 'Will you follow them, or stay here?'

She went giddy. She placed her free hand against the wall of her new house, which was warm like fresh baked bread. How to explain that the concept of total freedom was terrifying to one who had lived so long in a cage?

'I will have to ask the Queen's permission to retire from my post. She must release me.'

It would take a great deal of courage to make the request. And what would George think? Would he keep paying her if he did not see her, day after day? Without his generosity, she could not hold up the terms specified in her deed of separation. She was at his mercy.

Henrietta sighed, astonished to think how times had changed. Who would have imagined, all those years ago in Herrenhausen, that she would ever beg to leave the court?

'Come,' said Gay. 'Show us inside.'

The door was surrounded by rustic keystones and topped with a fanlight. Henrietta studied every tiny detail as she led her guests through, astonished to see her drawings brought to life. They entered the large square hall. It was fitted out in Roman style, with four Corinthian pillars supporting the ceiling. Black and white flags spread over the floor, reflected in two mirrors. Light flooded through the room, making the yellow walls glow like honey. Henrietta sighed, content.

'Palladian style,' Berkeley observed. 'Everything structured and orderly.'

Lady Betty widened her eyes. 'It is more masculine than I

expected, my dear. Where are all your pretty things?'

Henrietta laughed. 'Come and see.' She took them through to another room where they stopped and gasped. Set off against snow-white panelling, George's gift of mahogany had been shaped into a staircase. Its finely turned balustrades glowed from extensive polishing. Swirling floral motifs were carved into the side of thick, deep steps. Without waiting, Fop and Marquise pushed past Henrietta's skirts and hobbled up the stairs, their paws scrabbling on the wood. They were starting to show their age. 'Shall we follow?' Henrietta hitched her skirts and mounted the staircase. The bannister was cool and silky beneath her hand. This was *hers*; not a stairway creeping down to the servant's quarters or a fine case she tip-toed up in the wake of the Queen.

Nerves and a sudden shyness arrested her as they turned right into the Great Room. She walked over to the lacquered black screen in the corner and awaited her guests' reaction. Everyone stared. Lady Betty's head tilted back, taking in the two-storey room of intricate white moulding and burnished gilt. A flock of golden cupids soared over the marble fireplace. On the pristine walls hung paintings by Van Dyke; Stuart kings and queens the house of Hanover had replaced. Claret curtains framed a view of the grounds.

'Is it . . . too much?'

Lady Betty placed a hand to her breast. 'My dear . . . It takes my breath away.' She passed to one of Henrietta's gold and marble side tables, which were decorated with peacocks.

Pope watched her. 'Ah, the peacock. Symbol of the goddess Hera – or do you favour Juno?'

Henrietta blushed, feeling Berkeley's eyes upon her. 'Come, now. You are too much of a poet. Goddess of love and marriage? In my house? I may be pushing a little out of my place with this room, but I would not go so far as that.'

'You have an exalted place,' Berkeley said. 'Ladies of your

position have been the grandest in the land. You need not disclaim.'

'I seek no distinction.'

Berkeley disarmed her with his lopsided smile. 'Perhaps you should.'

Her laugh was brittle, hopelessly artificial. 'What nonsense you talk, Mr Berkeley.'

Lady Betty flicked her gaze between them and cleared her throat. 'Well, the peacock tables are exquisite, whatever they symbolise. Shall we go downstairs and eat? I saw some fruit tarts I am sure Miss Hobart will do justice to.'

Dorothy squealed and ran ahead, the dogs galloping at her heels. The adults filtered out behind, with Henrietta and Berkeley at the rear.

'Will you not take my arm?' He offered his free one. 'I may walk with the aid of a stick, but I am not an invalid.' Cautiously, she slipped her hand beneath his elbow. Her palm felt large, strangely clumsy. 'I wonder at your decision,' Berkley said, looking about him. 'This is such a lovely house. Why won't you leave the King and take up permanent residence?'

Henrietta hated it when he spoke to her of the King. She tried another laugh, but it came out as stupid as the first one. 'Does one do that, Mr Berkeley? Simply leave a King? Surely I must wait to be dismissed.'

'His recent behaviour suggests you will be.'

She reared back, stung. Was George's cooling affection so obvious? 'If we are speaking candidly, sir, I must say I wonder at you, too. Why do *you* visit court? You have no place and your brother was pushed out of the Admiralty years ago. I run a great risk in simply allowing you here. The King loathes the very name of Berkeley. Why stay to have him ignore you?'

His eyes, warm as a cup of chocolate, turned on her. 'I thought that was obvious. I stay for you.'

She stumbled on the step. The others were far ahead now, almost in the entrance hall. Berkley paused at her side, watching her intently. 'Goodness.' Her heart thumped, pushing all anger from her body. 'How you flatter me. What would the King think?'

Nothing pleasant, she feared. He had told her never to see the Berkeleys again. She was playing with fire merely by asking them to visit. If he saw this man flirting with her . . .

'You do not love the King.' He reached out and pressed her hand.

Henrietta closed her eyes, her breath jagged. 'I am under the King's protection.'

'Would you consider mine?'

Her eyes snapped open. 'What – what do you mean?'

'Leave the King. I will care for you.'

No man had ever looked at her the way he did, right now, not even George. Her chest clenched. Could she trust it? Of course not. That was not how the world worked. This man did not really know her; he was dreaming. She pulled her hand from his and buried it under her apron.

'Mr Berkeley, perhaps you do not understand the terms of my separation. My husband has no right to me or my goods but I am, to all other extents and purposes, still his. I am not free to remarry, nor leave the King and Queen.'

He leaned close to whisper. 'I am willing to endure any kind of shame or scandal for you.'

Her heart thrilled, but she shook her head. 'You misjudge me, sir. My position with the King is not of my own creation. I was pushed, through duty and necessity, into his bed. I will not be mistress to two men.' She thought of Henry and his disapproval. It hardened her resolution. 'I have *some* pride.'

To her surprise, he laughed. 'Oh, yes. I am coming to know your pride very well. But let me take some hope. May I come to see you privately, here, at Marble Hill?'

For the first time, she considered him seriously. She had not thought him in earnest before; only a man wooing her for his party. But now she saw the feelings bare on his face and realised that the attentions she had taken for gallantry were a symptom of something deeper. Something she did not want. Experience had taught her the idiocy of committing herself into the hands of men. 'You will be wooing as a hopeless knight errant, sir. My niece will remain with us at all times and you will receive nothing but smiles from me.'

He bowed. 'Ah, a smile. That, my dear lady, is all I ask.'

Hampton Court

They entered the Public Eating Room to a flourish of trumpets. The crowd buzzed, pressing against a wooden rail that held them back. Henrietta kept her eyes on Caroline's train as it whispered over the floor in flashes of gold. The smell of meat drifted on the air, curdling with the perfume of courtiers.

Sunlight flooded through the tall windows, sparkling on silver plate. Pyramids of crystallised fruit adorned the table, a welcome splash of colour next to the dull green walls. This meal would be another long, arduous task. Henrietta's legs and lower back twinged in anticipation of standing for hours. She was only grateful that her hearing impediment dulled the roar of chatter and whining notes from the band.

She no longer felt part of the fabric of court; her mind was always elsewhere, rowing down the river to Marble Hill, strolling in the orchard. It was time to leave. No matter how scared she was, she had to find a chance to speak to Caroline and George. She had to make an effort, at least one bid, to be free.

The King and Queen took their armchairs. Prince Frederick and the elder princesses sat down on plush seats, while the little ones

314

took stools. Dishes of stewed venison and potted pork came into the room, passed from hand to hand through the servant's chain of command. Henrietta braced herself to receive a platter; it was heavy and hot to the touch. She removed the silver cover, leaning back as steam engulfed her face. Then she passed it on for Lady Bristol to carve.

After the food had been tasted for poison, Caroline and George were served on bended knee. The flow of food kept coming. Henrietta couldn't stop for a moment. When the first course was finally on the table, a mountain of flesh with rich sauces, Caroline tapped a knife against her glass. A page scuttled forward, picked it up and handed it to Henrietta. With sweat pouring down her forehead, Henrietta filled it from a jug.

As she fell back into rank, a flicker of movement behind the rail caught her eye. She turned her head and blinked. Surely not? But it was: a man in the Howard livery. The glass nearly slipped from her fingers. She slopped a little wine over the top as she passed it to Lady Bristol.

'Careless girl,' the elder woman muttered.

The man searched the room, clearly looking for something. Someone. Her.

Henrietta served the second course mechanically, her eyes fixed on him. He was well turned out and had a patient, resigned air as he leant on the rail. He was too neat to be one of Charles's servants. He must belong to Charles's brother, the Earl Edward. Fear clattered in her head like a pebble in a jar. Was Henry ill? Did Charles want more money?

There was a long, low creak that cut through her worry and set her teeth on edge. It sounded like trees groaning in a storm, but the weather was hot and still. Henrietta turned just in time to see the mahogany rail bend and splinter to pieces. With an almighty cry, people tumbled through the gap, wig over heel. Ladies' skirts flew into the air, flashing thighs and unmentionables right before the royals. Caroline put down her cutlery and laughed. While guards surged forward to control the chaos, Henrietta seized her moment. She slipped out of line and passed behind the other household servants.

The man in Howard livery darted forward to meet her. He bobbed a hurried bow. 'My lady.'

'What is it? Did the Earl send you?'

He hesitated.

'Quick, man!' Henrietta glanced over her shoulder. 'They are settling down, I must get back to my place.'

'The Earl that *was*, your brother-in-law. He is – he is dead, my lady.'

She started. 'Dead?'

'Yes, my lady.'

'I am very sad to hear it. I hope he did not suffer?' Edward had been a good man, despite his brother. He had taken Henry in when they went to Hanover and he would always have her thanks for that.

'No. The end was swift. But I come to tell you of his Will. He left the remainder of his fortune to you, my lady. Three thousand pounds.' The man cleared his throat. 'He did not want it going to . . . *other* relatives.'

Three thousand pounds! With this money, and Marble Hill complete, perhaps she could afford to retire from court. Live, fully, as herself. The dreams she had kept caged for so long flexed their wings. Freedom. Independence.

Her hopes jerked back as the chains around their ankles reached full length. Caroline. She must ask Caroline first.

'I am touched by his remembrance. Thank you for letting me know.'

'My late master's lawyer will call on you, my lady – '

Henrietta stole a glance at the table. She had to go back. 'Yes, yes. You must not call me *your lady*.' She looked at Caroline's smiling face, flanked by sparkling diamond earrings. 'I am a mere Woman of the Bedchamber.'

'But – my – my Lady Suffolk . . .'

She moved closer. 'I beg your pardon?'

The man crumpled his hat in his hands. 'My master died with no living issue. Your husband . . .'

Understanding slammed into her. She gasped. 'Charles is the Earl now. Lord Suffolk.'

The servant nodded. 'And you are Lady Suffolk.'

The hot room whirled. Was it possible? Had she risen from the ashes of poverty and humiliation to become a countess? 'My husband and I are separated,' she told him. 'Surely I am not entitled to . . .'

The man flushed. 'The matter has been examined. The title is yours.'

It hit her bloodstream like a shot of neat gin. At long last, her marriage to Charles had brought her something worth having. A countess could not be a Woman of the Bedchamber. Caroline would have to let her go or promote her. She glanced back at Caroline, a wry smile twitching the corner of her lips. Little did her royal mistress suspect, as she popped a cooked ortolan into her mouth, that her days of crowing over Henrietta were at an end.

St James's Palace

Could the day get any worse? Caroline closed her eyes as the door clicked again, willing the new visitor away. These people were like woodpeckers; hammering insistently at her composure. Couldn't they leave her in peace? She cracked open her eyelids and saw Walpole waiting in the corner. She exhaled, relieved. He would support her against Fred's youthful obstinacy. 'Ah, here is our minister. Let him make you see reason, if you will not listen to your mother.'

Fred's eyes darted away like two silver fish. 'Can we continue this conversation another time? In private?'

'No. We will finish it now. You have gone too far, Frederick. It is one thing to play jokes on the servants, but I will not have you harassing people outside of the palace.' She looked him up and down, trying to make him out. It was hard to believe the slim, urbane young man before her could behave with such wild animal spirits. Already he had formed a riotous 'Henry the Fifth' club and lost his seal to a woman of pleasure in St James's Park. 'Come, Fred. You know better than this. Tussling with the night-watch? Smashing windows? Is this how a prince behaves?'

He sniffed. 'No one objected to my behaviour in Hanover.'

'This is not Hanover. Hanover is a dunghill compared with England.'

'At least in Hanover I had an establishment. The King won't even give me my own house.'

'This is not about the King. This is about *your* conduct. You have offended peers. People whose children will make up your parliament one day. You must apologise to Lord and Lady Buckingham for damaging their property.'

Those wide, grey eyes gleamed like mercury. Caroline had a feeling Fred was made of that liquid; ever changeable, poisonous in large doses. '*They* should apologise to *me*,' he said loftily. 'Their men fired grapeshot, you know. I could have been killed.'

'A ball through the skull might have knocked some sense into you!' she snapped.

'My grandfather never quarrelled with my conduct.'

Caroline gasped, indignant. Of all the dirty, mean tricks! He was purposefully goading her. Well, two could play at that game. She had years of experience on him. 'Your grandfather was an ass. The greatest ass and beast that ever lived. You were a fool to love him. He did not correct your behaviour because he wanted you to fail. Do you think he was trying to make you into the perfect prince? No. He wanted you to grow into a torment to your father.'

Rage contorted Fred's features. Reddening up to his ears, he turned his back on her and stormed out of the room. As the door slammed, Caroline sagged into a chair. Had she gone too far?

Fred did not understand the situation – how could he? In his memory, Georg Ludwig was a welcome face, the only family member who came to visit his lonely home in Hanover. He could not grasp why his parents hated his grandfather. He never saw little Georgie on his deathbed, or his young mother weeping her heart out.

'I have dropped the leading strings with that one,' she told Walpole as he sat down opposite her. 'I'll never reclaim him. I was a ninny to think he would slot right back into the family.'

Walpole pushed his legs out before him and laced his fingers together over his stomach. 'I would not mourn the loss of *his* regard. He is childish, obsessed with flattery.'

'He may grow out of it.' Idly, she picked up a hand mirror and regarded herself. Her once porcelain skin was blotchy and red. Sweat dripped off her forehead. She wound a curl of limp hair round her index finger. At this rate, she would lose both her son and her husband. Surely George wouldn't look upon this flabby monstrosity with desire for much longer?

How had it come to this? A short time ago, she had held everything safe in the palm of her hand. Now the days brought nothing but trial and pain. She felt like an old woman; bereft and tired, staring at the bony face of death. It terrified her. She was only forty-eight.

'You have heard, I suppose, that I have an opportunity to lose my rival?' She cocked an eyebrow at Walpole. 'Howard has become a countess. I can either promote her or let her retire.'

Walpole smacked his lips together. 'Well, promote her. Mistress of the Robes would do nicely. Let her play with silk and muslins – it will distract her from politics.'

She stared at him. '*Promote* her? She is a fruit ripe to drop. I must push her out before she grows too mighty, too . . .' *Beautiful.* The word was on the tip of her tongue, but she held it there.

'It is not like you to fear a little competition.'

No, but she had never been in this much pain before. The nub on her stomach burned and gout pricked at her skin like broken glass, day after day. Her spirits were exhausted. It was all she could do to stand upright. But she could never tell Walpole that.

'You still have influence with the King,' he continued, rubbing his nose. 'He is nothing if not a creature of routine – and you are his oldest habit. You must not expect the lusts of youth at your age. Rely on your head for managing him if your charms no longer work.'

She yearned to strike him for his insolence, but how could she? He was only telling the truth. It was not fair. Inside she was still that curvaceous beauty who could charm George into anything with a smile. 'How you flatter me, Sir Robert.'

His black eyebrows wiggled. 'Come, you are a rational creature. And you know it is in your interest to keep Howard close. Make it up with her, if you can. Be bosom companions once more.'

She could never do it. Every night George visited Henrietta's apartments was a slap in Caroline's face. 'My mother's second husband had a mistress,' she murmured. 'An infernal strumpet. She was with him before we came to the country, and she kept her claws in all through the marriage.' Memories oppressed her; her ribs seemed to cave in. 'It was she who took all his goods and love. My mother received nothing but bruises.'

'With all respect, Your Majesty, your mother should have befriended the harlot. Think of it. The King will keep a mistress, no matter what you do. Better to have my Lady Suffolk: deaf, mild and impotent. The King will never take her political advice now, no matter how the Tories court and cajole her. If you push the woman away . . .' Walpole blew out his breath. 'I can't imagine what young, ambitious vixen the King might take up with.'

Maybe he was right. Why had she not thought of this? Jealousy had blinded her as effectually as a fever. Wise queens made their resentment yield to prudence, their passion to interest. 'Better the devil you know.'

'Precisely.'

She swallowed her gorge. Was she really reduced to this? Clutching at her husband by the tails of his coat; bestowing honours on the trull who slept in his bed. She, who had once ruled them all. 'I thank you for your honest advice. I'm sure when I have had time to digest it, I will not want to kick you as heartily as I do now.'

1732

CHAPTER THIRTY-TWO

⌒ *Marble Hill* ⌒

Pattern books and ladies' magazines littered Henrietta's breakfast parlour. She held a square of Irish plaid at arm's length to inspect the chequered colours. Mistress of the Robes was a role suited to her talents; a preoccupation with the visual, rather than the audible. She enjoyed working with material; feeling smooth silks and rich piled velvets beneath her fingertips, blending hues to create the perfect effect. Trapped in the grey and bleached world of Beak Street, she had pined to own something with a bit of colour. Now the Queen's wardrobe was her playground.

She should be content. She knew that. Free from the usual chores, she could spend time at Marble Hill and entertain her friends. But she could not shake off the knowledge that she would have been far happier if Caroline had allowed her to retire. Still, she was not at liberty. Her leash was just a little longer.

'So what do you think?' asked Lady Betty. 'Will the plaid do?'

'Hmm. I don't know. The fabric may work on the princesses,

but horizontal lines will do nothing for the Queen's figure.'

'We had a similar problem in Queen Anne's reign, I recall. Plumpness is the fashion, but there are limits. How does one flatter a shape like that? It has no fixed lines; it is like a lump of snow.'

Henrietta couldn't help laughing. It gave her a devilish satisfaction to know she had retained her looks into middle-age, while Caroline wilted. 'What makes it worse is that she refuses to wear a busk or boned stays.'

Gay coughed beside her. His breath came raw and hacking, loud enough to penetrate Henrietta's woolly eardrums. She placed the plaid on the table before her and pressed her fingers to his forehead. 'You are clammy,' she fretted. 'And very pale.'

His chapped lips stretched in the imitation of a grin. 'I'll live.'

Would he? At nearly fifty, he wouldn't shake a fever quickly. Henrietta's parents had died of less, and younger.

She sighed and glanced out the window. Dorothy and Jack galloped round the pleasure ground, wrapped up against the cold. Her dear departed dogs slept side by side at last in the frosty clay. Molly's son stood near their graves with a bilboquet, his tongue poking through his lips as he concentrated on swinging the ball into the cup. Rapid growth wherever she looked; the unnerving passage of time. The new generation were pushing through like green spears in spring soil. For Henrietta and her friends, the golden days were drawing to a close.

Panic slid down her gullet. Time was running short and like a fool, she had spent the best years of her life as a slave; first to Charles, then to George and Caroline. But what else could she do? The Queen held her in iron chains. She insisted that she could not do without her good Howard.

'Would you leave me now?' Caroline had cried. 'Leave me all alone, when I need you?'

And of course, she had not had the heart to say *yes*.

The servant left to fetch Gay a glass of warm water and wine, mixed with nutmeg and feverfew. He left the door ajar. A smiling, impish face peeked round the jamb from the hall. It was Berkeley. Henrietta's heart turned over.

'Ah, my brother!' cried Lady Betty. 'Lurking in doorways as usual.'

Berkeley edged in, leaning on his stick. His dark eyes hovered on Gay for a moment. 'My dear Mr Gay, you look done up. Shall you go upstairs and rest?'

So it was not just Henrietta's fancy; he really did look that ill. She ran a finger over the checks in the plaid. The dazzle of jewels and satins had blinded her. Gay had been visiting for days; she should have noticed his condition before now. She should have done something.

'No, but I thank you for your concern. Lady Suffolk has just ordered a nostrum. I am sure any medicine of hers will cure me.'

'I trust it will.' Berkeley heaved himself into an armchair. 'I too come seeking my lady's good offices.'

She could think of nothing but the swinging pendulum of the clock. She cleared her throat, trying to shake off her morbid thoughts. 'What may I do for you, Mr Berkeley?'

'I have been sent to request your presence in the hall. Lord Chesterfield, Lord Argyll and Mr Pulteney want your opinion on our plan.'

'Plan? You mean they want me to wheedle the King once again.'

'Not at all.' He returned her gaze frankly. 'Only to see if your views are the same as ours. You must know that Sir Robert Walpole is proposing something monstrous. If we catch him out, it could mean the end of him.'

Henrietta exchanged a look with Lady Betty. 'What? What could possibly do that?'

'It is called an Excise Bill.'

She leafed through the pages of her memory. Something was

familiar . . . 'Yes. I heard him speak of it, years ago at Chelsea. It was merely a notion back then, but I recall nothing outrageous in it . . .'

Gay coughed. The servant arrived with his medicine and he took a shaky sip. 'The government will make it *sound* honest. They always do.'

'It is an inland tax,' Berkeley explained. 'Another encroachment on English liberty. Where will it end?'

Inch by inch Walpole's fat shadow crept across the country, swallowing money. He devoured the people's rights as eagerly as he munched on little Norfolk apples. It was unnerving for any man to hold such sway.

'Here,' Gay croaked. 'Walpole's impudence must end here. And surely it will. If the people can be convinced that his Excise Bill masks a darker plan, a plan to take what is theirs, they will rebel.' His voice dried up and he coughed again.

Henrietta looked away. Confusing emotions stirred within her. Walpole did not deserve his power; should not be allowed such a monopoly. For England's good, he had to fall. But as soon as she made up her mind the royal couple loomed, chastising her. Walpole was their man. Could she act against him? Could she displease George openly? Looking at Gay's skin, shimmering with sweat, she steeled herself. 'Gentlemen, I believe you are right. Sir Robert's time has come. And if we seek to throw him down, we have an ally right inside the royal camp.'

'Aye,' said Berkeley. 'You, dear Lady Suffolk, are our mascot.'

She grinned at him. Her pulse leapt like a nervous hound. 'Oh no; far better than me. Prince Frederick himself.'

Kensington

Caroline poked her breakfast around its dish. Juice oozed from the berries and made red tributaries through the white mess of sour cream. She had to let her anger out somehow, and this was the only route available to her: squashing fruit with the back of her spoon.

Events over the past few weeks had astounded her. How could the Tories turn something so simple, not to mention useful to the country, into a furious row?

'I must be missing something,' she said to Hervey. She leant back in her plush chair and watched him, the pretty young man who was her vice-chamberlain.

'Your Majesty?' Hervey's long, tapered fingers stilled on the single biscuit he took for breakfast.

'You know Walpole well. Tell me truly; what does he mean to do with this Excise Bill? I thought it simply a measure to reduce the Land Tax by a shilling in the pound.'

'It is, and it ought to be simple. If we turn the customs payable on tobacco and wine into excises – that is, collect the duty inland, rather than on importation – it would raise enough money to reduce Land Tax.' He broke off a morsel of biscuit and popped it into his mouth.

'But this is absurd. It is a useful, helpful measure. Why do we have mobs outside Westminster? How is it that impudent boobies like Lord Stair barge into my chamber and insult me over this? Have my subjects run mad?'

'Indeed, Your Majesty, I believe they have.' Hervey took a sip of fragrant green tea. 'The common people think everything they eat, drink or wear will be excised. Some say Excise Officers will enter houses in the dead of night to search and fine.'

Frustrated almost to tears, Caroline threw down her spoon. 'How can they believe such tales? We are trying to help the people!'

'Opposition in the court strengthens the rumours. I heard a Tory say the Bill will make the monarchy absolute, and strip Parliament of its freedoms.'

The Tories, always the damned Tories. 'Which Tory? Give me a name and I will have him whipped!'

Hervey shook his head. 'The soldiers would not do your whipping, madam. Someone has convinced them that the Bill will raise the price of tobacco.'

Anger trembled through her. With so much pain in her body, she couldn't handle upsets as well as she used to; every violent feeling broke her. 'We will push on,' she hissed through gritted teeth. 'The fools must see sense, eventually.'

'Even if it puts Your Majesty's crown at risk?'

Caroline pushed the fruit bowl away. The rich, peppered aroma of her drinking chocolate turned her stomach. 'Why should it do that?'

Hervey's small, pink lips compressed. 'The Prince of Wales has remained silent so far, but you must know he is thick with the Tories. Also those who supported the Pretender in the last reign – Bubb Doddington, Bolingbroke, Carteret. He wants to be a people's prince. He will seize his moment. If the people turn against the King, the Prince of Wales will be there, ready to step up.'

Gooseflesh ran along Caroline's arms. It could not be true. Fred was difficult, but surely not openly hostile? 'We cannot give way out of fear. Can't you lead Fred away from this bad company? I thought you were keeping an eye on him for me?'

Hervey wrapped his hands around the cup of green tea and stared into it. 'Not a close enough eye, it would seem. May I speak frankly?'

'Always.'

'Then I must confess that I have not kept company with the Prince of Wales for some weeks. He has taken a lady from me, like some common knave, and got a child upon her.'

Caroline gripped the table. Her delicate, puny Fred, a rake? Just like his father and his grandfather before him; these Hanoverian men couldn't keep their breeches buttoned up. 'I thought he had a good heart,' she murmured. 'But he is a scoundrel. Why did you not speak of this before? Who is the lady?'

Hervey wetted his lips. 'Mistress Anne Vane.' The name seemed to cost him pain. 'Your Majesty's aptly named Maid of *Honour*.'

Right under her nose! How had she not noticed? The idea of a grandchild did not cheer her in the least. If Fred was against her and he had a child on the way, he could be dangerous. An heir, illegitimate or not, was still a threat.

She thought over Fred's sickly childhood, plagued by rickets and sniffles. No sign of a black heart there; no hint of manly prowess. Yet he loved to pretend. When his nurse scolded, convincing excuses rolled off his tongue. He liked show; fine clothes and expensive toys.

'It's a trick,' she realised. 'He's goading us. He wants me to throw Mistress Vane out on the street so he can bemoan my cruelty. How better to ingratiate himself with the people than with pity?'

Hervey frowned. 'He already complains, to anyone who will listen, that Your Majesty prefers me and neglects him.'

'Precisely. He wants me to take your side on this too. But the irony is, Mistress Vane must be carrying *your* child. Fred cannot produce sons.'

'How do you know?'

'I do not *know*,' she admitted. 'But I believe it. He has always been puny. And he drank goats' milk all through his childhood. I objected, for it is known to make a man impotent, but Georg Ludwig overruled me.'

'Your Majesty forgets I am also unwell, and have consumed my share of goats' milk and crabs' eyes beside. Yet I have fathered sons.'

Caroline bit her lip. She could not swallow his words. She did not *want* to believe Fred would have an heir and oust dear William from his place. 'It is *not* Fred's child,' she said decidedly. 'And it is not Fred's country. I will make him see that, if it's the last thing I do.'

1733 – 1734
CHAPTER THIRTY-THREE

～ St James's Park ～

Freezing mist wound its way through London. Ghostly grey and flecked with soot, it veiled the streets where the great scenes had played out; the mob that had rushed at Walpole in the House of Commons, the petition from the City of London. Now the noise and light had retreated, it was cold around the palace; as cold as the corpse of the Excise Bill. Even George's bubbling rage had crystallised. He sat rigid, an ice statue of a King, as his hunter frisked across the grass beside Henrietta and Dandy.

The horses' shoes rang against the hard ground. Visibility was poor. Fat-bellied clouds and fog obscured the winter sun, leaving only a strange, pearl light. Henrietta did not mind. She didn't care to see the expression on George's face.

'Look behind,' he demanded. 'Are the guard close?'

She made a cursory glance over her shoulder. 'Really, how am I meant to see? Do not trouble yourself. No angry mob would be able to find you in this mist.'

'I'm not afraid of the mob,' he replied hotly. There was a chink as he reached for his sword. 'If they came for me, I'd give them a damn good thrashing.'

'I don't doubt you would try, George. But they would overpower you and roast you alive if they thought it meant the end of this Excise Bill.'

George's spurs glinted through the fog. His hunter danced to the side. 'They are fools! It is my bill and my country. Walpole is *my* man now. Impertinent paupers! They do not know what they're talking about.'

Dandy threw his head up, jangling the bit. Steam plumed from his nostrils. His brown ears flicked back and forth, unnerved by the tension. Once, the flare of George's temper had made Henrietta uneasy too; now it disgusted her. What a pathetic, childish thing it was for a man to scream insults. He could not use his wit and solve a problem; he merely yelled at it, as if he could blow it away with the volume of his voice. 'They are talking about their freedom. Even your poorest subject is qualified to speak on that topic.' .

George wheeled his horse back toward her. Its hooves churned up the scent of cold leaves and frosted grass. 'What?'

She pulled Dandy to a halt. Her heart raced. The drifting mist shrouded George and gave her the courage to speak her mind. 'Lowering the land tax. Who does that benefit? The estate owners, the country squires. Not the poor.'

'Have a care, madam.' The threat in his voice carried through the fog.

'You forget I have been poor myself. I know what an extra tax means. Oh, you might say it is only a custom, collected inland. No doubt that is what the Queen and Walpole tell you. But the truth is, many people can only afford to buy their drink and tobacco from smugglers. If you stamp out smuggling, you are as good as taking bread from their mouths.'

There was a swish and a thwack as George's whip came down on his horse's rump. He appeared gradually through the mist. Dandy sidled at the apparition. She put a hand on his neck to steady him.

'I have come closer,' George growled, 'because I think you have forgotten whom you are talking to.'

She gritted her teeth on a spurt of temper. Enough, for now. He could make her poor once more, if he chose to, and her deed of separation would be jeopardised. 'I am sorry that our opinions differ on this subject. Shall we make our way back?'

He considered her. She stared down at Dandy's mane, uncomfortable beneath his gaze. Despite her schooled expression, despite the fog, she was sure he would see that her heart had changed toward him. That there was another man, far dearer, hovering around her.

'It is the company you keep,' he said slowly. 'Those damned Berkeleys.' Leather creaked as he adjusted his position in the saddle. 'Oh yes, I know you have seen them, despite my orders.'

She held Dandy a few paces behind him, safe from his lashing whip and the hunter's rear hooves.

'There's no end to the strife you have caused at my court. Compton, Gay, the Berkeleys. And the separation from your husband! It is as if you live to shame me.'

'You cannot blame me for separating from Charles. You know how he treated me.'

His snarling expression made her recoil. 'I know I paid a fortune to keep him at bay, even before your damned separation. Why did you need a legal paper too?'

How could she make him see? Any tie to Charles, legal or religious, sullied her. Her honour, her very soul, yearned to be free of him. 'I needed security.'

'Wanted to trap me into keeping up the payments, did you? You doubt my honour, now? Perhaps you are right. God knows, you do not deserve the wage I pay you.'

'You do not mean that,' she whispered.

He grunted. 'Don't look at me like that. I am not a monster; I will keep paying your husband, as agreed in the settlement. That's all you really care about. That is the only reason you took up with me.'

Henrietta flinched. It was so close to the truth that her conscience stung. 'No! I care for you.'

'If you did, you would relieve my sorrows, not add to them. You were supposed to be a consolation for me, a place of retreat. Now you are against me, just like Fred.' His eyes were cold as chips of ice. 'I tell you plainly, your dog of a friend Lord Chesterfield will be dismissed for his part in quashing my Excise Bill. If you so much as look at him again, or the damned Berkeleys, you will be dead to me.'

～ ～

Drizzle beat down upon the cobbles. Moonlight winked off their wet glaze. A stream of mud and offal slid down the street, washing Caroline's hopes with it. 'So it is over. We must give way.'

Hervey and Walpole shuffled behind her. With her back to them, she let tears spill over her lashes and fall down her face. Foolish, to cry over an Excise Bill. But defeat weighed heavy upon her chest, forcing her to lean forward and press her forehead to the window's cool glass. How had it all unravelled so fast?

Walpole cleared his throat. 'I fear we must. The clamour is too loud. I cannot carry a majority.'

Golden streaks lit up the western sky. The setting sun, or another mob burning effigies of her and Walpole? She wished she had been at the riots with the constables, drumming her foolish subjects over the head with a wooden club. 'Well, then. Tomorrow we surrender.'

'The King!' A servant announced.

Caroline turned at the sound of her husband's footsteps.

'So, you have heard?' George stalked over to the window seat and sat with a huff. 'Puppies, blockheads and whimsical fellows;

that's all I have in my Parliament. They threw out a bill which was for their benefit! Well, let them pay a higher land tax and be damned!'

'But the people will think they have won in a battle of wills against us. This looks like weakness. You must not allow – '

He jerked, reddening. 'Don't you start, madam. I have had enough bold-faced cheek from your servant, thank you. I will not tolerate any more.'

'Which servant?'

'Which do you think? My Lady Suffolk.' George clicked his jaw. 'In all my life, I never heard her carry on like she does about this Excise Bill. Very high and mighty she is, too! Deaf, peevish old beast! The title of countess has gone to her head.'

Caroline caught Walpole's eye. His advice cawed in her ears like a flock of crows. *Befriend the harlot. Imagine what young, ambitious vixen the King might take up with.* Vultures circled already; the girls' governess would leap into George's bed, given half a chance. 'Have patience, my love. Lady Suffolk is not herself; her friend Mr Gay is seriously ill.'

'What!' The word exploded from him as he rose to his feet. 'That scribbler? That hack? Of all the friends to cherish! I know very well what his Beggar's Opera was about, madam.' He gestured to Walpole. 'Mocking my minister! My government! If he was not already at death's door, I would run him through myself!'

A wave of pain took Caroline unawares. She clenched her teeth, trying to make it look like a smile. 'I agree, my love. Lady Suffolk keeps strange company. And it is ludicrous of her to start having opinions at her time of life. But I'm sure she will settle down, once her grief subsides.' She hoped she was right. Since building Marble Hill, Henrietta was unpredictable. She had a retort for every chide and a brisk, outraged step that made her skirts swell with air. Caroline's mild lady had gone.

'She had better settle down or she will be out on her ear. I have made it clear I will not speak to her if she sees Lord Chesterfield again.' He rubbed his hands together with a froth of lace cuffs. 'He'll be dismissed immediately for the part he played in scuppering our Bill.'

Unease tugged on Caroline's skirts. They could hardly afford to make more enemies. 'Mutiny must be punished, of course. But do you think we ought to wait until the cry has settled down? Already, our standing with the people – '

'Damn the people!' George slammed his palm against the wall, making picture frames shake. 'They are *my* people. They should bow to my will.'

But they never would. Without the contrary nature of the English, George would not have a crown on his head in the first place. The people chose their own kings now; blood meant very little, divine right nothing at all.

Walpole wet his lips. 'Her Majesty may remember that I spoke to the King some time ago, about a marriage for the Princess Anne.' Caroline's stomach folded in. She didn't want to hear it. 'Earlier today, the King and I discussed the subject once more. We feel now may be the perfect time for a royal wedding.'

George nodded. 'Give the mobs something to gawp at. They will forget their blasted freedoms when the fountains flow with wine.'

Caroline had no plausible argument against it. Anne was desperate to wed; she always had been. But the idea of separation was unbearable. 'Whom do you consider?'

Walpole's eyes slid away. 'A fine Protestant match, Your Majesty. One always popular: the Prince of Orange.'

Her heart seized. The English loved the House of Orange for the sake of King William, who had saved them from Catholic despotism. But the current prince was no match for her darling. 'Is he not deformed? Or a dwarf? I heard something of the like . . .' She began to pace like George, her panniers swinging. 'This would be a fall in consequence for Anne. She will not do it. Why, he has not twelve thousand pounds a year!'

George stopped by the fireplace. 'She will marry him if I tell her to,' he grunted. 'Ring for her now – we will discuss it.'

A servant moved and a bell echoed in a distant part of the palace. Its sound throbbed through Caroline as though it were a tocsin. The thought of her daughter, stuck in some awful backwater with an ugly man . . . 'Shouldn't we marry Frederick instead?' she tried desperately. 'It is more fitting, for the succession.'

George goggled at her. 'Have you run mad? Give that puppy a co-conspirator? You would have some sassy, upstart princess winning over the people. We would have to increase his allowance and give him houses of his own. Has he deserved that, from his behaviour to you?'

'Very well. But if it *is* to be Anne, surely there must be some better match for her . . . '

'There is none,' Walpole admitted. 'Unless you want her to marry a Catholic.'

'No, that will never do.'

Anne's footsteps rang on the floorboards outside.

George looked at her earnestly. 'You know, Caroline, this prince's appearance might not be so bad. And our girl is hardly a beauty herself.'

Caroline's retort died on her tongue as Anne sailed into the room. Looking objectively, George was right. Anne's plump bosom burst over her bodice and her stays creaked as she walked. A lace cap hid her golden hair and fell into pleats framing her round face. Pits speckled her skin where the smallpox had been. The scars made her look wrinkled, older than twenty-five.

George sighed. 'Well, then. Sit, child.' Anne pushed up her carmine skirts and took a chair. 'We have been discussing your marriage, Anne.'

Her eyes glittered. 'At last! Will I be a queen?'

Something twisted within Caroline. She looked down and toyed with the lace at the crooks of her elbows, deliberately avoiding Anne's gaze.

'No,' George confessed. 'Though perhaps the wife of a Stadtholder, one day.'

'The Prince of Orange, then.' Anne exhaled. 'I thought so. There's not really another choice, is there?'

So she had been studying the houses of Europe. How pitiful to think of her poor daughter pouring over genealogies, desperate for a mate, finding only one solution.

'He is two years younger than you.' George's voice turned gruff; perhaps he had misgivings too, now Anne sat before him. 'But very amiable, by all reports. I fought alongside his father; he was a fine man.'

Anne shifted on her seat, sending up a waft of jasmine. 'Well, I must marry. I pray God will preserve you for many years Papa, but I cannot be here when Frederick's reign comes. I hate the fellow.' George snorted. 'Mama? What do you think?'

Caroline squeezed her eyelids shut. 'I understand . . .' Her voice drained away. She tried again. 'I have heard there may be some physical *abnormalities* about the man. But he is the only option you have.'

'That's settled, then.' Anne brushed her skirts. 'I must have a husband. The Prince of Orange is my only chance. I would marry him even if he were a baboon.'

'Well, it will be something from the menagerie,' George muttered.

CHAPTER THIRTY-FOUR

⌁ *Hampton Court* ⌁

Henrietta assessed Caroline's mantua, checking her subordinates had performed their duties. She nodded her approval. The taffeta was steamed and someone had brushed all the grease out from the lace with bran. They dressed Caroline in her private bedchamber, these days; a room of light, wood panels and gold carving.

Outside, metal clanged and saws rasped as workmen built a new wing for Prince William to entertain his teenage friends. Though George maintained he couldn't increase Fred's allowance and that the proposed excises had been entirely necessary for the economy, he was sparing no expense on his second son. Nothing but the finest materials – a whole suite of blue mohair.

Caroline stood by the bed like a dress-maker's poppet. Her chemise lay smooth and white against her wrinkled, greying skin. Only canvas stays, like those for a child, gave her body any shape. But without boning she was wobbly, ever shifting, her flesh like uncooked dough. Silver clocked stockings stretched taut over her feet. Beneath, the skin was swollen and shiny, reminding Henrietta of overripe fruit. Garters sat above her knees, but she did not need

them to hold her stockings up; the difficulty would be peeling th
fabric away from her legs at night. She winced as the ladies tied th
tapes of her panniers, settling a weight of whalebone and iron on he
hips. It seemed a shame to hurt her so in the cause of fashion. Sh
was wide enough without the cage. Once Henrietta had envied he
looks. She had thought the court and the princess the very essenc
of magic, glittering like diamonds, but now she scratched the sur
face and found it was mere paste.

She turned her attention to the jewel box, deciding which woul
go best with Caroline's dusky lavender gown. A silver broach for th
bodice, amethysts for the ears. She laid them out on a square o
velvet and presented them for Mrs Clayton to fasten on. How sagg
and loose Caroline's neck looked above the sleek bodice of her dress
Her once magnificent bosom still drew the eye, but it was no longe
a pleasure to look at. Henrietta tilted her head. A necklace wouldn'
do; it would only highlight the flaws. A fichu was the only option
She fetched one and smoothed the material around Caroline's neck
It felt like an act of charity to cover the aging Queen's shame. A
she went to tuck the fichu down the bodice, their eyes met. Th
sharp blue of Caroline's irises had drained; they were watery, bleed
ing into the whites. They held a desperate question Henrietta coul
not answer. Hurriedly, she looked away.

Just then the door slammed open and George swept into th
room. All the ladies fell into curtseys. Without speaking, he stalke
over, put up a hand and ripped the fichu from Caroline's neck. Sh
exclaimed as the material whispered across her skin.

'Get rid of this trash, Lady Suffolk,' George demanded. H
crumpled the fichu in his hand and tossed it to the floor. 'You onl
seek to hide the Queen's neck because your own is ugly.'

The ladies gasped and tittered. Mrs Clayton pushed to th
front, anxious to see.

Henrietta found his arrows did not hurt her; she had develope a shield. 'I was not hiding her neck,' she muttered beneath her breath. 'I was protecting it. I perceived Your Majesty was in one of your rages and feared you may worry the Queen by the jugular.'

George's eyes popped. 'What did you say?'

'Nothing, Your Majesty.'

What had happened to the George who wept to think of Henrietta parted from her son? Where was the prince who had showered her with gifts? Age changed a man, it seemed. Patience grew short, opinions became set in stone. As the years of his life fell away, there was less room for manoeuvre.

Caroline's hands fluttered like tiny birds. 'Softly now, George. There's no need to shout at Lady Suffolk. I asked for the garment, but of course I will leave it off if you wish.'

'You need to keep your staff in better order, madam,' he barked.

Caroline's voice rose up. 'The employees of my household are my own business. Lady Suffolk has been with me for years.'

Henrietta stared at her; that sloping nose, the defiant lift of her thin eyebrows. Where had this spirited defence come from? A few years ago, Caroline would have been glad to see Henrietta dressed down. Now she was protecting her.

'More fool you! She is not a loyal servant. You know she was against our Excise Bill. Why do you keep her?'

Caroline burst into tears. Mrs Clayton stopped snickering and turned white. The Queen had never cried over trifles before. 'Is it not enough that my own daughter is being taken from me?' she sniffed, eyes blazing. 'Can't you let me keep one attendant? Is that so much to ask?'

Henrietta retrieved a handkerchief and pressed it into Caroline's hand. She felt ashamed. This was a sick woman, desperate to keep a shred of familiarity in her disintegrating life. She should be taking better care of her . . .

A knock at the door.

'Who the deuce is that?' George ripped off a shoe and threw it at the startled page who appeared behind the jamb.

'F-forgive me, Your Majesty,' the boy stuttered as he ducked. His wide, brown eyes took in the outraged King and the weeping Queen. 'They told me the Queen was walking in the gardens with the princesses.'

'And so I should be,' said Caroline, blotting her face. 'I was delayed. Come in, child, do not be afraid.'

Gingerly, the page picked up George's scuffed shoe and sloped into the royal presence. He regarded the King like the tiger in Kensington's menagerie.

Henrietta took pity on him. 'Who have you come for?' she asked gently. 'You do not want the Queen, if you thought she was walking outside?'

He shook his head. 'No. I have a message for *you*, my lady.'

Her field of vision narrowed, focusing on the note in his hand. She held out a trembling palm for it. She did not recognise the writing. She tucked it into her pockets, where it hung burning against her thigh.

'I am ready,' Caroline announced. 'I will walk with my daughters. You may retire to read your letter, Lady Suffolk.'

Bobbing a curtsey, Henrietta pressed a coin into the page's palm and grabbed his shoulder, steering him out of the room with her.

'Aye, get off with you! Look how you have upset your kind mistress!' George's voice blared behind them. Henrietta kept walking without looking back. Something slammed into the wall as she crossed the threshold – perhaps George's other shoe.

When they were safe behind the closed door of the supper room, she turned to the boy, eager with questions. But the moment her hand left his shoulder he twisted and fled. Sighing, she settled herself into a crimson chair beside the empty fireplace.

She took the letter from her pocket and held it on her lap. Her index finger dithered over the seal, pressing the wax imprint. She took a breath and cracked it open.

It was from a law firm in Saffron Walden, near Audley End House. Her eyes skittered over the page. She would find it in a moment: some new demand from Charles, some clause that made their separation invalid. But then she focused on a word and her eyes skidded to a halt. Was it possible? She leapt up and stumbled over to the window, holding her letter under a pool of sunlight. Dear God! Charles was dead!

She dropped to her knees. Those hands that hit her were cold and still; that black heart extinguished. Finally, the chain coiled about her waist fell rattling to the floor. He was dead, and she was free of him.

St James's Palace

Of all the things Caroline had wanted for Anne, this was not one of them. Iced with diamonds, the princess drifted through the Chapel Royal. Blue silk swathed her frame, glinting where its silver embroidery caught the candlelight. Pearls fastened a cape to her shoulders. Her train flowed on for six yards, a shimmering river born by ten bridesmaids. Anne's golden hair glowed beneath her coronet. She had desired so much more than that delicate headpiece: a crown or sceptre. She would get neither.

Mr Handel's music swelled, trembling through the crowd. Crimson taffeta, studded with golden roses, transformed the chapel into a jewellery box. There were galleons, fringes, gilt lustres and tassels; everything Caroline could find to make the space beautiful. But there was no disguising that bridegroom. From her throne beside the altar, Caroline dissected him with her eyes. His face was not bad; pleasingly round with frank, arching brows and a small mouth. His chocolate eyes reminded her of William's spaniels. But if this poor Prince of Orange had been born a dog, he would have been shot. His body sprawled at odd angles like a tree twisted at the root. A peruke wig covered his hunched shoulder, yet it could not hide his odd proportions; a short waist, legs that seemed entirely thigh with no calf at all. Could such a monstrosity sire children? If so, what sort of animals would they be?

Caroline had wanted a handsome, dashing prince for her Anne. A man who would be strong and protect her, not one that fell ill with pneumonia at a breath of English wind. Fred appeared stunningly handsome by comparison, coated in cloth of gold. Only his thunderous expression marred his appearance as he escorted Anne toward her bridegroom, taking care to let only the tips of her fingers rest on his arm. His grey eyes, hard as steel, fixed on Caroline. *Where is my wedding?* they asked. *Where is my bride; my regular allowance?* She did not have room for his grievances. She was full to the brim with her own sorrows.

Pain rumbled through her stomach, down her legs. The old complaints. She would have to sit for hours yet, pretending she was well. But at least she did not have to feign happiness. George snuffled beside her. From beneath their canopy of state, little Mary and Louisa blubbered too. At last, Caroline could cry. All her fine dreams turned to this: a husband bored of her, a son who hated her and her daughter, married to a baboon.

Fatigue wrapped Caroline in a suffocating embrace as they escorted the newlyweds to their bedchamber. She had no stomach for wedding traditions: the loving posset; tossing stockings to see who would marry next. It was bad enough that Anne had to climb into bed beside this mangled combination of ill-fitting limbs. Could they not leave her alone with her shame?

'I have put up a screen.' George leaned in and spoke to her from the corner of his mouth. 'He can get changed behind a curtain and just slip into bed from there. The people will only see his cap and a flash of brocade nightgown.' Was it compassion, or embarrassment that made George so considerate? She hardly cared.

Courtiers gathered round the bed, each with an orange ribbon or cockade in honour of the groom. George scowled as he gripped the prince's short arm and steered him behind the curtain. Caroline, Emily and Carrie took Anne, drooping and ring-eyed from exhaustion, into a separate chamber to undress her.

The door was hardly closed before Emily burst out. 'Lord, Anne! Nothing on earth would induce me to marry that monster! Whatever will you do, with his pudgy fingers touching you?'

Quick as lightning, Caroline spun and slapped her around the ear. 'Insolent wench!'

Anne swallowed and held up her arms to be unlaced. 'Do not concern yourself, Mama. I am satisfied. He seems to be a good man and I will try to make him happy.'

Carrie sidled up to her sister and helped the ladies take off her gown. 'To be sure, his figure is not good. But I believe, in your situation, I should have come to the same resolution.'

'Exactly. Emily is only bitter. No man, monstrous or not, will take her.' Caroline spoke with a cheerfulness she did not feel. Now Emily had planted the image, she saw it: Anne's tender young flesh and his gnarly body, entwined.

Emily rolled her eyes. 'Oh, don't worry about me. Soon I will be in Bath, with all the beaux falling at my feet. But I would rather stay single than choose a husband from the Orange menagerie.'

Anne looked tiny and fragile in her nightgown. Caroline pushed forward and embraced her.

'I have never had any sorrows over you, dear heart. Even this first one is blended with pleasure. Orange seems a good man and will always be a favourite with me.' How easily the lies slid from her tongue. But there was no point in crying over what might have been. Anne had made her bed now, and there was nothing to do but teach her how to sleep in it comfortably. 'It will hurt at first,' she whispered through Anne's golden hair. 'But the pain eases. Pretend it is pleasurable to you. After a while, it will become so.' The cold shoulders stiffened beneath her arms. 'You have come through smallpox; this is nothing.'

Anne nodded. Resolution set in her face. If anyone could skim the cream from this sour milk, it was her. She would find a way to live in a dull court, love a deformed husband. Caroline only wished she could be there to support her through it.

'I am ready,' Anne croaked. Her step was steady as they left the chamber; she looked every inch a happy bride. Only Caroline felt her fingers fidget on her arm, clammy to the touch.

By the carved state bed, Lady Suffolk pulled back the sheets to let the bride in. Planting one last kiss on Anne's cheek, Caroline stepped away from the bed. George shoved the Prince of Orange into his side with a flash of stubby legs and curved shoulders.

Black spots danced before Caroline's eyes. Pain throbbed inside and out. Through the rushing in her ears, she heard ladies murmur, shocked by their glimpse of deformity. It was all she could take. She had to leave.

CHAPTER THIRTY-FIVE

~ *Marble Hill* ~

Henrietta and Berkeley sat together in the breakfast parlour. They were oddly shy. Her black skirts filled the space between them, a vivid reminder of the man who had once stood in their way and was no more. Everything had changed.

Light fell through the window, dappling plates of untouched meat upon the table. The sun was low in a pale blue sky; summer was dying fast.

'Please reconsider. Bath would do you the world of good. My sister and I could take you in our carriage.'

Something fluttered in her chest, like a bird trying to break free. She picked up the key to the tea chest and turned it over in her hands. 'I cannot. The King has forbidden me from seeing either of you.'

'Then why do you let me sit here now?'

She had no answer for him. Perhaps it was just her own foolish weakness, longing for someone kind to rely upon. Since Gay had passed away, she had felt strangely alone. Only Berkeley's presence brought any comfort.

'Perhaps I will go with you and Lady Betty next year. Since

Princess Anne's wedding, the Queen has been so distressed . . . '

'I do not understand, Henrietta.' He reached across the table and picked at a bread roll. 'You no longer need the King's money. Do you wish to stay in royal favour or not?'

How could she explain the complex tangle of emotions that bound her to the royal couple? 'It is hard to abandon the Queen, Berkeley. Especially in her illness. Besides, she is kinder to me now . . .'

'Until the next thing happens to annoy her.'

She grimaced. He was right, of course. Caroline had saved her from Charles, and she would always be in Henrietta's prayers for that. But whatever there was of friendship and loyalty had melted away in the heat of George's bed.

He watched her hand, turning the key over and over. 'I thought you disliked the Queen.'

'I dislike what the Queen has *become*.' Images of Caroline flashed before her; the blonde beauty laughing in the gardens of Herrenhausen, the grieving mother, drenched in blood. She was so close, so entwined with her memories, that she could be a physical part of her. 'She was not always so. At one time, she was all that stood between me and ruin.'

'Then she has purchased your gratitude. Not your life. Use Bath as a trial. See how she copes without you for a few months.'

Henrietta gazed past him to her display of willow pattern china. She had lived her life like one of the Oriental figures; forever trapped in one blue scene, eternally seeing the same trees, the same bridge, the one pagoda. She would have to smash the plate to break free. 'Next year. Next year I will go with you to Bath.'

He sighed. 'There comes a time in life when one must stop living for others and start living for themselves. But while you are in the mood to serve your fellow man, can I ask when you are planning to pour me some tea?'

She stopped, suddenly aware of the key in her hand. She laughed.

'I am a terrible hostess.' She unlocked the tea chest and busied herself with preparing the drink. 'I am sorry, Mr Berkeley. I don't mean to be obtuse. But the Queen is determined to keep me. To leave, I must anger the King beyond hope of forgiveness. I must leave her with no choice. Yet no matter what I do, she takes my part.'

'Come to Bath,' he urged again. 'When you are away, the Queen will hear gossip. And gossip can be controlled. Think of the rumours we could send back to court. The Opposition mass in Bath! We could say you are conspiring against the King, flirting with Prince Frederick.'

She swallowed. The tea leaves leached their sepia colour into the hot water. What Berkeley suggested would work, but it was a huge, daunting step. If she could only settle her emotions and summon her courage . . .

Henrietta looked up into Berkeley's face. While he held her gaze, she thought she could do anything. Taking a breath, she stepped over the precipice. 'Very well. Let us do as you say.'

She was rewarded with one of his boyish grins. 'And what then?'

She had no idea. Freedom was a foreign country. She poured a little milk into the empty cups. 'I expect I will live quietly. Have my nephew and niece down to stay with me. I have had many titles, but I cherish that of *aunt* the most.'

He moved in close, filling her nostrils with his sweet musk. 'What about *Mrs Berkeley*? Is that a title you might stoop to?'

Her heart turned over. She gripped a cup as milk sloshed onto the table. 'Anything is possible, Mr Berkeley.'

St James's Palace

Sweat poured down Caroline's neck as she struggled to keep up with George's brisk pace. The park was a mosaic of bronze, copper and bright red leaves but she could not pause to enjoy its autumnal beauty. Everything depended on her steering the conversation between father and daughter.

Emily galloped at George's side, hopelessly unladylike. She did not moderate her voice. 'I *saw* her, I tell you. She gadded around Bath, courting every wretch who voted against the Excise Bill.'

'That scoundrel Chesterfield?' George pounded his cane against the path as he walked.

'Yes! And *Bolingbroke*. I think my Lady Suffolk is becoming a Jacobite.'

'Oh, fie!' Caroline gasped. She jogged a few steps before pain seized her legs. 'Lady Suffolk has always kept company with Chesterfield; that is nothing new. They are friends. And I am sure she met Bolingbroke only by accident.'

Emily threw back her head and laughed. 'Well if she did, it was a *repeated* accident.'

'How could she do this to me?' George cried. 'After the kindness I have shown her? Ungrateful bitch! I thought she was my friend, but she conspires with my enemies.' He shook his head. 'She was using me. Playing me for a fool all along, just to pay off her husband. Now that he is dead, see how she changes!'

Birds flocked in the sky, headed for warmer climes. In a great black column they flooded over the park gates out into London.

'George, please consider. Lady Suffolk has been our servant for twenty years. I am sure this is all a terrible misunderstanding.'

Emily snorted. Caroline threw her an icy glare.

'You are a silly old girl,' George growled. 'What do you mean by defending her? Why, it was you who warned me about her and Chesterfield conspiring together in the first place. You saw him sneaking to her apartments by the secret passage.'

Caroline fought for breath. He spoke the truth. Prodded by jealousy and spite, she had tried her best to bring Henrietta down.

She regretted it now. 'Perhaps I was mistaken. After all, a pretty lady would hardly pick Chesterfield as a lover.'

'Oh, but she has found herself another now!' Emily trilled. 'Not much better, but less ugly.'

Caroline stumbled on an uneven paving stone. If she was not in crippling pain, she would seize Emily and box her about the ears.

It was hopeless. She would never save Henrietta now. But every racking breath of cold air she took, every step of agony pointed out how much she needed her. George would not want this broken, bloated body. And if he took a young, lithe mistress, how would Caroline compete? Would she have any strength left to control her?

George stopped dead, leaning on his cane. A breeze lifted the curls of his wig from his neck. 'Who? Who does she favour now?'

Emily's eyes danced. 'Mr Berkeley. I saw them dancing together. Talking in whispers. All of Bath was in uproar.'

'All of Bath?' He spun to face her. 'The whole town saw her betray me?'

'Oh yes, Papa. They were quite scandalised.'

Bellowing, George launched his cane down the path. Several pigeons took alarm and flew away.

'Come now, George . . .' Before Caroline could lay a hand on his shoulder he stalked off, turning right down another trail. Emily skipped after him, relaying the places she had seen Henrietta and Berkeley together.

Caroline could go on no longer. Exhausted, she fell against a box hedge. It was scratchy and full of insects, but she could not move. At least it was cool and shady there.

George's voice drifted over the gardens. 'I will have the minx horse-whipped!'

What would she do now?

⤳ ⤸

The drawing room was bursting with courtiers for the King's birthday. People could barely move. One man in a silver jacket bowed to an acquaintance and hit someone with his dress sword. A lady fainted from the heat and had to be carried, over the top of the crowd, out of the room. Yet somehow, as Henrietta walked, the company fell away from her path. She had no trouble moving the panniers of her elaborate purple gown forward. From the corner of her eye, she saw ladies tittering behind their fans. She swallowed. She had wanted this: to be the subject of gossip, to push George over the edge. So why did she feel so sick?

Hot wax dripped from the chandelier onto her arm. She flinched, biting her lip to stop herself from crying out. She would not leave in tears, no matter what happened. But it was difficult not to shake from emotion; even harder not to gag at the mixture of overpowering fragrances: orange-blossom, civet, frankincense.

Caroline stood with the princesses and Mrs Clayton beside the throne. She made a great show of listening to something Carrie was saying, but it was clear from the way her eyes flicked that she marked Henrietta's progress toward George. He was speaking to Lord Hervey, gesturing with his hands. Judging by his enthusiasm, Henrietta guessed the topic was another obscure branch of his family tree. He always looked handsome when animated. That boyish gleam of the eye made her remember why she had cared for him. If only it could have been different; if only they could part as friends.

Lord Hervey turned as she arrived beside him in a rustle of taffeta. George did not pause in his sentence, did not even glance at her. She was left waiting, on the side, looking thoroughly foolish while he finished his story.

Prince Frederick passed close by her. He leant in so near she could smell the powder on his wig. 'It is hurtful, is it not? He does the exact same thing to me. One might as well be a spirit!'

It was good-natured of him to try and cheer her, but she wished he would not. Kindness only made her feel worse. She forced a smile and squeezed out a false laugh.

For an instant, George glanced in their direction. Henrietta fell into a profound curtsey. She held her legs bent, braced for a scold. It did not come. Still he ignored her.

Lord Hervey took pity. 'Ah, Lady Suffolk. Molly is somewhere hereabouts. She will be glad to see you.'

'Perhaps you would go and fetch her for me, my lord?'

He blushed red beneath his porcelain paint. 'I . . . the King was just telling me – '

George cut across him. 'What do you want, Lady Suffolk?'

'Merely to wish Your Majesty felicitations on your birthday. And many happy returns of the occasion.'

His crack of laughter was so loud that a lady behind him jumped. 'Indeed? I thought you and your friends wished to put an end to my birthdays. Was that not your plan?'

She stood, drawing back her shoulders. 'I do not understand . . .'

'Tell me, Lady Suffolk,' he went on, projecting his voice so all around could hear. 'When you drink my health, do you pass the wine over a bottle of water?'

Her throat closed. That was what the Jacobites did; they drank to the exiled James Stuart, *the king over the water*. She could only shake her head.

'Pah!' he snarled. 'I have no time for your games. Get away with you!'

Sweat dribbled down her neck. She closed her eyes and tried to recall the speech she had rehearsed, but she couldn't hear her thoughts over the pulse drumming in her head. 'As Your Majesty has not called on me since my return from Bath, I must ask if –'

'Why do you still stand there? I told you to leave. I will not be calling on you again, rest assured.'

The courtiers around them fell silent. *Oh, George.* Now he was finally looking at her, she wished he would not. His eyes were icy, his lip curled in contempt. Of all the expressions to see on a once beloved face, hatred was the worst. 'Then I wonder if Your Majesty would be so kind as to let me know when it is convenient for me to leave your family. Since . . . since you no longer have need of my services.'

'Services! Hah! No, I do not require your *services,*' he leered, looking her up and down. 'I could get better from a two-penny whore.'

Somebody gasped. Henrietta's vision clouded. She put her hand to the string of pearls at her neck – they had been a gift from him. She ran her finger over the dip between her collarbones, remembered him kissing her there. She bobbed a hasty curtsey and walked backwards, away from the King. She had no difficulty reaching the door; people drew back as if she had the plague.

Just before she turned to hurry away, a hand caught her shoulder. She recognised the waxy, honeyed perfume of rose otto. It was Caroline. 'Lady Suffolk? Are you unwell, child?'

'I am exceedingly ill, Your Majesty.' Her voice bubbled. 'Once again, I must beg your permission to retire.'

'For the night?'

'Forever.'

Caroline's face fell slack. 'You are doing exactly what your enemies want. They have told the King lies about your behaviour in Bath, and by leaving you confirm them! And what will you gain? Your friends will drop you the instant you quit court.'

'Perhaps I am better off without such people.'

'You will repent of it. I cannot give you leave to go. Pray consider, be calm.' But Henrietta was calm. It was Caroline who sweated.

354

'Madam, I beg you. Let me retire. I must leave with or without your consent. I would rather have it.'

Caroline twitched. Strain pulled at the corners of her wrinkled eyes. 'Well . . . stay a week longer, won't you? Stay a week at my request. You will not refuse me this?'

Unexpectedly, tears started to Henrietta's eyes. How pathetic Caroline had become. 'No, Your Majesty. I will obey you, as always. But I shall not change my mind. After a week I shall leave.' Henrietta picked up her skirts and moved toward the door. She was heavy with the need to weep.

As she placed her fingers on the handle, Caroline's hand stopped her again. 'I am dying, Lady Suffolk,' she whispered. 'I do not have long. I cannot manage the King alone. What will I do if he takes another mistress, one I cannot trust?'

Henrietta froze. It all made sense now; the sudden swing to her side, the protests in her defence. She could feel Caroline's desperation leeching through her fingers, onto her skin.

'Think!' Caroline went on. 'You would nurse me in my last days and then . . . The King would turn to you for comfort. You would be the first lady at court.'

Henrietta wavered. She had never heard a plea for help and ignored it. But she had given and given of herself until she was nothing but a limp rag rung through a mangle. And neither Caroline nor George appreciated it. 'I will pray for you, Your Majesty. But I do not want your court, or your husband. I only ever asked for your protection. And you made me whore myself to get it.' Yanking the door open, she ran down the steps into Whalebone Court.

1735

CHAPTER THIRTY-SIX

～ Kensington ～

Caroline's advisors backed out of the Council Chamber, heads inclined. As they filed through the heavy, wooden door she saw another figure standing outside with a hand theatrically pressed to his forehead. Frederick.

'Do not tell me I am late!' He withdrew his pocket watch and stared at it. 'I thought the meeting was to start now.' For all his love of the dramatic arts, he was a bad actor.

She sighed. 'Come inside, Frederick. Close the door behind you.'

The ministers looked disappointed as he obeyed, leaving them shut out in the King's Drawing Room.

Caroline limped to a chair. Jagged pain in her legs forced her to sit down. She closed her eyes and inhaled the scent of cut grass drifting in from the open window.

'I do beg your pardon. So foolish of me, to mistake the hour. To think, if I had only left my rooms a little sooner – '

'Be quiet, Fred. You do not deceive me.' She stared up into his eyes. They were hard as grey iron. 'This is of a piece with the rest of your behaviour. You set out to humiliate me.'

His mouth curled at the corner. 'I? Would *I* dare show disrespect to the Regent of England?'

This again. He could not forgive her for holding power or influence while George was away in Hanover. He was insulted to think a woman was made Regent over him.

Was nobody on her side? Henrietta left her, Emily vexed her with scandalous flirtations and George . . . Well, she could not bring herself to dwell on George now. She was in too much pain already.

'Yes, you would. Although you are careful to seem full of duty in public, I know you are working against all that we do. My advisors tell me you plan to take the matter of your allowance to Parliament! Can you not give me an instant's rest?' She thought of her closet, where Mrs Clayton would be waiting with pails of ice water. She couldn't wait to plunge her raw feet into them and feel a moment of relief.

'The allowance is my birthright. The King is unjust to me. You know it.' He brushed back the skirts of his jacket and put a fist upon his hip.

Why couldn't he be reasonable? She was so tired. She needed a son to care for her, to lighten the load. Not this spiky, cuckoo of a young man transplanted into her family. William tried to help her, but he was only fourteen. He needed to be out riding with boys of his own age, not growing musty in a sick chamber.

'It *is* your right. But why draw the public eye toward a family tiff? It is . . . vulgar.'

He snorted. Something flickered over his face. '*Make them love you,*' he muttered

'What?'

'*Make them love you, Fred.* They were the last words you said to me before you left Hanover. I mean to do it. My subjects will not laugh at me as they do my father. And I will not offend them by complaining about every English fashion, dish and custom.'

His words took her breath. So he *had* thought of her, all those years apart. She had been dear to him – but why did he seem to hate her now? 'I am pleased you attended to me. Do it again. You will never rule if you undermine the crown you are to inherit. You must support the King and his decisions.'

'*Your* decisions,' he corrected. 'You rule the King. You will not rule me.'

It was as if he had punched her on a bruise. Yes, she had ruled George. But for how much longer? 'I am trying for you, Fred!' she cried, tears in her eyes. She reached into her pocket with difficulty and produced a crumpled piece of paper. 'Look, here is the latest letter from your father. He has been to inspect a bride for you. Augusta of Saxe-Gotha.' She smoothed out the passage. 'Blonde, young, handsome . . .'

He bit his lip. 'I wanted to marry my cousin Wilhelmina.'

'Strange, then, that you tried to elope with Lady Diana Spencer.'

'I was in debt! The King left me no choice,' he flashed.

'Well now you have one! Surely the King will raise your allowance when you marry and produce children. He might even give you a residence of your own, if you take care to show your support and prove that he can trust you.'

He considered, fiddling with his sword. 'This princess is not the bride I wanted, but I have heard no harm of her. I suppose I must be content.'

'That is all I ask. Settle down, have a family. Make it your chief object to care for them, not to disturb your father.' She only meant it in part. The thought of Fred or his offspring succeeding George made her mouth taste sour. But this Augusta was a small, frail creature. With any luck, the pair of them would prove barren and the crown would be where it belonged: on William's golden curls.

'I will try.' He did not meet her eyes. 'What else does my father say from Hanover?'

Heat rushed to her face. She balled the paper into a fist. 'Nothing. Nothing of importance.' If only the force of her fingers could crush George's words from existence and this new woman with it. Her dark hair, her twinkling eyes. The curves Caroline no longer possessed. *I know you will love Amalie Wallmoden, because she loves me.*

Sunlight glared through the window onto her back. Sweat trickled down her neck. It would start again: the jealousy, the fake smiles as she listened to George harp on another woman's perfections. But this time it was not a powerless, pliable lady. Wallmoden was the thirty-one-year-old granddaughter of a practiced mistress. A rival over the sea, where Caroline could not even touch her.

How ardently she longed for Lady Suffolk.

Cranford

Church bells pealed through the summer air. Henrietta paused beneath the lychgate to kiss her new husband. Her heart soared. These joyful chimes were the death knell for the woman that was: Henrietta Howard, Lady Suffolk. Mistress to the King, Mistress of the Robes. Rising from the ashes was a new woman: Mrs Berkeley.

Children from the village cheered and waved ribbons on sticks as they made their way to the bridal carriage. The shimmering colours were more beautiful than any she had seen in the Queen's wardrobe. She was done with the false glamour of court. Her dress was unpretentious; powder pink silk with rosebuds embroidered down the skirt to match the fresh ones in her hair. She had let it return to its natural chestnut colour. Her days of enduring the smell of horse urine to appease George's penchant for blondes were at an end.

Lady Betty pressed a handkerchief to her eye. Berkeley put out a hand to help Henrietta up into the carriage, but Dorothy and Jack burst out of the crowd and wrapped their arms around her. 'Aunty Hetty! When can we come to stay with you at Marble Hill?'

She laughed, stumbling under their embraces. 'Very soon, I hope. Ask your father.'

'Berkeley and I have already agreed – their main residence shall be with you.' John grinned at the surprised look on Henrietta's face. 'Business shall keep me busy in town . . .'

The rooms she had designed with such care would ring with the laughter of children. It was more than she had ever dared to wish for. Ecstatic, she returned Dorothy's embrace.

'Come now,' Berkeley smiled. 'We will celebrate this later. For the moment, our wedding breakfast awaits!'

'Oh, but can't we ride with you in the carriage?' Dorothy pleaded.

Henrietta shot a hopeful look at Berkeley.

He laughed and shrugged. 'How can I deny my beautiful bride anything?' He handed Henrietta and Dorothy up, then he and Jack scrambled in behind. A cheer arose from the villagers. Henrietta snuggled in close to Berkeley, her nostrils full of the scent of flowers. The coachman cracked the whip and the carriage whirred into motion. Lady Betty, Berkeley's brothers and John hurled shoes after them for good luck. Henrietta laughed as one hit the back of their vehicle and then bounced off into a hedge.

It was a glorious day; the sun seemed to be bursting right out of the sky. She had never felt so content. The years of abuse, poverty, adultery and humiliation fell away. She could leave it all in the past – even Henry. She was where she should have been all along – after a long and arduous detour.

She may be deaf and Berkeley might be a gouty, middle-aged man but in their hearts they were a young couple; the chattering teenagers opposite their surging family. Life had been put on hold for Henrietta until the age of forty-six. Now it was time to begin.

AUTHOR'S NOTE

Henrietta and Berkeley enjoyed a happy marriage for eleven years. Sadly, Berkeley passed away on 29th October 1746, in his mid-fifties. Henrietta devoted her remaining life to Dorothy, Jack and their children. Despite her frequent ill health, she survived until 1767 and died quietly at Marble Hill.

After Henrietta's departure from court, Caroline's life became increasingly difficult. Besotted with his new mistress, George was often rude and unfeeling toward her. Frederick continued to act against her wishes, and these episodes will be shown in my novel about his wife Augusta. Death came through the nub on Caroline's stomach, which was actually an untreated umbilical hernia. Thanks to the inept surgery of the day, Caroline endured an agonising last few days before expiring on 20th November 1737. George was distraught and refused to marry again. Henrietta's feelings on the occasion have not been recorded.

In telling Henrietta's story, I have taken liberty with a few of the facts. Although she sold all of her furniture to reach Hanover, she did not sell her hair. She did contemplate the transaction, and I have used the price she was quoted. Her departure from St James's Palace in 1717 was also a little different. After days of agonising decision, Henrietta left Charles and Henry in the full knowledge that she would be barred from coming back again. However, it seems she was far from giving up on Henry. Her correspondence shows that she had relatives visit his school and was always trying to get news of him. Unfortunately, the feelings were not reciprocated. Exactly what changed between mother and son is unclear, but in later years Henrietta went out of her way to avoid his company. The pair never met again. Tragically, Henry died in 1745 without issue, ending that branch of the Howard family.

I do not have any evidence that Caroline discovered Henrietta's abusive marriage early on, or that she asked Henrietta to become George's mistress. However, both of these occurrences seem likely to me. Caroline was extremely observant. After her mother's troubled second marriage, it is hard to believe she would not notice what Henrietta endeavoured to hide. There must have been a confession of some sorts, for Caroline certainly knew enough of Charles's nature to defend Henrietta against him, both when he plagued her with letters and broke into her apartments. Concerning the role of mistress, we know that Henrietta must have had Caroline's approval to take up the post, if not her decided blessing. Had the princess truly felt betrayed, she would have speedily found a way to disgrace and banish her rival. But it is clear that Caroline found Henrietta's services useful to her schemes. From Henrietta's hand-written account of their last interview, we know that Caroline tried to make her stay. However, Caroline's confession of her impending death and Henrietta's spirited response are my own additions.

There is some debate as to when the affair between Henrietta and George began. Some date it back to 1713, but gossip did not intensify until the summer of 1718. I find it easier to believe that Henrietta would wait until she was out of her husband's reach before taking such a dangerous step. Although George did not give Henrietta the dogs Marquise and Fop, his other gifts are accurately recorded. Such bounty from a famously stingy man makes me suspect that there was more than just a physical tie between the pair.

Writing from Caroline and George's point of view, King George I has inevitably come off unfavourably in this novel. Rest assured, his version of events will be told in another story.

ALSO BY LAURA PURCELL:

QUEEN OF BEDLAM

London 1788...
The calm order of Queen Charlotte's court is shattered by screams.
The King of England is going mad.

Left alone with thirteen children and with the country on the brink of war, Charlotte has to fight to hold her husband's throne. It is a time of unrest and revolution but most of all Charlotte fears the King himself, someone she can no longer love or trust. She has lost her marriage to madness and there is nothing she can do other than continue to fulfil her royal duty.

Her six daughters are desperate to escape their palace asylum. Their only hope lies in a good marriage, but no prince wants the daughter of a madman. They are forced to take love wherever they find it – with devastating consequences.

The moving, true story of George III's madness and the women whose lives it destroyed.

"...masterfully written and well researched... by someone who has mastered the craft of evoking readers' emotions." *Historical Novels Review*

"Laura Purcell's powerful new book... takes an eye-opening look at the triumphs and trials of Queen Charlotte and her marriage to 'mad' King George III."
Daily Express

ISBN: 978-1-910183-01-4   **Price: £8.99**

Hope Against Hope

Sally Zigmond

Yorkshire, 1838…

At the dawn of the Victorian epoch two young sisters, stoical industrious Carrie and carefree and vivacious May, lose home and liv hood when their Leeds pub is sold out from under them to make way the coming of the railway. They head for Harrogate to find work in the town's burgeoning hotel trade only to fall prey to fraudsters and preda before being driven apart by misunderstanding, pride and a mutual se of betrayal.

Estranged from one another, Carrie and May must each pursue t own destinies as they seek to overcome misfortune and look for love lasting happiness. Their separate paths will cross those of three men: Alex clair, a bold and warm-spirited Scottish railway pioneer; Charles Hammo the dissolute and tormented heir to a wealthy and manipulative mother, Byron Taylor, a ruthless entrepreneur and consummate womaniser.

Populated by a host of engaging characters and by turns poign warm and humorous, *Hope Against Hope* is a compelling tale of trium love and redemption that takes us on a ten-year journey through the sal and bordellos of Harrogate, the cholera infected slums of Leeds and bloody streets of revolutionary Paris.

> **"There is something for every reader: happiness, sadness, warm and a bit of humour, sisters, hotels, revolutions, railways, love and loss. It is beautifully written, very readable, powerful, and gritty. wonderful debut novel that keeps the reader enthralled and guessi It is very difficult to put down until the last page is turned, and th story will stay with the reader long afterwards."**
>
> ***Historical Novel Society***

Longlisted for *Romantic Novel of the Year*, 2011

ISBN: 978-1-905802-19-7   Price: £8.99
AVAILABLE AS AN E BOOK

Mrs Lincoln

Janis Cooke Newman

(May 20th)
Mrs Mary Lincoln admitted today – from Chicago – Age 56 – Widow of ex-President Lincoln – declared insane by the Cook County Court May 19th – 1875.
Patient Progress Reports for Bellevue Place Sanatorium.

Incarcerated in an insane asylum after committal proceedings instigated by her own son, Mary Lincoln resolves to tell her own story in order to preserve and prove her own sanity and secure her release. But can she succeed?

"…this epic drama exerts an exceptional pull… an impressive, engrossing and moving piece of historical imagining and characterisation." **– Holly Kyte, *The Sunday Telegraph***

"…a tender and thoughtful portrait of a 19th century woman severely misunderstood… *Mrs Lincoln* unfolds with plenty to inspire and is all the more poignant for a timely arrival." **– Sarah Emily Miano, *The Times***

"As I read it, I wept. I cannot recommend a book more… a very powerful novel." **– Pat Schroeder, President of the Association of American Publishers**

"…one of those rare books that turns the reader into an admiring fan of both the author and her subject. You feel a compulsion to urge others to read it. **– USA Today**

"…a gripping tale of scandal, war, intrigue, and séances… for sheer page-turning fun…" **– San Francisco Magazine**

"…thoughtful and thoroughly enjoyable… not only a fascinating read, but also a touching love story." **– Chicago Sun-Times**

"Moving and with an almost palpable compassion for its subject, yet clear-eyed and even humorous at times, this is a book I will be re-reading." *Historical Novels Review*

"...a daring novel about the inner life of Mary Todd Lincoln; an intelligent, sympathetic, well-written work of speculative fiction." – **Kevin Baker, author of** *Paradise Alley* **and** *Strivers* **Row**

ISBN: 978-1-905802-21-0   **Price: £8.99**

Searing and achingly beautiful tale of Sub-Saharan West Africa…

Harmattan

Gavin Weston

"Harmattan is just the novel that all readers need right now."
Glenn Patterson

Haoua is a young girl growing up in a remote village in the Republic of Niger. Spirited and intelligent, she has benefited from a stable home life and a loving and attentive mother and enjoys working and playing with her siblings and friends.

She worships her elder brother, Abdelkrim, a serving soldier who sends money home to support the family. But on his last home visit, Abdelkrim quarrels with their father, accusing him of gambling away the money he sends and being the cause of their mother's worsening health. It also emerges that their father plans to take a second wife.

Despite this Haoua finds contentment in her schoolwork, her dreams of becoming a teacher and in writing assiduously to the family in Ireland who act as her aid sponsors.

But for Haoua, there are new storm clouds on the horizon: as civil strife mounts in Niger, she fears for Abdelkrim's safety, her mother's illness is much more serious than anyone had recognised, and her father's plans are turning out to be far more threatening than she could have ever imagined.

Approaching her twelfth birthday, Haoua feels alone and vulnerable for the very first time in her life.

"*Harmattan* is a captivating and beautifully written debut novel. Gavin Weston's unique and distinctive style hails a new era in Northern Irish literature."
Kellie Chambers, *Ulster Tatler*

ISBN: 978-1-905802-75-3   Price: £8.99
AVAILABLE AS AN E BOOK

TAMING POISON DRAGONS

Tim Murgatroyd

Western China, 1196…

Yun Cai, a handsome and adored poet in his youth, is now an old man, exiled to his family estates. All that is left to him are regrets of a growing sense of futility and helplessness and the irritations of his feckless son and shrewish daughter-in-law. But the 'poison dragons' of misfortune shatter his orderly existence.

First, Yun Cai's village is threatened with destruction by a vicious civil war. His wayward second son, a brutal rebel officer, seems determined to ruin his entire family. Meanwhile, Yun Cai struggles to free an old friend, P'ei Ti, from a hellish prison – no easy task when P'ei Ti is the rebels' most valuable hostage and Yun Cai considers himself merely a spent and increasingly frightened old man.

Throughout these ordeals, Yun Cai draws from the glittering memories of his youth, when he journeyed to the capital to study poetry and join the upper ranks of the civil service: how he contended with rivalry and enmity among his fellow students and secured the friendship of P'ei Ti. Above all, he reflects on a great love he won and lost: his love for the beautiful singing girl, Su Lin, for which he paid with his freedom and almost his life.

Yun Cai is forced to reconsider all that he is and all that he has ever been in order to determine how to preserve his honour and all that he finds he still cherishes. Only then can summon the wit and courage to confront the warlord General An-Shu and his beautiful but cruel consort, the Lady Ta-Chi.

'A riveting story.' **John Green, *The Morning Star***

'An evocative and epic tale of love,honour and valour in the midst of civil war.'
femalefirst.co.uk

ISBN: 978-1-905802-39-5   Price: £8.99
AVAILABLE AS AN E BOOK